THE CARRIER NOVEL
EXCITING. EX...

The North Korean Navy ... ... a U.S. intelligence ship in international waters. They dare Washington to retaliate. The U.S. response? The ultimate military power play . . .

VIPER STRIKE
A renegade Chinese fighter group punctures Thai airspace— the spearhead of a giant invasion force streaming across the Burmese border. The skies are about to blow wide open . . .

ARMAGEDDON MODE
India and Pakistan are on the verge of nuclear destruction, and Carrrier Battle Group Fourteen must shift into Armageddon Mode—the ultimate battle by land, air, or sea . . .

FLAME-OUT
After a hard-line military takeover, the Soviet Union is reborn. Norway is invaded. Finland is crushed. And the President orders Carrier Battle Group Fourteen to smash the Soviet strike force at all costs . . .

MAELSTROM
The Soviet occupation of Scandinavia continues as Carrier Battle Group Fourteen struggles to keep up in conventional weapons combat, and avert all-out war . . .

COUNTDOWN
Carrier Battle Group Fourteen must launch marine and aerial assaults to prevent the deployment of Russian Typhoons. They are the largest submarines in the world. And they may have nukes . . .

AFTERBURN
As the Russian Civil War rages on, Carrier Battle Group Fourteen is ordered to the Black Sea as a show of American strength. But if the U.S. thinks they can sail into traditionally Russian waters without a fight, they're dead wrong . . .

Titles by Keith Douglass

THE CARRIER SERIES:

CARRIER
VIPER STRIKE
ARMAGEDDON MODE
FLAME-OUT
MAELSTROM
COUNTDOWN
AFTERBURN
ALPHA STRIKE

THE SEAL TEAM SEVEN SERIES:

SEAL TEAM SEVEN
SPECTER
NUCFLASH
DIRECT ACTION

CARRIER

Book Seven
AFTERBURN

Keith Douglass

JOVE BOOKS, NEW YORK

CARRIER 7: AFTERBURN

A Jove Book / published by arrangement with
the author

PRINTING HISTORY
Jove edition / July 1996

The Penguin Putnam Inc. World Wide Web site address is
http://www.penguinputnam.com

ISBN: 0-515-11914-8

A JOVE BOOK®
Jove Books are published by The Berkley Publishing Group,
a member of Penguin Putnam Inc.,
200 Madison Avenue, New York, New York 10016.
JOVE and the "J" design are trademarks
belonging to Jove Publications, Inc.

PRINTED IN THE UNITED STATES OF AMERICA

10   9   8   7   6   5   4   3

AFTERBURN

PROLOGUE
Friday, 30 October

Vitse-Admiral Nikolai Sergeivich Dmitriev looked up from his desk as his aide slipped into the office without knocking. The young *starshiy-leytenant* looked tired, drawn, like a man who hadn't slept for a week. That might well have been true, Dmitriev reflected as he studied the man. There weren't many loyalists left with the Black Sea Fleet these days, and the officers who had stayed at their posts were all working double and triple shifts to try to keep the fleet in something approaching a state of readiness.

A losing cause, Dmitriev thought bitterly. Transfers, desertions, and outright mutinies had left the Black Sea Fleet crippled.

"Comrade Admiral," *Starshiy-Leytenant* Anton Ivanovich Kulagin said formally. "There is word from the *Krimsky Komsomolets*. The American battle group is entering the Dardanelles."

Dmitriev looked away. "So it has finally happened," he said quietly, not bothering to hide his own fatigue. Even though he'd expected the news, the confirmation was bitter medicine indeed, confirmation that the Motherland had fallen yet another notch in power and prestige. An American aircraft carrier battle group would soon sail where no such force had ever sailed before, in the waters of the Black Sea.

1

Once, the *Chernoje More* had been a Russian lake. Not even
the Nazis had placed a fleet of any importance in those
waters. To find a comparable time in history would require
looking back a century and a half, to the days when British,
French, and Turkish invaders had besieged Sevastopol in
the Crimean War.

It was the end of an era. The West might have proclaimed
that the *Rodina* was no longer a superpower after the fall of
the Berlin Wall, the 1991 coup against Gorbachev, and the
end of Lenin's Soviet Union, but this was the final, the
undeniable proof of the fact, when the Motherland could no
longer even defend these waters that had for so long been
her own.

"Is the submarine maintaining contact with the Americans?" he asked slowly.

The aide nodded. "Yes, Comrade Vice-Admiral. The
Americans have been carrying out their routine antisubmarine operations, of course, but there has been no indication that the *Krimsky Komsomolets* has been detected. His
captain is more concerned that the Turks may detect the sub
if he moves into the straits behind the Americans."

"Not a serious problem, I think. The Turks are staying
quite neutral these days. The political situation between
Greece and Turkey is still somewhat, ah, strained. And that
has had serious repercussions for the Americans."

Kulagin sniffed disdainfully. "They might have blocked
passage," he said. "Denied the Americans the right to sail
through their waters."

"Turkey plays a careful game. They do not wish to
cooperate with those they believe to be allies of the Greeks,
but they will not defy the United Nations. Wheels within
wheels within wheels, Anton Ivanovich." He held up his
hands and shifted them rapidly back and forth, as though
juggling many precariously balanced objects. "The UN
passes resolutions concerning Armenia and Georgia, then
asks the United States to help enforce them. Turkey denies
the Americans the right to base aircraft on their soil, partly
because they still dislike American policies in Greece, but
also because allowing it would further inflame Turkish

Moslem fundamentalists. However, the Turks agree to the passage of the carrier through their territorial waters because if they do not, the UN may not see their point of view when it comes time to discuss the way the Turks have been handling their ethnic Armenian problem. Still, I doubt they will share information or assist the Americans in any way, so long as we do not force them to choose sides."

"Doesn't that rob us of our best chance to stop the Americans, Comrade Vice-Admiral?" Kulagin's eyes flashed. "They are vulnerable as they move through the straits." He moved his hands together, defining a narrow space. "*Concentrated* . . ."

"If our leaders were willing to authorize a nuclear strike against an American fleet in Turkish territory, perhaps." Dmitriev shook his head wearily. "Short of that, we cannot challenge them."

"But surely a strike with conventional forces, Comrade Vice-Admiral—"

Dmitriev sighed and got up from behind his desk, moving to the window overlooking the historic harbor beyond the waterfront below. Once, Sevastopol had been one of the Soviet Union's thriving ports, filled with commercial shipping and the naval might of a superpower. Though the harbor might now have seemed crowded to the untrained eye, Dmitriev knew better.

His eyes lingered on the imposing bulk of the *Pobedonosnyy Rodina*, the largest ship in the harbor. The sight of the nuclear-powered aircraft carrier brought back mixed memories for Dmitriev, fond and bitter. Just a few years before, he'd commanded a Russian naval squadron built around another carrier, the *Kreml*, working together with an American carrier battle group to keep India and Pakistan from escalating a conventional conflict into a full-fledged nuclear exchange. Ah, those had been heady days, back when Russians could still hold their heads high and proclaim that they, too, were a superpower, despite anything the West might say.

But those days were gone now. *Pobedonosnyy Rodina* was the only aircraft carrier still afloat out of the three

commissioned with the old fleet, and the rest of the
Motherland's naval power had shrunk proportionately. Dmitriev had been rewarded for his loyalty to Krasilnikov with
this promotion to command of the entire Black Sea Fleet.

An empty reward. An empty *fleet*, impressive on paper,
but rusting to scrap as he watched, with few men left to man
the few ships that could still put to sea . . . and with a
homeland that was tearing itself apart in blood and bitterness.

His country was dying.

He gestured for Kulagin to join him by the window.
"Even if we were willing to add to the list of our enemies by
mining or launching an attack in Turkish waters, it would be
a futile attempt. Look out there, Anton Ivanovich. What do
you see?"

"I see . . . the harbor. The fleet." Kulagin sounded
baffled.

"The fleet. The Red Banner Black Sea Fleet. During the
Cold War we maintained nearly two hundred warships and
submarines of all sizes in these waters, plus four hundred
aircraft, and that was just our naval force. Now we control
what you see out there, plus the handful at Balaklava and
Kerch. Less than fifty ships still seaworthy, all told, and I
doubt we have the trained men to man more than two-thirds
of those. Our air arm has been reduced even more, and the
Army would be fortunate to muster two full divisions in all
the Crimea. We could attack the American battle group,
perhaps even cause some damage, but all that would do is
bring down the full weight of the West on us . . . again, as
in the Kola. It is over, Kulagin. Our leaders have betrayed
us, and we can no longer hope to hold back the tide."

The *Rodina* was dying.

First had come the collapse of the old Soviet Union after
Gorbachev had withdrawn from Europe and lost control of
the reforms he'd tried to put in place to minimize the
damage from a failing economy. Yeltsin had done little
better than Gorbachev, allowing the Soviet Republics to go
their own way, making a series of fatal compromises with
the West, letting the economy continue its relentless slide

into the gutter. Hard-liners, old Communists and right-wing Nationalists united by their visions of restoring order, had ousted Yeltsin in due course, bringing in a figurehead ruler in the Gorbachev mold to head the revived Soviet Union. But that compromise regime hadn't been able to stabilize things either, and the real leaders of the new Union had turned to the one sure way of changing the balance of power . . . war.

Dmitriev wasn't privy to the machinations inside the Kremlin, but he suspected that the assassination of the Union's president in Norway had been an inside job, planned and executed by the KGB or perhaps the GRU. Within hours the tanks had started rolling across the frozen border between Russia's Kola Peninsula and Norway, supposedly in retaliation for the plot and to "restore order" in a dangerous neighbor. It might have worked, too; it *had* worked as a means of bringing the breakaway republic of Ukraine back inside the Soviet fold, at least temporarily. Certainly, the West had been slow to react, unwilling, perhaps, to see danger in a Soviet Union that everyone believed was already dead. The Norwegian gambit might have left the new Union poised to dominate a confused and irresolute Europe . . . until the Americans had thwarted the plan. Their aircraft carrier *Jefferson*, the same ship Dmitriev had cooperated with in the Indian Ocean, had crippled the Soviet naval forces off Norway and opened the way for a full-scale Western intervention. In the process both *Kreml* and *Soyuz*, two-thirds of the Union's available carrier force, had been lost in battle, the most devastating upset of naval power since the destruction of the Japanese carrier fleet at Midway.

Dmitriev turned away from the window, more discouraged than ever. That gamble in Norway had been the final blow to the Motherland. A populist leader named Leonov had seized control from the discredited hard-liners, but it was too late for a political solution to Russia's problems. Soon Leonov's Popular Democratic Front, the "Blues," had been locked in combat with Marshal Krasilnikov's hard-line "Reds" in an all-out civil war. As the revived Union had started to disintegrate, the Americans had intervened in the far north, seizing key military facilities in the Kola Peninsula. They'd claimed that Krasilnikov was planning to use submarine-launched nukes to blackmail Leonov into submission, through Dmitriev was convinced that their real intent had been to guarantee the success of Leonov and his anti-Communists. The Americans had a long history of anti-Communist sentiments.

The Kola Intervention, in fact, was the *second* time the West had put their troops on the soil of Holy Mother Russia in this century. The first had been in 1919, when they and a small international force had occupied Murmansk, Archanglsk, and Vladivostok in opposition to Lenin and the Revolution. Few outside of Russia remembered that particular chapter of history now, but the Russians had long memories.

And now that same American carrier, *Jefferson*, was leading a battle group through the Dardanelles and into the Black Sea. It would have been . . . satisfying to strike back, to smash this insult to Russian sovereignty, to Russian honor, but Dmitriev lacked the military strength to oppose them. The Red Banner Black Sea Fleet had been too hard-hit by defections and neglect to defend the coasts of the *Rodina* herself. Dmitriev's first duty was to preserve the fleet for the coming struggle with Ukraine.

As much as Dmitriev would have liked to bloody the Americans for their invasion of the Kola, he was a realist. The American presence in the Black Sea was almost certainly an artifact of the constantly churning politics between the United States and the United Nations, an unpleasant fact that might be wiped away by the stroke of a diplomat's pen tomorrow. The Ukraine was a more constant problem, one that was not so likely to simply go away.

Ukraine had never been wholly comfortable with its role as one of the largest and most productive republics of the Union. Ethnic Ukrainians were not Russians, whatever most outsiders might think. They had their own language, their own culture, and a history of independence extending back for centuries. Great Russians still remembered, with the

same loving attention to historical detail that recalled the
foreign intervention in the Kola in 1919, that millions of
Ukrainians had actually welcomed the Hitlerite legions as
liberators in the Great Patriotic War.

Now those same Ukrainians were taking advantage of
the Russian Civil War to strengthen their own position—
especially in the Crimea.

Geographically, the Crimean Peninsula had always been
considered a part of the Ukraine, which extended across the
mainland to the north; the Russian Federation bordered the
peninsula only to the east, across the narrow Straits of Kerch
and on the far side of the Sea of Azov. Politically and
militarily, however—which was to say practically—it had
always belonged to Russia, who'd seen the peninsula's
strategic naval value as far back as the early 1800s when the
czars were still fighting the Turks.

And then, in the 1950s, Nikita Kruschev had formally and
officially returned Crimea to Ukraine in a gesture of
international goodwill and fellowship. At the time, the
gesture had been just that, a gesture, a public relations
gimmick, as an American capitalist might say . . . and
meaningless in the realities of internal Soviet politics.

Now, though, with Russia unable to defend herself on a
hundred crumbling fronts, Kruschev's goodwill had become
a major problem, an invitation to the Ukrainians to settle old
scores and to enrich themselves at Mother Russia's expense.

Not that they needed the encouragement, Dmitriev thought
wryly. They would soon be turning their attentions southward.
The Ukrainian army was strong and well-equipped, and they
controlled more than half of the old Black Sea Fleet. They
were the real threat, not the Americans.

But how could he explain all of that to Kulagin? The
young aide had been raised and educated during the
seventies and eighties, when the West had been the enemy
that threatened the Soviet Union, and the breakaway republics and states were tools or dupes of Western adventurism,
a clear case of black and white, of good and evil. Though
Dmitriev had grown up with all the indoctrination of the
Cold War era teaching him those same lessons, he knew

from long experience that a broader interpretation was necessary. The forces of political and economic freedom unleashed by Gorbachev didn't need Western villains to make them dangerous. The genie could never be put back in the bottle. . . .

"No, Anton Ivanovich," he said again after a long and thoughtful silence. "We cannot stop the Americans. And I wonder if we really want to, after all. The West may find that intervention here is far more difficult and costly than they ever imagined possible." He paused, his eyes still lingering on the nuclear carrier out in the harbor that might never venture out of port again. "I do not envy these Americans. They may find that the *Rodina* in ruins is a far more dangerous enemy than she ever was when she stood proudly in strength and union."

Dmitriev turned away from the window and gave a gesture of dismissal. He felt weary, discouraged . . . a tired man who faced impossible odds. Still, he could not give in to his fatigue or his ebbing morale. There was still a job to be done here, and he could not let self-pity or weariness stand in his way.

Nikolai Sergeivich Dmitriev knew his duty, to the *Rodina*. And to honor.

CHAPTER 1
Friday, 30 October

1520 hours (Zulu +3)
Bridge
U.S.S. *Thomas Jefferson*, the Bosporus Strait

"I don't know," Captain Matthew Magruder said dubiously. He leaned forward to peer out of the slanted forward windscreen on *Jefferson*'s bridge, looking across the carrier's forward flight deck toward the dismal gray waters ahead. "You'd never catch me taking *my* aircraft carrier into that lake!"

"Ah, these young aviators nowadays," Captain Jeremy Brandt said, shaking his head in mock sorrow. He was sitting in the bridge's high chair, the leather-backed elevated seat with the word CAPTAIN stenciled across the back in yellow block letters. "No spirit of adventure at all!"

Magruder, call sign "Tombstone," turned from the windscreen and cocked a bantering eye at the ship's commanding officer. "'Spirit of *adventure*.' Is *that* what you call it?"

"Certainly! What'd you expect, youngster? Nice safe milk runs on the open ocean? Getting to be captain of a Love Boat? This here," he thumped his fist melodramatically on the arm of his chair, "is a *man's* Navy."

"Um," Tombstone said. "Don't let Brewer or the other Amazons hear you say that. She could take exception."

"Shit, you're right," Brandt said. "Though I'm more afraid of Madam SecDef and the PC Police. Promise not to turn me in?"

"I won't tell if you won't, Skipper."

"Deal." He grinned. "You know, Stoney, this is the sort of shit you have to learn to deal with if you want to play with the big boys up here."

It was a long-standing joke. Tombstone was CAG, commander of CVW-20, the air wing assigned to the nuclear-powered aircraft carrier *Thomas Jefferson*, CVN-74. Sooner or later, however, he would have to move on in his career . . . and for most aviators who made it high enough up the chain of command to run an air wing, that meant going on to command a carrier someday. It was possible—if not entirely likely, at this point—that Tombstone might one day be sitting in Brandt's chair, skippering this same CVN through some other strait in some other troubled part of the world. As training for that day, Tombstone was required to spend a certain number of watches on the bridge; at times, he served as acting captain under Brandt's tutelage. This time, though, he was strictly an observer. The situation, both tactically and politically, called for an experienced captain on the bridge as the supercarrier cruised majestically into new waters.

Like a vast, gray, slow-moving island, the *Thomas Jefferson* was making her way northeast, threading her way along the narrow channel of the Bosporus and toward the Black Sea proper. Over a thousand feet long, displacing 96,700 tons fully loaded, the nuclear-powered supercarrier U.S.S. *Thomas Jefferson* was heart and soul of Carrier Battle Group 14, a powerful naval squadron that included the Aegis cruiser *Shiloh*, the destroyers *William B. Truesdale, Alan Kirk*, and *John A. Winslow*, the frigates *Stephen Decatur* and *Leslie*, and the Los Angeles–class submarines *Galveston* and *Orlando*.

Immediately ahead of the *Jefferson*, and preceding her through the straits, was a Meko-class frigate, hull number F240, but she wasn't part of the battle group. Her name was *Yavuz*, and she was their military escort through Turkish waters. At the moment, the only other American ship visible was the *Truesdale*, a gray smudge on the northern horizon,

far out ahead of the *Jefferson* and already well into the
Black Sea.

It was unnaturally quiet aboard the CVN. Personnel on
the bridge stood to their stations, speaking little, and only
when required by duty. Outside, on the roof, flight deck
personnel gathered in small groups among the closely
spaced parked aircraft to watch the slow-passing shore or to
enjoy a rare moment of inactivity. The planes themselves
looked like so many huge, sleeping gray birds with their
wings tightly folded. Flight deck operations had been
suspended during the passage through the Bosporus. The
transit agreement with Turkey called for *Jefferson's* aircraft
to stay grounded while the vessel was in Turkish waters,
and that was part of what was making Tombstone uneasy.
With none of her aircraft aloft, *Jefferson* was completely
dependent on the electronic eyes and ears of those ships of
her battle group that had already entered the Black Sea.
Shiloh was already out there, beyond the *Truesdale* and over
the horizon, as were *Winslow* and *Leslie*, while *Decatur*
brought up the rear. If Washington had guessed wrong about
Russian intentions or Russian sensitivity to an American
task force entering their traditional waters, enough of the
CBG was already in place to protect the carrier as it moved
ponderously through the narrow straits.

At least, that was what the CBG Ops Staff hoped.
Tombstone, as CAG, had been in on all of the planning
sessions and knew the logistical and deployment rational-
izations by heart.

Stupid . . . stupid . . . stupid . . .

Leaning forward, he peered up at the sky, a jumbled mix
of towering blue-and-white cumulus clouds and patches of
blue sky . . . as if he could spot incoming aircraft before
the battle group's radar could. He shook his head at the
thought. An aviator's hands-on instincts . . . and impossible to ignore. This was a critical time for the CBG. If the
Russians were going to try something, they couldn't ask for
a better moment than *now*, while the *Jeff* was pinned in the
straits with her air grounded.

Were they still at war with Russia? Tombstone honestly

wasn't sure, and neither was anyone else in CBG-14. Most likely the politicians weren't sure either; officially a truce was on, and American forces had been directed to fire at Russian units only if the other guy fired first. The trouble was that things were rather confused inside Russia these days, and no one, inside the country or outside, knew for sure who was speaking for them. So far as Tombstone could tell, the truce was strictly unilateral, if only because no one knew whether the people who'd agreed to it in either the Krasilnikov or Leonov factions had the authority to do so.

In fact, the short, hard-fought naval war that had started just after the neo-Soviets had invaded Norway and led up to the Marine landings on the Kola Peninsula had finally ended more through Russia's internal collapse and exhaustion than anything else. Prisoners taken during that campaign had indicated that Russian morale was at zero, that their troops were short of food, of clothing, of ammunition, of boots, of everything, in fact, that a modern army needed in order to fight.

That was seven months ago, and things within the borders of the former Soviet state had gotten a hell of a lot worse since then. The civil war continued, bloody and relentless, and there was no clear-cut government to deal with, no one to sign a cease-fire or agree to a cessation of hostilities. The UN had been trying to bring about a truce for months now, and the closest they'd come was in establishing a tiny enclave in Georgia—nominally an independent nation but largely controlled now by one or another of the Russian army factions that were battling it out all across the length and breadth of the vast and once-powerful land of Russia. UN officials hoped, however, that a United Nations peace-keeping victory in those nations would open the way to a UN-bartered peace throughout the Russian Federation.

And that, indirectly at least, was why the *Jefferson* and her battle group were sailing into this landlocked potential death trap. They'd already arranged to have a Marine Expeditionary Unit—MEU-25—moved to the waters off the Georgian port of Poti, and now the *Jefferson* was going in to add her air wing to the UN's arguments. Whether or

not American forces should be put under the command of
UN commanders was an issue that had been debated for
many years now; a group of advisers close to the President
had acquired the nickname of the "Internationalists" because of their insistence that the long-touted New World
Order would evolve only when the UN possessed the
military teeth of a world power, while national armed forces
were weakened.

Personally, Tombstone didn't care for the direction things
seemed to be taking. A U.S. carrier battle group under the
command of a foreigner just wasn't right.

In fact, he thought it was downright dangerous.

A scant two hours earlier, *Jefferson* had cleared the
Golden Horn, that freshwater arm of the Bosporus lying just
north of the city of Istanbul proper, the Old City, and had
slipped into the narrow waterway separating Europe from
Asia. Technically, the buildings visible to either side of the
strait were still part of Istanbul. The four slender minaret
spires of the Sancta Sofia, rising above the sprawl of
Topkapi Palace and marking the heart of old Istanbul, had
long since receded out of sight astern, but the buildings
sliding past to the west, part of a community called Rumeli
Kavagi, could be thought of as part of Istanbul's modern
suburbs.

The Bosporus, the strait linking the Black Sea with the
Sea of Marmara, was eighteen miles long and averaged two
miles in width, though it was only half a nautical mile wide
at its narrowest. While the historic Old City was huddled on
the tightly crowded peninsula at the extreme southern end of
the waterway, Istanbul, the modern city, sprawled exuber-
antly clear to the airport fourteen miles west, north to the
shores of the Black Sea itself, and eastward, across the
Bosporus and deep into Anatolia. An important seaport and
trading center since the times of the ancient Greeks, it was
today a bustling, crowded metropolis, with modern sky-
scrapers vying for space with centuries-old Ottoman minarets and the onion-shaped domes of mosques.

Most unforgettable for Tombstone, however, had been the
waters just off the Golden Horn in the shadow of Sancta

Sofia. There, the garish spectacle of Old Istanbul had
crowded in on every side of the carrier, a cluttered profusion
of shapes and colors, the only city in the world straddling
Europe and the Asian mainland. Through the open window
at Brandt's elbow, Tombstone had heard the eerie, wailing
cries of the muezzins atop the city's myriad minarets,
calling the faithful to afternoon prayer, mingled with the
sound of horns and traffic in the city's crowded streets. The
straits themselves had been packed with boats and small
craft of every description, from modern yachts to sail-driven
coasting vessels that looked like galleys out of the *Arabian
Nights*. Fishing boats were especially thick here, for the
straits provided access for a number of species of fish that
migrated between the Black Sea and the Aegean; at times,
Tombstone felt as though the carrier were shooing whole
flocks of waterfowl out of her way as the fishing boats
scattered left and right just beneath the CVN's towering
prow.

The next two hours had been a period of slowly mounting
tensions as the carrier navigated up the waterway, slipping—
with just room to spare—beneath two of the three suspension
bridges spanning the Bosporus. The oldest and southernmost
dated only to 1973; the newest, stretching now across the
water directly ahead of the *Jefferson*, the final barrier between
the carrier and the open sea, had been opened only a few years
ago. To Tombstone's eye, none of those bridges looked high
enough to give the top of *Jefferson*'s superstructure and radio
masts clearance beneath their gray-silver girders. Ismet Ecevit,
the pilot who'd come aboard at Canakkale, had insisted that
there was plenty of room to spare, and so far, at least, he'd
been right. Just one more bridge to clear, now . . .

The straits had been tight and narrow, but at last they
were opening up and the waters of the Black Sea were
spreading out ahead. The sky had been partly cloudy all day;
at Istanbul, shafts of sunlight had sliced through high-
stacked blue-gray clouds, touching the centuries-old mosques
and towers and ancient-looking walls and the sails and
canopies of small craft in the harbor with liquid gold. The

clouds were beginning to close in now, but patches of blue sky continued to peep from among the towering piles of fluffy cumulus clouds. *Jefferson's* met boys were calling for clear weather for the passage, but probable rain tonight. It looked like this time they'd called it right.

Tombstone was glad the passage was almost over. Bringing a modern Nimitz-class aircraft carrier through the Bosporus wasn't quite as needle-threading a challenge as guiding the 1092-foot-long vessel through the Suez Canal, but in his opinion it came damned close. He hadn't felt this hemmed in since the *Jeff* had hidden from Soviet reconnaissance forces inside a narrow fjord in Norway.

Somehow, though, he didn't think he'd feel much safer when they entered the Black Sea . . . the *Chernoje More*.

Stupid . . . stupid . . . stupid . . .

Something about his expression made Captain Brandt chuckle. "It's okay, Stoney. We're past the narrow part. You can breathe now."

Tombstone grinned at him. "You know, sir, we missed a bet. Back there where the straits were really closing in, we could've tossed a handful of lira to the kids on either bank and had 'em scrape down and paint our hull as we passed."

"Shit," Brandt said with considerable feeling. "This is nothing compared to the Suez. Man, I *hate* taking a CVN through there."

"I don't know which would make me more nervous," Tombstone replied. "Scraping paint to port and starboard, or the security threat."

Brandt nodded toward the flight deck, where a number of U.S. Marines in full combat gear stood at key positions around the perimeter, facing outward. *Jefferson's* Marine contingent, together with an armed party of the carrier's sailors, were responsible for protecting her from any threat imaginable—or unimaginable, for that matter—from gunfire from either shore, to grenades dropped among the aircraft on the flight deck from those suspension bridges, to kamikaze speedboats, and they took their responsibilities very seriously indeed.

"Security, Tombstone," Brandt said, all trace of bantering gone from his voice. "It's *always* the security."

Then they were up to the final bridge, cruising into its shadow. Tombstone repressed an instinctive desire to duck as the shadow drifted slowly up the flight deck, then blotted out the sun as the bridge slipped momentarily out of the direct sunlight on the strait. Half of the Marines on the flight deck were scanning the bridge overhead, watching for threats . . . an impossible task, actually, since the span was crowded with Turks gathered to watch the passing of the American carrier.

Brandt cast a measuring glance toward the Turkish pilot. "I thought your people were supposed to close those bridges off, Mr. Ecevit?"

The pilot replied with an exaggerated shrug. *He* didn't care, that much was certain. He ignored Brandt after that, carefully pointing out a set of channel marker buoys to the helmsman, a quartermaster chief standing at the carrier's wheel. The chief tossed a covert glance at Tombstone and rolled his eyes toward the overhead; he'd obviously seen those buoys and made any necessary adjustments to their course long before. Ninety-thousand-plus-ton supercarriers did *not* stop on the proverbial dime; even at her current slow and ponderous crawl up the waterway, it would take her the better part of a mile to come to a complete stop if she needed to.

The sun came out again as they cleared the bridge. The shorelines to the east and the west were receding swiftly now. In another few moments, the carrier would be out of the Bosporus and inside the Black Sea.

Tombstone watched the pilot for a moment, trying to decide if he genuinely didn't care about the botched security arrangements or was pretending nonchalance to mask embarrassment. The latter, probably, Tombstone decided. He was only a minor functionary, a civilian pilot with the Turkish Port Authority, and quite far down in any hierarchy of command.

The Turks had been sticky about allowing a carrier battle group to traverse their territorial waters, formal and correct

in their dealings with Navy officials to the point of an
almost icy disdain. Their reaction, perhaps, was understand-
able. Turkey's government was strictly secular, but there
were powerful Moslem fundamentalist groups within the
country who would see the *Jefferson* as a golden target, a
symbol of the hated United States and her foreign policy, a
high-profile incident to capture a segment on *World News
Tonight*. Ankara did not want a terrorist incident . . . which
made the security failure on the bridge hard to understand.

   More than that, though, Turkish-American relations were
not good just now, partly because of U.S. support for the
Greeks in various recent wars, incidents, and territorial
disputes, but more because Turkey feared being dragged
into the rapidly spreading wildfire of war and insurrection
engulfing her once powerful neighbor to the north. Too,
Turkey's Kurd and Armenian minorities were growing
restless again and might use the chaos across the Russian
border to resurrect their own hopes of dismembering eastern
Turkey and creating states of their own.

   When the United Nations had passed Special Resolution
1026 five weeks ago, they'd turned to the United States to
provide the military and technological expertise necessary
to enforce the newly imposed no-fly zone over Georgia. The
United States, in turn, had begun pressuring Turkey to allow
the basing of U.S. warplanes on her soil in order to support
UN activities. That pressure, as Tombstone had heard it, had
damned near caused a complete and final break in Turkish-
American relations. Ankara feared that American aircraft
and personnel based on Turkish soil would cause an
explosion in the country's Moslem fundamentalists, and
they'd refused, point-blank. There'd followed several days
of acrimonious exchanges, until at last a deal to allow the
entry of a carrier battle group into the Black Sea had been
hammered out.

   Tombstone didn't know what deals had been struck or
what kind of markers had been called in to induce the
Ankara government to permit the *Jefferson* battle group to
traverse the straits to the Black Sea, but he imagined that the

promises made had been considerable, something bordering on extortionate. The Montreux Convention of 1936 specifically prohibited foreign aircraft carriers from transiting the Dardanelles and Bosporus. In earlier years, the Soviets had gotten around that restriction with their light carrier *Kiev* by identifying her as an antisubmarine cruiser; presumably they'd made other arrangements for passages by their larger, more recently built carriers.

What had Washington promised the Turks to get them to permit *Jefferson*'s transit? Or had the promise been something more on the order of a threat?

He glanced again at Ecevit. He seemed a decent enough sort, if somewhat restrained. Tombstone wondered what he thought of the political storm suddenly howling across his part of the world.

At last the shorelines of the Bosporus were passing abeam, little more now than gray smudges on the horizon. "We're out of the channel, Captain," the helmsman called. "Clear to navigate."

"Very well, Chief," Brandt replied. "We'll be heaving to while Mr. Ecevit transfers to the pilot boat."

"Aye, aye, sir."

"Commander Hadley?"

Jefferson's executive officer had been waiting in the wings for his cue. "Sir!"

"Perhaps you would be good enough to escort Mr. Ecevit to his boat."

"Aye, aye, Captain!"

"It's been a pleasure to have you aboard, Mr. Ecevit."

"Thank you, Captain," the civilian said in a thick accent, facing Brandt. "Permit me to say that this, this vessel of yours is truly remarkable. I've never had such a view of the water ahead."

"We like her," Brandt said.

Tombstone chuckled. "Conning a CVN has been compared to driving Manhattan Island from the top floor of the Empire State Building."

"I have never been to Manhattan Island," Ecevit said. "But this ship of yours does have the feel of an island." He hesitated, then licked his lips, a nervous gesture. "You should be careful out here. An island is an easy thing to find. It would be a pity if the wrong people found it."

"Just who do you mean, Mr. Ecevit?" Brandt asked casually. "Our status here will be as peacekeepers." He grinned broadly for a moment, showing clenched teeth. "See? We're friendly."

It was a variant on a joke popular aboard the *Jefferson*, but Ecevit either missed the point or ignored it.

"There are many in this part of the world who do not want peace. To them, this floating island of yours would be a most tempting target. And a vulnerable one." He shook his head. "I was directed not to discuss politics with you gentlemen. I've said too much as it is. But I . . . I *admire* this wonderful ship of yours and would hate to see her destroyed."

"A modern carrier takes one heck of a lot of destroying," Tombstone said. "The *Jeff*'s been through a few scrapes already and come through in one piece."

"That's right," Brandt said. "You should've seen the *other* guy."

"Well, I wish you good fortune. *Allaha ismarladik.*"

"*Güle güle,*" Brandt replied with carefully rehearsed formality. He'd been practicing the line on Tombstone; Turkish good-byes were two-part exchanges, with the person leaving saying "God remain with you," while the person staying behind replied with "Go with happiness." The phrase could literally be interpreted as "Go smiling."

As the pilot and the XO left the bridge, Tombstone wondered if Ecevit had been trying to deliver a message with his concern, perhaps an unofficial warning from people in the Turkish government or military who were unwilling to risk making an official one. More likely, Ecevit knew nothing specific beyond what everyone knew, that the Black Sea was a bomb with a short, lit fuse.

The officers and men of CBG-14 were under no illusions about the danger they faced inside the Black Sea. It was part of the duty of the U.S. Navy—and the tradition—to go in harm's way.

This was something different, however. In the past, "going in harm's way" meant stopping an enemy threat as far from the coasts of the United States as possible, but America's role as high-tech policeman for the United Nations was threatening to change that. The Republic of Georgia offered no threat to the United States at all, not to her population, not to her trade or even to her foreign policy, nor did it matter to American policy which of several Russian factions might be in control of the country at any given moment.

Russia, of course, was still a threat; they still possessed ICBMs that could obliterate most of the cities of North America, and with the accelerated fragmentation of order it had become impossible to know which faction in the civil war possessed how many working nukes—or to know where they were pointed. American peacekeeper operations in the Black Sea were certain to attract Russian attention for any of a number of reasons, and Tombstone wondered whether the UN mission was worth the inevitable clash.

Tombstone had been in the Navy long enough to know that the politicians back in CONUS too often either overestimated the ability of forces in the field to carry out the often vague, scattered, and mutually contradictory directives issued by Washington or else underestimated the ability, the strength, or the sheer resolve of a potential enemy. They'd already decided to send a Marine MEU into the Black Sea, and now some dim bulb in Foggy Bottom had decided that CBG-14 ought to be there as well. It was often said that any time there was a crisis, any time the United States needed to project military power to any part of the world, the first thing the American president would ask was "Where are the carriers?"

Well, now one of America's handful of precious CVNs was inside the Black Sea, with no certainty that they would be able to leave freely once the balloon went up in Georgia. Politicians who made the decisions responsible for getting their country's military forces into this kind of pocket ought to be made to serve alongside the service men and women who bore the risks and the hardships those decisions entailed.

Stupid, Tombstone thought again, and with deep and sincere bitterness. *Stupid . . . stupid . . . stupid . . .*

CHAPTER 2
Friday, 30 October

Lieutenant Commander Tricia Conway, "Brewer" to the other members of her squadron, stood in the shower stall, dripping and half-covered with soap. She looked at the snake in her hand, gave it a frustrated shake, and swore. The water was coming out, but in a weak and lukewarm trickle instead of a hot, dashing spray.

They called it a snake . . . and other things, most of them obscene. All of the showers aboard the *Jefferson* were equipped with the devices now, white plastic shower nozzles on flexible hoses designed to spray water only when the button on the side of the handle was held down. It was a means of saving water, but for Brewer it was one more way that the Navy was intruding itself into her life, her *private* life. Even that wouldn't be so bad, though, if the damned plumbing worked.

Water conservation was always of critical importance aboard any Navy ship; all crewmen, officer or enlisted, male or female, were treated to several training and indoctrination films before their first tours of duty aboard ship on the proper and approved method of taking a Navy shower.

First use just enough water to get your body wet.

She'd heard of some captains who cut the water to the shower heads if the usage meters showed someone spending more than five minutes under a running stream. It wasn't that bad on the *Jeff*, thank God, but the rules were strict, and if the nearly six thousand men and women aboard used the fresh water supplies too quickly, then there were standing orders posted for rationing.

Then, with the water off, work up a lather and soap yourself down.

Brewer had always been somewhat fastidious, and the thought of the population of a fair-sized city crammed cheek by jowl inside a steel can, most of them young and athletic, most of them putting in eighteen-hour days of some of the most grueling work in the world, and not enough water for daily showers was fairly disgusting. There was always a slight stink of sweat and humanity clinging to the carrier's berthing areas, the natural consequence of too many bodies in too little space.

After you've scrubbed yourself, turn on the water again, using just enough to remove the soap. . . .

The snake was a relatively new addition to the *Jefferson*, one installed just a couple of months ago during her last rotation back Stateside. Scuttlebutt had it that several city commissions and representatives from the California state legislature were interested in the thing, that there was talk of passing laws requiring houses in the southern part of the state to have them installed in order to enforce water conservation measures there.

Remind me never to live in California, she thought. One of the few sybaritic luxuries that she'd learned to enjoy during her lifetime was a good, long, piping hot shower—and since coming aboard ship that luxury had taken on the dimensions of an addiction, one that she could never get enough of. After spending sixteen hours or more wrapped up in a stinking flight suit, the thought of coming here to face the snake could be damned near unbearable.

The worst of it was that the snake didn't work all that well, though she didn't know if the flaw was in the snake's design or somewhere in *Jefferson*'s plumbing. The best the thing could manage was an anemic stream of tepid water, when it was supposed to blast the skin with a high-powered jet. When she'd complained about it to Group Seven, the ship's engineering and hull department, they'd laughed and told her to get in line.

"Shit, Commander, you want us to tear half the ship apart so's you can get a decent shower?" one old-Navy pipe fitter chief had asked, grinning at her around the stub of a reeking cigar. "Maybe you got yourself in the wrong career track, know what I mean?"

She could have reported the guy for that crack—published Naval standards about what constituted sexual harassment in the wake of the Tailhook scandal were exhaustive, specific, and draconian—but she preferred to handle that sort of thing with professionalism and wit, not a reliance on regulations. She'd replied with an icy, "And maybe your people are in the wrong jobs if they can't make the plumbing on this ship work," and let it go at that.

Grimly, she continued sluicing the soap off her body, occasionally giving the shower attachment another shake, as though the hose were blocked and a good shake might free it. Navy showers were just one of the countless adjustments Brewer and the other women serving aboard the carrier had had to make as the price of equality, and generally the feeling was that if the men could put up with it, so could the women. Still, she wasn't entirely certain whether the low pressure in the women's head was something everyone aboard suffered with, or whether it was a problem restricted to the shower head reserved for female personnel. If it was the former, there wasn't anything to be done about it. If the latter, then someone was having some twisted fun at the women's expense . . . or worse, they were using this particular form of harassment to let the women know that they weren't wanted aboard, and something most certainly would have to be done about that.

But Brewer wasn't sure how to go about finding out which it was. What was she supposed to do . . . walk up to the ship's Exec and ask him whether or not *his* shower was hot? Ask to inspect the enlisted men's shower heads? Or demand a return to the bad old days when men and women had shared one of the carrier's shower heads on a rotating schedule? God, that had been a nightmare.

Their last overseas deployment, earlier in the year, had been a comedy of inconveniences and logistical headaches. A shared shower head had been just one of the problems. After the Kola Peninsula deployment, *Jefferson* had returned to Norfolk for refits and resupply in May, while her carrier wing had transferred to NAS Oceana for training. Normally, a Stateside deployment would last for at least six months, but with things going to hell all over the world, the U.S. Navy's twelve-carrier fleet was stretched to the absolute limit . . . and maybe a bit beyond. After only four short months, *Jefferson* had been ordered to sea again; the men and women of CVW-20 had said good-bye to families and loved ones at Oceana, then flown their aircraft out to a rendezvous and trap aboard the carrier as it cruised several miles offshore in the Atlantic.

Some reworkings when the ship had been back in Norfolk over the summer had made things considerably better for the female contingent; they still were forced to take a multideck detour from points aft of the hangar deck, but they at least now had one whole, entire shower head that belonged to them and them alone.

She had to keep reminding herself that things *were* improving for the women aboard . . . but they still had a long way to go. The women had their own berthing and shower facilities now. Most of the men accepted them, too, despite the inevitable jokes about "Amazons" and "skirts." In most ways, it was no worse than being stationed ashore; an aircraft carrier was such an enormous place it was sometimes almost possible to forget that you were actually aboard a ship at sea.

A sudden thunder followed by a harsh rattling sound from overhead was an adequate reminder, however. The thunder had been suspended for most of the day by the lull in flight operations that had brought them through the straits from the Aegean Sea, but it was in full force once more, with a full flight schedule resumed almost the instant the *Jefferson* had left Turkish waters. It was even noisier one level up, on the O-3 deck, where most of the enlisted men were quartered directly beneath the "roof."

She released the sprayer's button and hung it back on the side of the shower stall, still feeling a bit gritty and soap-filmed. Her hair, she decided, would just have to wait for another time. She kept it cut short, the blond tresses reaching only halfway down between ear and shoulder so they wouldn't interfere with wearing a flight helmet, but even that much was a pain to keep clean when the water was as sluggish as this. The guys had the right idea there; most had crewcuts, and some wore little more up top than razor stubble, which made washing their hair as easy as passing a washcloth over their scalp. Some of the other women in the squadron had already taken that step and cut their hair so short the skin showed through. Brewer wasn't quite ready for anything that drastic . . . but each time she took a shower in here, the day got just a little closer.

Stepping out of the stall, she reached for the towel she'd left on the bench and started drying herself off, sparing only a brief glance for the off-white cork-tile panels of the overhead. During their first deployment, one of *Jefferson*'s horny male crew members had hidden himself up there with a spy camera; she'd seen the pictures just before the guy went to captain's mast. Close quarters and lack of privacy were still among the biggest problems with women serving aboard ship, and lonely guys could get pretty inventive sometimes.

The Great Experiment, it was still being called. The problem of female Navy personnel serving aboard ship or in combat had been plaguing the service for decades now. The Navy's first experiment in women serving at sea had been the result of one of then-Admiral Elmo Zumwalt's famous "Z-grams" in 1972, when 424 men and 53 women had been assigned together to the hospital ship U.S.S. *Sanctuary* for a four-hundred-day cruise. Officially, the experiment had been a success—"success" in this case being defined by those Pentagon bureaucrats whose careers and reputations depended on the mission's successful outcome. In real-world terms, however, the *Sanctuary* experiment had been a disaster, with frequent sexual liaisons between members of the crew, several pregnancies, a number of jealous fights over women, and lingering bad morale. In fact, *Sanctuary*'s cruise had ended after forty-two days, not four hundred, and she'd spent the rest of her career in port before she was finally quietly decommissioned.

And this with men and women who'd been carefully screened beforehand, in order to ensure that nothing would go wrong!

But the Navy had kept trying. Federal District Court Judge John Sirica in 1978 had held that banning women from serving aboard ship violated their Fourteenth Amendment rights, a ruling that had led directly to several more experiments . . . and an increasing number of Navy vessels referred to by an amused news media as "Love Boats." Despite this—and despite the civil rights ruling eventually being overturned by the Supreme Court—the Navy had taken the final step in 1993, when it lifted its ban on female combat pilots; less than a year later, female aviators and enlisted personnel had reported for duty aboard the carrier *Abraham Lincoln*.

The first time in combat for female aviators had come a few years later, when the *Thomas Jefferson* met neo-Soviet forces off the Kola Peninsula, and Brewer still thought herself lucky to have been in on that op. She'd proven herself in combat then, racking the six kills to become the Navy's first female combat ace. Right now, right *here*, she was at the very top of her own personal career pyramid . . . and she was poised to keep on climbing as the opportunities kept opening. Not for her the glass ceilings that women in mid-level management still complained about in civilian life. Not for her an executive's position in some corporation Stateside, where if she dressed and acted feminine her coworkers would think she was weak, and if she acted tough she was a bitch, and where success, any success at all, was assumed by her male compatriots to be her reward for sleeping with the boss.

Well, screw *that*. She was the very best at what she did, which was flying Navy combat aircraft. She loved flying, loved it with a passion she felt for nothing else in the world. The opportunity to be here, a pioneer for female naval aviators, made everything—the lack of privacy, the harassment and innuendo—all worth it.

But, damn, what she wouldn't give for a hot, high-pressure shower right now. . . .

1635 hours (Zulu +3)
Sonar
U.S.S. *Orlando*, the Black Sea

"Contact is turning right, Captain," Sonarman First Class Brian Davies said. He spoke softly into his lip mike, as though fearful that the target out ahead of the American submarine would hear. "Still turning . . . Okay. Contact on new heading, course one-seven-one."

"Very well, Davies," the voice of Captain Lang replied over the intercom. "Stick with him."

"Sounds like transients," Sonarman Second Class Wilbur Brown said, hesitant at first, but then growing more confident. "Like a . . . clanking sound?"

"Someone left a cable dangling," Davies told him. "An Irish pennant. When he changes course, it hits the bulkhead. Sloppy, Ivan. Sloppy."

They sat side by side in the alcove just off the *Orlando*'s control room, hunched over the array of electronics that were the Los Angeles–class submarine's primary sense at eight hundred feet. The cascade of light on the screen in front of him, the "waterfall" in submariner's parlance, gave a visual signature to the contact frequency by frequency, but Davies trusted his own ears and brain. His eyes were closed, his fingertips lightly pressing the headphones against his ears. Sometimes it was almost as though he could *see* that other vessel up ahead through what he was hearing now on *Orlando*'s passive sonar. Loudest was the gentle thrum of his prop, a tandem eight-bladed screw . . . but Davies, like a blind man who'd learned to see with his ears, could distinguish countless other noises as well, from the hiss of water flowing over the submarine's skin to the slight fluttering sound of a minor cavitation due to one of the screw's blades being slightly out of alignment to the intermittent clink of something — a loose cable, perhaps — swinging free inside the pressure hull and transmitting the sound of each contact with metal through the water.

They'd picked this sub up only three hours after entering the Black Sea yesterday, slipping in behind him as he, in turn, slipped into the wake of the Aegis cruiser *Shiloh*. It was like a return to the bad old days of the Cold War, when U.S. and Soviet submarines would play endless games of tag and double blind man's bluff, a game that American sub skippers — and their sonarmen — were especially good at. The Russian's signature — a sonar fingerprint unique to each different vessel — was already in *Orlando*'s electronic library. He was one of twenty-six submarines of the class known to the Russians as Project 671 RTM, and to the West as the Victor III. The oldest class of nuclear-powered attack submarines still in the Russian arsenal, it was nonetheless reasonably quiet, capable of making thirty knots submerged, and mounted four 650mm and two 533mm tubes firing a variety of torpedoes and missiles, with a total of twenty-four weapons carried aboard . . . and deadly when skillfully used.

Submarines — even Russian submarines — were not that common inside the Black Sea. Treaty constraints restricted the number of subs allowed to pass the Bosporus-Dardanelles waterway each year; more to the point, the Dardanelles were only thirty meters deep in spots, deep enough to hide a submerged sub — barely — but with precious little room for error. Subs trying to pass unobserved through the straits did so with the certain knowledge that the waterway was thickly laced with sound detector equipment and other sub-hunting gear . . . not to mention the less predictable hazards imposed by fishermen's nets. Since submarines survived in modern warfare by remaining unobserved, the old Soviet Union had never added many submarines to its Black Sea Fleet, and the majority of those stationed there were diesel electric boats out of the secret pens at Balaklava—Kilos, Tangos, and aging Foxtrots.

There were a few more modern, nuclear-powered boats in the Black Sea, however, and this Victor III was one. Obviously he'd been deployed to keep an eye on the CBG, and it was *Orlando*'s task to keep an eye on him.

Or rather . . . an ear. Davies remained motionless, not straining to hear so much as he was losing himself in the hissing, churning cascade of sound coming through his headset.

"Davies?"

He looked up, startled. Commander Peter Lang was leaning against the entrance to the sonar shack. "Yes, Skipper?"

"You're sure of that heading, son?"

He took a moment more before answering, listening to the churn of the Russian's eight-bladed screw. Yes . . . the sound was definitely moving off to the right now as *Orlando* continued forward. "Yes, sir. I make it between one-seven-oh and one-seven-three. He's on a straight heading now. It's not a crazy Ivan."

Lang ducked out of the compartment long enough to say, "Helm! Come right to one-seven-one. Gently, now!"

Davies heard the source of the noise drifting back to the left, until it was coming from directly ahead of *Orlando*'s bow. "That's it, Skipper," he said after a moment. "We're still squarely in his baffles."

That was where they wanted to be in this deadly game—inside the cone-shaped area astern of the Russian sub where her own wake and propeller noise made detection of the American sub almost impossible.

"Think we can release a message buoy without him hearing?"

"With all the racket he's making? Sure thing."

Twice so far in the hunt, *Orlando* had dropped off astern of the contact, letting the Russian sub move on ahead so that they could quietly slip close to the surface in order to radio the carrier group, then reacquiring the contact later. Releasing a tiny buoy with a radio transmitter and a canned, coded message, however, would permit the *Orlando* to stay on the contact's tail.

"I don't want to lose this bastard," Lang said quietly. "One-seven-one is going to put him right on the *Jefferson*."

Davies looked up, startled. "No shit?"

"No shit," Lang agreed. He looked up at a clock mounted on the bulkhead above the waterfall. "Your watch is up in fifteen."

"Supposed to be."

"You mind sticking around for a while, son? I want the best ears in the boat on this one."

"Hey, no problem, Skipper. I wouldn't miss this for anything."

"Good man. If that son of a bitch even twitches toward a weapons release, I want to know about it. Understand?"

"Yes, sir!"

Lang smiled and nodded. "Keep me posted."

Davies exchanged glances with Brown after the captain left. "They're going after the *Jefferson*?" the other sonarman said. "Shit!"

"Makes sense," Davies replied. "They're gonna want to keep assets close and ready, just in case another shootin' war breaks out."

"What about us?"

"I guess we've just got to be closer . . . and readier."

He closed his eyes, losing himself once again in the dark, swirling roar of sound from ahead.

CHAPTER 3
Friday, 30 October

The clouds had closed in completely as *Jefferson* turned into a freshening wind out of the northeast, dropping a low, gray ceiling across the sky. The overcast increased the sense of claustrophobia Tombstone had been feeling since entering this landlocked sea.

South, some twenty miles away, the northern coast of Anatolia showed as a streak of green and brown between gray sea and gray sky. Turkey claimed a six-mile limit on their territorial waters in the Aegean, which they shared with Greece, but twelve miles in the Med and in the Black Sea. It had taken *Jefferson* less than thirty minutes to work her way north out of Turkish waters, after transferring their pilot to the *Yavuz*. They were on their own now, though Turkish naval units continued to shadow the American force to the south.

"Feeling better, Stoney?" Brandt asked with a chuckle.

"I'm not sure, Captain," Tombstone replied. He thought a moment. "You know, sir, when you're in an F-14 coming in for a trap, a carrier looks damned small, about the size of a postage stamp . . . especially at night or in rough weather. Out here, though, I feel just about as small and as inconspicuous as an elephant in a phone booth."

"I know what you mean." Brandt chuckled. "Ain't hardly enough room out here to swing a Tomcat."

Tombstone laughed. He nodded toward the flight deck, where the normal bustle and excitement of air ops had resumed. "Or a Hawkeye."

Now that they were out of Turkish territorial waters, *Jefferson* was launching aircraft as fast as she could hurl them off her deck. Four F-14 Tomcats, her Combat Air Patrol, had been first aloft; now, a big E-2C Hawkeye was being readied on Cat One.

One of the carrier's four E-2Cs of VAW-130, the gray, twin-engined turboprop aircraft seemed anachronistic among all of the sleek, high-powered jets . . . not to mention a bit exotic with its large, flat, flying-saucer radome mounted on its back. That radome, or rather the powerful APS-125 radar inside, truly made the Hawkeye the eyes of the fleet. Its sophisticated electronics were capable of keeping track of air and surface targets across a circle nearly five hundred nautical miles in diameter and could control up to twenty-five simultaneous intercepts, making it an AEW—Airborne Early Warning aircraft—of awesome sophistication and abilities. Once on station, it would be able to see everything on and over a good two-thirds of the entire Black Sea and be able to peer deep into Ukraine and Russia in order to alert the battle group of gathering hostile aircraft.

On the deck, the launch officer, identifiable by his bright yellow jersey and green-striped helmet, made a last check up and down the length of the aircraft, then snapped off a crisp salute to the pilot. Dropping to one knee, he pointed two fingers down the length of the deck, then jabbed his thumb to steel, signaling the catapult officer to punch it. The Hawkeye, its props already howling, rocketed forward on a trail of steam boiling from the catapult slot. In two seconds, it was traveling at over 150 miles per hour; flaps down for maximum lift, it sailed off the *Jefferson*'s bow, hung there in the wet air for a moment as though unsure whether to climb or fall . . . then began climbing.

"I'm sure glad to see him away," Tombstone said with heartfelt relief. "I hate being blind."

"Amen to that, Stoney," Brandt replied. "At least now we can see 'em when they come after us."

Tombstone knew that the claustrophobia he'd felt about this op ever since its inception three weeks earlier was as much psychological as anything else. With a surface area of over 175,000 square miles, the Black Sea was only twenty percent smaller than the North Sea. In places it was three times deeper; the greatest recorded depth was some 1226 fathoms—better than 7300 feet, deep enough to be very black at the bottom indeed. There was enough water here for whole fleets of ships; certainly, Tombstone had never felt this hemmed in or restricted during his tours in the North Sea.

But throughout the years of the Cold War—indeed, since long before America had had any national interests in this part of the world at all, the Black Sea had been, by virtue of its geography, virtually closed off to the Western world, a body of water owned—dominated, rather, which was much the same thing—by Russia, whatever Turks, Romanians, or Bulgarians might have had to say about the matter. American ships occasionally passed through those straits for a game of show-the-flag, but in a typical year the number of U.S. naval vessels entering the Black Sea was likely to number fifteen to twenty . . . while ten or twenty times that many Russian vessels made the passage.

A Russian lake . . .

That description had been floating about the wardrooms and squadron ready rooms a lot lately, along with other names like "Lakeski Russki" and "Red Sea North." The Romanians, Tombstone reminded himself, still called it the "Friendly Sea," as had the ancient Greeks, but those cold gray waters ahead would be anything but friendly for an American battle group.

Stupid . . . stupid . . . stupid . . .

. What asinine, pencil-pushing, limp-dicked, shit-for-brains REMF, he wondered bitterly, had thought *this* bastard of an operation up?

Operation Sustain Hope was what the politicians and the news media were calling this mission Stateside, though the *Jefferson*'s men and officers had taken to calling it Operation Hopeless unofficially. The brainlessness of sending an aircraft carrier battle group into the Black Sea simply defied imagination.

There were all kinds of arguments against operating a CBG inside the Black Sea, arguments besides the painfully obvious one that, large as it was, the Black Sea was completely landlocked and ringed by hostile or potentially hostile nations. Carriers and their battle groups depended for their survival on mobility and on defense in depth; both of those factors would be severely limited once they were inside the Black Sea operational area.

Normally, in the open ocean, a carrier group was scattered across some forty *thousand* square miles, or nearly a quarter of the surface area of the entire Black Sea. An example often used to demonstrate the sheer scale of a battle group deployment imagined the carrier, the center of the CBG, located in Washington, DC. Her escort ships, destroyers and frigates, would be as far afield as Norfolk, Virginia, and Johnstown, Pennsylvania; her combat air patrol defending the CBG's airspace from enemy attack would be patrolling the skies over Bangor, Maine, and Charleston, South Carolina; while her attack submarines and her S-3 Viking ASW aircraft would be probing the waters ahead somewhere in the vicinity of Cleveland, searching for enemy subs.

And if she'd needed to launch an alpha strike with her A-6 Intruders, she could have delivered sizable force packages—bombs, in non-Navy speak—on Chicago or Nashville.

Transposing that one-to-one scale model to the Black Sea gave a rough idea of how crowded things were going to be here. With the *Jefferson* cruising in the western Black Sea just halfway between the Bosporus and the Crimean Peninsula, her screen of surface ships, at a radius from the carrier of 150 miles, would be entering the Crimean port of Sevastopol to the northeast, just exiting the Bosporus to the southwest, or hard aground on the coasts of Romania to port or Turkey to starboard. Her submarines would be hunting enemy subs in the Dnieper River somewhere near Nikopol, while her CAP orbited above Dnepropetrovsk over two hundred miles north of the Crimea.

And as for that alpha strike, it could be aimed at Kiev or Kharkov, deep inside Ukraine and two-thirds of the way to Moscow.

Obviously, CBG-14 was going to have to operate on a much smaller scale, pulling her escorting ships and her patrolling aircraft in close and tight. That would increase the group's ability to maneuver somewhat, but it would sharply cut into its ability to defend in depth. Rather than intercepting a first wave of incoming enemy aircraft at a range of over five hundred miles, they might have to set an outer ring of defenses at, say, three hundred miles . . . which meant more "leakers" slipping through the outer ring of defenses and a correspondingly higher chance that the carrier's innermost defenses, her Sea Sparrow missiles and CIWS high-speed guns, would be overwhelmed by the sheer number of incoming targets.

Arguably worse than being pinned down to such a small and landlocked AO was the fact that half of the encircling coastline belonged either to the Russian Federation or to former Soviet countries like Ukraine. Quite frankly, there was no help to be had in there if things got rough, no place to turn to, no source of supply or repair. Of the other three nations bordering the Black Sea, Bulgaria, Romania, and Turkey, only Turkey could be described as anything like an ally . . . and relations with Ankara had been so strained of late that no one was counting on help from *that* quarter.

As just one example, a modern carrier like the *Jefferson* required at-sea replenishment of expendables every two to three weeks. She was nuclear-powered and didn't require fuel herself, but her aircraft drank millions of gallons of the stuff. In combat, *Jefferson*'s onboard reserves of over three million gallons of JP-5 aviation gasoline wouldn't last more than ten days—less with a heavy flight schedule, a major alpha strike, or an extended, running battle like the one they'd fought months before off North Cape. Her only sources of resupply were the UNREP tankers that followed the battle group like a bride's train across the sea; if things got tight, if an enemy wanted to pin or incapacitate the carrier short of actually sinking her, an obvious move was to hit the choke point on the *Jefferson*'s supply line, those two damned narrow slots of waterways, the Dardanelles and the Bosporus.

Hell, the only thing that made this deployment even remotely possible was the fact that the Russians weren't likely to add Turkey to the list of nations that were mad at them right now. In fact, Russia needed Turkey's help—as Turkey needed Russia's—in coordinating operations against the Armenian nationalists who operated freely on both sides of the Turkish border. U.S. military intelligence thought that Moscow would be treading carefully around the Turks . . . and that ruled out provocations like air strikes against supply ships transiting the Hellespont.

They *thought*.

Tombstone loved it when the intelligence community made a definite and unambiguous statement like that. If the Russians decided they needed to bag a U.S. carrier battle group more than they needed to stop Armenian gunrunners in the Caucasus, well, *Jefferson* and her escorts were going to be flat damned out of luck.

Commander William Jeffries, the carrier's ops officer, walked onto the bridge, a computer printout in his hand. "Captain?"

"Whatcha got, Bill?"

"Flash from the *Orlando*, sir."

"*Shiloh* still has a tail, then, I take it?"

"Looks like they're giving up on the *Shiloh*, sir, in favor of a fatter target."

"Us," Tombstone said.

"That's about the size of it. But *Orlando*'s squat in their baffles, and the Russkis don't even have a clue."

Brandt grinned. Jeffries handed the printout to him and he glanced over it, then handed it to Tombstone. It was a terse and to-the-point message from Commander Lang, captain of the Los Angeles attack sub *Orlando*. Most of the message consisted of numbers and code groups, but the gist of the

thing was that *Orlando* was still tracking the Russian sub
that she'd picked up shortly after *Shiloh* had entered the
Black Sea late yesterday. The data had been recorded an
hour earlier and sent to the surface in a message buoy,
which had waited its programmed twenty minutes for the
Orlando to get well clear of the area before squirting its
coded and compressed digitized warning to the *Jefferson* by
way of one of the Aegis cruiser's SH-3 helos.

The tail was inevitable, of course, and the discovery of
the sub had come as no surprise. *Orlando*'s orders were to
stick tight to the Victor, to report on its position occasionally. If the Victor made a hostile move, such as opening her
torpedo tubes, Lang was under orders to kill her.

It was a damned precarious position to be in. The
American battle group's orders from both Washington and
the UN officials in charge of Sustain Hope were explicit on
at least one point: Under no circumstances were Russian
units to be fired upon unless the Russians fired first. Further
bloodshed, the politicians thought, would only make the
peace process more difficult, and a unilateral, watchful truce
by the Americans might convince the Russian factions to
back down and let the UN step in with a negotiated
settlement.

Those were tough orders to obey in modern warfare,
however, where ship-killer weapons could be deployed in
seconds, and where a mistake rarely permitted a second
chance.

"So," Tombstone said. "What are we going to do about
friend Victor?"

"Do? Not a hell of a lot we can do. We keep track of him
with Vikings and Sea Kings and trust *Orlando* to nail the
bastard if he so much as looks hard at the *Jeff*. Other than
that . . ." A shrug.

"Hell of a way to run a war."

"It would be, if this was a real war. Who knows? Maybe
the Russians just want to make sure we stay clear of their
bases in the Crimea. And you know, that Victor could be a
Ukrainian boat, too, out of Odessa."

Tombstone nodded. "Russians and Ukrainians, they've

both got to be a bit nervous with us here. About the way we'd feel if a Russian battle group steamed into Chesapeake Bay."

"Nah. There's a difference. Chesapeake Bay is U.S. territory, right down to the last soft-shelled crab. The Black Sea is international waters, whatever the Russkis and Ukes might think about the matter."

A telephone rang, and an enlisted rating picked it up. After a moment, he looked at Brandt. "Captain?"

"Yes."

"Commander Nelson, in Ops, sends his respects and says that all vessels are clear of the Bosporus now, and the battle group is in a standard port-heavy deployment."

"Very well."

Tombstone looked out the bridge windows. He could see two other ships, both very small and on the horizon. *Decatur* was to the north. *Leslie* was a gray smudge to the west, just off *Jefferson*'s standard bow. The sea appeared empty otherwise. So long as the *Jefferson* was hugging the Turkish coast, the bulk of her screening ships could be thrown out to north, east, and west, giving an added layer of defense across the most likely direction of an enemy's approach, a protective net that extended across the surface of the water, in a broad bubble in the air overhead, and beneath the waves as well.

Not that they ignored the southern flank. In these waters, the CBG had no friends, and no one else to trust.

"Wishing you were on a smaller target, Tombstone?" Brandt asked, twinkling.

"To tell you the truth, sir," Tombstone said, jerking a thumb toward the overhead, "I'd feel better up there. With my people."

"Now, now," Brandt admonished. "When you grow up, you put away your toys. You're a big boy now, Stoney. Time to stop playing with airplanes and take on some real responsibility, right?"

Tombstone wondered—not for the first time—whether he really wanted to go on to command a carrier like this one someday. He just wasn't certain, and that bothered him. A man should want that next step in his career, want it enough to taste it, to be willing to *fight* for it, not to simply wait for it to be handed to him on a platter. Not that command of a CVN was something that could be disbursed that way; there were thousands of eager young aviators in the U.S. Navy, every one of them on a career track straight for command of an aircraft carrier. In the entire U.S. Navy, there were exactly twelve supercarriers, some nuclear powered, others, like the *John F. Kennedy* and the three Kitty Hawk-class carriers, powered by conventional steam boilers. Even throwing in the various Marine amphibious assault ships and helicopter carriers, there were only a couple of dozen carrier commands in the entire Navy, and thousands of eager would-be skippers. His chances of landing a carrier command were vanishingly slim.

And there was something more.

He cocked an eye at Brandt. "Tell me the truth, Captain. Do you miss it now? The flying, I mean?"

"Every goddamn day of my life, Stoney, and that's the truth."

"That's what I thought. Maybe all the grown-up responsibility isn't such a great idea after all, huh?"

"Second thoughts, Tombstone?"

"I'm not sure, Captain. I just know I prefer blue sky to quarterdecks, and a Tomcat's ejection seat to the captain's chair on the bridge. Now, if you'll excuse me, sir, I think I'd better get down to CATCC. With our planes up, it looks like I'm CAG again."

"Well, son, thanks for keeping me company. Drop by anytime."

"You know I will, Captain."

"Oh, and Stoney?"

"Sir?"

"You tell your people to keep their Mark One eyeballs peeled up there. Hawkeyes or no Hawkeyes, I trust their judgment and their instincts more than all the electronics between here and Silicon Valley."

Tombstone grinned. He felt exactly the same way. "Aye, aye, sir!"

CHAPTER 4
Friday, 30 October

1735 hours (Zulu +3)
Carrier Air Traffic Control Center (CATCC)
U.S.S. *Thomas Jefferson*

It was almost time for evening chow, but work aboard a
Navy carrier continued nonstop, with no pause for food or
sleep, often with a near-constant cycle of cat launches and
recoveries carried out for hour after hour after grueling hour.
Save for rare instances such as *Jefferson*'s recent transiting
of the Bosporus, several aircraft were nearly always in the
sky, especially in potential war zones like this; minimum air
deployment at any given time for the *Jefferson*'s air wing
was a couple of Tomcats on Combat Air Patrol, and at least
one of the E-2C Hawkeyes. While the actual takeoffs and
landings were controlled by the *Jefferson*'s Air Boss from
his glass-enclosed domain high up on O-8 deck known as
Primary Flight Control, or Pri-Fly, aircraft already in the air
were directed from the darkened room on O-3 deck designated the Carrier Air Traffic Control Center. CATCC—
pronounced "cat-see" in the Navy's language of acronyms
and abbreviations—was a dim-lit, magical world of computers, monitors, and complex communications systems
overseen by a staff of the Navy's most skilled high-tech
wizards. Perhaps a dozen men occupied the consoles and
radar display screens scattered about the room, while
Lieutenant Fred Penhall, the duty officer in CATCC for this
shift, surveyed his domain from the lordly throne of an

elevated, leather-backed chair at the center of the compartment.

Tombstone was tired as he pushed aside the curtains that kept out the harsh light of the passageway outside and entered the room. He'd been going pretty much on adrenaline since the *Jeff* had entered the Hellespont the day before. Someone thrust a steaming mug of coffee—*his* mug, inscribed "CAG-CVW-20"—into his hands and he gave the sailor a brisk nod. Radio voices crackled from speakers on the bulkhead, terse and urgent.

"As you were, Lieutenant," he rasped as Penhall started to rise from his chair. He took a sip from the mug. It was a particularly strong brew this evening, the much-concentrated remnants of a pot put on the hot plate a long time ago. "Just passing through. What's the word?"

"We're on line now with both the *Shiloh* and Hawk One, sir," he replied. The duty officer gestured toward one of the several large computer display situation boards commanding the entire compartment. Drawn in zigzagging lines of colored light, crowded with small and cryptic symbols, each tagged by strings of alphanumerics, it was a condensation of tactical and map data relayed from several sources—in particular the Hawkeye's APS-125 radar and the high-tech array of search and tracking radars that made up the *Shiloh*'s electronic sensor suite—but it included data relayed to the CBG from other ships and aircraft and even from military satellites as well.

The scale at the moment revealed only a fraction of the display's reach, out to about one hundred nautical miles from the *Jefferson*'s position. At a glance, Tombstone could see the Turkish coast running southwest to northeast some fifteen nautical miles south of the carrier. The Turkish port of Zonguldak was prominent there, ringed by the glowing icons representing air defense, tracking, and surface scan radar. The various far-scattered ships and aircraft of the battle group were marked in green, while yellow symbols represented identified Turkish radar contacts, mostly military forces shadowing the American force.

One red-lit target stood out on the map display with

ominous clarity—the last known position and track of the presumed Russian submarine following the *Jefferson*, closely shadowed by a green icon for the *Orlando*. Tombstone pointed at the submarines, which were being paced by two pairs of green aircraft. "I see you have our tail bracketed."

Penhall grinned. "Sure do. The word just came through from Top Hat. We're gonna give him a concert. A rock concert."

Top Hat, also known as Alpha Bravo, was the code name for Admiral Douglas F. Tarrant, CO-CBG-14, who was currently running the operation from the Combat Direction Center aboard *Shiloh*. Those aircraft, according to the information appearing next to them on the display, were a pair of SH-60 Sea King ASW helos, part of *Jefferson*'s HS-19, plus two Vikings from VAW-42, the King Fishers. Though belonging to *Jefferson*'s contingent, the sub-hunters were operating under the direction of *Shiloh*'s CDC now, while the CATCC and Air Ops people aboard *Jefferson* simply listened in. The voices coming over the radio speaker were contact and vectoring information, for the most part, between the ASW aircraft and *Shiloh*'s CDC.

"Sounds like a plan to me," Tombstone said, smiling. "If the guy's a classical music lover, maybe he'll give up and go home."

Penhall laughed. "With luck, we'll jangle his sonar and make his operators' ears ring. They won't be able to hear the *Jeff*'s screws from ten meters off our stern."

It was in many ways, Tombstone reflected, an operation similar to the Bear hunts he'd participated in when he'd been a Tomcat driver flying with VF-95. During the Cold War, the Soviets would routinely test an American carrier battle group's readiness and alertness by vectoring one or more of their big long-range Tu-95 Bear-D reconnaissance planes toward the CBG. Just as routinely, F-14 Tomcats would deploy to meet the incoming Bears as far from the carrier as possible—usually several hundred miles—and force them to change course.

The same mock-war feints, threats, and counters were

part of the repertoire of the carrier's antisubmarine units as well. The "concert" Penhall had mentioned would be a special, high-volume broadcast from the Sea Kings, using their powerful AQS-13 dipping sonars, set to active mode to ping the Victor III and let him know, in no uncertain terms, that he'd been spotted. And if the sub's skipper refused to take the hint, firmer measures would be applied.

Tombstone continued studying the map display. "Let me see the Sustain Hope AO," he told Penhall.

"Yes, sir. Markowitz! Punch up Sierra Two on the main display."

"Aye, aye, sir."

The map view shifted, showing now the eastern rim of the Black Sea. The scale changed as well, covering the entire east shoreline, running from the Turkish port at Hopa northwest all the way to Kerch at the extreme east tip of the Crimea and guarding the narrow straits into the Sea of Azov. Especially prominent was the small port city of Poti, on the Georgian coast fifty miles from Hopa and the Turkish border. A cluster of green icons lay thirty miles offshore, identified by the alphanumeric MEU-25.

Tombstone pursed his lips for a moment as he studied the display. The Marine Expeditionary Unit was not technically part of CBG-14 at all, though MEUs were attached to the battle group from time to time, depending on deployment and mission. This time, MEU-25 was operating under UN auspices as part of the Georgian relief program. With Operation Sustain Hope, the old question of U.S. forces serving under United Nations leadership had come to the fore again and was rapidly proving to be a disaster.

MEU-25 consisted of the LPD *Little Rock*, the LHA *Saipan*, and the LPH *Guadalcanal*, plus a small fleet of transports and escorts assigned to carry a reinforced Marine Battalion Landing Team anywhere in the world at short notice as a rapid-response peacekeeper force. The expeditionary unit had arrived in the Black Sea a few days before the *Jefferson* with orders from the National Command Authority—meaning the President—to open up a secure port at Poti in the former Soviet Republic of Georgia so that

UN humanitarian aid could begin to flow into the war-ravaged little country lying on the southern slopes of the Caucasus Mountains.

It was supposed to be a routine operation—routine, that is, save for the extraordinary fact that U.S. military force was being projected into this corner of the world for the first time in history. A British peacekeeping force under direct UN control was already on its way to take over, but as usual the U.S. Marines would bear the brunt of the initial operation.

It was all quite a tangle, Magruder reflected. Who would have thought, just a few years back, that when American troops stood on soil that had belonged to the Soviet Empire they'd be doing it as glorified security guards? Or that in the end Russia and her former satellites would turn into just so many more Third World hot spots where the UN formula of humanitarian aid, peacekeepers, and no-fly zones would be applied the very same way it had been in Iraq, and Bosnia, and Haiti, and Macedonia?

But the world was changing fast, sometimes so fast that it almost seemed to outpace American foreign policy itself.

The Republic of Georgia was mirror to the drama that was being played throughout this part of the world now and for most of the past decade. Once a federated S.S.R., Georgia had declared its independence from the old Soviet Union on April 9, 1991. Even as the nation fought for freedom, however, the autonomous provinces of Abkhazia, Adharia, and South Ossetia were fighting for independence from Georgia. By 1994, Georgia's President Shevardnadze had agreed to a cooperation pact that increased Russian military influence in the country, a frank exchange of freedom for security, and Georgia joined the Moscow-led Commonwealth of Independent States soon after. By the time the Soviet Union was briefly reborn and the tanks had been rolling into Norway, Georgia was again solidly under Russian control.

But then the Scandinavian campaign had collapsed, the Russian military had been proven a hollow shell, and American forces were landing on the once sacrosanct soil of

the Kola Peninsula. Leonov and Krasilnikov were battling
one another in the streets of Moscow and a hundred other
Russian cities, and the entire nation was sliding relentlessly
toward the yawning chasm of total anarchy. States that had
enjoyed a brief freedom in the era of Gorbachev and Yeltsin,
states like Ukraine and Belarus, the Baltics and Georgia,
were shaking off the neo-Soviet mantle and reasserting their
independence. In one ex-Soviet state after another, popular
uprisings were driving out garrisons weak enough or discouraged enough to give way.

But independence is never cheap. There were still plenty
of neo-Soviet units scattered across the length and breadth
of the former empire, controlled by hard-liner Reds and
pro-Krasilnikov factions, and the fledgling rebel movements were rarely strong enough to break the militarists'
control by themselves. One after another of the newborn
governments had applied to the United Nations for support;
at the same time, the UN was trying to keep up with the
spreading chaos by inserting peacekeepers and taking steps
to ensure the delivery of humanitarian relief as the dreaded
Russian winter loomed near.

In Washington, the President had agreed to honor the UN
Secretary General's request and ordered MEU-25 and CBG-14
into the Black Sea, once it became certain that Turkey was not
going to permit foreign military forces to be based on their
soil.

On paper, Operation Sustain Hope seemed no more
outlandish a proposal than had Operation Restore Hope, the
abortive and expensive Marine operation—again at the
UN's behest—in Somalia in 1992 to 1994. The National
Command Authority had been specific in its directive:
Under no circumstances would U.S. forces involve themselves in the fighting between the Red and Blue Russian
factions. The Marines would go ashore at Poti only after a
UN Crisis Assessment Team could demonstrate that both
the Reds and the Blues were out of the picture in Georgia,
leaving the way clear for the Georgian Freedom Party to
cooperate with the UN mission. If and when the CAT gave
the go-ahead, Marines would start going ashore, securing

port and airfield facilities in and around Poti so that relief supplies could begin arriving by ship and plane.

Meanwhile, the *Jefferson* battle group's aircraft would impose a UN-dictated no-fly zone over western Georgia. By stopping all air traffic within a triangle marked out by the cities of Batumi and Sukhumi on the coast, and Kutasisi, about fifty miles inland from Poti, a fragile peace might be eked out among the warring tribes and factions; if it worked in western Georgia, the UN sanctions would be extended, taking in all of Georgia and the neighboring states of Armenia and Azerbaijan as well. *That* region was still a running sore in this part of the world, and a successfully enforced UN-mandated peace there would go a long way toward legitimizing the notion of a United Nations with teeth.

The UN also hoped to use a strong military presence to defuse other problems in the area as well. Turkey had threatened more than once to invade former Soviet Armenia in order to quell the restlessness of its own Armenian population and the threat of a single Armenian state carved from both sides of the border; Iran, too, was a regional wild card, with troops poised on the Iranian-Azerbaijani border threatening to intervene in that country as well.

It was enough to give anyone one hell of a headache.

"Have there been any threats to Twenty-five?" Tombstone asked Penhall.

"No direct threats," the lieutenant replied. "A number of radar sites all along the coast have been keeping tabs on them, of course, but no weapons radar signatures, and nothing that could be interpreted as a hostile move. Yet."

That final word was offered as an afterthought, and Tombstone nodded understanding. No one in this part of the world really wanted them here in these waters, and all parties concerned would be very glad to see the Americans leave.

And that goes for me, too, Tombstone thought. He pointed to a cluster of yellow symbols over the Black Sea, south of Kerch and the straits leading to the Sea of Azov. "And who are those guys?"

"They've been IDed as another military flight out of Krasnodar," Penhall said. "Reinforcements for Sevastopol, I expect."

"I think," Tombstone said slowly, "that the Crimea is going to sink if they pile anything more in there."

Penhall smiled. "What was it the Russian general said about Stalingrad, sir, back in World War II? That it was one big prison camp?"

"I'm not sure the Russians said that," Tombstone replied, "but I take your point."

The ongoing war between Russia and Ukraine was what made the American incursion into the Black Sea particularly dangerous. More so than even the civil war between Blues and Reds, the Russo-Ukrainian War carried with it the seeds of a general conflict throughout this part of the world, one that might well spill over into both Europe and the Middle East.

It had, in fact, all of the makings of a new world war.

"Top Hat, Top Hat," a radio voice called from a nearby speaker, carrying more urgency now. Tombstone cocked his head, listening, as Penhall switched the map display back to a view centered on the *Jefferson. "This is Sierra One-five. We're over the target area at seven-five feet and we're trolling for big ones, over."*

"Ah, roger that, Sierra One-five. Commence active sonar."

"And a one, and a two . . ."

The sonar pings weren't transmitted over the open communications channel, but Tombstone could imagine what it must sound like aboard the Russian sub. That SH-3 was hovering just above the sub's location, its sonar dangling at the end of a long cable, dipping beneath the surface of the water like bait on the end of a line. When the sonar started broadcasting—"going active," as opposed to passively listening—every man aboard the sub would hear it as a sharp, ringing chirp transmitted through the bulkheads of their tiny, enclosed world, proof positive that they'd been spotted and were in someone's gun sights.

"Any idea yet whose sub that is?" Tombstone asked.

"Not really," Penhall replied. "Our best guess is that it's

Russian. The signature matches a Victor III that's been operating out of their sub pens at Balaklava for some time now. It's not conclusive, but . . ." He shrugged.

"Understood. Hardly matters, anyway. Nobody out here likes us much."

"They might like us even less after this," Penhall said. "We're telling them, in effect, 'Go away!' Not exactly neighborly, you know?"

"More neighborly than an ADCAP torpedo," Tombstone said. He hesitated, watching the unmoving graphics symbols, green and red, on the screen. He grinned. "Wonder how they're enjoying the concert down there?"

1757 hours (Zulu +3)
Control room
Russian Submarine *Kislovodsk*

Ping! . . .

Scowling, Captain First Rank Aleksei Aleksandrovich Vyatkin looked up toward the control room's overhead, past the maze of conduits, wirings, and piping that ran fore-and-aft through the compartment like a writhing bundle of spaghetti.

Ping! . . .

Louder this time, loud enough to hurt sensitive hearing. *Kislovodsk*'s sonar officer, Valery Sofinsky, had already pulled off his headset and was ruefully rubbing his ear. Even at a depth of four hundred feet, it sounded as though the American helicopter-mounted sonars were right on top of them, scant meters from the outer hull.

It hadn't taken the bastards long to find them, either. Another Russian sub, the *Krimsky Komsomolets*, had been shadowing the American battle group up the Aegean; orders had come through from Balaklava just hours ago for the *Kislovodsk* to pick up the group and continue shadowing it inside the Black Sea. Their orders were to remain unobserved, but to get as close to the major ships of the CBG as possible—especially either their Aegis cruiser command ship or the carrier itself.

Ping! . . .

"They have us bracketed, Comrade *Kapitan*," Captain-Lieutenant Yuri Aleksanyan, the boat's first officer, said. "I think they must have known we were here all along."

"The bastards have the devil's own ears," Vyatkin spat. But it was more than the vaunted American technology. He knew that.

In the old days, in the Soviet days, Russian crews had not quite been the match of their American counterparts. Now, with morale at rock bottom, with machinery falling apart and no spares to be had anywhere save, just possibly, on the black market, things were much worse. His crew was sullen to the point of mutiny, and as likely to drop a heavy metal tool in protest to some unwanted order as out of stupidity or neglect. Equipment designed to run quietly didn't. Sensors designed to monitor sound aboard the submarine didn't. Officers supposedly trained in the skills necessary to navigate efficiently and silently while submerged weren't. Service aboard a Russian submarine, always both dangerous and uncomfortable, was fast becoming a nightmare.

Ping! . . .

"That was from directly ahead, Comrade Captain," the sonar officer said. He didn't even need his headset, so loud and bell-tone clear was the American transmission.

"They are warning us, Captain," the first officer added.

"They are telling us they want us to come no closer to their precious nuclear carrier," Vyatkin said.

PING! . . .

"Comrade Captain—"

"We will fox them, Yuri Aleksanyan," Vyatkin said. "Ready *Kukla*."

"At once, Comrade Captain."

The submarine known to the West as a Victor III was the oldest class of SSN still in service with the Russian navy. The first Soviet undersea vessel to be a match for the sophisticated submarine technologies of England and the United States, it was nonetheless the result of a number of compromises . . . not the least of which was the fact that the same power plant used to drive the smaller, lighter Victor II was used on this larger submarine, which translated to a slower top speed and more sluggish handling.

Worse, *Kislovodsk* had been one of the last of the Victor IIIs to come off the ways at Komsomolsk in 1985, and he—Russians always thought of their ships as he—was decidedly showing his age. There were few alternatives, but Vyatkin found the obvious one of flight to be distasteful in the extreme. To allow the hunter wolf to be chivied away from its prey by the squawking of *crows* . . . no. There was another way. A better way, one that might help unite this crew that had been beaten on the day it had set out to sea, and perhaps instill in these men confidence in their commanding officer.

"Torpedo room reports *Kukla* loaded, Comrade Captain."

"Open outer torpedo doors, and prepare to fire."

"At once, Comrade Captain."

He might be old and slow, Vyatkin thought, but the creaking *dedushka Kislovodsk* had a few tricks left in him yet. . . .

1758 hours (Zulu +3)
Control room
U.S.S. *Orlando*

"Captain! Sonar! He's opening his outer doors!"

"Damn!" Lang slapped the intercom switch on the console just above his head. "Torpedo room! Stand by tubes one and three!"

"Tubes one and three ready, Captain," a seaman's voice came back. He sounded young . . . and scared. "ADCAP, standard war shot."

"Sonar! What's he doing?"

"Hard to tell, Captain," Davies replied. "It's hard to hear through the pinging."

Lang cursed. This was bad, damned bad. Range to the *Jefferson* was still over twenty nautical miles, too far for a

standard 533mm torpedo, but easily within the range of the
big Russian 650mm monsters. Those babies could travel
over fifty miles at thirty knots . . . or twenty-seven miles
at fifty, and they packed one-ton warheads, powerful
enough to do serious damage to the *Jeff* if one connected.

Fire only if fired upon. . . .

But that particular Rule of Engagement couldn't apply
here, not to submarine combat. To wait for the other guy to
get the first shot in was suicide. *Orlando* was here, astern of
the Victor, precisely to keep the son of a bitch from firing
the shot that might sink or cripple the *Jefferson*.

And all Lang had to go on was what his sonar operator
was hearing amid the churning, ping-echoing water ahead.

Naval careers were made and broken by decision points
like this one. He was in a perfect firing position. Moments
before, when the helicopters had started their deafening
pinging of the contact ahead, he'd ordered *Orlando* to drop
back a ways, partly to stay out of the sonar barrage, partly
to set the *Orlando* up with a good shot if the need arose.

The need, apparently, had arisen; if he guessed wrong,
though, firing recklessly before he was sure, he could start
a war. . . .

The hell with that. If he guessed wrong, erring on the side
of caution, he would be responsible for the deaths of
hundreds aboard the *Jefferson*. "Weapons Officer!" he
snapped.

"Tubes one and three, loaded and ready, sir."

"Fire one!"

Orlando's weapons officer slapped the topmost of four
red switches on the bulkhead console. The deck lurched
slightly, and a light on the console winked red.

"One away, sir. Running hot and true."

"Fire three!"

Again, the lurch transmitted through the deck.

"Three away. Running time for number one is twelve
seconds."

He found himself counting off the seconds in melodra-
matic anticipation. . . .

CHAPTER 5
Friday, 30 October

Kukla—the Russian word meant *puppet*—was a decoy, a standard 533mm torpedo with the warhead removed and a sophisticated packet of microelectronics tucked away in its place that broadcast a convincing facsimile of the submarine's sound signature. The ploy would not be successful with active sonar, of course—the Americans would be able to tell from the echoes whether a target was 6.4 meters long or 104. Still, Captain First Rank Vyatkin had enormous faith in the effectiveness of confusion as both weapon and tactic in combat. If *Kislovodsk* cut his engines at the same moment he launched the *Kukla,* there would be several moments of confusion. When their passive sonar receivers picked up the sound of the SSN moving off at top speed, they would almost certainly stop pinging and listen, trying to get what information they could about the sub's new course and speed.

And in those critical few moments, before they realized that they were tracking an electronic decoy, he would bring *Kislovodsk* onto a new heading and slip out from beneath the very noses of the American ASW forces. A simple maneuver, but an effective one. He'd seen it used successfully more than once, on boats he'd served aboard as a junior officer during the Cold War.

"Fire *Kukla*!" he ordered. There was a hiss as the torpedo slid clear of the tube on a blast of compressed air. . . .

Aleksei Vyatkin and the men with him on the *Kislovodsk*'s control room deck never heard the approach of the two American torpedoes. They were coming straight out of the sub's baffles, for one thing, and for another the water around the submerged vessel was filled with the echoing pings from the helicopters' dipping sonars, and the Victor III's aging electronics suite was hard-pressed to separate the cascading signals from one another in any kind of order that made sense to the human listeners.

The first ADCAP torpedo, wire-guided by an operator aboard the *Orlando*, passed just beneath the *Kislovodsk*'s starboard stern plane and slammed into the aft trim tank about ten meters forward of the screw. Three hundred kilograms of high explosive detonated with a roar of white noise detected by every sonar within hundreds of miles.

The second Advanced Capabilities torpedo struck the Victor III's vertical stabilizer, vaporizing the teardrop-shaped towed-array sonar housing, smashing the steering mechanism and tearing away the eight-bladed screw.

Normally, one submarine firing at another from the target vessel's baffles would have sent the wire-guided ship-killers on long, looping courses that would bring them in on the target's port or starboard side. This increased the likelihood of a kill, both by presenting the incoming torpedoes with a larger target, and by exposing the most vulnerable sections of the target sub, the large compartments forward and amidships, to attack. This time, however, the attacker had gone for a straight-in shot; steering the ADCAP torpedoes in by wire across a roundabout attack path would use up precious minutes during which the Victor III could launch his own torpedoes at the *Jefferson*.

That single small note of urgency saved the Victor's crew—some of them, at least. As the after trim tank and three after bulkheads collapsed, a wall of water smashed its way forward through the main engine room, the switch-board room, and the reactor compartment. Twelve of the eighty-five men aboard were killed as the after compartments flooded, but watertight hatches were dogged shut and the sea's invasion of the Victor was halted just abaft the auxiliary machine room, stores hatch, and aft escape trunk. The lights failed, plunging everyone aboard into a screaming, panicking darkness, then returned as emergency batteries came on-line.

Vyatkin's palm came down on the alarm Klaxon, and he scooped up a microphone. "Emergency surface!" he yelled, as the Victor lurched heavily to port, trembling with the inrush of hundreds of tons of seawater. "Blow all ballast!"

Kislovodsk shuddered again, harder, and the deck canted sharply as the stricken attack sub rolled back to starboard, flinging crewmen and anything else not tied down across the deck. With a shrill scream of escaping air under high pressure, the water in the sub's ballast tanks was blasted into the surrounding sea.

"Pressurize the aft compartments!"

"Sir, the pressurization feed pipelines—"

"Force air into every compartment you can, damn it! We've got to fight the flooding!"

Vyatkin clung to the railing circling the periscope well as the vessel's bow came up. Everything, *everything* depended on how much of *Kislovodsk*'s stern was flooded, on how many compartments might yet be sealed off and still contain air, on whether or not the flooding could be contained by forcing at least some of the seawater out of compartments already flooded. He became aware of Yuri Aleksanyan clinging to a stanchion a meter away, his eyes bugging from his paste-white face as he stared at the overhead. "Easy, my friend," Vyatkin said softly, and the first officer flinched as though he'd been struck. "Easy. We live or die on the laws of physics. It's out of our hands, now."

"We are rising!" the rating manning the sub's blow planes yelled. "One hundred twenty meters . . . and rising!"

The angle of the deck increased as the bow came up higher. The stern, smashed and waterlogged, was dragging at the *Kislovodsk*, trying to pull him back into the black depths tail-first. The vessel lurched sharply, flinging Vyatkin away from the periscope, smashing him painfully against the main ballast control console as the lights flickered and dimmed once again until the only illumination

was from small, self-contained emergency lighting units
near the deck. A terrible grating, shrilling noise filled the
near-darkness, coming from beyond the aft bulkhead. At
first he thought someone was screaming back there, but the
scream grew louder, and still louder, reaching a pitch and a
volume that no human throat could possibly manage. The
scream gave way to thunder . . . and the sub jolted hard,
whipsnapping from starboard to port to starboard again, as
though it were a bone being worried by a particularly large
and playful dog.

The scream, Vyatkin realized with something like sick-
ness in his soul, was *Kislovodsk*'s death cry, the shrilling of
steel tearing like cloth.

1759 hours (Zulu +3)
Control room
U.S.S. *Orlando*

"I'm getting break-up noises, Captain!" Davies reported. He
had to listen hard, pressing the headphones against his ears
to shut out the cheering of the crew.

"All right, people!" Captain Lang shouted. "Quiet down!"

"As you were, there!" Callahan, the Chief of the Boat,
added. "Stand to!" The noise subsided.

Lang was standing just behind Davies's chair. "A kill?"

"Captain . . ." He shook his head. "Damn."

"What is it?"

"Okay . . . it's a bit confused out there. The blasts
scrambled the water, y'know? For a minute, I thought I
heard two subs, though."

Lang's eyes widened. "Two—"

"No, it's okay. I think the torp launch we heard was a
decoy. I can still hear it . . . running at zero-nine-eight, at
about thirty knots. Making noises like our contact, but I'm
also getting definite break-up noises. I think the contact
launched a decoy just before our ADCAPs took him down."

"Oh, *shit*!"

"Sir?"

"We may have jumped the gun a bit on that one. Okay, Davies. Is he going down?"

"Up, I think." The sonarman listed a moment longer. "Yes, sir. I'm not getting any engine noise, but there's lots of bubbling, hull stress and structural flexing sounds. And it's headed toward the roof."

"Diving Officer! Bring us up . . . slow. Follow the contact up."

"Coming up slow, Captain," the diving officer of the watch repeated.

Lang felt the deck tilting up beneath his feet. He felt sick inside, a mingling of combat eagerness and shock at what had just happened. "If that poor bastard didn't launch on us," he said softly, "we'd better be on hand to render assistance."

1804 hours (Zulu +3)
Russian Submarine *Kislovodsk*

For a time, the *Kislovodsk* hung suspended between the surface and the black depths below . . . caught in a very temporary balance between buoyancy and flooding. Then, with a final grinding shudder, the keel parted just beneath the sub's reactor compartment; hull plates and ribbing shredded like paper as the aft third of the Russian submarine tore free and plunged into unrelieved night, trailing bubbles, oil, and a thin, spreading plume of radioactivity from the ruptured reactor containment vessel.

The forward part of the sub leaped toward the surface with an explosive jolt. Moments later, the crippled vessel's prow burst up through the surface and into the air above in a vast explosion of spray. It was already well past sunset and the sky was overcast, but enough twilight remained to gleam from the white foam breaking across the bow and past the low, rounded sweep of the sail. In seconds, the aft, forward, and sail hatches had been cracked, and crewmen were scrambling out into the cold, wet, and windswept near-darkness, battling the black waves breaking over the submarine from bow to shattered stern as they ripped open deck panels and broke out the life rafts. Their task was made more difficult by panic, and by the fact that the deck was canted sharply aft and to port; the sail was listing at a forty-five-degree angle, and each swell of the sea breaking over and past it sent torrents of water cascading down the after escape trunk hatch.

Vyatkin clung to the railing at the side of the bridge, high atop the sail, and watched miserably as his crew fought to save themselves. For a time, he'd thought, possibly, that *Kislovodsk* might be saved. He'd known the damage to the engineering spaces and propeller shaft must be grave, but if the sub could be kept on the surface, a tug out of Sevastopol could have them back in port by morning.

But that final shock that had catapulted them to the sur-face—that had been the final blow. He could tell by the wallowing feel of the vessel that he would remain at the surface only a few more moments before making his final dive.

Vyatkin only hoped that all of the crew could get out first.

He heard the thuttering roar of helicopters . . . probably the Americans who'd been pinging them. The nearest Russian ships must be a hundred miles away. If only—

Light exploded from starboard, a dazzling whiteness that, at first, he thought was a flare. Then the beam swept across *Kislovodsk*'s hull, illuminating dozens of life-jacketed sail-ors already afloat in the water, the soft orange shape of a raft already smothered by desperate men, and the black sheen of oil. It took Vyatkin a mind-numbing moment to realize that another submarine had surfaced a hundred meters abeam, that it was playing a searchlight across his dying command. By the back-scatter of that light, he could see one of the helicopters approaching, its rotor noise growing louder as it gentled toward the stricken *Kislovodsk*. A second light winked on, gleaming from the helo's side. Something spilled from the open door, expanding as it fell.

A life raft. The Americans were dropping life rafts.

"Comrade Captain!" Aleksanyan called, shouting into his

ear to be heard above the wind and the growing thunder of the helicopters. "We must leave! Now!"

Grimly, Vyatkin nodded. For a moment, he'd entertained romantic notions of going down with his command . . . but he found that, after all, he wasn't quite ready to die.

Aleksanyan handed him a life jacket and he began to strap it on.

1840 hours (Zulu +3)
Flight deck
U.S.S. *Thomas Jefferson*

Commander Willis E. "Coyote" Grant strapped on the safety helmet, known aboard ship as a "cranial," before stepping out of the Mangler's O-4 compartment and onto the carrier's flight deck. The air inside the compartment was crackling with radio calls; the Deck Handler—more familiarly called the "Mangler"—and his crew were frantically repositioning aircraft silhouettes on the big Plexiglas diagram of *Jefferson*'s flight deck, updating the model to reflect the realities of aircraft positions outside.

He stepped through the doorway and onto the flight deck; the gathering night was held at bay here by the glare of spotlights, both from *Jefferson*'s island and from the helicopters overhead. Most deck operations had been suspended half an hour earlier when the word had come down that a Russian sub was in trouble twenty miles to the northwest. SH-3 Sea Kings were shuttling back and forth between the *Jefferson* and the sub now, bringing in another handful of wet, oil-smeared survivors with each trip.

It was a painstakingly slow process. The Sea Kings of HS-19 were ASW aircraft, their cargo compartments crammed with so much electronics gear that there was precious little room for passengers above and beyond the usual four-man crew.

Still, there was a little space aft of the sensor suite, and each aircraft was fitted with a winch and sling to haul people out of the water. They were ferrying survivors back to *Jefferson*'s flight deck just as quickly as they could harvest them from the oil-slicked waters of the Black Sea.

With a thunderous roar, a Sea King gentled itself toward the deck just ahead, guided down by a deck handler waving a pair of glowing, yellow Chemlite wands. The SH-3 touched down, bouncing slightly against its hydraulics as a dozen men hurried across the deck, heads bent low to avoid the descent of the slowing rotors. The side door was already open, and a crewman was helping the first of several black-coated men stumble off the aircraft and onto *Jefferson*'s flight deck. Helmeted American sailors reached him at the same moment, helping him walk clear of the helicopter. Others moved in with wire-frame Stokes stretchers to take off the men unable to walk. It took only a few minutes to off-load the survivors. Then, as deck personnel scattered and the handler raised his lighted wands, rotating them rapidly, the Sea King lifted off once more, making room on the deck for the next incoming flight.

Thirty or forty Russian submarine crew members were gathered already on the deck in the lee of the island, some lying sprawled on oil-smeared blankets, others, unhurt but clearly in shock, sitting slumped with their backs against steel, heads cradled in their arms. *Jefferson*'s complement of hospital corpsmen moved among them, making those that appeared to be in shock lie down, handing out blankets, talking reassuringly to others, even though few spoke English. The more seriously injured men had already been moved below to *Jefferson*'s sick bay.

Coyote spotted a familiar figure squatting next to one of the survivors and walked over. "Stoney!" he called.

Tombstone looked up, then stood. "Hey, Coyote. How's things in the Deputy CAG department?"

"They were quiet until a few minutes ago. I was just getting ready to go to chow when I heard the incoming helo call."

Tombstone grinned. "Me, too. No rest for the wicked, I guess. When's your watch?"

"Twenty-hundred hours. What the hell happened?"

"We're still sorting it all out. As far as I can tell, though, we were playing tag with a Russki sub, pinging him hard to make him unwelcome."

"A concert, huh?"

"That's right. He popped a decoy, hoping to confuse things enough to make a getaway. *Orlando* was in his baffles and thought he was loosing a war shot."

"Oh, God."

"*Orlando*'s on the surface now, taking survivors aboard. The Russian sub's gone. It only stayed on the surface for a few minutes before taking the big dive."

"How many survivors?" Coyote asked.

Tombstone shook his head. "Hell, they're still fishing them out of the drink. A Victor III has a complement of about eighty-five. We've got maybe a quarter of them on board so far. But the evening's still young."

Coyote nodded, then dropped to a crouch next to a Russian officer. His face, hands, and uniform tunic were coated slick-black with oil, and the stuff was thickly matted in his hair and beard, contrasting startlingly with the whites of his eyes. He scarcely looked human. "Hey, *tovarisch*," Coyote said. "You understand what I'm saying?"

"*Shtoh*?" the man asked. His eyes looked tired, and very, very old. "*Ya nee paneemayu*."

"You speak English?"

"*Meenya zavoot Kapitahn pervogo ranga Aleksei Aleksandrovich Vyatkin*," the man said with quiet, exhausted dignity. "*Podvodnaya lodka* Kislovodsk."

"Did he say 'Captain'?" Coyote asked.

"Captain first rank," Tombstone replied. "See the shoulder boards? He must've been that boat's skipper." He squatted next to the man. "*Ya plaha mayu*."

"Damn, you speak *Russian*, Stoney? You never cease to amaze me!"

Tombstone shook his head. "Not more than a few words, I'm afraid. I just told him I don't speak it very well. What did you want to ask him, Coyote?"

Coyote stood up, hands on hips. "Well, this'll sound crazy."

"Yeah?"

"I was just wondering if we were at war with them. With Russia, I mean."

"I doubt that these guys know any more about it than we do, actually. My guess is that we're both waiting to hear from the big boys up our respective chains of command."

"Anybody been talking to them yet? Their fleet, I mean. About this . . . incident."

"I really don't know," Tombstone replied. "I think Tarrant's been on the horn, but I haven't heard the word yet."

"Damn," Coyote said. "So here we don't even know if these guys are guests or POWs."

"I imagine we'll find out soon enough," Tombstone said. He shouted, to make himself heard above the clatter of the next incoming helicopter. "Maybe sooner than we really want to know."

And Coyote knew he was right.

2245 hours (Zulu +3)
Office of the Commander, Crimean Military District
Sevastopol, Crimean Military District

"Come in, Nikolai Sergeivich."

Vice-Admiral Dmitriev entered the ornate, luxurious office. The place was richly furnished, paneled in dark red wood, and with an elaborate and expensive parquet wood floor. General Sergei Andreevich Boychenko was not known for his abstemious or purse-pinching habits.

"You sent for me, Admiral?"

"I did. I did. Sit and be comfortable." Boychenko, a lean, hawklike man with silver hair and a vast array of medals on his uniform coat, was sitting behind the expanse of his desk. An elaborate silver samovar rose from a wheeled cart beside the desk. The commanding officer of the entire Crimean Military District gestured at a glass. "Tea?"

"Thank you, sir." As he helped himself to the tea service, Dmitriev wondered why he'd been summoned here. He assumed it had to do with the sudden loss of contact with the *Kislovodsk* . . . and the subsequent loss of contact with the American carrier group. He tried to read Boychenko's manner but failed utterly. The man betrayed no emotion—if, indeed, he possessed any at all in the first place. Boychenko had always struck Dmitriev as something of a cold fish.

With the dark Russian tea steaming in his glass, he took a seat opposite the desk. Boychenko's corner office overlooked the port of Sevastopol, as his did, but had larger windows and a more expansive view. The harbor was spread out practically at his feet; normally, city and waterfront together made a splendid sight, colored lights agleam on still, black water, but a blackout was in force and there was little to see now. The entire district was on full alert, of course, with the threat from Ukraine hanging over the Crimea. Too, the Crimea was suffering from a general power shortage, and the blackout helped save electricity. Dmitriev thought it a singular mark of disgrace that so great a city as Sevastopol, or the fleet anchored there, could no longer afford to keep its lights on at night.

A third wall of the wood-paneled office was taken up by a large framed map of southern European Russia and Ukraine. Unit positions were plotted by pins bearing tiny colored flags, red or blue for Russian forces, gray for Ukrainian. The gray flags were heavily clustered along the northern Black Sea coast, from Odessa in the west to the shores of the Sea of Azov in the east. Dmitriev noted, with a cold, sinking sensation, the number of Ukrainian flags clustered north of the Crimean isthmus . . . and how few red flags opposed them.

"We have had word from the *Kislovodsk*," Boychenko said without further preamble.

"What!" Dmitriev sat up straighter in his chair, nearly spilling his tea. "How? When?" As commander of the Black Sea Fleet, he should have been the one to hear, not Boychenko, his immediate superior.

"About an hour ago. Ah, do not worry, my friend. You were not cut out of the chain of communications. It was not the *Kislovodsk*, precisely, that contacted us."

"Not the *Kislovodsk*. What do you mean, Comrade General?"

"My office received a radio communiqué, in the open, from an Admiral Tarrant, aboard the American cruiser *Shiloh*. The *Kislovodsk* was sunk—by accident—at about eighteen hundred hours this evening."

"Sunk!" Dmitriev's eyes narrowed. "An accident, you say?"

"That is what we were told, and I am inclined to believe the story. Captain Vyatkin, apparently, was being urged to leave the area by antisubmarine warfare forces. He chose to fire a noisemaker torpedo in order to deceive the Americans and was torpedoed when they assumed he was firing on their carrier."

"Were there . . . were there survivors?"

"Surprisingly, yes. Apparently the Americans initiated rescue operations as soon as they realized that a mistake had been made. At last report, sixty-eight officers and men had been pulled from the sea. Fifteen were seriously injured and are receiving treatment in the carrier's onboard medical facility."

"Has this been reported to Novgorod?" The headquarters of Krasilnikov's neo-Soviet government was currently in Novgorod, about four hundred kilometers east of embattled Moscow.

Boychenko did not answer immediately. Though something, in his normally impassive expression put Dmitriev on his guard.

"General?"

"It has not been reported, Nikolai Sergeivich. Not yet. I need . . . I need to discuss something with you first."

"Yes, sir?"

"Just where is it you stand in the current difficulties?"

Dmitriev thought carefully before answering. "Current difficulties" had become the catchword recently for all that was wrong with Russia . . . and most especially for the civil war of Red versus Blue.

"I would like to see them ended."

"A diplomatic answer. And a safe one." Boychenko sighed. "Perhaps it doesn't really matter. What I am about to do could not seriously be considered to be treason, no matter which side we stand on. In a way, I will be acting to save the Crimea. For Russia."

"What is it you intend to do, Comrade General?"

"Nikolai Sergeivich, the Crimea is doomed. A blind man could see that. Novgorod has been sending us supplies and men, but not enough. Not enough by far."

"The Ukrainians may not attack us here, sir. Not if they see we are dug in and willing to defend ourselves."

"They will attack. Intelligence is convinced of that. And so am I. They have no option, really, if they intend to intervene in our war." Turning in his padded chair, he gestured at the wall map with its pins and colored flags. "They could invade Russia proper, of course, but would soon find themselves heavily outnumbered, either by our forces, or by the Blues. With luck, they might make it as far as Volgograd. And what would it profit them? Hitler made the same mistake, you may recall." Volgograd had once carried another name, before the name had fallen out of favor—*Stalingrad.*

"They would be foolish to attack us in any case, with or without Hitler's example."

"Perhaps. They would also be foolish to extend themselves too far to the east, leaving the Crimean bastion here, in their rear." Standing, Boychenko walked to the map. He pointed to the forces near Odessa and the mouth of the Dnieper River. "You've been reading the intelligence reports, I'm sure. Two army groups stand ready to attack the Crimea, Nikolai Sergeivich. They have assembled over one hundred landing craft, and a large number of naval vessels . . . mostly small combatants, true, but enough to cover an amphibious operation on the Crimean west coast, north of Sevastopol. Intelligence believes they will move within a week."

"A spoiling raid, perhaps—" Dmitriev began. His fleet might be in tatters, but he could still put together a hard-hitting strike force, one that might splinter the Ukrainian invasion fleet before it was loaded and ready to move.

"No. There is another way. A better way."

"Sir?"

Boychenko hesitated. Dmitriev had the feeling that the general was studying him closely, measuring him.

"I intend," Boychenko said after a moment, "to surrender the Crimea to the United Nations. And you, Nikolai Sergeivich, must help me."

The glass slipped from Dmitriev's fingers and shattered on the general's parquet wood floor.

CHAPTER 6
Saturday, 31 October

Commander Edward Everett Wayne completed the aircraft checkout. He was strapped into the cockpit of his F-14 Tomcat, nose number 201, parked in the early morning shadow of *Jefferson*'s island, and he'd just brought both engines on-line.

"Clearance to roll, Batman," the voice of his Radar Intercept Officer, Lieutenant Commander Kenneth Blake, said over his ICS.

"Here we go, then." He nudged the throttles, and the F-14 nosed forward, following the vigorous hand and arm movements of the yellow-jerseyed plane director who was guiding him out of his parking place, a holding area behind a red-and-white safety stripe painted on the dark gray deck just aft of *Jefferson*'s island. Their destination was Cat Three, the inboard of two catapults leading across the carrier's angled flight deck amidships.

"The met boys are still calling for CAVU," Blake, call sign "Malibu," said. "Perfect weather over the entire AO."

"That's something, anyway," Batman replied. "At least we'll be able to see where we're flying."

The Tomcat shuddered as another aircraft, an F/A-18 Hornet of VFA-161, cranked up its engines on Cat Four, ahead and to Batman's left. Hot air roiling back from the aircraft's twin engines made the air above the deck dance and shimmer. Deck personnel, their duties identified by the color of their jerseys and helmets, moved clear of the Hornet and crouched low on the deck. The launch director dropped to one knee, then touched thumb to deck.

Instantly, the Hornet slid forward, accelerating to flight speed in less than two seconds as steam boiled from the cat track in its wake, a seething, straight line of white fog swiftly dissipated by the breeze coming in over *Jefferson*'s bow. From Batman's vantage point in his Tomcat, the Hornet appeared to slide off the end of Cat Four and vanish, dropping off the end of the rail as though plunging toward the waves far below.

Then, as if by magic, the Hornet reappeared, climbing up from behind the edge of the flight deck that had briefly hidden it from view, climbing higher, dwindling in seconds to a speck in the blue sky above the blue horizon.

Launching off a carrier, Batman reflected, was the only time when the aviator didn't have full control over his aircraft.

Most aviators feared the trap at the end of a mission more than the launch—night traps or recoveries during bad weather were the worst of all—and Batman shared that common dislike with all other naval pilots. At least during a trap the aviator was in control of his machine, guiding it down the glide slope, adjusting position and speed and angle of attack in response to the LSO's radioed commentary, and to his own eye, hand, and judgment. But the launch was the one time during the mission when the man in the cockpit was literally a passenger. Just beneath the carrier's roof, in the catapult room, steam pressure was fed into two enormous bottles, with pistons attached to the shuttle, which rested in its track on the deck overhead. The FDO—the Flight Deck Officer—was responsible for calling for just the right amount of steam, an amount that varied depending both on the type of aircraft being launched and on its launch weight, which might vary anywhere from 42,000 to 82,000 pounds. Too much steam pressure, and the aircraft could be torn apart; too little, and it would not build up enough speed to become airborne and would trundle off the front of the catapult and into the ocean below. There wasn't much room for error; typically, cats were set to launch aircraft at about ten knots above the minimum speed necessary to get them airborne.

Sometimes—not often, but sometimes—something just plain went wrong with the equipment, and the aircraft was given a nudge instead of a kick. Batman had seen it happen more than once. On one occasion, pilot and RIO had ejected as their Tomcat fell toward the sea. The RIO had survived, but the aviator had been recovered from the sea by helicopter later, dead, his neck broken.

Even in peacetime, flying jets off a carrier was one hairy way to earn your paycheck.

It was always a bit unsettling then to sit and wait in line for your turn at the cat. Batman liked being in control; he was very good at what he did—which was flying a high-performance Navy fighter—and he disliked just sitting there, strapped into his ejection seat hoping that somebody else got their figures right and pushed the right sequence of buttons.

He'd been giving a lot of thought to control, lately, especially as it related to his future. Aboard the *Jefferson*, Batman had a playboy's rep; when he'd first checked in with the VF-96 Vipers, several years earlier, he'd been something of a hot dog, young, brash, and just a bit too eager to bend or break the regs when it suited him, especially when he was flying.

No more. He'd met a girl two months ago, a *wonderful* girl . . . and he was seriously considering giving up the Navy and settling down.

There'd been a time, not so many years back, when Batman would have howled with derision at the thought that he could ever be anything other than a naval aviator. He loved flying, loved it with a passion that put flight at the very core of his entire life. He'd joined the Navy in the first place precisely because, in his opinion, naval aviators were better than any other military pilots; they had to be, to let themselves be hurled off a pitching flight deck at 170

knots . . . or to trap on the carrier deck after hours in the
air, often in the dark and in stormy, wet, or visibility-poor
weather.

But after more than ten years in the Navy, he was
beginning to look for something more than the heart-
pounding slam of acceleration when he pushed the throttles
to Zone Five burner.

He was beginning to realize that Sunny Tomlinson might
just be that something more.

Ahead, another F-14 waited on Cat Three as the dance on
the deck continued, White Shirts completing their safety
checks, red-shirted ordnancemen checking the aircraft's
weapons, making certain the arming pins with their red-
tagged wires were pulled, making double-certain each of the
F-14's missiles—Sidewinder, AMRAAM, and Phoenix—
was secure. Then the jet blast deflector, the JBD, slowly
rose from the deck into an upright position squarely behind
the Tomcat, obscuring it from Batman's view.

In less than a minute, however, the F-14 ahead thundered
off the angled flight deck, its F110-GE 400 engines glowing
like twin bright orange eyes as the catstroke hurled it off the
waist and into the sky, following the Hornet. In a swirl of
steam, the JBD folded back down to the deck, and Batman
eased Tomcat 201 forward, guiding it over the slot where
green-shirted hookup men ran the catapult shuttle back to
the start.

Everywhere on the deck around him, the dance continued, an ant-heap scurrying of rushed but purposeful behavior. Four to five hundred men were working together on the
deck, moving in close synchronization, the entire produc-
tion directed by the Air Boss in his glassed-in aerie high up
on the island, in Pri-Fly. Things were moving fast this
morning, as if to compensate for the unexpected interrup-
tion in flight activities last night. With the survivors of the
sunken Victor III's crew aboard now and with the *Jefferson*
well into her operational area in the eastern end of the Black
Sea, the launches and recoveries were going like clockwork,
the carrier flexing her airborne muscles.

A Green Shirt standing to the starboard side of the F-14

held up a board reading 62500, providing Batman with verification of the Tomcat's total weight in pounds— aircraft, fuel, and weapons. He nodded agreement; the same weight would be fed to the catapult officer in his domed-over hideaway on the deck, letting him know just what settings to call for from the cat crew below. *Get it right, guy,* Batman thought with a flash of gallows humor. In fact, every man and woman aboard the ship knew his or her job as well as he knew his.

But there were so many things that could go wrong. Not even the instruments were fast enough to keep up with everything that happened during the catstroke; launch was a supreme gesture of blind faith in shipmates and in technology.

A Red Shirt held up a bundle of wires, each with a red tag fixed to one end. There were six of them, representing two AIM-9M Sidewinders and four AMRAAM radar-guided missiles . . . correct. A clatter of chains beneath Batman's feet told him the hookup men were securing his nosewheel to the cat shuttle.

The final checklist run-through proceeded swiftly and with a taut economy of motion. The launch officer held his hand high, circling tightly, and Batman eased his throttles forward to full military power. He checked the motion of his stick, forward, back, left, right . . . then the rudder pedals, left, right. All clear, all correct. A red light high on the carrier's island next to Pri-Fly winked over to green.

"Green light," Malibu called.

"Hang on to your stomach, buddy. Let's find us some elbow room!"

"Roger that."

The launch officer, standing to the F-14's right, was taking a last look around, checking the aircraft, checking to make sure deck personnel were clear. He looked up at Batman and saluted.

Batman returned the salute, a final exchange indicating readiness for launch. The launch officer dropped to his knee, pointing down the deck as the Green and Yellow

Shirts nearby crouched low. He touched the deck with his thumb. . . .

An explosion of acceleration slammed Batman back against his seat as the catapult hurled him down the deck. In two seconds he was traveling at 170 miles per hour, past the island, off the angled flight deck, and flashing past the overhanging cliff of *Jefferson*'s towering gray bows close off his starboard wingtip. The catstroke's acceleration was so hard it actually seemed as though he slowed down once he was clear of the track and airborne; he felt the aircraft's controls biting the air—nothing soft or mushy, no red-light indicators of engine failure or control fault. "Good shot!" sounded in his headphones as the Assistant Air Boss confirmed his launch.

It always took him a second or two to recover mentally from the cat launch, to "get behind the airplane." Gently, he brought the stick back and started climbing. Blue sky and sunlight shone above and around him with the unearthly, dazzling intensity of flight.

"Whee-*ooh!*" Malibu exalted from the rear seat. "I think we left the old stomach back there on the deck someplace."

"Too late to go back for it now, Mal," Batman told his RIO. "Let's see if we can find us some mountains."

"I'm with you, dude. Try east."

"Into the sun." He brought the stick gently right, watching his compass heading change on the HUD as the sun, still low in the sky, shone with a brilliant, golden light above a low-lying ripple of clouds on the horizon.

He thought of Sunny, and the last time they'd been together.

0905 hours (Zulu +4)
UN Flight 27
Poti, Republic of Georgia

First Lieutenant Marty Cole, U.S. Army, opened the pilot's-side door and clambered awkwardly into the cockpit of the VH-60 Black Hawk. He was stiff and sore from two days of hard flying mixed with nights of sleeping on hard cots in dilapidated shanties. Cold and hard as they were, folding cots brought in off the *Guadalcanal* and set up in a drafty tent were infinitely better than the parasite-infested bedding that was the norm in most of the buildings he'd seen since being assigned to the UN Crisis Assessment Team. But this morning Cole was starting to wish he'd taken his chances with the insect life.

"How's it looking, Ski?" he asked, suppressing a yawn. Another thing he was wishing for was a decent cup of coffee, even a *bad* cup of coffee, to help him wake up. The stuff they served locally was worse than Turkish coffee . . . and a good explanation for why most people around here seemed to drink tea. Normally he was up before dawn, but he'd been out later than expected last night and not made it back to Tara until nearly zero-three-hundred.

Tara—the name of the mansion in *Gone With the Wind*—was what the American forces in Georgia were calling their camp ashore, a tent city just outside a ramshackle native village of stinking huts made of sod, clapboard, and sheet tin damned near as ritzy-looking as some of Rio de Janeiro's poorer slums. Poti, the nearest city hereabouts, was almost as bad, shot to hell and almost abandoned.

Second Lieutenant Paul Dombrowski looked up from the copilot's position and frowned over the top of the dog-eared preflight checklist. "You look bright-eyed and chipper this morning. Where have you been?"

"Crashed. Crashed and burned."

"Big date last night, huh?"

"Don't I just wish. *God*, I hate this place!"

"Well, we're preflighted and ready to go. We're gonna be late, though. We're running two hours behind our flight plan, at least."

"The damned blue-hats don't give a shit if they're on time or not," Cole said bitterly, ignoring for the moment the fact that both of them had been issued flight helmets painted the brilliant baby blue of the United Nations Peacekeeping

Forces. "Don't see that it makes any difference to us how late we are."

In his five years in Army aviation, Cole had served on his fair share of shit details, but this one, he figured, ought to satisfy his quota for at least the next seventy years or so. This whole operation was one big cluster fuck from start to finish, a monster conceived in good intentions, born in politics, and nurtured in the hellish clash of committees, boards, and panels that dominated every policy-level Pentagon decision made these days. The cross-service problems alone were staggering; Sustain Hope had started as a joint Navy-Marine operation, but the Army, unwilling to let itself be cut out of the potential treasure trove of political largesse, name recognition, and program funding that the UN mission represented, had wormed its way in through the back door. While CH-53 Sea Stallions had been ferrying Marines ashore yesterday, Cole and Dombrowski and their aircraft's crew chief, Warrant Officer Palmer, had flown one of two Army UH-60 Black Hawks into Poti's airfield.

They'd come to Georgia loaded for bear. Their Black Hawk had been equipped with ESSS—an acronym meaning External Stores Support System. A deliberate copy of the external weapons mounts employed by Russian Hind helicopter gunships, the ESSS would let the Black Hawk ride shotgun for the UN Crisis Assessment Team's Hip. There'd been a lot of sniping at UN air traffic over western Georgia lately, chiefly from Russian mobile antiaircraft units under the control of one or another of the militia or Russian army forces in the area; one UN helo had been shot down the week before, and two others damaged. The Army Black Hawk's ESSS, loaded with sixteen Hellfire air-to-ground missiles, would be one hell of an incentive for those units to stay under cover and leave UN aircraft alone.

Dombrowski touched the side of his helmet, listening closely. "Uh-oh. Here it goes."

"What?"

"Two-seven finally checked in over the radio." The code group referred to the Assessment Team, and their helicopter. "They're saddling up."

Cole glanced at his watch. "Only about two hours late. That must be a new speed record for a Crisis Team."

The tall Pole's frown turned into a grin. "All we have to do now is pray that nobody goes and insults the local honcho's sister before we get out of here. They've got our flight plan so screwed up now I'm beginning to wonder if we'll get back home before our enlistments expire."

The Crisis Assessment Team had been on the move for over a week now, since long before the Americans had arrived. They were traveling from town to town throughout western Georgia, trying to determine from interviews with the locals—and by whether or not anybody took a shot at them as they passed—whether this wretched country had indeed been abandoned by the more organized Russian units, or whether Reds or Blues were still here in force. From what Cole had seen over the past couple of days, there wasn't *anything* organized about Georgia . . . except possibly for the misery of its inhabitants. The towns were war-shattered, with little left but rubble and vast, sprawling, disease-ridden refugee camps and tent cities. The team they were escorting was a varied lot—two U.S. Army officers who'd arrived with Dombrowski and Cole, two Marine officers out of MEU-25, three British army officers, a French air force man, two Turks, and an Ethiopian UN Special Envoy with the tongue-twisting name Mengistu Tzadua—not to mention the ragged, heavily armed Georgian freedom fighter who'd insisted on accompanying the team as it made the rounds of the countryside, plus two people from the American Cable News network, a reporter and a cameraman. The whole operation was a bizarre melting pot. They could barely share ideas among themselves, much less quiz the locals on how the UN could better deliver humanitarian aid. Cole didn't know how much more of this assignment he'd be able to put up with before he did something most undiplomatic. He was all for helping the victims of war by delivering humanitarian aid, but so far he'd seen more bureaucrats than relief workers, and it seemed like there was no end in sight.

Cole grimaced. You usually knew why you were on an

op, and who your enemies were, and what the risks were likely to be, whether it was delivering food to Somalia or stopping the neo-Soviets in the snow-covered mountains of Norway. This was something totally different, however, a tangled web of crossed interests, cross purposes, and particularly unpleasant men with guns who weren't always pleased to see the U.S. troops or UN peacekeepers.

"Here they come," WO Chris Palmer called from the rear compartment.

"Finally!" Cole muttered, powering up the Black Hawk and gently feeding the twin T700-GE-700 turboshafts, listening to the rising whine of the rotors with a practiced ear. "Radio silent routine, people, once we're airborne."

Their orders had specified staying off the radios once in the air. The idea was to surprise Russian forces who might otherwise track them by their radio calls.

Moments later, another helicopter flew past, an odd-looking, ungainly beast with an elongated, rounded fuselage and prominent round windows along the sides. The Mi-8 Hip was an old Soviet design and was seen everywhere in this part of the world, especially for transport duty. This one had the blue UN flag painted on its side. "Hang on, everyone," Cole said, and he engaged the collective, lifting the Black Hawk clear of the dirt.

Poti spread out below, shattered white buildings crowded against the sparkling waters of the Black Sea, a ruin that looked as dilapidated from the air as it did from the ground. Cole could almost imagine the stink of the place fading away as he followed the Hip toward the northeast.

"That guy's really traveling," Cole said. The Hip was already a good three miles ahead of them, a black spot just above the horizon. "Wonder if he's trying to make up for lost time?"

"Maybe so." Dombrowski pulled out a map from under his seat, folded and attached to a clipboard. "So where to today? Cha-something, they said?"

"Chaisi," Cole replied. Another last-minute change, decided on just last night by the team's leaders. "Little village up in the mountains, just outside the NFZ."

"Outside the no-fly zone? Oh, joy. We get to play tag with Hind gunships today."

"None have been sighted so far," Cole told the copilot. "In fact, from everything I heard last night, it looks like the Russian regulars really have pulled up and stolen away into the night. Not so much left behind as a crust of black Russian bread. Piece of cake."

"Shit. That just means we're gonna be staying here, L-T! Maybe we should scare up a Hind or two. Might mean we get pulled back to the ships."

"I'm not sure which is worse," Cole said. "Sleeping on those damned cots at Tara, or being cooped up aboard a hip-pocket aircraft carrier."

"Man, look at those mountains," Dombrowski said, changing the subject. One particularly rugged range was thrusting up in front of them, its jagged brown walls only a few miles distant now. "We're not going *over* that thing, are we?"

"Nah. There's a valley." He pointed at the Hip, now reduced to a tiny spot far ahead and to the right. "See? Two-seven's headed straight for it."

"Christ," Dombrowski said as the valley opened up around them. Trees flashed past to left and right, some reaching well above the Black Hawk's cockpit. "Just like the trench on the Death Star in *Star Wars*."

"At least," Cole said with a grin, "we won't have Imperial fighters on our tail!"

He wished, though, that Two-seven would slow down a bit. He didn't want to get lost in these mountains, and with radio silence, he couldn't call the bastard and tell him to slow down.

Muttering an imprecation against all bureaucrats, Cole opened the throttle a bit wider.

CHAPTER 7
Saturday, 31 October

"Bird Dog, Bird Dog, this is Watch Dog Six-one. Do you copy, over?"

The E-2C lurched as it hit a pocket of turbulence, but Lieutenant Arnold Brown was as oblivious to the jolt as he was to the steady drown of the Hawkeye's twin turboprops. He was hunched over his radar console, his full attention focused on the smeared yellow splotches of radar returns painted there.

"Bird Dog, Bird Dog, this is Watch Dog Six-one. Do you copy, over?" he called again.

The E-2C was orbiting a fixed point fifty thousand feet above the Black Sea, its sophisticated electronics keeping track of air activity across a circle nearly five hundred nautical miles in diameter. As an Airborne Early Warning aircraft, it wasn't quite as versatile as the land-based AWACS, but the Navy "Hummer" could do things no other AEW plane could do. Specifically, it could fly off of a carrier deck, and with a tracking capacity of over 250 targets it was well suited to warn the ships and planes of a carrier battle group of any activity that might pose a threat to their operations. As the aircraft's Air Control Officer, Brown was responsible for the coordination of air activity throughout the carrier battle group's sphere of operations.

The E-2C and her crew, Brown decided, were really pulling down their pay today, that was for damn sure.

"Watch Dog, Bird Dog Leader" sounded over his helmet earphones. "We copy. Whatcha got?"

"Bird Dog, Watch Dog. We have a hit on our screens here. Unidentified contact, bearing zero-eight-five, range eight-eight miles, over."

"Ah, roger, Watch Dog. We don't have him on our display. Over."

"Bird Dog, the target is flying at extremely low altitude. Contact is intermittent, and we think he may be right down on the deck, zigzagging through the mountains. We'll vector you in."

"Roger that, Watch Dog." There was the slightest of pauses. "So tell me, have you seen any flying saucers lately?"

Brown grinned. The flying saucer gag was one of a number of running jokes aimed at the Hawkeye and its peculiar look with the saucer-shaped radome up top. Sailors aboard the *Jefferson* made jokes about the little green men who flew it . . . or called it a Frisbee and asked Brown if he'd like to join them for a game of catch on the flight deck.

So far as Brown was concerned, it didn't matter what the aircraft looked like. It *worked* . . . flew like a dream, if a bit on the sluggish side. In fact, the flattened-dish shape created as much lift as was needed to counteract the parasitic drag of the entire assembly and neither helped nor hindered the plane in flight, even during takeoffs and landings. More important than flight characteristics, though, nothing could move on land, on water, or in the air throughout a volume of three million cubic miles and not be instantly pinpointed by the E-2C's APS-125 radar. Through a wide-ranging suite of communications equipment, including UHF, HF, and high-speed data links, the Hawkeye could pass coded data to any of the *Jefferson*'s aircraft, engage in a two-way exchange with the Tomcats, and serve as the primary eyes and ears for Alpha Bravo, the battle group's commander. So far as Lieutenant Brown was concerned, the entire air wing was structured around the Hawkeyes, like the rim of a wheel connected by spokes to the hub.

He watched the blip crawling across the tangled web of returns off the mountains. As far as he could make out, it was about thirty miles out of Poti and moving away from the city at 150 knots. He adjusted the gain on the set, willing more information from the pulsing smears of light before him. It was hard to tell; there might be *two* aircraft there. According to the schedule passed to the CBG from the UN liaison office ashore, there were supposed to be a couple of friendly helos flying out of Poti this morning . . . but that flight had been scheduled for a couple of hours ago. And neither of these guys was showing IFF.

Ah, no! There *were* two aircraft . . . and the leader's IFF had just been triggered by the touch of the Hawkeye's farseeing radar. Sierra-Delta-Three-Tango . . . He checked the code group with a list on a clipboard at his side: UN Flight Two-seven, a CAT mission. Flying under radio silence.

But who the hell was the untagged bogey on Two-seven's tail? . . .

0816 hours (Zulu +3)
Tomcat 201
Over the Black Sea

Batman was holding his Tomcat steady at 25,000 feet, flying south some ninety miles off the Black Sea coast. He'd been aware of Malibu in the backseat talking with Watch Dog, but not really listening in. So far, their flight had been singularly routine. Glancing back over his right shoulder, he saw that his wingman, in Tomcat 218, was in position twenty meters off his wingtip at four o'clock. The helmeted figure in the other aircraft's pilot's seat must have seen the movement, for he raised one hand and touched his visor in a bantering salute.

Lieutenant Tom Mason, "Dixie" to the other aviators in Viper Squadron, was a nugget, a new arrival aboard the

Jefferson and CVW-20. The kid seemed to know his stuff. He'd been teamed up with one of the women aviators in the squadron, Lieutenant Kathleen Garrity, as his RIO, and so far they seemed to be working well together. Batman hoped, though, that this deployment wasn't as rough as the last one; nuggets tended to get excited in *real* combat, like the furballs the Vipers had participated in over Norway and the Kola. They could do something harebrained, like leave their wingmen, or they could freeze up. Either way, the statistics relating to their surviving that first taste of combat weren't all that good. Cat Garrity had proven herself over the Kola, though, and ought to provide a good, steadying influence if anything nasty went down this time out.

He glanced left. The Georgian coast was just visible to the eye, a gray-and-purple smear on the horizon beneath the rising sun. It would be so nice if someone would explain, just once and in terms that people other than State Department policy wonks could understand, what America's strategic interests in this part of the world could possibly be. Thanksgiving was just three weeks away, but it looked as though *Jefferson*'s crew was going to spend the holiday season away from homes and families. And for what? To enforce the UN's no-fly zones in the Black Sea? It was hard to think of that as vital to the national interest.

He wondered if the incident with the Russian sub might change things. Scuttlebutt aboard the *Jefferson* had it that the Russians fished from the sea last night might be returned home soon . . . and that the agreement being worked out with Russian officials might even lead to a downscaling of the hostilities in this region. One rumor floating about VF-95's ready room had it that the Russians were about to surrender the whole damned Crimea to the UN.

If that happened, maybe they wouldn't need a carrier out here anymore. The no-fly zones could be enforced by Air Force planes operating out of Sevastopol.

Not, Batman reminded himself, that things ever worked out that smoothly.

"Contact, Batman," Malibu said from the backseat. "We've

got a bogey in the NFZ, probable helicopter. Watch Dog is vectoring us in."

"Roger that." He opened the tactical frequency with Mason. "Bird Dog Two, this is Bird Dog One. Did you copy that contact? Over."

"Ah, roger," Cat Garrity's voice came back over the radio. "We copy."

"And it's about time," Dixie's voice added. "I was starting to doze off up here."

"Well, it's time for reveille, people," Batman said. "On my mark, come to zero-eight-five, and ready . . . break!"

He brought his stick over to the left and gave the Tomcat some rudder, dropping his left wing as he slid into a hard, tight turn. Dixie and Cat followed, the two Tomcats turning into the sun in air-show perfection.

"Update coming through from Watch Dog," Malibu said.

"Okay. Patching in."

"Bird Dog Flight, this is Watch Dog," the voice of the Hawkeye's air controller said. "Listen, we have two contacts now. We've IDed one as UN Flight Two-seven, out of Poti. He's being followed by a bogey, designated contact Sierra One. Negative IFF on the bogey. Repeat, bogey is not transmitting IFF."

"Roger that, Watch Dog," Batman said.

IFF—Identification Friend or Foe—was the means by which ships and aircraft could recognize one another across distances or in conditions where visual identification could be a problem. Back in the old glory days, when air-to-air combat was a matter of getting close enough to the other guy to use your machine guns on him, target identification was a matter of recognizing a silhouette. Nowadays, though, when a Tomcat could down a target at 120 miles with an air-to-air Phoenix launch, something better than Mark One eyeballs was necessary. IFF had been part of the electronic arsenal of warfare for years and was similiar in most respects to the equipment used in civil aviation to identity aircraft on air traffic control radars. When an aircraft was touched by friendly radar, a transponder aboard automatically replied with a string of coded pulses. Those pulses were picked up by the radar receiver and matched by computer to a list of known codes; friendlies could instantly be identified simply by painting them on radar. The transponder codes, of course, were carefully kept secret, as were the interrogation frequencies and any other data that might be of use to an enemy in combat. Codes were changed frequently; the distribution of those codes among all of the participants in a given mission was an important part of ops planning.

If the UN flight was transmitting its IFF and Sierra One wasn't, it was a good bet that Sierra One was a bad guy on the UN chopper's tail.

Still, in wartime nothing can be taken for granted. It would be nice if they could get a positive visual ID on Sierra One as well. It was always a good idea to know just who or what you were shooting at, especially in a situation like this one, with tangled politics and the inherent, bureaucratic confusion of a joint-service, international operation like this one.

Ahead, the purple-gray smear of the horizon was rapidly taking form and substance. Mountains, gleaming white in the morning sunlight, rose from the azure waters of the Black Sea.

"Mal? Better check in with Dog House. Let 'em know what we're at."

"I'm on it." Dog House was the op's code name for the *Jefferson*.

A thought occurred to Batman. He opened the channel to the orbiting Hawkeye. "Watch Dog, this is Bird Dog Leader," he called. "Is Sierra One trying for an intercept on UN Two-seven?"

"Ah, that's hard to say, Bird Dog," the Hawkeye air controller replied. "He's definitely trailing Two-seven and seems to be closing. Looks like he's about two miles behind right now. It doesn't look like a typical intercept, though. He may just be shadowing the blue-hats. Over."

"Roger that. We're going to try to set up an eyeball, over."

"We copy that. We'll talk you in."

"Thank you, Watch Dog. Bird Dog Two, this is One."

"Bird Dog Two," Dixie replied. "Go ahead, Batman."

"Two, I want a visual confirmation on this one. We'll go in with an extended formation. You're the eyeball. We're the shooter."

"Aw, shit, Batman. You're saving all the fun for yourself!"

Like hell I am. "You want to discuss this, son?" He put a growl behind the words.

"Uh, negative," Dixie said. "We'll spot for you."

The deployment was a common one in fighter combat, especially in situations where welded wings—wingmen sticking close together—weren't necessary. One aircraft, the "eyeball," was sent several miles ahead of the second plane, or "shooter." The eyeball could use his position to get a positive ID and could also illuminate a target with his radar for the shooter's radio-homing Sparrows or AM-RAAMs. Batman wasn't hogging the fun, as Dixie had suggested. The fact of the matter was that he didn't quite trust Dixie yet as shooter; if the kid launched early because he got excited or because he'd misheard a sighting report, a friendly aircraft might be downed. On the other hand, Batman trusted Cat to back up any sighting report that Dixie might call in.

Dixie's Tomcat accelerated, afterburners glowing briefly as he arrowed ahead and down, dropping toward the deck.

Batman checked his time display. Zero-eight-twenty. Actually, it was zero-*nine*-twenty now, since they'd crossed a time zone on their way to their patrol station, from GMT plus three to GMT plus four. Air ops were always conducted in the local time zone of the carrier, however. Combat was confusing enough without bringing conflicting time zones into it.

"Anything on the scope yet, Mal?" he asked his RIO.

"Negative, Batman. We're getting the track feed from Watch Dog, but the bogey's not on our scope yet. It's pretty rugged up ahead."

"You got that right." The mountains were growing larger and sharper second by second. The Caucasus Mountains

followed the Black Sea's eastern shoreline from the Sea of
Azov southeast to Gagra, then angled toward the east as the
coast bent away toward the south, so the range appeared
nearer and higher to the left. The highest of those peaks
brushed fifteen thousand feet, a rugged stone wall separating Georgia from its war-torn neighbor to the north.

"Let's come right a bit, Batman," his RIO said. "Bring her
to zero-eight-eight."

"Rog."

"Bird Dog Two, feet dry," Cat's voice called over the
radio. Two-one-eight had just crossed the beach and was
over land now.

Seconds later, Batman's Tomcat was across the coastline
as well, hurtling inland as just below the speed of sound.
"And Bird Dog One going feet dry," Malibu reported.

They were now over what amounted to Indian territory.

0821 hours (Zulu +3)
Operations, U.S.S. *Thomas Jefferson*
The Black Sea

"Commander? There's been a new development on the Bird
Dog patrol, sir."

Commander Grant joined Lieutenant Chadwick in front
of the large screen that displayed tactical data relayed from
the Hawkeye. Chadwick had just taken over the watch as
Ops duty officer. Though he was the senior officer present,
Grant wasn't standing watch. He was in Ops this morning as
an observer, part of a crash course in how to carry out his
new assignment as Deputy CAG. Observer or not, however,
he'd be drawn into any situation that might develop this
morning, at least until Magruder arrived and took over.

Coyote Grant had commanded a Tomcat squadron for
nearly two years, now, and he'd been an aviator for a lot
longer than that. Making split-second decisions and taking
the responsibility for them was part and parcel of being an
aviator, something you learned to deal with if you wanted to
keep flying. But there was something intimidating about Air

Ops, about its myriad display monitors and banks of consoles and computers, about the technicians hunched over their screens and speaking in low tones, about the crackle of static and the radio calls coming over the speaker system. This was the heart of the whole operation, and he never felt the pressures of command as keenly as when he was in this place. Sometimes, when he was standing watch here, Coyote had to tell himself that the whole compartment was nothing more than a high-tech video arcade. The technicians, most of them, were kids; the average age of the enlisted men aboard was something under twenty years. It was easy to imagine them all as bright-eyed video game fanatics feeding quarters into their machines.

But it wasn't a game. This time it wasn't even a simulation.

"What is it, Lieutenant?" he asked Chadwick, his eyes scanning the monitor. A rough map—drawn all in straight lines and sharp angles—showed the coast of the Black Sea. Dozens of coded lights marked radar contacts, known and unknown, scattered up and down the coast.

"Watch Dog picked up an unknown aircraft, probably a low-flying helo," Chadwick said crisply. He jabbed a stubby finger at the display monitor. "Here . . . a few miles northwest of Poti. Bird Dog is deploying for intercept and requesting instructions."

Grant leaned forward to study the screen. Bird Dog Two was well ahead of Bird Dog One now, arrowing across the coast toward the interior. Inland, one of the IDed blips showed a UN designation. "Flight Two-seven?"

"Right there," the lieutenant said, pointing again. "He's showing IFF. The word from the Marine liaison ashore is that it could have an Army gunship flying escort."

"Could have? Does it or doesn't it?"

"They're not sure. In any case, we only have the one friendly on the screen. If there are two helos there, they're so close together we're only getting one return from them."

Coyote nodded. It was a common phenomenon; often one radar blip would resolve into two or more, once you closed with the target a bit. And in rough terrain like that . . .

"It's this guy a couple-three miles to the southwest we're worried about," Chadwick continued. "He's not showing IFF. Watch Dog thinks he could be a local, maybe a helo flying low to avoid the radar. If so . . ."

"If so, it's a violation," Grant said. "What are their orders?"

"To check 'em out and enforce the edict. If that bogey's a bandit, we take 'em down."

In the language of naval aviation, a *bogey* was an unidentified target, while a *bandit* had been positively identified as hostile. And according to UN resolution 1026, aircraft violating the Georgian no-fly zone were to be considered hostiles.

"Where's CAG, anyway?" Coyote wanted to know.

"Getting ready for a meeting with Top Hat, last I heard, sir. You want me to get him down here?"

Coyote shook his head. "You've got the deck, Chad. And you've got your orders."

"Yeah, I know." Chadwick licked his lips. "You know, Commander, it gets damned scary down here sometimes."

"I know what you mean, Lieutenant. I know exactly what you mean."

0923 hours (Zulu +4)
Tomcat 218
UN No-Fly Zone, Republic of Georgia

"Hot damn!" Mason said with boyish enthusiasm. "Just like *Star Wars*!"

Lieutenant Kathleen Garrity, call sign "Cat," smiled behind her oxygen mask with mingled condescension and amusement. Technically, the man up front outranked her. Tom Mason had made lieutenant six months back, while she'd received her promotion from j.g. to full lieutenant only three months ago, while *Jefferson* had been undergoing her all-too-brief refit at Norfolk. Still, Dixie was a nugget, a new arrival to the air wing who'd transferred in from a reserve air group Stateside. Cat, on the other hand, was a combat veteran who'd seen action in the Kola Peninsula.

She recognized Mason's eagerness, though. Nine months back, she'd felt the same way.

Cat had battled to get where she was now. She'd battled harassment, battled prejudice, battled the sneers and jibes of fellow aviators to get what she wanted—an assignment as a naval flight officer, as an RIO in the backseat of an F-14 Tomcat, instead of a routine billet as just another tech specialist in some rear-echelon base. She'd battled, she'd gambled . . . and she'd won.

And now she was the old hand, the vet, listening with wry amusement to the excited edge in her partner's voice.

She and Dixie had a lot in common, she decided. A decade back, naval aviation had largely been a private club reserved for white males with the right connections. A few black and Asian and Hispanic officers made it into carrier air, but not many, and damned few as NFOs. Those minority Naval Flight Officers who did make the grade more often than not ended up flying CODs or other support aircraft. Things had finally started to open up, though, and if she and the other women on the *Jefferson* were a success story, then so was Tom "Dixie" Mason.

Because Dixie was a black—no, an "African-American," she wryly corrected herself—his battle had been at least as rough as hers, in a Navy that still sometimes had the air of an exclusive, all-white country club at the highest levels of the command hierarchy. There'd been black admirals and female admirals for some years now, but much of the Navy was still run by the old boys' network, a network that could be damned vicious sometimes when it came to an aviator's sex or color . . . or even the fact that a man's name ended with a vowel.

Mason had graduated near the top of his class at Annapolis and again at flight school in Pensacola. For the past four years, though, he'd been struggling against the odds to win acceptance as an aviator. Shunted into a RAG for most of his career, he'd finally managed to land carrier duty . . .

which any flier in the squadron would insist was the one assignment that separated *aviators* from mere *pilots*.

And she had to admit that Mason was a superb flier, one of the best she'd ever seen. Despite the enthusiasm, technically he was an iceman, cold and hard and precise. The emotions showed through when he was under stress, but all he really needed there was some seasoning.

"Bird Dog, this is Dog House." That was Lieutenant Chadwick's voice, from Ops. "Do you copy, over?"

"Bird Dog Leader copies, Dog House," Batman replied over the open channel. "What's the gouge?"

"Bird Dog, we confirm your bogey, but we still don't have an India Delta yet. Repeat, no confirmed identification on the bogey. Nothing on radio and no IFF signal. Before we take further action, we need a positive visual ID. Until we do, we're calling it a possible hostile. Over."

"Ah, roger that, Dog House," Batman replied. "With stress on the *possible*, right?"

"That's affirmative, Watch Dog. You've got weapons free, but stick to the ROEs. Get a positive visual identification before you do anything. The last thing we need is a friendly fire incident to lead the news stories today."

"Understood," Batman said. "We're on it, Dog House. Bird Dog clear." He paused. "Dixie, you still with me?"

"Bird Dog Two, roger," Mason answered.

"You hear all that? We've got weapons free, but mark your targets."

"That's a roger." Cat heard him pause. "Uh, Skipper? You think this one's for real?"

"Hell, that's what we're here to find out. You keep your eyes peeled up there, or I'll have you in for another session of sensitivity training."

"Oh, no, not that, Skipper," Mason said, his tone mock-serious. "Anything but that!"

Cat laughed. The politically correct crowd back in Washington had been leaning hard on the Navy to provide sensitivity training to teach tolerance, understanding, and acceptable behavior toward women and minorities both. It was thoroughly loathed by all concerned and didn't seem to do very much good, though the people issuing the directives seemed less concerned with results than with the actual issuing of the directives.

It was a strange world, sometimes. . . .

"Don't worry, Dixie," she said over the ICS. "Even if this run turns up dry, I'm sure we'll see action pretty soon. Up at North Cape and the Kola, it was one damned crisis after another. I'm beginning to think the old *Jeff* just kind of draws trouble like a magnet."

"Just my luck if everything goes quiet as soon as I get in the game," Mason told her. She could hear just a trace of bitterness in his voice. "You train every day of your life for something that never comes . . . know what I mean?"

"Hey, don't forget who you're talking to back here. Of *course* I know what you mean. And believe me, if *women* can get a piece of the action out here, your turn's bound to come up!"

0928 hours (Zulu +3)
UN Flight 27
UN No-Fly Zone, Republic of Georgia

Cole had never particularly liked low-altitude flying in rough terrain, and today was no exception. But the Hip with its VIP passengers up ahead was flying NOE so that they could get a good look at the terrain below as they passed, and Cole knew better than to argue with the brass. Especially when most of the brass belonged to self-important UN twits who tended to retreat behind language problems anytime they didn't want to understand a complaint or a protest.

"Keep your eyes on the road, L-T," Dombrowski said. "That's about the only way to tell we're on course."

"Yeah. Right." The road, in this case, was a track that might have been paved once, but which had deteriorated under harsh weather, hard use, and lack of maintenance. According to the map, it followed this valley all the way up to Chaisi, up among those ice-capped peaks ahead.

He saw something up ahead, a squat vehicle parked alongside the road. He touched Dombrowski's arm and pointed. "Shit, Ski, that looks like a Zoo down there."

"Got news for you, man. It *is* a Zoo." Dombrowski grinned at him. "One of our freedom fighter buddies told me about 'em last night. His people have a few of them, compliments of the Reds when they pulled out. It knows we're coming, and it won't fire. Probably."

Cole muttered a curse. "You might tell a guy, you know. The altitude we're pulling now, we'd be dead meat before I could get us high enough to dodge those suckers."

The "Zoo"—slang for the ZSU-23-4—was a deadly air defense weapon that was one of the most dangerous pieces of equipment in the ex-Soviet arsenal. A self-propelled tracked vehicle mounting quad AZP-23 cannons, it fired 23mm shells directed by the B-76 radar code-named Gun Dish by the U.S. military. A Zoo could wreak havoc with any low-flying aircraft unlucky enough to stray into its line of fire.

Neither man spoke for a long moment. Then Cole looked across at Dombrowski, scowling. "And just what the hell do you mean by 'probably,' anyway?" he demanded.

Dombrowski laughed.

0929 hours (Zulu +4)
Tomcat 218
UN No-Fly Zone, Republic of Georgia

The blip winked onto Dixie's Vertical Display Indicator with the suddenness of a thrown switch . . . a hard signal from the Tomcat's own AWG-9 radar, not a data link feed from the Hawkeye. "Contact!" he yelled. "I've got him now! Bearing oh-one-oh, range four miles."

"I keep losing him in the ground clutter," Cat added. "Getting an eyeball on this guy's going to be tough."

"Yeah. Tell me about it." The typical helicopter cruised at less than 150 miles per hour, a snail's crawl to a Tomcat howling in at just below Mach 1. And with the helo flying down on the deck in these rugged mountains, spotting would be that much harder.

Mason craned his neck, straining to get a visual on the bogey even though he knew they were still too far out. At four miles, an aircraft was a speck when it was backlit by the sky; this clown would probably be wearing camouflage, and he'd be down on the deck. But at almost six hundred miles per hour, they would cover four miles in just twenty-four seconds. In that same period of time, the bogey would cover just about another mile; thirty seconds and he and Cat would be smack on top of them.

Mountains rose to left and right, gray granite walls, some cloaked with pine trees, others barren. He was following a river valley now, relatively flat and a couple of miles across but bounded by sheer cliffs and woods-cloaked slopes. Snow flashed at the highest elevations.

"Hey, Dixie?" Cat called from the backseat. "Maybe we should back off from the wall a bit."

She wasn't referring to the valley wall, he knew, but to their speed. Flying slower would be safer . . . give them both a chance to *see* something.

But he was eager. He wanted to get there, *now*.

"Just another few seconds, Cat. We're almost there. . . ."

The radar contact vanished off the screen, less than two miles ahead. Dixie could see why—the valley took a sharp turn to the left up there, and the slopes to either side went vertical, turning the valley into a tight, rock-walled canyon. The bogey must have just gone around the bend.

"Keep your eyes sharp," he told Cat. "The bastard's just around—"

"Radar contact!" Cat cut in. "We're being painted!"

"The helo?"

"Negative! Negative! I read it as Gun Dish!"

"Christ!" Dixie swore. "A *Shilka*!"

Shilka was the Russian name for the quad-mount ZSU-23-4. Dixie's first instinct was to haul back on the stick and grab some sky, but he held the Tomcat's altitude steady as he eased into the dogleg of the canyon. *Shilkas* were relatively short-ranged and couldn't reach targets at altitudes of more than a mile or so, but Dixie knew that he would offer a perfect sighting picture if he suddenly popped his Tomcat up out of that valley.

Instead, he increased the speed a notch, whipping around the twist in the canyon, coming up just a little to give himself some more maneuvering room if the ground rose sharply around the bend . . .

. . . *and there was the contact!*

He had only a glimpse, and from a difficult angle. The Tomcat was coming up on the helicopter from behind, about in the seven o'clock position, but he had time enough to see the heavy weapon pods mounted to port and starboard, the long, low, smooth curve of the fuselage. It was painted in a green-and-brown camo pattern that blended well with the valley floor.

"I see him!" Dixie called. "Target is a Hind gunship!"

Then he pulled the stick back, rammed the throttles all the way forward into Zone Five afterburners, and kicked his Tomcat into open blue sky.

CHAPTER 8
Saturday, 31 October

"Jesus H. Christ!" Cole shouted, jerking the control stick over and banking sharply as a silver shape thundered past the helicopter a few hundred feet overhead, then broke into a sharp climb. "What the hell was *that*?"

Dombrowski shook his head. "Oh, shit, man! Who told those Navy bastards they had the right-of-way?"

"Navy?" It took Cole a moment for that to register. "Oh, yeah, sure, the flyboys watching the no-fly zone. Man, that guy scared the shit out of me!"

"Guess he got bored flying CAP and decided to come hassle us," Dombrowski said.

Cole swore and brought the helicopter back on course. "Man, the moment we get back, I'm reporting this one! That guy could've smashed us into a cliff with his jet wash!"

But something was nagging at him. According to the op plan he'd seen, the Navy fighters were supposed to fly racecourse tracks out over the sea unless there was a specific reason for them to fly inland.

A reason like a no-fly zone violation.

"Dom," He said, feeling cold. "Get on the horn. Raise Tara. Find out what the hell a Navy F-14 is doing in here."

"Radio silence, L-T. Remember?"

"I don't give a shit about radio silence! I want to know what the hell is going on!"

0930 hours (Zulu +4)
Tomcat 201
UN No-Fly Zone, Republic of Georgia

"Bird Dog Two, this is One," Batman called. "Say again your last!"

"One, this is Two," Dixie's voice said, harsh with urgency and with the stress of a high-G climb. "Target Sierra One is a Hind gunship. I say again, Hind gunship."

Batman pulled back on his stick, taking the Tomcat to eighteen thousand feet. His VDI showed three targets now, Mason and Garrity's F-14, the UN helo, and the bandit.

"Cat," he radioed. "Do you concur?"

"Sorry, Batman. I didn't see it. We've got a Zoo down here in the rocks and I was working my board."

"Bird Dog One, this is Dixie. I only had a glimpse but it was pretty close. I made the weapons pylons."

"Do you have it in sight now?"

"Negative," Dixie replied. "Still in my climb. He's behind us somewhere."

At the top of his climb, Batman eased the stick left and put the nose over, lining up the shot. On his HUD, the targeting pipper drifted toward the bandit, moving up the mountain valley. At a range of just over five miles, he still couldn't actually *see* the target, but the Tomcat's computer had painted it on his VDI and again on his heads-up display, a tiny circle of green light. Pipper and circle connected.

"Batman," Malibu said over the ICS. "I've got something from UN Two-seven. It's garbled . . . something about they're under attack."

That Hind must be taking shots at them. "Tell 'em the cavalry's on the way," Batman said. "I've got the bandit lined up. Target lock!"

He decided to go with a heat-seeker rather than a radar-guided AMRAAM. With the target between his AWG-9 radar and the valley floor, there was too great a chance that the missile would accidentally lock onto the ground instead of the

Hind. The helicopter's engine exhaust was hot, the ground cold. It would make a perfect target beacon for the AIM-9.

He snapped a selector switch and immediately heard the high-pitched warble as one of his Sidewinder missiles "saw" the heat emitted by the helicopter.

His thumb closed on the firing switch. "Fox two!" he called, giving the alert that told all friendly aircraft that a heat-seeker was in the air.

With a piercing *shoosh*, a Sidewinder slid free of its rail beneath his starboard wing, streaking toward the valley five miles away. As its exhaust flare dwindled, Batman suddenly remembered the date and broke into a grin behind his oxygen mask.

"Trick or treat, you sons of bitches," he said.

0930 hours (Zulu +4)
UN Flight 27
UN No-Fly Zone, Republic of Georgia

"You raise Tara yet?" Cole demanded.

"Yeah, but things are all screwed up. Sounds like a Chinese fire drill back—" Dombrowski stopped. He'd turned in his seat to illustrate his point and stopped in midsentence, staring out of the Black Hawk's cockpit toward the rear.

"Dom?"

"Shit! Missile! Missile! *Incoming!*"

Cole acted on instinct alone, bringing the Black Hawk's nose up and over in a hard turn to the right. No helicopter in the world could outrun a missile; their one chance was to turn into the missile and pray that it smacked into the ground before it could correct.

They almost made it.

The AIM-9 Sidewinder streaked in at 660 miles per hour, arrowing down from above and behind the Black Hawk, homing on the bright, hot flares of exhaust spilling from the two engine exhaust shrouds beneath the big four-blade rotor. The missile's tiny brain was correcting the weapon's course, bringing the AIM-9 up to match the target's forward vector when it struck . . . not the engine, but the tip of one whirling rotor blade.

The explosion was shattering, but not as deadly as it might have been if the warhead had detonated inside the target's engine, as it had been designed to do. Cole felt the aircraft lurch suddenly, and then the helicopter was violently oscillating, the entire ship jerking back and forth with each turn of the rotors. He battled the stick, trying to bring the ship back under control. The landscape was whirling past the cockpit now as the Black Hawk spun dizzyingly into the valley.

It felt as though they'd lost all or most of one rotor blade; the imbalance would tear the engine apart in seconds, but with luck and some decent piloting, Cole thought he might be able to save enough collective to make it to the ground all in one piece. Nursing the engine, battling stick and pitch and collective, he brought the spinning aircraft down. In the last second or two before touchdown, however, the machine started to go over onto its right side, and nothing Cole could do would right it. The spinning rotors chewed into earth and the Black Hawk's fuselage counterrotated. An instant later, the engine blew, and a ruptured fuel line spilled aviation gas across a red-hot manifold.

They struck hard, plowing into soft earth, the impact softened somewhat by the right-side ESSS crumpling with the crash and breaking away. Cole gasped as he slammed against his safety harness, then again as his seat tore free of its mountings and slammed him forward into the instrument console. The fuselage bounced once, then rolled partly upright; the change in attitude let the pilot seat collapse backward into an approximation of its original position.

Stunned, his chest shrieking agony with each breath, Cole still managed to hit the release and drag himself free of the seat. Dombrowski's head lolled to the side; Cole couldn't tell if the copilot was dead or unconscious. Blinking back tears against the pain, he unstrapped Dombrowski, tried to drag him free . . . and failed. The man's weight was too much for him to handle with what felt like several broken ribs.

Then Chris Palmer was with him, his face a mask of blood from a nasty cut on his scalp up near his hairline, but otherwise intact. Smoke boiled into the cockpit from the aft cabin.

"The ship's on fire!" Palmer yelled. "We've got to get out!"

"Help me with him!"

Together, they dragged Dombrowski out from between the cockpit seats, aft into smoky darkness, and out the right-side door. They hit muddy earth and kept moving; Cole glanced back once and caught a glimpse of the entire engine housing aflame, as black smoke spilled from the downed aircraft's interior. A few seconds later, the flames reached the fuel tanks and the Black Hawk erupted in a searing yellow-and-orange fireball that roiled into the morning sky.

The two of them dropped to the ground on either side of Dombrowski's body, gasping for breath. "God, what happened?" Palmer asked.

"We just got shot down, is what happened," Cole said. He winced as pain lanced through his side. "Damn, I think we just got shot down by the fucking Navy!"

It was a miracle that any of them had survived.

0933 hours (Zulu +4)
Tomcat 218
UN No-Fly Zone, Republic of Georgia

Mason pulled up gently, putting his Tomcat into a terrain-hugging flight across the hills. At the far end of his climb-and-turn when the missile had struck, he'd seen the flash and the smoke. Now he was angling back into the valley for a closer look.

"Target Sierra One is down!" he radioed, exultant. "Scratch one Hind!"

"Roger that," Batman replied. "Good spotting, Dixie!"

But Dixie didn't respond, not immediately. As he passed low over the valley, he had a clear view of the downed helo. Most of the main cabin directly beneath the engine compartment and the twisted, shattered rotors was gone, crumpled up in a fire-blackened skeleton that was rapidly being consumed by fiercely burning flames. The tail section was more or less intact, however, extending out of the fireball at a jaunty angle. He could just make out the words UNITED STATES ARMY stenciled in yellow on the olive-drab paint.

Nearby, a Russian-made Hip Mi-8 was settling to the ground, and figures were running from the open rear door. Then the F-14 was past the valley, and he couldn't see anymore . . . couldn't see if there were survivors, couldn't see the flames.

"Oh, my God . . ."

Cat's words over the ICS said it all. Dixie felt a cold, hard lump in his chest and throat, felt sweat slicking the skin inside his helmet, felt the hammer of his heart beneath his safety harness.

Years of training, years of work, years of battling idiocy and prejudice to get him his one golden chance as a Navy combat aviator.

And it had just ended with a downed U.S. helicopter.

"No," he said, shaking his head. *"No! . . ."*

0954 hours (Zulu +3)
Tomcat 201
One mile abeam U.S.S. *Thomas Jefferson*

"Tomcat Two-oh-one, Charlie now." The voice of Commander William Barnes, *Jefferson*'s Air Boss, sounded over Batman's headset, giving the order to commence his final approach to the carrier.

Batman pulled the control stick over, guiding the Tomcat into a 4-G turn toward the carrier deck. He cut back on the throttles and hit the Tomcat's speed brakes to slow the fighter to below three hundred knots. The computer started to reset the position of the wings to a forward position to compensate for the reduced speed, but Batman overrode the controls without really thinking about it. Most naval aviators liked to come in with the wings in their swept-back position, claiming the computer's preferred wing setting made the Tomcat look like an oversized goose. Batman's actions were virtually automatic after years of handling carrier landings, but this morning he was doubly distracted.

He still couldn't believe that he'd just scored an own goal . . . downing an American helicopter. Damn . . . damn . . . *damn*! How in hell had that happened? . . .

He forced himself to concentrate on the approach. Batman flicked on the switch to lower the Tomcat's landing gear as he continued the turn. His HUD display showed his speed falling below 230 knots, and Wayne dropped the wing flaps to further reduce the speed of the aircraft. He scanned his console readouts, noting the rate of descent, 615 feet per minute, and the range to the carrier, just over three-quarters of a mile. His angle-of-bank was twenty degrees as he finished his turn and lined up on the flight deck, making his approach from astern.

Jefferson was making fifteen knots, steering east through relatively calm waters under a clear blue sky. Landing conditions were almost ideal, and for a pilot who had made landings in the most difficult weather conditions—and, worse yet, at night—it should have been an easy approach. But Batman Wayne was finding it hard to stay focused, and on something as tricky as a carrier landing that could be deadly. From his vantage point behind and above the carrier, the flight deck seemed an impossibly small target set in the wide blue expanse of the sea.

He could see the ship's Fresnell landing system mounted on the squat tower on the port side of the carrier, the "meatball" that helped a pilot estimate his glide slope. "Tomcat Two-oh-one, seven point one, ball," he radioed. Calling the ball was the signal that he had the meatball lined up and was starting his final approach with 7100 pounds of fuel on board.

"Roger ball," Barnes acknowledged. That passed control

of the approach from Pri-Fly to the Landing Signals Officer stationed on a platform just below the Fresnell lens.

"Glide slope's a little steep, Batman." The voice of Lieutenant Gene "Lassie" Lassiter, the LSO on duty for the Vipers this morning, was flat and calm. "More power."

He pushed the throttles forward and pulled the Tomcat's nose up, cursing under his breath. There was no reason for this to be anything but a routine trap on the flight deck.

No reason beyond the simple fact that he couldn't get the image of that burning helicopter out of his mind.

"Easy now," Lassiter said. "Don't overcompensate now. . . ."

The very best LSOs in the fleet were the ones like Lassiter who could keep calm and unflappable, giving guidance without sounding like world-class nags.

"Ease off, Batman!"

Shit . . . he *had* overcompensated. The fighter was coming in too high now. The red lights on either side of the meatball came on, but he was almost up to the carrier's roundoff and there wasn't a damn thing he could do about it now.

"Wave off! Wave off!"

His landing gear shrieked as they touched the deck, too far forward for the arrestor hook to snag a cable. Batman pushed the throttles forward and pulled up on the stick, cursing aloud this time. The engines thundered, the acceleration pressing him into his seat as the plane lifted clear and headed back into the open sky once again.

"Bolter! Bolter! Bolter!" the LSO called. Batman felt himself flushing behind his oxygen mask. Of all the stupid rookie tricks to pull!

"Take it easy, man," Malibu said behind him. "Don't let it get to you. Just circle around and get your focus back."

"Shit, Malibu! If you don't like my flying, you can get out here and *walk* back to the boat!"

"Chill out, dude," the RIO responded with a trace of his usual bantering style. "Just stay frosty, right? You can cool off while they bring Dixie down. Nothing to worry about . . ."

"Yeah. Nothing to worry about."

Except for the fact that he'd just downed an American aircraft, maybe killed its flight crew.

Nothing to worry about at all.

1007 hours (Zulu +3)
Tomcat 218
Flight Deck, U.S.S. *Thomas Jefferson*

The Tomcat snagged the arrestor wire with a jolt that flung Tom Mason hard against his shoulder harness. "Good trap! Good trap!" the LSO was calling on the radio as he cut the throttles back. The roar of the engines faded to a low rumbling whine. A yellow-shirted traffic director ran onto the flight deck in front of the fighter, waving his twin rods to guide Mason on his taxi path.

He backed the plane up far enough to take the strain off the arrestor cable and let it drop to the deck, "spitting out the wire," as it was called. Then he folded the fighter's wings and started slowly forward, following the Yellow Shirt.

"Good trap" echoed in his mind. He'd made it down in one try, at least. After Batman's bolter, Mason had been worried he'd have trouble, too. After all, if the commander had been shaken up by the downing of a U.S. chopper, how much worse should it have been for the man who made the bad call in the first place? Somehow, though, when the time had come to start the approach, Dixie had been able to push his concerns aside and concentrate on the landing.

Does that make me a good aviator or a callous one?

"I'd vote for callous," Garrity said from the backseat.

Mason suppressed a curse. He hadn't realized he'd been thinking out loud. "Hey, lay off, Cat," he said. "I made a mistake back there. But just because I didn't bolter . . ."

"Relax, Dixie," she said. "I didn't mean anything by it. Pressure hits different people in different ways. The Batman was probably shaken up by a lot more than that Black Hawk. He's got a whole squadron to worry about."

"Yeah," Mason said. He pulled into the space reserved for his plane and killed the engines, then paused before opening the canopy. "Just between us, Cat, what do you think's gonna happen? . . ."

She didn't answer for a long moment. "Look, I don't have any answers," she said at last. "I didn't get a good look at that helo when we made the pass. From back here, though, it looked to me like you saw exactly what you wanted to see, and that was a hostile bird you could go after."

"But—"

"You asked for my opinion, Dixie. I'm not saying you were making things up, or anything like that. I just think you were a little too eager, that's all." She paused. "If CAG thinks the same, he could throw the book at you. If there's one thing I've learned since I started carrier duty, it's to play everything as chilly and professional as possible. Magruder doesn't tolerate anything less . . . and he shouldn't."

"Cat, I *know* what I saw. . . ."

"Yeah. Yeah, I'm sure you're convinced of it now." There was an even longer pause. "But I've got to tell you the truth, Lieutenant. I'm going to ask to be assigned to another plane for a while. I don't think I want to ride with somebody I can't trust to keep his head in a tight spot."

The canopy lifted slowly, and the plane captain was alongside to unfold the ladder so Mason and Garrity could climb out. He didn't answer her.

The problem was, he wasn't sure he *could* answer her.

Because, deep down, Tom Mason was very much afraid she was right.

CHAPTER 9
Saturday, 31 October

Coyote Grant paused outside the locker room where Viper Squadron kept their flight gear, prey to a confusing mix of emotions. He had been a part of VF-95 for more than four years, and CO of the squadron since their deployment to Norway nearly eighteen months ago. It was still hard to adjust to his new role as Deputy CAG, no longer flying Tomcats almost daily alongside his men but instead a staff officer who had to think of the entire Air Wing, the interaction of all the different aircraft in *Jefferson*'s formidable arsenal.

He missed the Vipers. He saw them every day, of course, and even flew with them when he could, when he needed to log some flight time, but it wasn't the same.

Aviators, more than most, showed that peculiar human trait that classified other people as "them" or "us." It could be an especially cold-blooded fraternity. A fellow aviator might be a close buddy, a wingman, a fellow member of the squadron until the night when he lost his nerve in a particularly hairy recovery on board and turned in his wings. After that, he was an outsider, greeted, perhaps, in friendly fashion . . . but always with a lurking trace of condescension, a knowing smile that said, *Shit, he didn't have what it takes, after all.* The guy might still be flying, but it would be as a *pilot*, not a naval aviator, definitely a cut below the best of the best.

Coyote was still rated for carrier duty; he flew whenever he could get out from behind his desk, every chance he could find in an increasingly paper-logged schedule. But he was no longer a member of the Vipers. He could see it in their eyes when he greeted one in a passageway, or when he was delivering a briefing. His feet were firmly planted now on the same career ladder Tombstone was already climbing. Down the line he might be a CAG himself, and someday he might even rise to command a carrier like the *Jefferson*. Every naval aviator's dream . . .

For the moment, though, his sights were fixed on the immediate future. He could expect to follow this Deputy CAG assignment with a tour of duty Stateside, possibly on the command staff of a Naval Air Station. That meant time with his wife and daughter, time to try to rebuild a marriage that was already in tatters.

It had been especially bad during this last deployment back to Norfolk. Lots of tears, lots of recriminations, and the knowledge that there really wasn't much he could do about it, unless he was willing to resign from the Navy and get a nice, normal, steady, *safe* civilian job. In some ways, Coyote had almost been glad when the unexpected orders came through, sending the CBG to the Med . . . and informing him that he'd just been moved to the carrier's Deputy CAG slot.

Most of Julie's worries were those typical of a woman left alone to raise a three-year-old girl by herself while her husband spent months on end at sea, risking his life every day. The presence of women on the *Jefferson* hadn't helped things, either. When he was still CO of the Vipers, Coyote had usually flown with Cat Garrity as his RIO, and during that last rotation home he'd made the mistake of telling Julie how much he respected the woman as a naval flight officer. That, coupled with some of the more lurid stories filtering back to the States through the media—stories about sexual harassment cases and the goings-on among the mixed crew—had raised all kinds of unfounded suspicions in

Julie's mind. They were the sort of fears he could have allayed in seconds if he'd just been there with her to show her how much he still loved her.

But that simply hadn't been possible. When the Navy said go, you went; he loved Julie, but he also had a career to consider. *If the Navy had wanted you to have a wife, they would have issued you one with your seabag* ran the old saw among enlisted men. *Sex and saltwater don't mix* was another.

Maybe, just maybe, his recent promotion would prove to be the first step in putting his marriage back together again. In the meantime, though, it was a letdown working on the CAG staff instead of flying with the Vipers. Worst of all were the days like this when he had to watch one of his old friends sit in the hot seat.

Grant double-checked to be sure the sign saying WOMEN was neither posted by the hatch nor lying on the deck. There weren't enough female enlisted personnel to assign to watch the ready rooms on every shift when female flight officers might need to change, so unlike the showers the ready rooms functioned on an honor system, with the aviators taking turns . . . except, of course, when there was a scramble and every man and woman had to be suited up as fast as possible. The sign was a courtesy, used when there was time to observe the niceties of civilized behavior.

So far there hadn't been any deliberate violations of ready room privacy, though there had been that one time when the sign had fallen down and one of the men from the War Eagles had gotten an eyeful when he went to suit up. Apparently, though, Cat Garrity had already finished changing and was on her way to debriefing.

He heard Malibu talking as he entered the changing area. "Look, all I'm saying is you've got to ease up on yourself," the RIO was saying. "Quit acting like the weight of the world's on your shoulders."

"Good advice," Coyote said. Malibu was already in his khakis, hanging up his flight suit in his locker. Batman was sitting nearby, still wearing his own flight gear.

"Coyote!" Malibu said. His features broke into a grin. "What're you doing in here? Slumming?"

"Just making sure you two get your sorry asses up for debriefing," Grant said. He studied Blake for a moment. The RIO had been uncharacteristically quiet lately, almost withdrawn, but he seemed more animated now. Coyote suspected he was worried about how Batman was dealing with his new role as CO of the Vipers. The two had been inseparable friends for years, with a bond that sometimes seemed almost psychic.

"I'm on my way," Malibu said. "The Bat here has a bad case of the slows."

"I'll get him over that." Grant waited until Malibu had left before turning to Wayne. "Bad time this morning, huh?"

Batman fumbled with the zipper of his suit as he replied. "There's an understatement," he said. "Sort of like saying Krasilnikov's a troublemaker."

"Look, I just got a report down from Ops," Coyote told him. "Thought you'd like to hear right away. The flight crew on that helo's okay. They're pretty dinged up, but they got picked up by a Marine medevac and flown out to the *Guadalcanal*. The word is they'll be okay."

Batman let out a long, slow sigh. "Thank . . . God . . ."

"You can also thank the Army pilot on that Black Hawk. He gentled his machine down after you popped one of his blades."

"Army? Shit, what's the *Army* doing over here?"

"Damfino. I thought the *Canal* was just carrying Marines this time. We don't have the full story yet, but Ops is working on the theory that we weren't given all of the IFF computer recognition codes . . . which would explain why they registered as a hostile."

"God."

Someone rapped on the door, then stuck his head in. It was Lieutenant Randolph Wojiewski, one of the assistant LSOs. He held a clipboard in one hand. "Commander Wayne?"

"Yeah."

"Okay, got your scores, sir. Two bolters. Mr. Lassiter says it happens to the best of us."

"Right."

"On your landing pass, you were still a little high, a little tight. You were showing a tendency to overcorrect when the LSO fed you the word." Wojiewski continued ticking off the flaws in Batman's trap. This was a routine that followed every landing aboard a carrier, and the results were posted on the big greenie board outside each squadron's ready room. It was a way of showing each aviator where he stood with all the others, and giving him instant feedback that would let him improve his technique.

"All in all, not too bad, though," Wojiewski concluded. "Mr. Lassiter's giving you a 'fair.' Okay?"

Batman scowled, and for a moment Coyote thought he was going to lash out at the ALSO. In the highly competitive world of carrier aviation, each landing could receive one of four possible grades. Best of all was "okay," and a green square on the greenie board. Next was "fair," with a yellow square. "No grade" and no color on the board meant the trap had been dangerous to people or to aircraft on the deck. Lowest of all was a red square with the letter "C" marked in, for "cut." That grade was reserved for a landing so dangerous it could easily have ended in disaster.

Batman, Coyote knew, carried a fierce pride in his abilities as an aviator. It would take a while to wash that yellow from the record book he kept inside his skull.

"So, what happened?" Coyote pressed him, after Wojiewski had left the compartment. "What's your side of the story?"

"*Mason* happened. Shit, Coyote, I don't know what went down out there. The kid IDed the bogey as a Hind. I got weapons clear and went Fox two. Next thing I know, I'm hearing about a downed American helo over the radio and I'm being ordered back to the bird farm." He managed a wry, drawn grin. "And two bolters to get me down."

"We all have our day inside the barrel," Coyote said, using the expression that referred to an aviator who made pass after pass on the deck but couldn't connect with the arresting wire . . . each failure making the *next* failure that much more likely. "But this own goal you scored, that's serious, even if the crew's okay. Stoney's about to go ballistic. He was over on the *Shiloh* when word came through, conferring with Admiral Tarrant. He was *not* pleased, let me tell you!"

Batman didn't reply right away but continued changing to his uniform. "How did you handle it, Will?" he asked after a long moment. "Being skipper of the squadron, I mean. How did you know when to get tough and when to go easy?"

Coyote raised an eyebrow. "Are you asking me if you should cover for Mason and Garrity?"

"I didn't say that," Batman said.

"You want to tell me what happened up there? I mean exactly."

Batman shrugged. "Dixie was eyeball, I was shooter. He led the way in by three miles or so. Watch Dog wasn't picking up IFF on the target. Neither did we, when we got close. Then Cat reported that they were being painted by a Zoo, and I guess she was busy turning knobs about then, because she didn't see the target. Dixie reported a Hind.

"About that time, Malibu picked up something about the UN flight being under attack. Since the bogey was trailing UN Two-seven, I assumed, I mean, it looked like the bogey was after the UN bird, right? Anyway, I launched."

"Was there any way you could have checked on Dixie's ID?"

"What was I supposed to do? Ignore him because he's a rookie and insist on another pass before I made up my mind? I might've flown us right into triple-A if that Zoo had turned out to be a hostile. Anyway, I can't treat the rest of the squadron like they're a bunch of idiots."

"No, you can't," Grant agreed. "You have to trust their training. I remember Tombstone chewed my ass once in Norway because I wasn't letting the other guys do their jobs while I did mine."

"Well, the leader still has the responsibility, right? I was supposed to be looking out for him." Batman gave a hollow laugh. "Great job, huh?"

"New guy. Just out of a RAG and trying to prove himself." Grant paused. "Is he wearing a chip? Black guy in a white-bread world?"

"I wouldn't say he's got a chip on his shoulder, no. He's all right. Seems to fit in with the others okay. But he does work extra hard to prove he can cut it."

"Yeah." Grant looked away. "Look, Ed, I wasn't out there. I don't know what I would have done in your place . . . but I don't see where you made any wrong decisions. Mason missed the ID call. Hell, that can happen even to a veteran. But you can't second-guess your people all the time, veterans or newbies. If you do, you'll burn yourself out—and you'll take the squadron with you."

Batman nodded. "You're right. But, God, I could've *killed* someone, one of our guys. . . ."

"Well, you didn't. Concentrate on that. If you let it get to you, it'll screw your head up so bad you'll never pull out of the spin. You're too good an aviator to lose your wings because of something that *almost* went down."

"I may be a good flier," Batman said. "The question is how good a CO I am. When I was your XO, it was pretty easy, you know? I fielded some gripes for the guys, I helped you with the paperwork, I did my turn on CAP or on combat ops. No big deal. Shit, Coyote, you should've told me what you were going through, running the show. Then maybe I'd've told them what to do when they decided to stick me in this slot."

"You'll handle it, Batman. Trust me. Inside a few weeks, you'll be the same old arrogant, cocksure hot-dog bastard we all know and love."

Batman finished dressing and closed his locker. "Maybe you're right," he said. He managed a grin. "Of course, first I have to survive whatever old Stoney decides to throw at me. If I don't make it out of debriefing alive, Coyote, you can have my CD collection."

Tombstone Magruder looked up at the four officers standing in line in front of his desk. He didn't speak right away. His emotions were in turmoil, caught between horror at the incident that had so nearly turned tragic and relief that the ultimate tragedy had somehow been averted. The fact that two of the four were among his best friends didn't make his job this morning any easier. *Friends are a luxury you can't always afford in the Service,* his uncle, now a desk-bound admiral in Washington, had told him once.

He took a deep breath. "Okay. Let's have it," he said.

No one answered. He studied them, one after another. Mason and Garrity were at rigid attention, looking far too young and vulnerable to be part of the carrier's front line of defense. Batman and Malibu were older, steadier hands, officers he had long relied on. Friends . . .

Coyote shifted in his chair to Tombstone's right. "Friendly fire happens sometimes, Stoney . . . CAG."

"That's not an explanation," he shot back. "You can't just say 'Shit happens' and leave it at that."

Still, Coyote was right. He knew that. Friendly fire, accidental attacks against your own people, had probably been a factor in warfare since the first cavemen duked it out over the local water hole. In the Persian Gulf War some of the most serious battlefield casualties taken by Allied forces had been the result of friendly fire, especially when fast-moving ground support aircraft misidentified vehicles on the ground. The press had spent a lot of verbiage and agonizing over those incidents, of course, but anyone with combat experience knew they were inevitable. The fog of war was as real on today's electronic battlefield as it had been in the days of Napoleon . . . or Sargon the Great.

He was thinking in particular of an incident hauntingly like this one, back in 1994, when two U.S. Air Force fighters had engaged and destroyed two Army helicopters in the no-fly zone established over northern Iraq. The pilots had been edgy, the AWACS procedures had broken down, the IFF systems on the choppers had been turned off. And then, as now, someone had confused the U.S. Army Black Hawk with the Soviet-made Hind. That time, over twenty men had died.

Murphy's Law still ruled, especially when men were excited, frightened, or tired. But there were supposed to be safeguards in place to keep these things from happening, and Magruder needed to know just what had gone wrong.

"Sir, I take full responsibility . . ." Batman began.

Magruder cut him off. "You bet you do, Commander," he said harshly. "But that's not much better than 'Shit happens' either! Do you know the difference between a Hind and a Black Hawk?"

"Yessir," Batman said quietly.

Mason cleared his throat. "I made the ID, CAG," he said. "It was my fault, not the skipper's."

"You made the ID," Magruder said, turning his angry gaze on the younger man. He let the words hang there for a moment before reaching into his top desk drawer and extracting a manila folder. Inside were several photographs, drawn from the files of *Jefferson*'s OZ Division, the carrier's intelligence department.

He spread the photos out on the table, turning them so Mason could see. "This is a Hind," he said, tapping one of the photos. "Recognition features: five-bladed rotor; tapering, anhedral stub wings shoulder-mounted on the fuselage; separate, stepped pilot's and gunner's cockpits; cannon mounted in a nose turret; three-bladed tail rotor mounted to the port side of the boom." He tapped another. "This is a UH-60 Black Hawk. Recognition features: four-bladed rotor; large, single cockpit with broad windows; four-bladed tail rotor mounted to starboard of the tail boom, and canted at twenty degrees to provide additional lift; *large* tail planes. Is there anything here you don't understand?"

"No, sir. I know what a Black Hawk looks like. I know what a Hind looks like. I only saw the target for a second or two, and from behind, so I couldn't see the double cockpit. But I *did* see the weapons pylons on either side. I've never heard of a Black Hawk with weapons pylons."

"For your information, son, what you saw was an External Stores Support System, ESSS." He looked at Cat. "What about you, Garrity? Did you see it?"

The woman shook her head slowly. "No, CAG," she said. "My head was down at the time."

"Your head was down. So you were the only one who saw it, Mason?"

"Yes, CAG," Mason said. "I . . . I really thought it was. The aspect was from the rear and above, and it really looked like a Hind configuration to me. I honestly thought . . ."

He held up a hand. "We've established what you thought you saw."

"They were being painted by a Gun Dish signal from the ground, CAG," Batman said. "Probably a ZSU. I made my decision based on the report of one of my aviators. I could have ordered a double check of the target, but thought it would be unwise to risk possible triple-A from the Zoo. There was also the possibility that the enemy was engaging the UN flight. Time was critical."

Tombstone let himself relax a little. "You're right. You made a mistake. Wrecked an aircraft that cost the taxpayers something like fifteen mil. And before any of you points it out to me, I'll say the rest. It would also have been a mistake to get confirmation if those Zoos had opened fire and brought one of you down. And it would have been a mistake if you'd let the sucker go on about his business and he turned out to be a Hind on his way to shoot down the UN Hip."

"Hell, CAG, we can't win for losing," Cat Garrity said. There were a few chuckles in the room, and the tension eased a little.

"That's exactly right, Cat," Magruder said. "This no-fly zone crap is one of the trickiest damned ops we've taken on. There's no clear-cut enemy out there, nothing but a set of vague rules that we have to interpret well enough to keep everybody off our backs while we try to do our job at the

same time. Right now, our biggest worry about this incident
is the fact that there were reporters on that UN helo."

"Reporters!" Malibu said.

"Oh, shit!" Dixie added.

"The headline news tonight may lead off with a real
humdinger of a story. Something like 'Navy Downs Army
Helo Over Georgia.'"

"If we're lucky," Coyote said with a grin, "they'll play it
on the sports segment. 'Navy Scores Over Army, 1–0.'"

"More likely we're going to get a storm of inquiries.
Congressmen calling. Interviews. Hell, maybe somebody
will start asking some intelligent questions. Like what the
devil is a carrier battle group doing way the hell out here?
But in the meantime, we have to do our part to make sure
this doesn't happen again."

"What the hell happened with the helo's IFF?" Batman
wanted to know.

"As near as we can tell, no one bothered to tell us that a
couple of Army helos had been sent into Georgia to work
with the UN team."

"I thought the Navy was supposed to be handling no-fly
zone security?" Garrity said.

Tombstone shrugged. "You know how it goes. One
service gets a plum assignment, and suddenly everyone
wants a piece of the action."

"Grenada," Coyote added, and Tombstone nodded.

That monumental foul-up was still a reminder—and a
warning—of how not to conduct joint military operations.
When America decided to invade the tiny Caribbean country in 1983, the op had started off as a relatively small
mission. Then invasion fever had started spreading through
the Pentagon. One service after another had wanted in . . .
as did each of the elite combat units within the larger
branches. The SEALs. Delta Force. Army Special Forces.
No one knew what anyone else was doing, radio frequencies
and call signs weren't distributed to the proper people, and
in one classic case of idiocy, orders describing an air assault
gave a time but failed to say whether that was EST, GMT,
or local time.

A lot of Americans died unnecessarily in that invasion.

Tombstone let out a sigh. "Okay, people. There will be no disciplinary action from my office. I should warn you all, though, that I don't have the last say here. Depending on how big a noise this makes with the brass Stateside, or with the news media, there could be a further investigation."

"You mean we're still on the hook," Batman said. He looked resigned. "What do you want us to do, CAG?"

"First thing, I want reports. All four of you get a complete report on the incident done and on my desk by 1600 hours. And I mean *complete*. I don't want excuses, but I damn sure do want anybody who reads these reports to know what we're going through to police these damned zones. We've got Zoos and helos . . ."

"And bears, oh my," Cat Garrity put in with a grin.

Tombstone caught Batman's eye and smiled. "No, thank God, no Bears this time." Both men had been through some harrowing encounters with the Russian aircraft code-named Bears. As a matter of fact, the first time Magruder had ever chewed out Batman Wayne was over a Bear hunt, back when Tombstone was the squadron CO and Batman a young hot dog just joining the squadron. Some things, it seemed, never changed. He let the smile drop. "Next. Dixie, I'm taking you off the zone patrols for a few days. You'll be limited to flying CAP until further notice."

"Sir—"

"No arguments. I know your record; I know you think you're the hottest pilot Viper Squadron's ever seen; I know how much you want to be out there. But until this has a chance to settle out, I don't want you in the no-fly zone." He looked at Batman. "You'll see to the scheduling?"

"Aye, aye, CAG," Wayne said. He sounded unhappy.

"All right, then. Case closed, at least for the moment. You're all dismissed."

The four from Bird Dog Flight filed out of the office, but Coyote didn't leave. "You have a problem?" Magruder asked him when the door closed behind Garrity.

"More than you can imagine," Grant said. "But a couple of immediate concerns. Don't you think you could've been a little nastier? Like maybe call off Christmas or some-thing?"

"We've had this talk before, Will," Magruder said with a sigh. He leaned back in his chair. "CAG staff's not like being in the squadron, not even like being squadron CO. You know how I feel about Batman and Malibu. And those two kids are going to be hot when they get some seasoning, as good as we ever were."

"Better, maybe."

"Maybe. But I can't be their *buddy* anymore. Neither can you. Our responsibility isn't to the individuals, or to the squadron. It's to the whole Air Wing, to the *Jefferson*, and to the mission. If this incident had resulted in Americans being killed due to friendly fire, I'd've been forced to recommend relieving them of duty. A court of inquiry. You think I'd want something like that hanging over Batman? Next to you, he's the best friend I've ever had."

"I don't like it much," Coyote said quietly. "Sometimes I think I wasn't cut out for this staff shit. Maybe I should've turned you down."

"You can't sit in the cockpit forever, Coyote," Tombstone told him. He jerked a thumb at a mug that sat on the corner of his desk. A dozen cigars stuck out of it, still in their original wrappings. The had belonged to Tombstone's predecessor as CAG, the man who'd taught him at Top Gun school years before. He kept them on his desk as a reminder of the lessons the man had taught him, both at Top Gun and later, when Magruder was his Deputy CAG and *Jefferson* was sailing into the Norway crisis. "Stinger Stramaglia made my life a living hell when I was his deputy. But he also taught me that if I didn't grow I'd end up being left behind. The first time I realized just how *big* this damned job was I almost cracked. All I wanted was a chance to strap on a Tomcat and go up with the Vipers again. Trouble is, that isn't an option. Sometimes you have to sit behind the desk and cope with all the petty little details so the other guys can get in the air."

"I'm just not sure I can cut myself off from everything that's gone before," Grant told him. "I'm not a machine."

"Neither am I. I'm worse. I'm the CAG." Magruder looked away. "You said there were a couple of things bothering you. What else?"

Coyote frowned. "Just wondering if you knew what you were doing with Mason."

"By rights, I should've grounded him. I have the impression he saw exactly what he wanted to see out there, and we damn near lost an American air crew. I took it easy on him because . . . well, because I'm not a machine. He's got the makings of a good aviator, but he needs some drudgery to put things into perspective."

"I read his file. He's got friends in high places."

Magruder raised an eyebrow.

"His sponsor when he applied to Annapolis. Sammie Reed represented his district and made the recommendation."

"Well, well. Our brand-new Secretary of Defense." Magruder shrugged. "If I read Mason, he isn't the sort to run for help just because he gets his ears pinned back."

"Yeah, but you know how these things get out. He mentions it in a letter, somebody back home gets outraged, phone calls get made . . ."

"You really think it could be a problem?"

"Come on, Stoney, wake up and smell the avgas! George Vane resigned as Secretary of Defense because of policy disagreements with the President. Mostly the Kola deployment, but also all the damned social experiments. Our new fearless leader doesn't share any of his reservations. Look at Directive 626."

"I try not to," Tombstone said wryly. Directive 626 was a new order from the upper levels of the Pentagon requiring women in combat units to be worked into command slots on a quota basis, regardless of relative seniority or experience. The Air Wing had been forced to make a number of adjustments to accommodate the order, and it was one more blow to the unit's morale. "And Mason?"

"Is a minority, in case you were too color-blind to notice it. Sam Reed would love to have a cause like that to get behind if it would make the Navy look bad. You remember the trouble a couple of years back? The Top Gun graduation?"

Magruder nodded. Before moving to the cabinet, Reed had been on the House Armed Services Committee, one of the liberal voices pushing hard for unpopular reforms in the military. After the committee had recommended relaxing the standards for female pilots to compete for slots at Top Gun and other advanced schools, a graduating class had displayed banners calling Reed some extremely derogatory names. That had sparked an ongoing feud between Reed and the Navy, particularly in Naval Aviation.

Now Samantha Reed was America's first female Secretary of Defense, and she was well placed to carry on that feud.

Magruder frowned for a moment, then shook his head. "I appreciate the advice, Coyote. I really do. But I'll take my chances on this one. If I have to look at an officer's gender or color or sexual preferences before I can hand down discipline I might as well just pack it in. If Madam Secretary Reed wants my head, she can have it . . . but she can't make me screw up this unit in the name of political correctness."

Coyote grinned and shook his head. "You always did have a bad attitude, Stoney. Head hard as a rock. Not exactly good for the career track, but——"

"Screw the career track," Tombstone said. "If they take this job away from me, maybe I can go back to flying airplanes!"

"*Now* you're talking!"

CHAPTER 10
Saturday, 31 October

"Mind if I join you, Skipper?"

Batman Wayne looked up. It was Brewer Conway, his XO, standing beside the table with a tray in her hands. He hesitated a moment before replying, torn between a need for sympathetic company and a dread of having to go through another round of questions about the helicopter incident. Finally he shrugged. "It's a free country. Drag up a seat."

Brewer sat down across from him, looked at his plate, then looked at her own, making a face. Gingerly, she lifted one corner of her hamburger bun and peered uncertainly at the meat inside. "Well," she said, "at least I know now why they call these things 'sliders.' There's enough grease in here to clog every artery on board this bucket."

"Hey, all the comforts of life ashore. You know how many fast-food burgers you have to eat to get the same cholesterol spike of one of these babies?"

"I'd hate to think." She set the bun aside and began blotting at the meat with her napkin.

"Just drown it in ketchup. You'll never taste the difference."

"You mean I'll never know what hit me." She dropped the wadded-up napkin on her tray, then helped herself to the ketchup bottle. "Hey, Batman?"

119

"Yeah?"

"How long you think this deployment's going to last?"

"What, our Black Sea cruise? Beats the hell out of me."

"I mean, they cut our rotation Stateside pretty short. I was wondering if we'd be out for a full six-month deployment, or if they might rotate us back early."

"You're asking the wrong guy, Brewer. Nobody ever tells me a damned thing."

"*Nimitz* was supposed to take this assignment, wasn't she?"

"That's the scuttlebutt," he said. "That's the way it goes, though. Too many commitments, too few carriers. Maybe the *Nimitz*'ll relieve us after that mess in Africa gets resolved. On the other hand, maybe by then there'll be some new crisis and we'll be stuck here for months."

"You *are* cheerful today."

"Yeah, well. Two bolters, a 'fair' for my recovery, and I get to paint a little silhouette of an American helicopter on the side of my plane. Kind of hard to top that, right?"

"Hey, the day's just half over."

"That's what I'm afraid of."

Conway was silent for a long moment, eating her hamburger and looking thoughtful.

"Okay, Commander," he said. "Out with it."

"Out with what?"

"You've got something churning between your ears, and it looks serious. Want to talk?"

"Well . . ."

"Look, it can't make my day any worse than it already is. Go ahead. Hit me."

She sighed, then nodded. "Okay. Skipper, I think we've got a problem with the squadron, and I don't know how to handle it."

"Let me guess. You heard about Nightmare and Big D."

She nodded. "That's part of it. But a lot of the guys have been sidestepping me, not just those two. I can't do my job if nobody will accept me."

"I know." Wayne frowned. He had seen this situation coming for a long time, another of the petty frustrations that were making it hard for him to get a handle on the squadron commander's job. "Look, Brewer, you know every man in the Vipers respects you and the rest of the . . . women." He stumbled over the word. It was so damned hard to choose words carefully to avoid giving unintended offense. You could refer to "guys" or even "boys" without a second thought, but never to "gals" or "girls." Even after months serving together, the men and women of the Air Wing were finding it hard to keep the gender wars from flaring up over the most trivial excuses. "The Kola fight proved you've got what it takes to be aviators. But you've got to understand what it's like for some of these guys. They've never had to deal with a female Exec before."

"I didn't ask for the job," Brewer said.

"No, but you got it, courtesy of Directive 626. You get extra points for being a woman with combat experience, so you get pushed ahead of men of comparable rank. Nightmare Marinaro has been in the Vipers almost as long as I have. He flew with us in Korea and India and all those ops off Norway. And Dallas Sheridan has a lot more time in rank, even though his combat duty was limited to Norway and Russia." He paused, then pushed on. "Look, you asked me, so I'm going to be blunt. Either one of them deserved a shot at the XO slot more than you. Hell, Malibu deserved it even more. He's just not making a big thing out of it. But they are. Those two guys are ambitious. They know a shot at Exec will lead to bigger and better things down the road."

"And if Malibu had it?"

Batman shrugged. "They'd both know he earned it," he told her.

"And I didn't."

"Look, Brewer, this isn't some male chauvinist thing. They don't resent you because you're a woman. Not anymore. You're a naval aviator, one of the—" He stopped. He'd almost said "guys." He took a deep breath and started over. "What I mean is, you're an aviator like the rest of us. What they don't like is the idea of someone getting special treatment that makes the work they've done all these years count for nothing. If you were a man and you were given a leg up because you were a minority, they'd feel the same way." He shrugged. "So if Big D and Nightmare are a little sullen, can you really blame them?"

She looked away. "I guess not. But what about the others? Lieutenant Davis went behind my back to see you last week. So did Whitman. I didn't take the Exec job away from them. They weren't even in the running."

Batman rubbed his forehead, his eyes closed. "Some of the men have trouble dealing with a female Exec," he said at last. Before she could protest, he held up his hand. "Think about it, Brewer. One of the main jobs of the XO is to deal with the people problems in the squadron. *All* kinds of problems—professional, personal, you name it. It isn't easy for a guy to come to a woman and tell her that he's, oh, having marital problems back home, say. Or . . . listen. Would you expect any of those guys to come talk to you because they're worried about what kind of diseases they might have picked up when they were on liberty? There's lots of stuff men don't want to tell a woman, especially an attractive one, and even more especially one they have to work with in close quarters every day."

"Male ego," she said with a frown.

"Call it what you want, Brewer," he told her. "But you can't just dismiss it. Think about the personal things you wouldn't have wanted to come to me with when I was the Exec. I know you and the other women held back a lot of complaints when you first came aboard. The harassment. Personal stuff that, well, people thought wasn't any of my business. Remember Lobo and Striker?"

She nodded, her eyes sad. Christine "Lobo" Hanson and Steve Strickland—Striker—had developed an intense personal relationship in the first few weeks of the deployment. Lobo had been shot down over the Kola Peninsula and captured. Strickland had refused a recall order and circled the crash site, trying to provide covering fire, until his plane was shot down. Unlike Lobo, he hadn't survived the crash.

"Striker came to me early on," Batman went on. "He didn't know how to handle the whole thing. I advised him to break it off, but he didn't. Thing was, it wasn't that hard for him to come to me man to man. I sure never saw Lobo. Either she never had any doubts—"

"She did," Conway told him.

"Well, she may have confided in you, but not me. See what I mean?"

"Yeah. I hear you. But where does that leave us? Do we have to start appointing two Execs in every mixed squadron, one per sex?"

He shook his head. "All we can do is try to do our jobs. I'll talk to Sheridan and Marinaro. They have a right to put in for transfers, but in the meantime they're damn well going to treat you like this outfit's Executive Officer. As for the rest . . . you can't force a man, or a woman either, for that matter, to share confidences with somebody he or she isn't comfortable with. But I'll try to discourage them bringing their problems to me behind your back."

"They'll probably just stop coming for help at all," she said. "That'll screw up morale even worse."

"Welcome to the wonderful world of the new, improved, politically correct Navy," he said, and he didn't bother hiding the bitterness he felt. "Where everyone is equal. Equally miserable."

1342 hours (Zulu +4)
Flight Deck
U.S.S. *Thomas Jefferson*

The C-2A Greyhound made a perfect trap, snagging the carrier's third wire and rolling to a stop, its twin turboprop engines slowing as the pilot cut his throttles. The plane rolled backward, pulled by the tension of the steel cable it had snagged, until it dropped from the hook. Crewmen started forward, a Yellow Shirt to guide the transport to an open spot on the deck, and men in green shirts bearing black letters to check the arresting gear before the next plane started an approach. Watching the activity, Coyote Grant never failed to be amazed that the dance on the deck involving so many men, so many aircraft, and so little actual room for maneuver could proceed so smoothly.

The Greyhound rolled to a stop and shut down its engines. Unlike the planes of CVW-20, the transport aircraft was not permanently assigned to *Jefferson*. It was part of VR-20, a Fleet Logistic Support squadron based in Sicily. Planes from VR-20 and other support squadrons were a vital link in maintaining America's carrier battle groups at sea. Though bulk supplies were transferred from Underway Replenishment ships, small cargo shipments, mail, and personnel were sent out by Carrier Onboard Delivery planes like this one.

Coyote advanced across the deck as the rear ramp was lowered slowly. A work party was already assembled to unload the plane's cargo, but Grant was here to meet some of the passengers. The Air Wing had been shorthanded for weeks, and this COD flight was supposed to carry the personnel they needed to bring the various squadrons up to full strength.

Several officers appeared, walking with the usual stiff, exhausted gait of Greyhound passengers. The planes were built for cargo and passenger capacity, not comfort, and after a few hours cooped up in the windowless passenger compartment, jolted by every air pocket along the way, even the most enthusiastic flier was happy to feel a ship's deck underfoot again.

"Listen up!" he shouted over the noise of the flight deck. "Replacements for CVW-20, follow me! The rest of you should see Master Chief Weston." He pointed to the carrier's Chief of the Boat, who was standing nearby waiting for newly arrived carrier crewmen to finish disembarking.

"Commander Grant! Good to see you again, sir!"

Coyote hadn't been paying much attention to the new arrivals, but now he recognized the petite redheaded woman striding across the deck to meet him with a smile on her freckled face. Lieutenant Commander Joyce Flynn, "Tomboy," had been part of the original female contingent with Viper Squadron during the Kola campaign. She'd flown as

RIO with Magruder when the CAG had taken out a Tomcat during the last desperate fight over the Polyarnyy sub pens. When their aircraft took a hit and the two bailed out, Flynn had wound up with a broken leg. After the two had been rescued, she had been put aboard a medevac flight for the States and an extended hospital stay. Now she was back, looking fit and ready to fly. "Well, Tomboy, looks like they couldn't keep you away from our little luxury cruise ship," he said. "What was it? The colorful ports? The ambience?"

She laughed. "Face it, Commander, you're not getting rid of any of us Amazons."

He chuckled. The female combat fliers had earned that nickname in the early days of the deployment, but it was hard for him to picture the petite Tomboy Flynn as a woman warrior. "Good to have you back," he told her. "There've been a few changes, but you'll still know your way around."

"Great." They started across the deck toward the island. "Oh, hey," she said, catching his arm. "Thought you might like to know. You remember Lobo?"

"Of course!"

"I got a letter from her just before I left the States."

"You don't say!" Coyote's eyes widened. "How's she doing, anyway?"

Tomboy grinned. "Instructor's slot, no less. At Top Gun!"

"Well! Good for her! That's great!"

But the mention of her name raised a small shadow in the back of Coyote's mind. There was a dark side to women serving in combat, a topic not often discussed or even acknowledged among the men or the women aboard the *Jefferson*, but always, always there. *Rape.*

Lieutenant Chris Hanson, running name "Lobo," had been one of that first batch of female aviators aboard the *Jefferson* last March. Shot down over the Kola Peninsula, she'd been captured and gang-raped by ill-disciplined militia. Hours later, she'd been rescued by U.S. Marines; they'd found her on display in a Russian village, locked inside a wire cage, naked, bruised from a savage beating, and shivering with the onset of deep shock. While her physical wounds could be treated easily enough, there'd been considerable question about the deeper psychological trauma she'd suffered. Her medical report had openly questioned whether she would ever fly again . . . especially in a combat role where she would have to face the possibility of going through the same ordeal again.

"There was talk for a while there, while she was in the hospital, that maybe she'd have to resign her commission," Tomboy explained.

"I heard something about that," Coyote said. "I gather she fought it, huh?"

"She's tough. Tough enough she was fighting to be placed back on combat status, last I heard."

Coyote didn't reply. From what he knew of the Navy establishment, it wasn't likely that Lobo would see combat again. Back in World War II, five brothers had all died on the same day when the ship they were serving aboard together was sunk by the Japanese. As a result, the Navy had made as standard policy a rule against close relatives serving aboard the same vessel.

When Lobo had been captured in the Kola, the Navy had suffered a public relations defeat very nearly as severe as the one they'd faced with the death of the Sullivan brothers. She'd been featured in a *Timeweek* article, interviewed on ACN, and the entire nation had been outraged . . . and horrified that such things could happen to its fighting women. The Navy, Coyote was certain, would not allow Lieutenant Hanson to fly combat missions again, not unless the *wanted* a conservative backlash to reverse all of the gains women had made in the service in the past few decades.

And that was damned unlikely, because too many high-ranking careers at the Pentagon were already at stake over the issue of women aboard ships and in combat roles.

And maybe it was just as well. Coyote tried to imagine what it would be like to be abused the way Lobo had been . . . then have to climb back into a cockpit and go face the same people who'd done that to you the first time. He couldn't picture it. In fact, the only reasons he could imagine for even wanting to do such a thing were either to prove something to yourself—like getting back on the horse after it threw you—or for revenge.

He didn't like either thought at all. He thought of Mason, jumping the gun on that helo ID because he was too eager to make his mark. A naval aviator needed to be a professional, to put aside love and hate, glory and fear.

There simply was no room for obsession in the cockpit of a Tomcat.

1508 hours (Zulu +4)
CAG Office
U.S.S. *Thomas Jefferson*

"Okay, Coyote, what else do you have for me?" Tombstone Magruder leaned back in his chair, feeling weary. Sometimes it seemed as if the paperwork and the endless details of running the Air Wing were far more difficult to cope with than the intensity of battle. He couldn't remember being this tired after the hottest combat ops he'd been in, even during drawn-out situations that had tested him to the limits of physical endurance.

Flying a desk might not be as much of a strain on his body, but it certainly left him feeling tired, irritable, and thoroughly fed up with his lot in life. Tombstone was starting to hate the inside of the CAG office, the sight of stacks of paper and computer monitors and all the rest of the paraphernalia of bureaucracy. He was an aviator, by God, not a clerk, but lately it seemed like he never had time for even a quick flight to keep his cockpit hours current.

Coyote was sitting across from him this time, holding a clipboard and ticking off points with a pen. "COD flight's in. We got eight officers all told. That'll fill out the Vipers, the Death Dealers, and the Javelins, but we'll still be two short in the Prowlers. I've assigned them quarters and given them their squadron postings. You'll probably be getting a string of courtesy calls this afternoon." Coyote paused, frowning.

"You're holding something back, Will," Magruder said. "Spill it."

"One of 'em's Commander Flynn."

Tombstone's eyes widened. "Tomboy? She's here?"

"Yup. Leg's healed and she's rarin' to go."

"You don't seem pleased."

"Oh, I was happy to see her. It's just . . . well . . ." He slapped the palm of his hand on Tombstone's desk. "Damn it, CAG. I keep wondering about the advisability of women in combat. She was telling me about Lieutenant Hanson. She's doing fine, according to Tomboy. Trying to get put back in a combat assignment, of all silly dumb-ass things."

"That's the career path, Coyote." Officers who'd actually experienced combat were preferred for promotion . . . and for choice assignments later in their careers. Female service personnel had long complained that men had an unfair advantage there; it was one reason why they'd been insisting all along that they should be allowed to assume combat status.

"I know, I know. But, well, what happened to Lobo in the Kola, it could happen to any of them. Call me old-fashioned, but I can't shake the feeling that that's the sort of thing we're out here protecting them from."

"You can take that up with Madam Secretary Reed," Tombstone said. "I'm sure she'll be delighted to hear your feelings on the matter."

"Yeah. Right. Oh, damn! Almost forgot." He leafed through the papers on his clipboard, found what he was looking for, and passed it over to Tombstone. "This came in from the *Canal* today. They're looking for aviation stores. Spare parts. Sidewinders. They're wondering if they can scrounge some from us."

"Not damned likely."

"Yeah, well, there may be a pronouncement on that from on high. I gather there may be some problems getting enough UNREP stuff through the straits. The Turks could balk at letting all that stuff through."

Tombstone looked at his friend for a long moment. "Goddamn."

"Oh, nothing serious. Yet. But there's talk. And I guess the jarheads are stretched pretty thin right now."

"You got that right. A little bird told me they're already scraping the bottom of the barrel for equipment and spares. They got deployed short." Magruder shook his head. "Sometimes I think our only real enemy is in Washington. The guys shooting at us are nothing but petty little annoyances, but those bastards on Capitol Hill are out for blood."

"A little bird?" Coyote raised an eyebrow. "Don't tell me you're starting to play Navy politics."

"Nah, this was just an old friend. The skipper of the *Canal*, no less. We had a chat this afternoon." Magruder smiled. "He wanted me to say howdy for him. Steve Marusko. *Captain* Marusko, now."

"Marusko's got *Guadalcanal*? God, that makes me feel older than I felt already."

Steve Marusko had been CAG on the cruise where Magruder and Grant had seen action in Korea, Thailand, and the Indian Ocean. Now he'd moved further up the career ladder, skippering one of the Marine carriers. Someday he might wind up as captain of a supercarrier like *Jefferson*.

"Maybe we'll get a chance to see him before the cruise is over," Coyote said. He looked down at his clipboard. "Well, that's all I've got for now, Stoney. Anything you need me to take care of this afternoon?"

"Just the maintenance logs on the War Eagles. Light a fire under those guys and get those reports on my desk tomorrow morning at the latest."

"Or heads will roll?" Grant asked with a smile.

"Starting with yours, so make sure they hop to it down there." He stood up as Coyote did. "Dinner tonight?"

Coyote shook his head. "I'm going to beg off, Stoney. I want to write a letter to Julie."

"Things still not so good, huh? If there's anything I can do . . ."

"Unless you can get them to send us home, there's nothing," Coyote told him. "But thanks, man. Thanks."

As Coyote left, Tombstone settled back into his chair and

picked up the picture on the corner of his desk. His fiancée, Pamela Drake . . .

She was a devastating combination of beauty and brains, an award-winning reporter for American Cable News. After a long and often stormy relationship, they'd finally agreed five months ago that they would set a wedding date after *Jefferson*'s next cruise. But then he'd received orders for an early redeployment, and Pamela had exploded. It seemed like she always saw the Navy as a rival, and she'd frequently urged him to give up his career, to settle down with a nice, safe airline job. He'd always protested strongly, saying that the Navy was his life, but sometimes, like now, he had his doubts.

He set the picture down. Magruder was starting to wonder just where his career was really heading. Working to break in Coyote as Deputy CAG had reminded him of all the things about staff work that he hated. But even with his record, it was possible, even probable, that CAG was as high up the ladder as he'd ever get. There were a lot more candidates for the high-powered postings than there were available billets, and frequently merit gave way to politics when it came to picking people for that handful of openings. Steve Marusko had been lucky to get the *Guadalcanal*. Magruder had an uncle who held an important Pentagon post in Washington and had advised two presidents, but Thomas Magruder had also made a lot of enemies, people who would be looking for an excuse to keep his nephew from rising any higher.

Well, that was the way it worked in the Navy sometimes.

He looked at Pamela's picture again. Marriage and career . . . neither one looked very solid right now. If he got stuck in some safe but dull staff position, Pamela would be happy, but Magruder knew he'd go crazy if he didn't feel like he was *doing* something. But if he got a ship of his own, another tour of sea duty policing some hot spot at the ends of the earth, could Pamela put up with it?

If Coyote couldn't hold onto his marriage with Julie, was there any real hope for him and Pamela? Julie had started with a lot more in common with Will Grant than Tombstone and Pamela had ever had.

Tombstone found himself thinking about Joyce Flynn, about the shared danger that day on the Kola Peninsula. Tomboy was no on-camera beauty like Pamela, but there had been a real connection there. She understood what Magruder felt when he was in the cockpit of a Tomcat, what it was like for him to really put his life on the line for his country. Things Pamela Drake would never really understand.

He loved Pamela, maybe more now than he had in the early days of their relationship. But the women he'd come to know in the Air Wing, Flynn and Brewer Conway and the others, were something special. They shared his world, his dreams and his hopes and his fears.

Sometimes Magruder wondered if love was enough.

CHAPTER 11
Monday, 2 November

1047 hours (Zulu –5)
Cabinet Room, The White House
Washington, D.C.

"Mr. Waring, this could be the most important opportunity we've seen since the fall of the Berlin Wall. We'd be fools not to take advantage of it."

Admiral Thomas Magruder looked from the speaker, Secretary of State Robert Heideman, to the President's National Security Adviser, Herb Waring. He was used to the Secretary's stance on foreign affairs questions but found it hard to believe that even a dedicated liberal globalist like Heideman could be urging a policy at odds with everything the United States had stood for since the days of the Founding Fathers.

He was even more surprised at Waring's evident interest. The President had been taking a real beating lately in foreign policy, and the smart money said he should stick with domestic problems rather than getting involved in yet another ill-advised adventure abroad. Magruder would have expected Waring—who always had an eye for the main chance—to back off from another round of foreign intervention, if only to appease the growing numbers of isolationists among the President's noisier critics.

Clearly, though, Heideman's presentation had struck a chord with Waring.

"Let me see if I understand what you're saying, Bob,"

Waring said. "This Russian general, Boychenko, will surrender to the United Nations, but the UN will only go along if our carrier battle group is part of the process."

"That's essentially it, Mr. Waring—" Heideman began. His measured, precise voice was overridden by another, louder and less cultivated.

"Mr. Waring, I want to go on record as having disagreed with this entire idea. It is a mistake from first to last, and it flies in the face of everything this country has ever stood for."

Magruder found himself nodding in agreement. The Chairman of the Joint Chiefs of Staff, Admiral Brandon Scott, leaned back in his chair. With his mane of white hair and his flashing eyes, Scott looked like a biblical prophet. His angry words seemed to hang in the room.

"I'm sorry you feel that way, Brandon," Waring said slowly . . . and with an oiliness that warned of masked feelings. "But I think Secretary Heideman may be right, here. This situation offers some interesting possibilities we really should explore. . . ."

"Going along with this is tantamount to giving up our sovereignty," Scott maintained harshly. "A U.S. carrier battle group cannot simply be loaned out to the United Nations this way, any more than we would consider loaning out part of our nuclear arsenal! It violates two centuries of policy—damned good policy. Throwing it all away is nothing short of idiotic!"

"If I may, Mr. Waring?" Heideman cut in. "Admiral, we all know your views. You've expressed them often enough, and loudly enough, for all of us to know where you stand. But this is a political decision, not a military one."

"It means putting more American servicemen in harm's way, Mr. Secretary," Scott said. "And that is *always* a military decision, regardless of the politics involved."

"Damn it, Scott, this perennial foot-dragging is getting damned old!" Gordon West, the White House Chief of Staff, exploded. "If you can't get with the program, for God's sake, at least get out of the way so the rest of us can do something constructive for a change!"

"Take it easy, Gordon," the Security Adviser said. "I invited his opinion, and he gave it. We have enough hot spots around the world without turning the Cabinet Room into another one, okay?"

West didn't answer, but he visibly controlled his temper and settled back in his seat. The other presidential advisers gathered around the long oak table relaxed, but there was still an air of tension in the room. After nearly two years of this administration, quarrels like this one were an almost routine part of any foreign policy meeting. This one, though, had all the earmarks of a really serious fight—the kind that ended in resignations offered and accepted, and in Senate hearings over new nominees for top-level government posts.

It wouldn't be the first time, either, Magruder thought as he glanced around the table. As a matter of fact, Admiral Scott wouldn't have been quite so touchy if it hadn't been for the last such argument, the one that had led to the resignation of Secretary of Defense Vane six months previously. Vane had always backed his military experts when it came to questions of foreign policy and American power projection, but those days were gone now. Scott wasn't exactly a lone voice in the wilderness, but sometimes it must have seemed that way to the man. It couldn't be easy working for the new secretary.

Magruder's eyes rested on Secretary of Defense Samantha Reed, former congresswoman from California, one-time member of the House Armed Services Committee, and powerful friend to the feminist left and champion of a liberal social agenda. Her appointment to the Cabinet had barely squeaked through the required Senate approval process despite the political pressures that made it all but impossible for many senators to vote against her. The nomination of the first woman ever considered for a powerhouse Cabinet position like Defense was one of those historic moments for women everywhere, and headline-conscious politicians weren't about to go on record as voting against the tide of history. Too many of them remembered the "They just don't get it" mentality engendered in the early '90s by incidents like the Anita Hill allegations against Clarence Thomas, and the fight over the retirement of Admiral Frank Kelso, the Navy Secretary who had presided over the Tailhook scandal.

Even so, the vote to confirm her in her new position had been a close one.

Tall, dignified, and with the experienced politician's charm and ready smile, Samantha Reed turned to face the President's chief adviser. "Mr. Waring," she said. "As far as I can see, this could be an excellent trade. We remove a potentially dangerous military force from the Crimea, and the UN moves in and takes charge. The UN's prestige is enhanced as a world peacekeeper. I don't need to remind anyone here that the American public is not enthusiastic about our becoming the world's policeman, do I?"

"Madam Secretary," Scott said. "With all due respect, where's the difference? If our military is policing the world as a part of U.S. foreign policy or at the behest of the United Nations, we're still footing the bill."

"Not at all, Admiral," she replied, her voice silk-smooth behind a glacial smile. "The UN would pay the costs of the deployment. A share of that is ours, of course, ultimately, but it won't be as though the American taxpayer is shouldering the entire burden."

"The bill I was referring to, Madam Secretary, was the *butcher's* bill. The cost in American lives. Putting our people under the command of foreign officers is nothing short of a military disaster waiting to happen."

She seemed to consider this for a moment, then turned and spoke softly to one of the aides flanking her. The man reached inside a briefcase and produced a manila folder. She accepted it, leafing through several pages inside before finding what she wanted. "Admiral, it seems to me that our current policy of supporting UN operations but maintaining separate and distinct lines of command and communication offers an even better opportunity for 'military disaster,' as you put it. You've seen this?"

She slid the paper across the table. Scott barely glanced at it and did not pick it up. "Of course, Madam Secretary."

"Gentlemen," Reed said, addressing the entire room.

"Two days ago, as any of you who watch cable news is *well* aware by now, one of our Navy jets shot down a U.S. Army helicopter that was flying a UN mission. No one was killed, fortunately, but the incident has pointed up the flaws in interservice operations. There were breakdowns in communication up and down the entire chain of command. It seems that the naval personnel making the decisions in the carrier battle group had not been notified that Army helicopters were operating in the no-fly zone and had not received the computer codes that let their radars recognize those helicopters as friendly.

"The day before that, this same carrier group sank a Russian submarine, *again* by accident. At least fifteen Russian nationals were killed.

"Now, it seems to me that putting all of our forces under one command infrastructure would be the best possible way of avoiding unfortunate mistakes like these in the future. Placing our forces under UN command will simplify the lines of communications. It will simplify intelligence and ensure that our military forces know who is in the area and what they are doing.

"I must say, it also sets a worthwhile precedent for the future. If we start putting larger numbers of troops under UN authority, it would give the organization some real teeth. That would save the United States from more embarrassments like Somalia and Haiti."

Magruder resisted the urge to speak up, to argue against what he saw as a blatant misuse of American military forces. His position was an unusual one. At the time of the Norwegian War he'd held the post of Director of Operations for the Joint Staff, but during that crisis and the Russian Civil War that followed it, the President had come to depend on him as a personal military adviser. Now he was attached to Admiral Scott's personal staff, a position that gave him access to these high-level meetings but no real authority. Anything he said now would be viewed as a "Me, too" echo of Scott's position.

Damn it, he wished the gold on his shoulder boards and jacket cuffs counted for something in this roomful of career politicians. For years globalists had been talking about increasing the authority of the United Nations and giving it control over larger and more powerful military units. They pointed to the organization's complete helplessness during the Cold War era and to the fiascoes of the early days of the New World Order as good reasons to stiffen UN power and prestige with troops, equipment, and armaments controlled by the Security Council. They pointed out that UN attempts to engage in nation-building in Somalia in 1993 had been derailed by the U.S. decision to withdraw all ground troops from the nation after a firefight where American troops had been killed and their bodies dragged through the streets in front of TV cameras for all to see. And UN Haiti policy had never quite gelled because of vacillating American leadership.

But the thought of handing over a sizable portion of American military power to the United Nations was, for Magruder, a chilling one. If the UN could send Americans into Georgia . . . or the Crimea . . . how long would it be before they sent troops into Los Angeles to quell the next round of rioting? Or into American homes to search for handguns? Or to arrest American citizens for speaking out against this dark and twisted vision of the New World Order? . . .

Admiral Magruder had too fond a regard for the lessons of history to ignore the possibility—no, the probability— that such power, once granted, would grow, corrupt, and ultimately enslave.

Unfortunately, he and Scott were very much in the minority at this table.

"I'm not sure giving the UN more power is a very good idea," Scott said, leaning forward in his chair and clasping his hands on the table before him. "In any event, this is a surrender of American sovereignty. We have never agreed to such a thing in our entire history. American forces have never been placed under the operational control of foreigners. The French tried it in World War I, and Montgomery wanted to try it in World War II, but in each case we did everything in our power to maintain control over our own

people. The closest we ever came was in Somalia, and
I'll point out that it was the UN component there that got our
people involved in that firefight that killed our boys . . . and
then failed to support them when they got into trouble."

"Admiral," Heideman said, "I respect your views, but I
cannot agree with them. We cannot live in the past any
longer. National sovereignty is a nice, high-sounding phrase,
but it's soon going to be as antiquated as Communism. Look,
you know how hard it is to get Congress or the public to back
an intervention effort. Even when that intervention is in the
national interest."

"In other words, you intend to sidestep the Constitution
by putting our troops under the UN," Scott said bluntly.

Heideman flushed. "Stop twisting my words, Admiral.
Troop commitment is a foreign policy decision. Executive
Branch has the authority."

"Except that Congress has the War Powers Act sitting
there waiting for you, and you don't want to force a
confrontation on whether it's legal for the Executive Branch
to exercise the kind of authority you're talking about." Scott
shook his head. "The simple fact is that UN intervention
often has nothing whatsoever to do with our national
interests."

"It does in the Black Sea," Waring said. "Right now the
whole of the former Soviet Union is balanced on the thin
edge of complete anarchy. Our presence in the Black Sea
will serve to stabilize the area."

Reed nodded. "My point exactly, Herb. I'll also point out
that intervention in this case helps our interests in the short
term."

Short-term interests, Magruder echoed in his mind. *Penny-
wise, pound-foolish.*

If the other people at the table were looking for disasters
waiting to happen, they didn't need to look beyond the
current situation unfolding between Ukraine and the frag-
menting Russian Federation. Magruder glanced at Roger
Lloyd, the new director of the CIA. He'd already given his
briefing on the geopolitical situation in that part of the world

and did not look happy with the way the discussion was going.

And Magruder didn't blame him one bit.

The vast expanse of rolling, fertile, black-earth prairies that was Ukraine had been one of the original founding states of the Soviet Union in 1922, but its people had never fully reconciled themselves to Russian domination. Ethnically, Ukrainians were not Russians; they remembered still with blood-soaked bitterness Stalin's forced collectivization during the 1930s, a policy of genocide by starvation that may have killed as many as twenty million people. Glasnost had come slowly to Ukraine; long after Gorbachev came to power, the head of the Communist party there had been one of Brezhnev's cronies, and the arrests, repressions, and police harassments had continued until his dismissal in 1989.

After extended flirtations with various union treaties, Ukraine had declared complete independence in 1991, shortly after the failed coup attempt against Gorbachev, then turned around and signed the Minsk Agreement with Russia and Belarus, creating the Commonwealth of Independent States. For a time, during the Norwegian War, Ukraine had again been part of the Soviet empire, but with the collapse of Moscow's central government and the outbreak of a general civil war, Kiev had again declared independence . . . and this time around seemed downright eager to redress old wrongs.

Unlike many other autonomous regions throughout the old Soviet Union, Ukraine had few internal ethnic conflicts. Most of the region's large Tatar populations had been forcibly resettled in Central Asia during the 1940s; the only real ethnic hostilities remaining were those between Ukrainians and Russians. Eastern Ukraine had a high percentage of Russians in the population, most of whom favored strong ties with Moscow; from the few reports coming out of Russia to the West, strongly nationalistic Ukrainians had precipitated a bloodbath among ethnic Russians, killing hundreds of thousands—perhaps millions—and sending millions more fleeing across the border into the already devastated lands of the Russian Federation.

Besides that, the old dispute between Kiev and Moscow over the ownership of the Crimean Peninsula and the Black Sea Fleet remained. With Russia involved in its civil war, Ukraine appeared poised to settle the issue once and for all . . . by threat if possible, by military force if necessary. According to the most recent intelligence available to the *Jefferson* battle group, the Ukrainian Fifth and Seventh National Armies were in position at Odessa and at Melitopol, ready to move in and seize the Crimea from its Russian caretakers. Amphibious landing craft were being gathered at Odessa and at both Ocakov and Svobodnyj Port at the mouth of the Dnieper, lending credence to CIA and U.S. Naval Intelligence predictions that an invasion of the Crimea—both overland across the narrow isthmus to the north and by sea, along the beaches north of Sevastopol— was imminent.

Though distracted, the Russians had been trying their best to bolster their defenses in the Crimea. Since Ukraine blocked all approaches across the isthmus, their main line of communication ran across the narrow straits of Kerch, from an arm of the Russian Federation that flanked the Black and Azov Seas from Novoazovsk to the Georgian frontier at Gagra. Most of that bolstering had taken the form of military flights—transports and their escorts—flying in from Krasnodar. No one was quite sure at the moment whether Red or Blue forces held the upper hand, either in the Crimea or at Krasnodar. For a time, there'd been speculation among U.S. intelligence officers that those flights out of Krasnodar were in fact an invasion, one civil-war faction moving in to take Sevastopol away from the other in a three-cornered tug-of-war between Reds, Blues, and Ukrainians. So far, though, there was no indication that this was the case. Supply flights were moving in and out of the various Crimean military and commercial airfields with an almost clocklike regularity, and so far the Ukrainian forces had not attempted to hinder them . . . or to deliver the expected attack on the peninsula's defenders.

But the situation was becoming more dangerous—explosively so—day by day. If the northern half of the Black Sea, from Odessa to Gagra, became a war zone, it would be difficult, perhaps impossible, for the UN-U.S. forces in the area to stay clear of the fighting.

And now, three days after the accidental sinking of a Russian sub in the southern Black Sea, a Russian general named Boychenko, the de facto military ruler of the Crimean Peninsula, had just offered to surrender military control of the district to the United Nations. One of Boychenko's people had approached the U.S. ambassador to the UN with the proposal during discussions of the return of the Russian submariners now aboard the *Jefferson*.

"I really wonder if it's our interests that are being served here," Scott said. "Let's put this in perspective. First off, Boychenko is the Military Governor of the Crimea. After Krasilnikov declared martial law during the coup against Leonov, he became what amounts to the absolute ruler of the entire Crimean region. We're not talking about some small unit commander wanting to turn over a few pieces of heavy artillery here. This is the equivalent of having an entire country ask for UN intervention."

Lloyd nodded agreement. "Admiral Scott's right," he said. "It's completely unprecedented. If the UN accepts this arrangement, they're in effect declaring the Crimea to be under the authority—and the protection—of the United Nations Security Council."

"That's what Boychenko's counting on," Scott went on. "The only reason he's decided to make this offer is the fact that he's got a Ukrainian army knocking at his front door. The Ukrainians want the Crimea, and they want it bad. They want the prestige of controlling what they consider to be Ukrainian territory. They want the military supplies and matériel there. The bases. The ships of the Russian Black Sea Fleet that haven't been seized or defected to them. Most especially, they want the *Pobedonosnyy Rodina*."

"Excuse me?" Reed looked baffled.

"*Pobedonosnyy Rodina*, Madam Secretary," Magruder offered. "It means 'Victorious Motherland' in Russian.

That's the name of the largest remaining ship in the Red fleet, a nuclear carrier as big as any of ours."

"I thought we took out their carriers in the Norwegian War," Waring said.

"We accounted for two out of three, sir," Magruder said. "*Kreml* and *Soyuz*, their first two carriers. This one wasn't ready for action when the fighting broke out in Norway, though. She was still undergoing sea trials in the Black Sea. You can be sure the Ukrainians would love to add her to their fleet. There's nothing like a supercarrier to enhance a country's image as a world power."

"Unless it's a nuclear arsenal," Reed said, her mouth twisted in distaste. "Which Ukraine has, I might add. And Russia. All of this simply supports my argument, that we must intervene to maintain the peace."

"*What* peace, Madam Secretary?" Scott demanded. "The whole area is tearing itself apart now."

"Ukraine has not attacked yet," she said. "By taking control of the Crimea, the UN will help ensure that the war does not spread. As it would if Ukraine attacked Russian possessions in the area. They would *not* risk angering the United Nations with an attack."

"Madam Secretary," Admiral Scott said wearily, "how can you *possibly* know what the Ukrainians will or will not do?"

"There are also humanitarian considerations at stake here," Heideman said with a disdainful look at Scott. "The Ukrainian government seems to have embarked upon a program of ethnic cleansing against the non-Ukrainian population within their borders. A large number of ethnic Russians have been killed or driven out already. And the population of Crimea is mostly ethnic Russian. Allowing the Ukrainians to take over the Crimea unopposed would open the floodgates to genocide."

"It would make Bosnia look like a picnic," Reed added.

"So by allowing the Reds in the Crimea to surrender to the UN, we keep the Ukrainians out," Waring said. "We stop a bloodbath, we reduce the risk of a general war between Ukraine and Russia, and we stop Kiev from seizing military assets in the Black Sea that could further destabilize the region. I'm not sure I understand your objection, Admiral Scott."

"And think of the opportunity we have here," Heideman said. "An *historic* opportunity! Since the end of World War II, we've been looking for a way to make the UN a strong voice for world peace, and this could be just what we need to do it. The picture of a Red officer surrendering to the United Nations, not to any one country but to the world itself, that would be a symbol that would *count*."

Reed nodded. "I agree. For years now Admiral Scott and others like him have been telling us that the U.S. can't keep playing the role of world policeman. That's true. But it's also true that the world *needs* a policeman, and the only way I can see us getting one is to give the UN both the power and the prestige to do the job. This would be an ideal first step."

"Be careful what you wish for," Magruder said quietly. "You just might get it."

Reed raised an eyebrow. "You've been quiet this morning, Admiral Magruder. I suppose you share Admiral Scott's viewpoint in this? Military tradition and national sovereignty and historical precedent and all the rest?" There was a note of contempt in her voice. Of all the services, the Navy was widely known to be Reed's pet peeve, and she made little effort to hide how she felt.

"I'm as much concerned with practical questions as I am with tradition and precedent, Madam Secretary," Magruder said slowly, keeping his voice flat and emotionless. "Since Desert Storm, everyone's looked on the UN as the ideal foundation for the 'New World Order.' But for most of its history the UN has been anything but a reliable friend to the United States. How many times did we have to impose our veto to protect our national interests, or our allies'?"

"That was in the Cold War, Admiral," Heideman said. "Now that we're the world's only superpower, we're in a much better position to influence the UN agenda."

"And when China is powerful enough to influence the agenda, are we going to feel the same way? Or Japan? Or Europe? If the twentieth century has taught us anything, it's the fleeting nature of power blocs and alliances and national status. Before World War I, England, France, and Germany were the world's superpowers. Less than a hundred years have passed, and look at the world today. Major powers have come and gone, alliances have changed, priorities are different. The world has changed in ways they never could have imagined a century ago. And it will keep on changing. New World Orders may be politically fashionable now, but don't gamble our freedom on short-term fashions that could change tomorrow!"

"Your fears are groundless," Heideman said. "The UN would never intervene against the United States."

"That's right," Reed said. "We'd still have our power of veto."

Magruder paused, his fingers drumming the tabletop. "I wonder. Does anybody here remember when the UN passed sanctions against Australia to force them to overrule one of their state governments when it passed laws against sodomy?"

"It was an archaic attitude . . ."

"Madam Secretary, it was an internal matter that the UN blatantly decided to get involved in. They might just as well have decided to pass sanctions against us because of the antisodomy laws still on the books in Mississippi or Alabama. And the time could come when a United Nations with all this symbolic prestige and real military power you want to give it could turn that power against us for reasons that are just as trivial."

"Admiral, I think we all take your point," Waring said. "Certainly the question of giving the UN control over any part of our military forces is one we shouldn't decide on hastily. But I think you're overreacting when it comes to this Crimean matter. Frankly, the President is concerned about the buildup of tensions in this part of the world. He wants to send a message to the warring factions that this sort of anarchy can't be tolerated, not when the rest of the world's population could be at risk if this thing turns nuclear. Anything, *anything* that will defuse this unfortunate situation should be seriously considered." He paused, frowning, then rapped twice on the tabletop. "I will recommend to the President that our battle group in the Black Sea be placed under UN command and cooperate with them in receiving the surrender of the Crimea."

"Sir—" Admiral Scott began.

"That is all," Waring said. "This meeting is adjourned."

With a rustling of papers and the scraping of chairs, the men and women in the conference room began gathering their things and getting up from the table. Scott exchanged a long, weary look with Magruder. Neither man said anything, however.

One long-standing tradition of America's military remained firm and unshaken, and that was the tradition of political control of the armed forces. Determining policy was the job of the politicians, not of the military; admirals and generals could advise, but when the policy decisions were handed down, it was their duty to shut up and carry out their orders.

Magruder just hoped that this wouldn't turn out to be one policy decision that the United States would end up bitterly regretting.

CHAPTER 12
Tuesday, 3 November

Jefferon's main briefing room was part of CVIC, the Carrier Information Center, and, like the department, was generally known as "Civic." It was located aft of Flag Plot, where the admiral in command of the battle group maintained his command center when he was aboard. Rows of folding chairs were set up facing one end of the room, which was dominated by a podium and a rear-screen projector. The walls were hung with artwork—a large painting of the *Thomas Jefferson* underway, and smaller framed prints of various scenes drawn from U.S. naval history. One painting, hung near the larger one, was a recent addition. It depicted *Jefferson* in the narrow confines of a rugged fjord during the desperate fight for Norway. Tombstone Magruder studied it for a moment before finding a seat, remembering the day it had been presented to Admiral Tarrant and Captain Brandt by the men and women of the Air Wing. Lieutenant Commander Frank Marinaro, call sign "Nightmare," liked to paint in his off-duty hours and was quite an accomplished artist. It had been a gift to commemorate the end of *Jefferson*'s last eventful cruise.

Now it was another cruise, a different sea. Some of the men and women were the same; others were new. The *ship*, however, carried on.

Glancing around the large room, Tombstone thought of the other times he had been summoned here. An admiral's CVIC briefing for senior CBG personnel usually signaled the beginning of a major new operation, often one involving combat. He caught sight of the air department's senior staff near the front of CVIC and moved down the center aisle to join them. Coyote was there, along with Lieutenant Commander Arthur Lee, the CAG's department intelligence officer, and Lieutenant Commander David Owens, the OC chief of staff. Owens looked up as Magruder approached.

"Have a seat, CAG," he said. "We've got the good seats, for a change."

"Is this a briefing or a movie premiere?" Lee asked with a grin. "Maybe I should've brought popcorn."

"I doubt the admiral would approve," Tombstone replied, sitting down. "You're in charge of intelligence, Art. Any idea what's going on?"

Lee shook his head. "Not a clue, CAG. I heard tell the admiral's staff was up half the night with a long decoding job from Washington, but nobody's leaking."

"That's ominous all by itself," Coyote commented. "Either we just got some pretty hairy new orders, or Sammie Reed's issued another set of sensitivity guidelines!"

"Please, not that," Owens said in mock horror. "Anything but that! I'll spill everything I know, but spare me another sensitivity class. . . ."

Some of the officers nearby chuckled. In the last few years the Pentagon's increasing shift to political correctness had made the institution a laughingstock in the front lines. "I've been waiting for a directive telling us we've got too many ships named after men," someone said. "But I'll be damned if I'm going to let them rename the *Stephen Decatur* after some feminist icon!"

Tombstone looked at the man and grinned. It was *Decatur*'s captain, Commander Richard Hough.

"They'll probably rename it the *Sammie Reed*, Dick," another man said.

There were groans from some of the officers, and a few scattered laughs. Tombstone looked away. The banter had an air of gallows humor to it. These were men who already felt all but abandoned by their country, whose government cared more about budget cuts and social experiments in political correctness than in their welfare.

Tombstone shook his head. This wasn't the Navy he'd joined more years ago than he cared to remember just now. That had been a close-knit fraternity of men and women who'd dedicated their lives to the Service and to the nation. There'd been some lingering inequities, yes, but for the most part it had been an institution where hard work and devotion to duty were the paths to success. Hell, it had been a Service where millions of minority men and women had gone to get a better shake than they would be able to on the outside. He wondered sometimes how an American military more worried about minority quotas and sensitivity to the feelings of others than about solid career experience would handle the next crisis that came down the road.

"Attention on deck!"

They all surged to their feet as Rear Admiral Douglas F. Tarrant entered the room, followed closely by Captain Brandt. Their appearances contrasted sharply—Tarrant was tall, silver-haired, aristocratic, while Brandt was shorter, with close-cropped hair and a bulldog-ugly face—but the two men had proven to be a superb team in Norway and the Kola Peninsula. A knot of staff officers followed them, finding seats near the front of the room.

"As you were," Tarrant said quietly as he reached the podium. Chairs scraped against the deck as the assembled officers of the battle group sat down again. The air was tense with anticipation.

"Good morning," Tarrant said. "There have been some developments that impact on our operations. We have new orders from Washington and will be redeploying the battle group to extend our operational area north and west. Commander Sykes will cover the details of the situation. Commander?"

He nodded toward Commander Daniel Sykes, the Flag Intelligence Officer, who walked up to take Tarrant's place at the podium. He laid a thick file folder in front of him and produced a telescoping pointer from his pocket. A petty officer set up an easel beside him and put up a chart of the Black Sea.

"Gentlemen," Sykes began. "Our original purpose for this deployment was to oversee the no-fly zone over Georgia. This was necessary because of Turkey's decision to deny both basing privileges and permission for overflights of their territory in protest over the UN's policy of encouraging ethnic minority separatist movements. The MEU operating with the *Guadalcanal* group was to be the initial ground component for the humanitarian effort in Georgia, with a British peacekeeping unit taking over in about two weeks." The intelligence officer paused. "As of this morning, however, all operations in Georgia assume a lower priority. They are not suspended, but our new operational orders have precedence."

Magruder heard coughs, groans, and restless movement around him. It wasn't uncommon to have the White House change a mission profile in midstream; indeed, that sort of thing was all too common. But evidently they were being asked to take on additional duties, stretch their resources thinner to try and keep doing their original job while taking on a whole new task as well.

Sykes waited for quiet before going on. "You all know the chaotic situation in the former Soviet Union. The Reds and the Blues are still fighting in Russia proper, while the other republics are for the most part declaring independence and throwing out whichever faction has troops on their soil. In many cases those troops are simply going home, or defecting en masse if they contain local contingents." The pointer indicated the territory of the Ukraine, colored gray on the map. "By far the best organized of the breakaway republics at present is Ukraine. They have the largest army and a lot of first-line equipment inherited from the Reds, and their government seems to have the only clear-cut agenda of any of the contenders. Unfortunately, that agenda is one Washington regards as dangerous."

Tombstone found himself nodding. The latest group to seize power in Kiev had been led by right-wing extremists who preached the twin sermons of security and nationalism with an all-too-familiar and chilling fervor. They had already been accused of attempting a program of ethnic cleansing inside their borders, and they made little effort to hide their intentions of expanding Ukrainian territory at the expense of their war-torn neighbors.

"High on the list of Ukrainian priorities is the conquest of the Crimean Peninsula," Sykes went on. His pointer tapped the map to indicate the rough diamond shape dangling from the underbelly of Eurasia. "Traditionally, the Crimea has been part of Ukraine from the time modern Russia first began to take shape, at least for geographic and administrative purposes. But the ethnic composition of the Crimean population contains a higher proportion of Russians, and after Gorbachev dissolved the Union there was considerable friction between Russia and Ukraine over the fate of the peninsula. To make matters worse, the Crimea contains some of the most important military bases in the Black Sea region, as well as one of its finest ports, at Sevastopol."

Sykes paused to allow the enlisted man to put up a new map, this one a more detailed view of Crimea proper.

"The, ah, political future of the Crimea has continued to remain in doubt. Most of the peninsula's population actually favor Russian control. However, the Red faction, which maintains control of the peninsula, is too weak and too occupied with the Blues elsewhere to adequately defend the place. The man in charge is General Sergei Andreevich Boychenko. Intelligence tells us he was something of a compromise for the post, a man trusted by both the fleet and Red Army elements in the area.

"In fact, Boychenko has been rather cool toward the Red cause. He sided with the Reds initially, but he suffered a lot of defections and at least one fair-sized mutiny within the fleet, and he's voiced opposition to the Krasilnikov regime more than once."

Sykes paused as if for dramatic effect. "Last weekend, while negotiating for the return of the Russian nationals from that Victor III we sank, he put out feelers to both the

United Nations and to Washington, offering to surrender the
Crimean Military District to international control. His stated
reason is a desire to avoid an expansion of the civil war, but
we believe his real fear is that the Ukrainians might be about
to assert their claim to the peninsula. Intelligence sources,
including satellite surveillance, suggest that the Ukrainians
may be about to move, probably through an amphibious
landing on the Crimea's west coast. Boychenko's forces would
be completely inadequate to stop a determined attack.

"Washington and the UN have decided to honor General
Boychenko's request."

The briefing room dissolved in a chaotic babble of many
noises. "Christ, CAG!" Owens said. "They're getting us
involved in the Russians' war again!"

Admiral Tarrant stepped up to the podium once more,
waiting patiently until the noise died down. "There's no
doubt," he began, then stopped, waiting until absolute
silence descended on the room before continuing. "There is
no doubt at all," he continued, "that if the Ukrainians take
over the Crimea, they will bring their ethnic cleansing
operation right along with them. In that sense, at least, this
will be a humanitarian effort. The United Nations sees
Boychenko's offer as an opportunity for the cause of
international peacekeeping. But it is also a huge responsibility. Basically, if the UN takes Boychenko's surrender,
they're guaranteeing the Crimea against outside attack,
and that's a far cry from sending in humanitarian aid to
some third-world nation still locked up in tribal warfare.
The Secretary General won't accept that responsibility
without a firm commitment of American support. That's
where we come in."

He paused, and to Tombstone it felt as though he were
wrestling with something unpleasant . . . and trying not to
show it.

"The UN has asked for," he said quietly, "and Washington has granted, operational authority over U.S. forces in the
Crimean Peacekeeping Operational Zone. For the duration
of this mission, my immediate boss will be the UN Special
Envoy in Sevastopol. He will determine exactly how, when,

and where we will be used in support of the other United Nations personnel that will be deployed into the region."

A babble of protest erupted throughout the room. "UN control!" Commander Hough shouted. "What dim bulb thought *that* one up!"

"I thought we'd settled that in Somalia!" someone else cried.

Tarrant raised a hand. "Quiet!" he roared. "Quiet down there! This is a briefing, not a free-for-all!" He waited for the room to be silent again. "Okay, people, I know how you all feel. This breaks with our whole military tradition. It's not what any of us bargained for when we signed on. But the Administration, the *President*, has his reasons for agreeing to these terms. Maybe you don't agree with him, but by God he's our commander in chief, and when he gives an order, each of us is going to obey it, or die trying!

"We will, therefore, operate under United Nations command until the President says otherwise. In the interim I expect my officers to uphold the standards of military decorum. That means you keep your comments to yourselves . . . and you treat United Nations personnel, military or civilian, with the same respect you would treat fellow American servicemen. Do I make myself clear?"

There were muttered responses and a distinct lack of enthusiasm. Apparently, though, it was enough for Tarrant . . . possibly because he'd gauged the emotions in the room and decided that it was the best he was going to get. Or possibly, Tombstone thought wryly, he agreed with them but couldn't admit to the fact.

"Very well," he continued. "That's the background to this operation. We are naming it, incidentally, Operation John Paul Jones. Those of you up on your Navy history will remember that after the American Revolution, John Paul Jones accepted a commission as a rear admiral with the Russian navy, under Catherine the Great. It was a difficult period in his life, one during which he was forced to serve under the orders of a foreign sovereign. It was also, I might add, a time when he was struggling against adverse politics as much as he was against any maritime enemy.

"Now, here's the gouge. Our initial orders call for MEU-25 to reembark its Marine forces and join this battle group. Together, we will take up a new position, designated Victor Station, one hundred miles south of Sevastopol. Technically, we are still responsible for the Georgian no-fly zone, but in practice we're going to ignore it, at least until additional forces join us. The Marines will remain aboard ship as a mobile reserve until the UN decides where they may be best employed. One possibility now being discussed is a Marine amphibious landing north of Sevastopol. This landing would be aimed at securing the port facilities at Sevastopol, the large airport inland at Simferopol, and, incidentally, denying the Ukrainians a landing beach on the Crimea's west coast. The idea is that if the Ukrainians know we're already ashore, they'll give up on their plans as a bad business."

Tarrant looked down at his notes on the podium. "At this time, there are still some details to be worked out with Boychenko and his people. A UN diplomatic mission is on its way to handle the final negotiations. Until those are completed, our role is mostly passive. We're here to show Boychenko—and the Ukrainians—that the UN has a carrier battle group in its pocket to back up the surrender agreement when and if it is signed." He spread his hands and gave the room a wintry smile. "What happens after that is anybody's guess. When I know what our role is, I'll let you in on it. Questions?"

Hands went up. Tarrant acknowledged Captain Henry Dorset, the new CO of the Aegis cruiser *Shiloh*. "Sir, how are the Ukrainians going to react to this? I mean, if they really are claiming ownership of the Crimea, aren't they going to be pretty damned pissed at the UN stepping in like this?"

Tarrant didn't answer, but Sykes, standing to the side with his arms folded, nodded. "It'll certainly complicate the whole issue," the intelligence officer said. "The best guess we can make is that Kiev will try putting political pressure on the UN as soon as the surrender goes through. Exactly how they'll frame it . . . well, that could go a lot of different ways. They might try to press their claim directly, or they might come forward with an offer of taking the lion's share of the peacekeeping burden themselves, possibly in the name of looking out for Ukrainian nationals."

"It all comes to the same thing in the end," Tarrant added. "It'll be critical that the surrender and the transition to UN control both go smoothly, because you can bet that if there's any kind of trouble—riots, or another neo-Soviet mutiny, or whatever—the Kiev government will jump in with both feet. They could claim they're moving into the Crimea simply to stabilize the region or to protect Ukrainian nationals."

"Do you think the UN will go along with their demands?" Dorset pressed.

"That will depend on who the Special Envoy is, and what kind of instructions he has from the Secretary General," Tarrant replied. "I'd say the odds are that the UN will want to keep the Crimea an internationally controlled zone, at least over the short haul. They have a vested interest in looking strong, well organized, and tough enough to make this whole thing work. But that's just my read on it."

"A lot will depend on just how Ukraine applies pressure," Sykes added. "It may amount to nothing more than saber-rattling, or they could try testing the UN's resolve directly with an attack. None of us have crystal balls good enough to make any really solid predictions right now. Hell, Boychenko might not go through with the surrender after all, especially if Krasilnikov gets wind of it before everything's in place."

"Krasilnikov doesn't know?" someone asked.

"We don't think so," Sykes said. "After all, the Reds have been funneling what troops and supplies they can into the Crimea for several weeks now, at least. That suggests they'd like to hang onto the place. One possible explanation for Boychenko's move, incidentally, is that Krasilnikov told him to hold at all costs, or else. Now, Boychenko has a rep as a humanitarian commander. Always trying to get the best for his men, that sort of thing. Could be he looked at the Ukrainians getting ready to pounce and knew that he and his

people didn't stand a chance. By surrendering to us, all of
his people get to go back to Russia and continue the fight
there. Of course, he'll probably claim amnesty and defect.
He won't be able to go back to Krasilnikov, that's for sure.
Not unless he's eager to face a firing squad."

"How long will our people be on the ground there?"
someone in the back of the room asked.

"Don't know," Tarrant replied. "The Brits, who were
originally slated to relieve our people in Georgia, are going
straight into Sevastopol as soon as the surrender is signed.
A battalion of the Black Watch, for starters. There are
pledges for more troops from Britain, France, Canada, and
Italy, but Washington didn't send me any kind of timetable.
The Marines will be on hand if the Special Envoy decides
we need them, but I think everybody's hoping they can go
ahead with the relief mission in Georgia as soon as we've
got the Crimea situation under control." He glanced at his
notes again. "You'll all be getting your orders, such as they
are, before you leave. Meanwhile, Commander Sykes and
the rest of my staff will be glad to answer any other
questions you might have. . . ."

Eventually, the questions ended and the meeting came to
a close. Tombstone sat for a moment as the other officers
stood and began filing out. Admiral Tarrant had left, but
Commander Sykes remained at the podium.

"What do you think, Stoney?" Coyote asked.

"Damn. Hard to know what to think. Looks like Washington just dropped us into another war zone. I'm beginning
to get the feeling that they want to get rid of us."

"Captain Magruder?" Sykes called. "Can I talk to you for
a moment, sir?"

"Catch you later, CAG," Coyote said.

"Yeah." Tombstone turned as Sykes approached. "What
can I do for you?"

"Admiral Tarrant wanted me to ask if you wanted to go
ashore with him."

Tombstone raised his eyebrows. "Ashore? What—"

Sykes grinned at his evident confusion. "The admiral will
be going into the Crimea to receive Boychenko's surrender,

of course. Yalta, to be specific. Wonderful symbolism there, you know. He'll be sending me and some of his staff officers in ahead, to lay the groundwork, as it were."

"Go on."

"He told me to ask if you'd like to ride along."

"Did he say why?" Tombstone was genuinely puzzled. Admirals generally didn't ask captains if they wanted to do something or not. "I'm not much of a diplomat, Commander. And I have an air wing to run. . . ."

"Of course. And this *is* rather irregular, I admit. But, you see, Admiral Tarrant is concerned about the view the American press will be taking in regard to the Navy. There was the sinking of that Russian sub. Then the helicopter shoot-down. Now the press will be wondering just what we're doing here, and if we can handle the job."

"I'd been wondering about that myself, actually."

"Aren't we all? But the news people are going to be flocking around the admiral's staff as soon as they hit the beach. Admiral Tarrant would like you to be his special liaison with the media, as it were."

Tombstone opened his mouth to give a sharp retort, then closed it again. Damn it, why the back-door approach? "If the admiral wants me to do this, why doesn't he—"

"Order you himself. Of course. This is strictly a volunteer assignment, Captain. And *very* much off the record."

Tombstone shook his head. "Damn it, Commander. Maybe I'm dense or something today. But I don't understand."

"There were two ACN personnel on that UN flight the other day, a reporter and his cameraman. He filed a story about the incident, of course."

"Of course."

"American Cable News evidently decided to follow things up with one of their top people. Ever hear of a news anchor named Pamela Drake?"

Tombstone's mouth gaped open. *Pamela!* . . .

"Anyway, the admiral seems to think you might have some influence with the woman. She's coming here to—"

"What? Pamela is coming here?"

"To Sevastopol. Yes. With a crew. Admiral Tarrant

thought you might be able to field her tough questions. Again, it's volunteer only. But . . ."

"Of course, of course," Tombstone said. He was dazed. Pamela, *here*!

"Then I'll tell the admiral it's settled. The staff group will be assembling to go ashore tomorrow afternoon. You'll want to have some things packed."

But Tombstone scarcely heard him.

Pamela was coming *here*!

CHAPTER 13
Wednesday, 4 November

1047 hours (Zulu +3)
Office of the Commander, Black Sea Fleet
Sevastopol Naval Base, Crimean Military District

"All is in readiness, Comrade *Vitse-Admiral.*"

Dmitriev looked up from the papers on his desk. *Starshiy-leytenant* Kulagin was not looking at him but remained fixed at attention, his eyes locked on a spot on the wood paneling somewhere behind Dmitriev's left shoulder.

"Excellent," Dmitriev replied. "The crews have been briefed on what they are to do?"

"Yes, sir." He sounded almost bitter. "Though it was . . . difficult finding volunteers."

"We expected as much."

"Yes, sir."

"And I suspect that what you mean is that it was difficult finding volunteers loyal to *me*, rather than to General Boychenko."

"Actually, sir, the majority of the naval personnel opted to follow you. The army, of course, is loyal to the general almost to a man. Putting together so many pilots who could be trusted was the most difficult part."

"That, too, was expected. When the Ukrainians come, the fleet, at least, would be able to retire to Novorossiysk, while aircraft could simply fly out."

"Yes, sir. The army would be forced to remain in this, this *trap.*"

158

Dmitriev sighed. "Anton Ivanovich, there are many kinds of trap. Some are more subtle than others. What I do, I do first out of loyalty to the *Rodina,* then out of respect for the oath that I took as a Russian officer. That, in a sense, is the trap that holds me."

"Yes, sir."

Kulagin was retreating once more behind the unreadable facade of the mindless subordinate, attempting to mask his own thoughts. Dmitriev leaned back in his chair, studying his aide. "You don't approve of this plan, do you?"

"Sir, it is not my place to—"

"*Talk* to me, Anton Ivanovich. I need to know what you are thinking." He nodded toward the window, and the ships gathered in the harbor. "What *they* are thinking."

"Sir . . ." He stopped, and the stiffness of his posture relaxed a bit as he moved his hands helplessly at his sides. "Sir, there are those within your command who see this as a desperate gamble, as something very much like deliberate suicide. Suppose this operation gets us into a general war with the United States? We could find ourselves fighting Leonov's rebels, the Ukrainians, the Turks, and the Americans all at the same time!"

"The Americans will not go to war over this, Anton. It will be in their interests to resolve this matter peacefully."

"How can anyone make predictions about what their government will or will not do, sir? Cowboy diplomacy—"

"Their president is in considerable trouble because of his foreign policy just now." He chuckled. "Or perhaps I should say he is in trouble because of his lack of anything like a coherent foreign policy. He will not risk a war with us, because that would deepen his problems with the American electorate, which is notoriously isolationist."

"Well, then, the Turks—"

"Will allow things to be smoothed over. They need us to solve their problems with their Armenian minority more than we need them. When our representatives have quietly explained why we were forced to do what we did, they will understand and accept it. A war with us would not serve their best interests, either."

"Wars rarely serve anyone's best interests, Comrade Vice-Admiral. Except, of course, for the arms manufacturers and the politicians."

"Why, Anton! You have the true Russian's soul of the poet!"

"You told me to speak freely, sir. I am. It could be that those members of your command who disagree with your plan see General Boychenko's initiative as their only real hope for survival."

"I see. And how do you feel about it?"

Kulagin looked acutely uncomfortable. "I really don't—"

"Come, come! You may speak freely here. It's not as though I'm about to ship you off to some gulag, eh?"

"Comrade Vice-Admiral, General Boychenko is a popular officer."

"One of the few. Yes, I know."

"The men and junior officers trust him. They trust him to get them home."

"And what of the officers and men whose homes are *here*, Anton? In the Crimea?"

"Ah." He seemed surprised at the question, but he nodded. "They . . . they are not so eager to leave, sir. Most worry about what will happen to their families when they are ordered to leave, to go back to Russia. The Ukrainians are not known for their forgiving natures."

"And what about you, Anton Ivanovich?"

The aide hesitated a long moment before answering. "I will tell you the truth, Comrade Vice-Admiral. I worry about *my* family, my wife and two daughters. They live in Volosovo. That's a town not far from St. Petersburg, a very great distance from here. The war inside Russia threatens them directly, far more than what happens to us here in the Crimea." He spread his hands, helplessly. "If the Crimea falls to Ukraine, how does that hurt them? How does it take bread from their mouths . . . unless, of course, I should die here. *That* would cause them hardship."

"You don't wonder if Ukrainian aggression might be encouraged by a display of cowardice in the Crimea?"

"I don't think any reasonable person expects the Ukrainians to invade Russia proper! In any case, their border is much closer to Moscow than to St. Petersburg." He sighed. "In any case, sir, I would feel much better if I thought my service, my actions, were protecting them directly. This, here . . . the Crimea . . . may I speak bluntly?"

"Of course."

"I feel, sir, that it is a lost cause. Nothing we do, nothing we can even consider doing here, will keep the Ukrainians out in the long run. Even the Crimea's population is divided over its loyalties."

That was certainly true enough. During the last free elections held here, a slight majority had voted to remain with Ukraine, rather than be readmitted to Russia. The region's current status, as an autonomous district loosely tied to Ukraine but still administered by Russia, by the Russian military no less, satisfied no one.

Dmitriev studied his subordinate's face for a moment. Kulagin's expression was that of a man who expected to be struck. Dmitriev only nodded, however, and gave the aide a reassuring smile. "I appreciate your candor, Anton. And I understand your concern. You must trust me, however, when I say that Operation *Miaky* is the one hope we have now. It will be our salvation, not a mass retreat, not abandoning our duty, and certainly not Boychenko's *treason*."

Miaky was the local name for a cold wind that blew south across the beaches near Yalta, sweeping down out of Angarski Pass in the chain of mountains that created a stone wall across the southern Crimea. That wind, though, was not so cold as the sound of the word "treason," as it hung there in the room between them for long seconds after Dmitriev spoke it.

"Is that how you believe Krasilnikov's people will see it?" Kulagin asked. "As treason?"

"Certainly. General Boychenko was tasked with the responsibility of defending the Crimean Military District against all enemies . . . against all threats, whether they be Blues, Ukrainians . . . or Americans. He proposes to abandon that responsibility, to turn it all over to the United Nations. To foreigners. What is that, if not treason? You might mention that to those personnel you speak with who are so eager to return to the *Rodina*. They seem to think Krasilnikov's people will receive them back gladly. It could be that they would be seen back there as accessories to Boychenko's crime."

Kulagin swallowed. There was a thin sheen of sweat on his forehead. "I, I see, sir. I understand."

His veiled threat, Dmitriev knew, was exaggeration, almost certainly. The days were long gone when an entire military unit numbering some tens of thousands of men would be rounded up and imprisoned or shot en masse because of its commander's inadequacies. Terror might have worked as a means of inspiring men in Stalin's day, but the breakdown in command authority within the former Soviet military hierarchy, from top to bottom, made such measures counterproductive at best. Besides, trained manpower was too scarce within the *Rodina* these days to carelessly squander it to satisfy ego or wounded vanity.

But he desperately needed to hold his command together for a short time longer. Operation *Miaky* had been scheduled for two days hence . . . as soon as final preparations could be made for readying the Black Sea Fleet for what would probably be its final sortie.

Miaky would be a cold wind indeed this time, one that would make its chill felt clear across the Black Sea . . . and beyond to the rest of the world.

1332 hours (Zulu +3)
Yalta
Crimean Military District

"ETA six minutes, gentlemen." The noise of the helicopter's engine made it hard for Tombstone to hear the pilot even over his headphones. "I've got clearance from the Russkis to land at the airport."

"Then take her the hell on in," Captain Greg Whitehead shouted into his headset mike. "The faster we get out of the air, the better I'll like it!"

Tombstone leaned back in his hard seat. He had to agree with Whitehead's assessment of the situation. This whole idea of accepting the surrender of an entire Russian military administrative district had come up on such short notice that no one really knew what was happening . . . and if that was true for the Americans in the battle group, it must be even more so for the Russian forces. The chance of yet another accident in this deployment—this time of Russian antiaircraft downing an incoming unidentified helicopter— was greater than Tombstone really cared to think about. He would have infinitely preferred flying in on an F-14 to this slow, bumpy, and terribly exposed approach in one of *Guadalcanal*'s CH-53 Sea Stallion helicopters. At least he could have distracted himself by concentrating on the controls.

But he wasn't an aviator today, or even CAG. He was—*God help me*—a diplomat and a news media liaison, and neither diplomats nor media liaisons came roaring into hostile territory in an F-14 with afterburners blazing, however attractive the image might be.

Magruder looked around the compartment, studying the other passengers—all bundled up in flight suits and life jackets and bulky *Jefferson*-issue cranials. Most of the others in the group looked as uncertain as he felt. Captain Whitehead was Admiral Tarrant's chief of staff, and as such was the man in command of the shore party. He looked collected enough, but the faces of the rest showed a mixture of worry, nervous expectation, and emotions rigidly held in check. He wondered if he was as transparent as the others.

Commander Sykes was present, of course, and four other staff officers, ranging from another full commander named Sedgwick to a lowly lieutenant j.g. from *Jefferson*'s OZ division named Eugene Vanyek. Enlisted personnel included Chief Radioman Joseph R. Geiger, a short, thickset man with heavy features and the indestructible look of chiefs throughout the Navy, and seven Marines in full battle dress who'd been asked to come along to provide security. All together, counting Magruder, there were fifteen men and two women on the flight, which meant that the huge transport helo's cargo bay was about half-full. The CH-53 wasn't normally carried aboard the *Jefferson*, which relied on the smaller Seahawks for most of its helicopter needs, but with so many people going ashore at once, *Jefferson* had borrowed the CH-53 from the Marine carrier, which had joined the *Jeff* on station the afternoon before.

He glanced across the Stallion's huge cargo compartment and caught Joyce Flynn watching him. She grinned at him, with perhaps a trace of nervousness behind her dark eyes, and winked. The enlisted woman sitting beside her, an ordnanceman second class named Natalie Kardesh, had her arms folded across her chest and appeared to be asleep, though the front of her cranial was down so far Tombstone couldn't see her eyes. She'd been included on this flight because she spoke fluent Russian.

It was Flynn who concerned him, though. Why, *why* had it been Tomboy who'd volunteered for this party?

Tarrant, he knew, had specifically wanted some women along on the flight, especially one of fairly senior rank with flight status, and Tomboy certainly qualified on both counts. The admiral's reasoning, Tombstone assumed, was that there would be lots of news personnel ashore—including ACN's Pamela Drake, of course—and he wanted to be sure that the U.S. Navy's progressive attitude concerning women in combat roles was well documented. The coming negotiations with Boychenko's people would have a high profile in the media, and Samantha Reed and her cronies back Stateside would see and approve. Politics, pure and simple . . . and it grated against Tombstone to see political standards—worse, standards of political correctness—used to make decisions such as who would go ashore on this mission, rather than more straightforward considerations such as who was best qualified.

And of all the women aboard the *Jefferson*, why did it have to be Joyce?

She'd flown as his RIO over the Kola Peninsula seven months before, when the squadron had been shorthanded and an alpha strike had been needed against a Russian Typhoon submarine base. They'd been shot down, had punched out together, and she'd broken a leg on landing. When he'd reached her, a Russian soldier was already there, standing over her; in a blurred confusion of a firefight that would have been funny had the situation not been so deadly, Tombstone and Tomboy both had shot the man with their service pistols before he could reach his AK. A recon force of U.S. Marines had arrived shortly afterward, beating a large Russian unit in a race to the downed fliers by two minutes.

The two of them had shared . . . something. Call it the camaraderie shared by all warriors who face fire and death together. Or the camaraderie of people who owe one another their lives; in that last desperate firefight, as they'd tried to bring the Russian soldier down with pistols before he could bring his AK to bear, they'd saved each other's lives. She'd then demanded he leave her and save himself, and he'd refused. There was a bond there, as undeniable as it was deep. It was not sexual, either, though Tombstone could easily imagine it becoming such.

But he was engaged to Pamela Drake. At least he assumed they were still engaged. They never wrote much in the best of times, and after that last quarrel . . . Well, he guessed they'd both needed time to cool down. Perhaps they could patch things up now that she was coming out here. He grinned to himself as he wondered if Pamela would understand the warriors' bond, the mutual friendship of military professionals that he shared with Tomboy Flynn.

Tombstone often thought of those hours on the Kola Peninsula . . . just as he tried not to think about what would have happened if the Russians had gotten there first. Lobo—Lieutenant Chris Hanson—had been captured that same afternoon.

It wasn't, he told himself, just the fact that female combat personnel might be—often were—raped or otherwise sexually assaulted when they were captured. Despite the Geneva Convention, a protocol that somehow seemed almost quaint nowadays in its assumptions that signatories would obey the limits it set, POWs could be subjected to a variety of indignities, assaults, and outright tortures, both physical and mental, regardless of their sex. No, his concern went deeper, to the very basic question of whether women should serve in combat at all, partly because of the physical threat to them, of course, but more because of the damage it did to the military system that Tombstone was a part of.

Tombstone was still old-fashioned enough to believe that biology had assigned men the task of defending home and hearth . . . a decidedly sexist attitude that he'd learned to keep to himself in these days of political correctness and enlightened attitudes toward women at the higher levels of both the military and the political bureaucracies. He was more than willing to admit that many women tended to be not only the equals but the superiors of men in some combat-related skills, especially technical skills like flying an aircraft, which required dexterity and brains as opposed to the upper-body strength demanded of grunts on the ground. They resisted G-forces better, were often more dexterous, and frequently dealt with stress better than their male counterparts.

But no matter how many directives there might be descending from Washington, the fact remained that men were men, and men acted differently when women were present. All the rhetoric about equality and all the regulations and orders in the world couldn't overcome the biological instincts that led men to want to protect women when they were in danger, instincts that could completely scramble a mission. "Striker" Strickland had disobeyed orders trying to protect Lobo after she'd been brought down, and he'd paid for it with his life and the life of his RIO. A ZSU had knocked them out of the sky as they came in low for a strafing run.

There was no question at all in Tombstone's mind that this visit ashore was dangerous. While not technically a war zone, the Crimea could become one at any moment. Worse, the Russian men and officers present would have nervous trigger fingers—and might be less than pleased to see Americans on Russian soil. Seven U.S. Marines with M-16s would not be able to provide much in the way of a defense if things turned sour.

There were, of course, the UN personnel already on the ground in the Crimea. According to the word Tombstone had gotten last night, they'd flown in yesterday from Turkey, part of the same contingent slated for peacekeeping activities in Georgia. Most were administrators and negotiators, but there were supposed to be about fifty Spanish troops along to provide security for the group.

Not a hell of an army, no matter how you looked at it.

"Hey, CAG?" It was Tomboy's voice, speaking over the Sea Stallion's intercom. "What kind of a reception do you think they'll lay on for us?"

Before Magruder could answer, Sykes spoke up. "Probably pretty low-key at least for now, Commander," he told her. "General Boychenko doesn't have anything to gain from moving too fast or too far."

"There could be some question about how many of his people know what's going on," Vanyek added. His voice didn't carry well against the sound of the rotors, and Tombstone had to strain to catch the words. "Boychenko is technically committing treason. Some of his people may not care for that."

"We're going to have to watch our steps down there," Tombstone told them. "Watch what we say, and watch who we talk to, at least until the surrender is official and we have a sizable UN contingent in place."

"Do you think Krasilnikov will attack Boychenko, once he finds out?"

"The Ukes'll save him the trouble," Whitehead said. "Unless we can convince them that invading the Crimea is a bad idea."

"Final approach, people," the chopper's pilot informed them from the cockpit. "Grab onto something and hang on. Please observe the seat-belt and no-smoking signs!"

The SH-53 came in fast and low, as if the pilot were determined to impress the Russians with his style and panache. Looking out the side door's window, Tombstone caught a blurred impression of blue sea, rock cliffs, and a small airport, with gray-purple mountains visible in the distance. Then they were down with a gentle bump, and the engine noise dropped in pitch as the rotors started to slow.

"End of the line," the Sea Stallion's loadmaster called cheerfully. He touched a control and the helicopter's rear ramp began opening with a grind of electric motors and the clatter of chains. Tombstone, with his personal effects and clean uniforms in a seabag over his shoulder, was first down the ramp and onto the tarmac. Captain Whitehead was close beside him.

As Sykes had predicted, there wasn't much of a welcoming committee on hand. A couple of elderly limousines were drawn up on the tarmac a few yards away, with a handful of Russian soldiers clustered around them. As Tombstone cleared the rotors and straightened up to his full height, two figures detached themselves from the waiting group and advanced toward the disembarking naval personnel.

The one in the lead wore a Russian army uniform with insignia that identified him as a colonel. He saluted Whitehead stiffly and spoke in careful, precise English. "Captain . . . Whitehead. Welcome to Yalta. I am Bravin. General Boychenko has asked me to see you and your party to your accommodations."

Whitehead returned the salute with a smile. "Thank you, *Tovarisch Polkovnik*," he said. "And please convey my thanks to the general, as well."

Before the stilted conversation could go any further, the second man stepped forward. He was in civilian dress, a short, slight man whose quick movements and brisk manner made Tombstone think of a bird searching for worms. "Captain Whitehead," he said. He spoke with a distinct Hispanic accent that sounded jarring in these surroundings. "I am Jorge Luis Vargas y Vargas, personal aide to Special Envoy Sandoval. He has placed me at your disposal until you have settled in and there is time to arrange a meeting with him and the rest of the United Nations delegation." The little man studied the new arrivals for a moment, his forehead creasing in a distinctly disapproving frown. "Captain, you and your people must not appear again without proper uniforms. His Excellency will be most displeased. Most displeased."

"Proper uniforms?" Tombstone asked.

"Your carrier group is attached to the UN command. You should wear the proper blue berets or combat helmets, and UN armbands." He gestured at the Sea Stallion, in its dark gray livery and muted roundel. "And for that matter, your helicopter should not display American insignia. Please be sure to let your people know what is expected. His Excellency is very precise when it comes to questions of protocol." Before either Magruder or Whitehead had a chance to reply, Vargas turned to the Russian lieutenant and spoke in rapid-fire Russian.

The young officer nodded. "*Da*," he said curtly. "Captain, if you and your party will accompany me, we will go to your hotel and allow you a chance to refresh yourselves. According to the schedule, there will be no meetings requiring your presence until tomorrow. If you please? . . ."

Whitehead turned and looked at the group, then locked gazes with Tombstone. "Well, CAG," he said. "I thought there was more of a hurry to this thing."

"Hurry up and wait," Tombstone said with a grin. "It's the same in every language." He looked at the UN man. "Señor Vargas, I'm Captain Magruder. I'm supposed to liaise with the press. Are there any members of the media here yet?"

Vargas rolled his eyes toward the sky. "*Aye, Madre de Dios*, you cannot go anywhere in the city without bumping into them and their equipment. They are staying at the same hotel where you will be staying. I'm sure you will have more to . . . to *liaise* with, as you say, than you really care to! Now, if you please? . . ."

Tombstone was intrigued by the little man's brusque and impatient manner . . . not exactly what he would have expected from a diplomat. True, Vargas wasn't exactly a diplomat—no more than Tombstone himself was, actually—but Tombstone had been expecting a little more in the way of common courtesy.

It seemed that he had a lot to learn about the gentle art of diplomacy.

CHAPTER 14
Wednesday, 4 November

1515 hours (Zulu +3)
Yalta
Crimean Military District

It was a mild and delightful seventy degrees—warmer certainly than Tombstone had expected for any part of Russia in November. Palm trees swayed in a line along Drazhinsky Boulevard below his window, and the scores of people he could see on the promenade beyond wore shorts or swimsuits. Bikinis were much in vogue with women, especially the young and attractive ones, and Tombstone had to remind himself that this was part of Russia—or Ukraine, depending on your point of view—and not some beach in Mediterranean France. Aboard the *Jefferson* one hundred miles at sea that morning the air temperature had been fifteen degrees cooler—not unpleasant, certainly, but not warm enough to prepare him for this subtropical Eden.

The Crimea, he decided, was going to prove to be full of surprises.

Most of the Crimea Peninsula, Tombstone had learned from a guidebook he'd picked up in the ship's store the day before, was actually hot, dry steppe, something that did not mesh easily with his mental image of the vast and sprawling land that was Russia. Like most Westerners, Tombstone had always pictured Russia as basically *cold*, in the grip of General Winter from October through April, and his experience over the far-northern tundra wastes of the Kola

170

Peninsula in the still-winter month of March had only reinforced that impression.

He'd *known*, certainly, that the former Soviet Union wasn't just ice and tundra, and the balmy temperatures and crystal blue skies of his first day in Yalta were enough to convince him that there was more to this land than Siberian wastes.

In fact, though the northern two-thirds of the Crimea was arid, the chain of mountains stretching from Balaklava in the southwest all the way to Kerch in the extreme east created a natural barrier that kept the southern coast subtropically pleasant. The sun along that coast was warm, even in early November, and the sea breeze was delightful, cool and moist and salt-tangy. The climate and the palms reminded Tombstone a lot of southern California; the south Crimean coast was known, in fact, as the Crimean Riviera. For decades, the elite of the old Soviet Union's vaunted classless society had come to this region on holiday, and the most powerful of Moscow's rulers had maintained their *dachas* and summer homes here. During the abortive 1991 coup, Gorbachev had been placed under arrest and held in his dacha estate not far from Yalta, while events elsewhere in the nation had spun far beyond the reach both of him and of the coup plotters.

The air of affluence that permeated much of the southern Crimean coast had marked the region since long before the Soviets had come on the scene. Czars had kept their summer palaces here, and Lenin had issued a decree to the effect that the palaces of the Russian aristocracy in the region should be turned into sanatoria for the people.

The ongoing troubles in Russia, however, had been felt here as well. From the hotel window, at least, there was actually surprisingly little evidence of the civil war that had been tearing at Russia's guts for the past months. The buildings were intact, there were no soldiers in the streets, no signs of fortifications or defenses. But the entire city had a *depressed* air, a depression of the spirit as well as of the economy. The region had depended on tourism for capital, but, reasonably enough, tourism had been in sharp decline for some time now. Most, maybe all, of the people visible on the street were native Russians; there'd been no foreign visitors for some time now, not since the attempted reintegration of the Soviet empire, and the city was showing the absence of their hard currencies. It looked shabby and a bit run-down. There was garbage in the streets—something unthinkable in the socialist paradise that once had employed women to sweep each street with brooms—and many of the people Tombstone could see from the window looked less like vacationers than gangs, groups of tough-looking kids in jeans and T-shirts loitering in public areas with the same swaggering aggressiveness Tombstone had seen in their counterparts back in the United States. He'd heard, too, that the region was a magnet for the darker elements of Russia's disintegrating economy. The Russian Mafia, he'd been told, controlled many of the businesses and most of the business transactions that went on here, while the southern Crimea was a principal meeting place for Armenians, Georgians, Uzbeks, Tatars, and renegade Russian military officers engaged in black market trade.

He turned away from the open window and looked over the room he'd been given . . . clean and pleasant enough, but modest by American standards. Rooms had been reserved for the United Nations personnel at Yalta's largest hotel, the Yalta—a Stalinist horror of concrete in classic Communist-modernist-monolithic architecture. All of the foreigners were being kept here, and Tombstone hadn't quite decided whether that was for their protection . . . or because it made it easier for the authorities to keep an eye on them. Both, probably.

His roommate was lying on the bed reading a guidebook. He was sharing the room with Greg Whitehead, the other captain in the group . . . and the place was almost certainly wired for sound. The Federal Bureau of Security—or whatever the old KGB was calling itself now—would be interested in any conversations the two of them might have during their stay.

"I'm going downstairs, Greg," he told Whitehead, picking up his jacket and shrugging it on. "Maybe stretch my legs."

"Okay, Matt. Watch out for the roaches." They'd flushed a few already in the room's antiquated bathroom, and they put Florida's finest to shame . . . not quite strong enough to take on a healthy cat, they'd decided, but large enough to require respect.

At least, Tombstone thought as he pulled the door shut behind him, they had their own bathroom; lots of Russian hotels still believed in communal toilet facilities down the hall. Outside, the floor concierge, one of the small army of women hired by Russian hotels apparently for no other reason than to keep an eye on the comings and goings of the guests, eyed him narrowly and suspiciously from her chair by the elevator. He nodded pleasantly, then took the stairs instead of the elevators, which neither looked nor sounded trustworthy. The stairwells were dark and filthy, stank with the mingled odors of mildewed rags and urine, and were lacking fire doors, but at least he didn't run the risk of getting stuck in one. The woman barked something in Russian at him as he started down the worn concrete steps . . . probably something in the nature of "You're not allowed to do that!" or "Official use only!" but he ignored her and kept going. Let her yell. Tombstone could handle being flung off the bow of an aircraft carrier at 150 knots with complete aplomb, but Russian hotel elevators were something else.

He was going to be very glad to get back aboard the *Jefferson.*

"Hey . . . you Am-yerican? You want fuck?"

The woman was small, blond, and painfully thin, dressed in a tight gown that tried to display her breasts but succeeded mostly in displaying how skinny her arms were, while the heavy eye makeup and lipstick emphasized her hollow cheeks. She stood squarely in the open doorway to the stairwell, blocking his way.

"What?"

"You want . . . fuck?" The obscenity was less shocking

on her lips than it was pathetic. "Or do other things. Five dollars?"

"No," Tombstone said.

"I suck you, two dollars."

He felt pity, and a moment's stumbling uncertainty. Should he just brush past this pathetic creature? Or offer her a few dollar bills as he would a beggar? Glancing past her shoulder, he saw a crowd of other women waiting in the corridor just outside the stairwell, all thin to the point of gauntness, dressed in clothes intended to be provocative, and wearing what they must imagine was sexy-looking makeup. And they were all watching his encounter with the first woman with predatory gleams in their eyes.

Shit. If he tried handing the woman money for no service, that bunch would descend on him like a wolf pack, targeting him as an easy mark. Better to shake his head no and shove past the woman without another glance.

And, he told himself, it might be best to avoid situations here where he was alone and could be cornered somewhere away from the main drag. Tombstone was under no illusions about his ability to fend off an attack by a half-dozen desperate women.

It was a sobering encounter. He'd known the Russian economy was bad, but no written description could have prepared him for the sight of those pitiful human wrecks accosting men in the hotel's stairwell. He steeled himself to walk past the women outside without meeting their watching eyes. He wished there was something he could do to help them . . . something other than actually doing business with them, which he knew would be dangerous on several counts.

But there was nothing he could do, nothing anyone could do.

The Yalta Hotel's lobby represented an unpleasant compromise between faux-neoclassical grandeur and Stalinist utilitarianism: large, ugly, and shabby. In some ways, it was like an American shopping mall, with hard currency shops and cafés. There were several tennis courts and swimming pools, amenities not normally associated with Russian hotels, and over twelve hundred rooms, most with their own plumbing and most wired for cable TV.

But it also showed the decay touching everything that once had been part of the Soviet system. Furniture was worn, mismatched, and dirty; the chandeliers were missing many of their crystal ornaments; the carpets were faded and showed worn tracks along the routes of heaviest traffic; and the clerks at the big front desk were conspicuously absent, though several guests were obviously waiting—clamoring, even—for attention. The place, Tombstone reflected, was probably busier today than it had been for some time, with the entire UN contingent quartered here, as well as, no doubt, the Russian security people assigned to keep track of them.

As Tombstone stepped into the main lobby near the elevators, his attention was immediately caught by a group of people in the sitting area, next to a scraggly collection of potted palms. Joyce—Commander Flynn—was standing there in full uniform, bathed in the glare of a pair of handheld camera lights. A man with a shoulder-held mini-cam bearing the ACN logo was filming her and another woman, who held a microphone to her face. The second woman's back was to him, but Tombstone recognized immediately her blond hair and slim figure. With only the slightest hesitation, he started walking toward the brightly lit tableau.

"And what's it like," the reporter was asking Tomboy, "being one of a few hundred women living with five thousand men aboard a nuclear-powered aircraft carrier?"

"It's actually not much different from being stationed on a Navy base ashore," Tomboy said. "You just can't go into town when you want to."

"And what do you think of the Crimea?"

"Well, we really haven't had much chance to see a lot of it yet. It's exciting being here, though. Kind of like history in the making."

Pamela Drake turned from Tomboy and nodded at the cameraman. "That's a take," she said. She smiled at Tomboy. "Thank you, Commander. That was great."

"My pleasure, ma'am."

"Hello, Pamela," Tombstone said, walking up behind the reporter. "You're certainly a long way from home."

Pamela turned sharply, eyes wide, blond hair swirling past her ears. "Matt! What are you doing here?"

He shrugged. "Actually, I'm supposed to be here as the Navy's liaison with the news media. Care to do some serious liaising?"

"I . . ." She stopped, then glanced at her cameraman. "Let's take a break, Phil."

He grinned at her. "Sure thing, Ms. Drake. Whatever you say."

She looked at him, her expression unreadable. "I hadn't really expected to find you here, Matt."

"No?" She didn't seem particularly pleased to see him. *Damn.* . . .

"I thought you were on the *Jefferson*."

"You knew we were deployed to the Black Sea, didn't you?"

"Yes. I also knew the battle group was coming to the Crimea. I guess I just, well . . . I just didn't expect you to come ashore."

"You don't sound that happy to see me."

"Of course I am." But the look in her eyes said otherwise. "You just caught me by surprise, is all." She looked at her watch. "Listen, I've got a meeting to attend, but maybe we can get together a little later, huh?"

"Certainly." Why was she being so cool? Was she still mad at him? It wasn't like her to hold a grudge. He knew that everything wasn't right between them, but right now he had the impression she'd have rather he'd not shown up at all. "Dinner, maybe?"

"That would be nice. Meet you here in the lobby? About six?"

"Eighteen hundred hours."

She made a face at the militarism. "Whatever."

He was pretty sure that she was still upset about his staying in the Navy. Damn it, why couldn't she see that he had a career, just as she had? They'd had this argument over and over again during the past three or four years, and it seemed like she could never see his side of things. He never squawked when she went gallivanting all over the world gathering news stories. Why couldn't she just accept the fact that he had the same kind of dedication and drive, the same kind of responsibility?

Tomboy stepped up next to him as Pamela walked off. "You know her?"

"Pamela Drake? Yeah, I've known her for, oh, four years, I guess. Met her when the *Jeff* was in Thailand."

Her dark eyes widened. "Oh, that was *that* Pamela! I never made the connection."

Tombstone chuckled. "I have trouble with that, too. Connecting the woman I see when I get back off a deployment with the face on the evening news. Yes, that's Pamela." He'd told Joyce about the love of his life, back when they'd been flying together. Aviators and RIOs often shared more or less intimate details during long flights—or during the longer watches in the ready room.

"An ACN anchor, yet," she said. "I'm impressed."

"Nothing to be impressed about. She's got a job. Just like the rest of us."

Tomboy glanced in the direction in which Pamela had gone. "Well, flyboy, it looks to me like you've been stood up." She jerked her head toward the lobby entrance. "Want me to show you the town?"

Tombstone considered the offer, then grinned. "Why not?" He offered her his arm. "Let's see the sights."

As they started out the front door of the hotel, however, a lanky, swarthy-skinned man with black curly hair and a closely trimmed mustache almost collided with them. "You like guide? See city?"

Tombstone looked the man over. He *might* just be an eager entrepreneur, but there was something about him, a sharpness of character, a focus behind those liquid brown eyes, that suggested he was also a watchdog.

Possibly he was only on someone's payroll, Tombstone thought. More likely, he was working for either the FBS or for military intelligence—the GRU. In any case, both he and Tomboy were wearing their dress Navy uniforms, making them somewhat conspicuous. Tombstone decided he would actually feel safer wandering the town with someone who belonged here. "How much?"

The man broke into a toothy smile. "For you, ten dollars American, each day! I have car, A-okay!"

Their guide's name was Abdulhalik, and it turned out to be a remarkably pleasant afternoon. They ignored his car for the time being in favor of a stroll along the waterfront.

It was a bit disconcerting, walking through the town with Joyce at his side. He was remembering when he'd first started falling in love with Pamela . . . while walking with her through the streets of Bangkok, seeing the sights of Thailand's exotic capital, and exploring Thonburi's floating markets.

Yalta was not as glamorous as Bangkok had been. The climate might have been like southern California, but the town itself reminded him of the more depressing and concrete-clad parts of Atlantic City, without as much in the way of advertising or gambling casinos. There were occasional surprises. Many of the buildings showed a distinct Turkish flavor, especially on the western side of town, and in some areas it was almost possible to forget that they were in the former Soviet Union, but for the most part the buildings were drab, Stalinist-utilitarian and in a depressing state of decay. There was a boardwalk, of sorts, along the waterfront—though there were no boards in sight. Instead, the strip between highway and water had been paved over, an endless expanse of sterile concrete . . . sterile in the aesthetic sense, at least. The uncollected garbage had attracted clouds of flies; in the full heat of summer, Tombstone thought, the stink must be atrocious. From time to time, he relieved his eyes by looking up at the Crimean Mountains, bulking huge against the horizon northwest of the town. Some of the tallest peaks there reached to over fifteen hundred meters, and the breeze coming down off their slopes was fresh and pleasantly cool. Tramlines were in place to take tourists up to the top of the mountain overlooking the town, but the queues were impossibly long.

"So why'd you join the Navy, Captain?" Tomboy asked.

He made a face. "Not 'Captain,' please. Or 'CAG.' Not when we're out like this, just you and me."

"Tombstone, then?"

"Or 'Stoney.' Or 'Matt.'"

"I like Matt. And I'm Joyce. If that doesn't bend the regs too far."

Official Navy protocol required personnel to call one another by their last names only, a regulation that was rarely followed outside of the strict limits of duty. "Oh, I think the regs can stand that. Joyce."

"So how come?"

"How come what?"

"How come you joined the Navy?"

He grinned. "Because I always wanted to fly jets. As far back as I can remember, I wanted to fly."

"So why not the Air Force? They do jets."

"Well, I had some relatives that wouldn't have let me forget that."

"Ah. Your uncle, the admiral."

"Navy family," he said, nodding. "Going way back. I guess I was just continuing the tradition." He sighed. "Sometimes I wonder if it's worth it, though."

"How come?"

He glanced around at their "guide." Abdulhalik was trailing behind them along the promenade, keeping them in sight but granting them privacy. When they had a question, he was right there with an answer, but the rest of the time he kept his distance. A nice guy, Tombstone decided, whatever his true colors.

"I guess I've always felt a need to make some kind of a difference," he admitted after a moment.

"I'd say you have," she said. She took his arm and snuggled up to him as they walked. "I wouldn't be here if it wasn't for you."

He looked down at her sharply, but she wasn't even looking at him. She'd said it in a simple, matter-of-fact way, no coyness, no hidden messages.

"Well, if it hadn't been for me, you might not have ended

up sitting on the tundra in the Kola Peninsula with a busted leg in the first place. And *you* shot the guy first, as I recall."

She glanced up at him and grinned. "Yeah, but you distracted him. How many times did you shoot at him and miss?"

"Hell, I lost count," Tombstone admitted. He grinned back. It *was* funny . . . now. It hadn't been funny then, though, as he'd tried to shoot a Russian soldier with a pistol while running flat out across a field—definitely a no-good way to practice marksmanship. It worked in the movies, all right, but in the real world, handguns were appallingly inaccurate in anything other than a static, proper stance on a target range.

"And you took him down after I slowed him up a bit, as I recall."

"Teamwork."

She snuggled a bit closer. "Teamwork," she agreed.

CHAPTER 15
Wednesday, 4 November

God, I'm not ready for this, Pamela told herself as they rode in the backseat of the car up a winding, cliff-top road. *Why did he have to be here? Why was I so* stupid *as to agree to meet him for dinner?*

She really wasn't ready for the confrontation she knew was coming.

Looking sideways at his profile, she had to admit that she still liked him . . . a lot. Hell, she loved him, but love wasn't always enough. It would have been great if they could've made things work out, but by now Pamela knew that they wouldn't be able to. She wasn't about to give up her career, and though she'd been trying for years now to convince Matt that his career was a dead end, she'd finally woken up and realized that the man was simply never going to change.

Matt Magruder was married to the U.S. Navy. It had been that way since she had met him, and so far as she could tell it was *always* going to be that way. Sometimes she thought the guy had saltwater in his veins instead of blood. Or jet fuel; he loved flying as much as he loved the sea, though he didn't get to fly as much these days as he had in the past. Still, she'd found the combination of sea and flying impossible to compete with.

And Pamela knew that she was simply not cut out to be a Navy wife.

"You're awfully quiet," he told her. He sounded worried, on edge. Maybe he'd already guessed what she was thinking. He'd always been pretty quick on the uptake.

Except when she was trying to get him to see the futility of his continuing career with the Navy.

"I'm pretty tired," she told him. It wasn't entirely a lie. "They've had us on the run ever since the Georgia thing came up."

"Is that what you were coming over to cover in the first place?"

"Sort of. The UN peace initiative was being covered okay by Mike Collins and some of our other field people. But then that Army helicopter got shot down. . . ."

He nodded. "Big news Stateside, huh?"

"Navy jets shoot down Army helo? I should say so. Those were your planes, weren't they?"

"They were off the *Jefferson*, yes. Remember Batman?"

"Of course."

"He pulled the trigger."

"God. What happened?"

"Is this an official interview?"

She sighed. He tended to get so touchy when she asked probing questions. "Strictly off the record. I was just wondering."

"It was an accident," he said.

Well, she'd *known* that. She made a face. "I didn't think you'd done it on purpose."

"Someone screwed up between Washington and the Black Sea," he said, looking away at the landscape passing outside. "The IFF codes for that Army helicopter didn't get delivered. We're taking steps to make sure the same mistake doesn't happen again."

She glanced up at the driver, sitting behind the wheel of the Zil. He was obviously listening in on the conversation.

Tombstone saw her look and smiled. "Don't worry about the driver. He's just the FBS's local spy. Isn't that right, Abdulhalik?"

"Hey, I just work here," the swarthy man said, flashing a dazzling grin. "Your secrets are safe with me!"

"Right." He turned back to her. "I assume he's FBS, anyway. But what happened to that helo's no secret. They probably know all about that. Right, Abdulhalik?"

"Low-grade stuff," the driver replied. "Doubt that they pay me more than eight, ten thousand ruble. Now, if you want to tell me how many nuclear weapons are on aircraft carrier . . ."

"Not a chance. Drive, okay?"

"I drive!"

Pamela looked away in disgust. Silly macho games. Those two were actually enjoying their banter!

It was growing dark by the time the aging Zil rental car got them to the cliff-top aerie known as *Lastochinko Gnezdo*, the Swallow's Nest, perched high atop the rocky Ai-Todor cliff overlooking the sea.

"It looks like a German castle," Pamela said as Tombstone held the car's door open for her. "Or someone's twisted idea of what a German castle should look like."

"It is," he said, grinning. "It was built for Baron Steingel, a rich German oil magnate, back in 1912. Photographs of this place must grace every Crimean travel brochure printed since World War I." He turned to the driver, pulling his billfold from his jacket and extracting some bills. "Here you go. You'll pick us up?"

"I be right here, Tombstone." He dug an elbow against Tombstone's ribs. "Hey, don't know how you American Navy do it," he continued, lowering his voice . . . apparently on the assumption that Pamela couldn't hear his conspiratorial semiwhisper. "Two girls in one day! A-okay, man!"

"Never mind the performance critique," Tombstone told him brusquely. "Give us a couple of hours, right?"

"A-okay! I be here!"

Pamela pretended to study the architecture. It really did look a little like a fairy-tale castle, perched on the very edge of the cliff. The western sky, beyond the town of Gaspra and the peaceful waters of the sea, was turning pink and blood-red. "It looks familiar," she told him.

"Did you ever see the movie *Ten Little Indians*? Agatha Christie?"

"Yes."

"This is where it was shot. There's a café and restaurant here now." He took her arm. "Come on."

And that, Pamela thought with a tightening of her lips, was exactly like the man, always sweeping in and taking charge, as though she and everyone else were just more aviators in his air wing.

The interior was overdone, heavy on the schmaltz and red carpeting. "The people at the hotel said they get a lot of tourists here," Tombstone told her. "If we get a waiter who only speaks Russian, I'm going to be lost."

"Well, it's nice to know you're not perfect at everything."

"Sorry?"

"Never mind."

The waiters did speak English—or at least the one who served them did. Most Russian food was actually rather bland, but the Turkish influence in the Crimea could not be missed. They both had *shashlik*—chunks of seasoned lamb grilled on a skewer, like Turkish shish kebab. Conversation was limited to news topics—the new woman Secretary of Defense, the UN mission in Georgia, the return of the Russian submariners to the Crimea.

They stayed away from anything personal, as if by mutual consent.

"So the Russian submarine sailors are all back in Sevastopol?" she asked him, spearing a chunk of lamb.

"As far as I know. They started ferrying them in from the *Jefferson* early this morning and were scheduled to be finished up by now. I haven't heard one way or the other, though."

"And that was really an accident, too? Like the helicopter?"

His fork paused halfway between his plate and his mouth, then completed the trip. He chewed thoughtfully for a moment before answering. "Kind of," he said. "Our sub was acting within its rights, and within the limits of its orders. Its sonar picked up what sounded like a torpedo launch."

"Wasn't it already too late, then? Sinking the Russian sub was just vengeance by that time, wasn't it?"

"Not really. If it had fired a torpedo at that range, it probably would have been wire-guided, which meant that sinking the sub would stop the torpedo. Our people acted exactly right." He hesitated again, then tried a disarming grin. "You're not accusing me of being a warmonger now, are you?"

"No, of course not. But it does make me wonder what the Navy is doing out here. You chalk up two kills, and both of them are mistakes."

"Believe me, I've been wondering the same thing."

"You sound bitter."

"I guess I am. There are people in Washington, our defense secretary among them, who still want to use the U.S. military for social experimentation. That's wrong. They want to loan U.S. troops out to the UN for humanitarian projects."

"Like Georgia and the Crimea."

"Like Georgia and the Crimea. Why don't they loan us out to the Red Cross and the Camp Fire Girls as well?"

"What's wrong with humanitarian programs?"

"Nothing. Except that that's not what we're for, not what we're *trained* for. It's a waste of resources, misusing us this way. It's also dangerous."

"Dangerous?" She thought he was exaggerating. "How?"

"Because each warm and fuzzy mission like this one, each make-work deployment, extends our resources a little farther. Weakens us a bit more. And because somewhere back in Washington, someone is trying to hammer our square peg into his round hole. When mission parameters are vague, when orders are jumbled or self-contradictory, when there's more politics involved than fighting, well, that leads to mistakes. Bad ones."

"Like the one that got the helicopter shot down."

"Exactly. It also means that someday a real crisis is going to come up, one that only the military can solve. And we won't be able to do it because we're going to be tied down with relief efforts in Mongolia, or carrying out a UN mission in Uzbekistan, or God knows what else."

She shook her head. "It won't get that bad."

"Won't it? Reagan wanted to build a fifteen-carrier, six-hundred-ship Navy. He wasn't able to, and his successors in office, along with Congress, managed to gut the Navy building program, especially once the Soviet Union fell apart and everybody was looking for the so-called peace dividend."

"It was decided twelve would be enough."

"Who decided?" He shrugged. "Congress, I guess. We've never had more than twelve carriers, and with the need to send them in for refit and modernization every so often, what's called the SLEP program, we usually don't have more than ten on active duty at any one time. Ideally, half of those carriers are deployed around the world, while the other half are home-ported, engaged in training exercises, taking on new personnel, and so on. So we have what, five? Five carriers at any one time to handle crises from the Med to the North Sea to the Indian Ocean to the Persian Gulf to the Far East. In fact, we often have to cut the Stateside rotation short, like we did for the *Jeff* last time in Norfolk. Anyway you cut it, though, we're stretched way, way too thin. Tie up just one of our supercarriers with something like delivering food to Ethiopia, and we could have big problems if some two-bit tyrant somewhere decides he's going to take us on."

She shook her head. "I'm still not sure I understand why you're upset. I mean, a mission's a mission, right? And it's not up to you to worry about the politics of the thing. The military is supposed to stay separate from politics."

"Pamela, the five-thousand-and-some men and women aboard a carrier can't just turn their personal feelings off. We're not allowed to, oh, stage a protest in front of ACN cameras, say, or call the President a scumbag on national TV, but there's nothing that says we can't have our own opinions. About the decisions that hang us out to dry in impossible situations. And about the politicians who put us there."

"But surely you don't have to—" she began, then cut herself off. It was always the same whenever they talked about politics, particularly politics as they affected the military. They were worlds apart in their ideas, and while there was nothing that said that husband and wife had to always agree on things, when the things they disagreed about affected their daily lives . . . Well, it was just another indication of how this relationship would not, *could* not work.

"Matt," she said, looking across at him and then quickly down at her plate. She'd been avoiding this all evening. She couldn't put it off any longer. "Look, Matt," she said. "I've been doing a lot of thinking since you left last time. I just . . . I just don't think it's going to work out for us."

He said nothing, and when she looked up and met his eyes, she saw only a carefully maintained mask, with no emotion whatsoever.

"I am not Navy-wife material," she continued. "I need a *relationship*, not an occasional houseguest. I need a person, not letters that leave me wondering if I'm ever going to see you again. I need someone who's there for me, not some guy who just shows up on my doorstep once every six or eight months for a quick bang and maybe breakfast the next morning." She stopped, breathing hard, her fists clenched. Now that she'd started letting out the anger and the hurt and the gnawing frustration, it was almost more than she could do to hold the flood in check. Damn, she hadn't realized there was so much bitterness penned up inside of her!

"I never thought that what we had was just a 'quick bang,' Pamela." He sounded hurt. There was no petulance there, but she could hear a coldness, a hardness that she'd never heard in his voice before.

"How do you think it is for me? You're home for maybe six months. I'm just getting used to having you around, and then I blink twice and poof! You're gone. For six months. Maybe nine months. Damn it, Matt, I can't *live* like that!"

"Pamela, I—"

"A friend of mine, Mike Berrens, did a human-interest story last spring when your battle group got back from the Kola. On the wives and sweethearts waiting at home. And on what a hell their lives were, particularly the wives, trying to run their homes, trying to keep their families together, when their men were gone half the time or more. I took another look at that story after you left, and that's when I knew I could never live like that."

"But, Pamela, it's different with us—" He put up a hand as she started to continue. "Damn it, let me get a word in! I know most Navy wives have a really hard time. Coyote's marriage is pretty rocky right now, and for just the reasons you've been talking about. I was best man at his wedding, and it really hurts to see things falling apart for them.

"But, look, you're different from Julie. I mean, she's a wonderful woman, but she has nothing outside her family. You have a career, and you're damned good at what you do. I would never ask you to give that up, you know that. Yet you expect me to be willing to give up my career for you!"

His voice was rising as he spoke, and growing more and more angry. Maybe she wasn't the only one who'd been bottling things up.

She shook her head, the worst of her own anger already drained. "I'm beyond that, Matt. I know you won't give up the Navy. It's a *part* of you, and you wouldn't be who you are, wouldn't be the . . . be the man I love, if you were the kind of guy who could give it up easily. But it's one of the things that just makes us completely incompatible."

He looked up sharply, a glimmer of hope in his eyes. "You still love me? Then . . ."

Pamela took his hand and held it for a brief moment. "Sometimes . . . sometimes love just isn't enough, Matt."

She released his hand and sat back. "Matt, I'm sure we'll be seeing each other while you're here in Yalta, but I really think it best if we not see each other . . . that way again. It's . . . it really has been wonderful knowing you, and I'm sorry it has to end this way. But it *does* have to end. Now."

The rest of the dinner was completed in an uncomfortable

near-silence and was cut short before dessert or the obliga-
tory after-dinner tea.

All the way back to the hotel, she could feel the tension
winding up inside of him.

2315 hours (Zulu +3)
Yalta Hotel
Crimea

Tombstone was still digesting what had passed between him
and Pamela that evening. He didn't know what to say, was
afraid to say anything for fear that either he or she would
explode.

He'd known she was hurt by his frequent absences, knew
she didn't like them, knew she'd rather he left the Navy . . .
but he'd never imagined it coming to this.

"Good night, Pamela," he told her in the hotel lobby.
"I . . . I'm sorry. . . ."

"It's not your fault, sailor," she said with something
approaching her old twinkle. "It has been fun. At least until
recently."

"Yeah. . . ."

She turned and walked away toward the elevator.

Tombstone turned and started for the stairwell, less
because he still mistrusted Russian elevators than because
the thought of riding up several floors in close proximity to
Pamela was suddenly unendurable. The prostitutes were
gone, at least, he was relieved to see.

As he started up the first flight, however, he was aware of
a sudden movement at his back.

"Stoy! Nee sheeveleetes!"

Tombstone turned, looking down at a young man—he
probably wasn't out of his teens—with long, wildly disheveled hair and a knife held threateningly in his right hand.

"Rukee v'vayrh!" His right hand held the knife, weaving
it back and forth at Tombstone's throat. The left was
extended, palm up. *"Ya hachu den'gee!"*

"I don't speak Russian," Tombstone told the youth,

keeping his voice cold and level. "Understand? *Ya plaha,* uh, *ya plaha gavaryu!*"

"Money!" the boy repeated, and he rubbed the fingers of his left hand together in a universal sign. "Money! Dollar! You give!"

It was almost ridiculously easy, given that he was already on the first step of the stairway, and the kid was waving the knife carelessly less than a foot away, well inside Tombstone's reach. Had it been a pistol the kid was waving, Tombstone would not have considered doing what he did next. He was neither a brawler nor a practitioner of martial arts, but he outweighed the kid by at least thirty pounds, and his reflexes were those of an aviator.

Besides, he was in no mood to be pushed around.

"*Da,*" he said, nodding and reaching up with his left hand to open the front of his jacket. "*Da*. I give."

The kid's eyes gleamed and he stepped closer as if to grab the expected wallet from the inside jacket pocket himself. Instead, Tombstone lashed up and across with his left forearm, blocking the knife hand and smashing it aside; he pivoted left with the movement, shooting his right fist up and hard against the underside of the kid's jaw.

The blow smashed the would-be mugger backward and into a cement-block wall. Tombstone was on him an instant later, slamming him twice more against the cement, hard, as the knife clattered to the floor. He threw another punch and the kid's head lolled to the side.

He let him slide to the floor then, face bloody. Tombstone picked up the knife, rammed the tip hard into a crevice between two concrete blocks, then applied pressure until the blade snapped with a sharp, metallic report.

He dropped the useless hilt on the unconscious kid's chest. "Sorry, fella," he said. "But I've had a *really* bad day. . . ."

CHAPTER 16
Thursday, 5 November

Tombstone had to admit that there was a tremendously rich symbolism in Boychenko's choice of a meeting place for the surrender ceremony. The *welcome* ceremony, he corrected himself wryly. The Russians weren't thinking of this as a surrender, but as a simple transaction, with the United Nations taking responsibility for the security of the peninsula in exchange for guarantees that the Russian soldiers would be repatriated.

Livadia was a village less than two miles west of Yalta where the czars had begun building summer palaces in the 1860s and where Nicholas II had erected his summer residence in 1912. That sprawling, luxurious building, known as the White Palace, had been the site of the famous—the infamous, rather—Yalta Conference of February, 1945, where Roosevelt, Churchill, and Stalin had carved up postwar Europe and unwittingly launched the Cold War that followed. It was here that yet another era of Russian history was to be inaugurated, as General Boychenko turned over the Crimean Military District to UN control.

A stage had been erected in the broad, level park in front of the White Palace, with plenty of chairs for the various UN and Russian officials and a massive wooden podium already arrayed with dozens of microphones of various types, their cables snaking off through the grass. A large number of people were in attendance, standing in front of the stage in a large, milling throng; though most were civilians from Yalta, the crowd included a generous number of reporters as well. As Tombstone climbed the three wooden steps to take his seat on the stage, he caught sight of Pamela and her cameraman there. He felt a pang as he caught her eye and saw the coldness there, but he pretended not to notice and kept walking. His helmet, the regulation helmet painted baby blue to identify him as a member of the UN contingent, chafed uncomfortably where the canvas circle inside rubbed against his head.

He still felt stunned by Pamela's change of heart. Not for it suddenness; now that he looked back on it, he realized he should have seen this coming since last summer, or even before. But he'd been so delighted at the chance to see her here . . . and it seemed a kind of betrayal that a romantic dinner in an exotic setting should turn into the end of their relationship.

In a way, he supposed, it was amusing. Aboard the *Jefferson*, one of the most common problems among the enlisted personnel, especially the younger kids, was the Dear John letter, the dread correspondence from home explaining that the Stateside partner couldn't continue this way, that she'd found someone else, that "it"—whether marriage, relationship, or affair—was over. Revelations like that could be deadly when the guy was far away from home, alone, vulnerable, unable even to make a phone call to straighten things out. It was, Tombstone knew, one of the problems most frequently encountered by the ship chaplain's department, as well as by the XOs of both the *Jefferson* and of the various squadrons.

As he found his seat, a folding metal chair in a line behind the podium, he thought of Brewer, the new XO of the Vipers, and wondered how she coped with the kids who must be coming to her with problems like his every day. Or . . . He frowned, puzzled. Were they? Admitting that your girlfriend or wife thought you were a jerk and was leaving you didn't exactly match up with the calculated macho image that most guys tried to present to the women stationed with them aboard ship. He made a mental note to talk with Brewer about that, to see if she needed a hand.

One common way of helping sailors who'd been blind-sided that way—a technique first employed at the two Navy recruit training centers where new sailors were first separated from the outside world—was the Dear John board, a large bulletin board in some prominent, public place where those who'd received such letters could post them if they wished. *Jefferson* kept one in the enlisted recreation lounge aft; there was, Tombstone thought, no better way to find out that you were not alone, that you weren't the only one who'd had to face this particular problem, as you found space to pin up your own letter amid the forest of similar letters already there.

The other participants in the morning's UN ceremony were assembling, both on the stage, in the area roped off for the crowd, and beyond, where both Russian and UN troops patrolled the park's perimeter. Admiral Tarrant and some more members of his staff had flown in from the *Jefferson* early that morning, and he'd already briefed the admiral on what he'd seen so far in Yalta . . . especially the crime. UN peacekeepers, whatever their nationality, were going to have their hands full when Boychenko's people relinquished control.

Tombstone could hear a faint, far-off thunder—aircraft. *Jefferson* had put up a CAP of Tomcats, just in case the Ukrainians or anyone else decided to try to break up the proceedings.

"Captain Magruder?"

Tombstone turned and was surprised to see Abdulhalik, his guide and driver from the day before. He was wearing a conservative dark suit this morning. The jacket was open and there was an obvious bulge beneath his left arm.

"Abdulhalik!" Tombstone said. "How's the spy business?"

"Dangerous," the man said, not bothering to contradict

Tombstone's assumption. "Especially when the general gives his little speech in a few minutes."

It was also interesting, Tombstone thought, how the man's broken English had mended quite a bit overnight. No more "A-okay" slang or dropped articles.

"I need to ask you, Captain, how long the helicopter flight to your carrier will take. "

Tombstone looked at the man curiously. "Didn't the general's staff cover all of this after their briefing?"

Abdulhalik gave Tombstone a narrow, inscrutable look. "I feel safer sometimes if I can . . . confirm information I have been given."

Though he hadn't been in on the original planning, Tombstone had seen the day's schedule, worked out item by item by UN and Russian personnel several days earlier, and approved by both him and Captain Whitehead yesterday. Boychenko would make his speech, followed by a speech from Special Envoy Sandoval on behalf of the UN, and another by Admiral Tarrant. There would be a brief opportunity for questions from the press, and immediately afterward, Boychenko and his senior staff officers, along with Tarrant and *his* staff, would be taken to a CH-53 Sea Stallion waiting on the east side of the White Palace grounds. The group would be flown out to the *Jefferson*, where Boychenko would officially request asylum.

As CAG, Tombstone had been consulted on the aircraft timetables, especially in regard to the CAP that would cover the helo on its flight back to the *Jefferson*. Tombstone had assumed that the necessary information had been passed on to Boychenko's security personnel. Apparently, though, Abdulhalik wanted to make sure that the information he'd heard was the same as what Tombstone had provided.

Which suggested the possibility of informants or worse within Boychenko's own planning staff. It wasn't a pleasant prospect.

"Well," he said, "the *Jefferson*'s about one hundred nautical miles out right now. If the helo pilot goes flat out? Call it thirty-five, maybe forty minutes. You sound like the general's going to need a quick getaway after his speech. You're afraid of critics?"

He'd meant it as a joke, but Abdulhalik nodded gravely. "Just so. We have word that a large part of the navy does not approve of the general's plans. They might try something to block them."

"I know. I was making a joke."

Abdulhalik did not look amused . . . but after a moment he cracked a thin smile. "I see. You will forgive me if my sense of humor is lacking this morning. It has been a long night."

"Just who are you working for, anyway? The FBS?"

Abdulhalik considered the question for a few seconds before answering. "Actually, I am on the general's personal staff. Security. At the moment, the Federal Bureau of Security is the opposition."

"I see. Why were you keeping an eye on me last night, then?"

A shrug. "If the general is to have his 'quick getaway,' as you call it, it is important that nothing happens to you. Yes?"

Tombstone considered telling him about the knife-wielding mugger in the stairwell, then thought better of it. Abdulhalik looked like he had enough on his mind already without having Tombstone bother him with irrelevant might-have-beens.

A stir in the crowd and a rising murmur of conversation marked the appearance of General Boychenko, Admiral Tarrant, and Special Envoy Sandoval at the front of the White Palace. Boychenko was tall and silver-haired, with a beaklike nose that gave him the look of a bird of prey. Sandoval was shorter and dark-haired, with a sketch of a mustache and a self-important air. Tarrant looked business-like and matter-of-fact, even a little bored. Accompanied by several aides and a small army of security troops, the three made their way up the steps and onto the stage. Captain Whitehead stood to greet Boychenko and shake his hand. The others stood until the VIPs took their places behind the podium, then sat down with a creak and scrape of chairs on wood.

The speech was in Russian, and Tombstone understood not a single word.

Not that he was particularly interested in the content. Had he wanted one, there were translations available in various languages, but he already knew the overall topic and didn't particularly care if he could follow the reasoning or not. Boychenko was talking about the need for international arbitration, the importance of the UN, the need for world peace. . . .

Not that anything being said had meaning. The UN hadn't enforced a working peace anywhere in the world yet . . . not until all parties in a given dispute had their own reasons for stopping the fighting. Ukraine would be watching these proceedings with considerable interest, and Tombstone was pretty sure that they, at least, would soon be testing the UN's resolve.

As the speech-making droned on, Tombstone looked away from Boychenko and let his gaze move across the crowd. Pamela, he saw, was watching Boychenko raptly, though he knew that she spoke no Russian either; a battery of cameras, both still and video, were trained on the Russian general as he spoke, and Tombstone could hear the ratcheting whir-click of automatic winders as the cameras fired. There must have been fifty or sixty reporters present, and easily ten times that many other people—dignitaries, civilians, and soldiers. Tomboy was also in the crowd, over with the civilians and those members of *Jefferson*'s company who weren't up on the stage.

The seat was uncomfortable, and Boychenko's droning monotonous. How the hell had he gotten into this situation?

Perhaps because he was watching the reporters instead of Boychenko, Tombstone saw the movement first, a crucial second or two before anyone else was aware. Three men detached themselves from the closely packed group of reporters, advancing toward the stage. They wore long-hemmed trench coats, and each was extracting something hard and metallic from beneath his garment's open front as he moved.

Someone was shouting. A woman screamed. Two of the running men had their weapons out and clearly visible now—AKMS firing port weapons—basically AKM assault rifles with folding steel-frame butts to make them smaller and more concealable under a trench coat. The third was waving a handgun; Tombstone couldn't see what kind it was.

Abdulhalik was leaping forward toward the front of the stage, fumbling inside his jacket for his own weapon. Other security men were also reaching for their guns, but slowly . . . too slowly. Except for Whitehead, who sat stunned and unmoving, Tombstone was closest to Boychenko. He leaped forward with the suddenness of an F-14 catapulted from the bow of a carrier, his chair flying off the back of the stage; he hit Boychenko low and from behind, driving the man forward into the podium and the forest of microphones, then toppling man and podium together in a splintering crash.

Gunfire cracked, a thundering, stuttering fusillade as the trench-coated assassins opened up with their weapons on full auto. Tombstone heard the bullets snapping through the air overhead or thumping loudly into the heavy podium. Microphones clashed together, and the sound system gave a shrill squeal of feedback that mingled with the steady *crack-crack-crack* of automatic weapons. Shrieks from the audience rose to a shrill, terror-stricken cacophony mingled with cries of pain.

Everything was chaos, raw and uncontrolled. He was lying on top of Boychenko, one arm thrown protectively over the Russian's back. Rolling to the side, he looked up, past the toppled podium and off the stage. One gunman was going down under the combined gunfire from Abdulhalik and another security man. The man with the pistol was out of sight at the moment, but Tombstone could see the other assault-rifle–armed assassin clearly as he ran up to the edge of the stage, firing wildly as he ran. Abdulhalik staggered, dropped his weapon, and collapsed onto his back, legs sprawling. Captain Whitehead flailed his arms and fell off the back of the stage, his face a mask of blood. Tarrant was down, too . . . and Sandoval. The assassins had sprayed the entire front row of VIPs, killing or wounding eight or ten of them in one long burst.

There was the man with the pistol, collapsing under a hail of automatic fire as he exchanged shots with the security guards. But the running man was closer, much closer now, so close now Tombstone could see his bushy mustache, see the wild light in his Oriental-looking eyes. Reaching the stage, he leaned over the railing, aiming directly at Tombstone and Boychenko from a range of less than five feet.

He pulled the trigger and nothing happened.

Tombstone was up and on his feet in the same instant, scooping up an overturned metal chair, pivoting, and hurling it as hard as he could. The gray chair struck the gunman and momentarily tangled with his weapon, knocking him back a step and confusing him. Tombstone was in the air right behind the chair, lunging for the man's throat even as he tossed the chair aside and tried to bring his AKMS to bear once more. He hit the man high, hands lancing toward the throat, his arms held stiff before him; the impact of his legs splintered the frail structure of the railing as he crashed through and knocked the assassin down. The gunman continued fumbling with his weapon, dragging a loaded magazine out from inside one of the capacious pockets of his trench coat. Tombstone battled him for that heavy black magazine, wresting it away from him, picking it up like a flat rock and bringing it down on the side of the man's head with tremendous force. The gunman raised his arm, trying to block the attack. Tombstone struck him again, and the man's head lolled to the side.

Tombstone looked up, blinking. People were still screaming, shrieking, and running in all directions as security troops converged on the stage. Half a dozen civilians were down on the grass, faces and clothing smeared with bright scarlet blood. Pamela! . . .

There she was, apparently all right, kneeling on the grass a few yards away next to the body of her cameraman. She looked up and locked gazes with him, but there was no recognition in her eyes, none at all. She looked like she was in shock.

Then a half-dozen troops arrived, muscling Tombstone aside and pouncing on the semiconscious would-be assassin with an almost gleeful viciousness.

"Don't kill him!" Tombstone shouted as one soldier hammered at the man with his rifle butt, but he didn't even know if any of them spoke English. He reached out and grabbed the soldier's arm before he could strike again. "*Nyet!*" Tombstone yelled. The soldier spun, face a twisted mask of anger. "*Nyet!*" he yelled again. Damn, how did you say "Don't kill him" in Russian? The foreign country guidebooks never gave you the really useful phrases.

One soldier, though—a lieutenant—barked orders and cuffed two of the soldiers aside. In a few moments, they'd sorted things out and half dragged, half carried the man away.

Tombstone scrambled back onto the stage and raced to Tarrant's side. The admiral had taken one round through his chest, up high, and was unconscious.

"Tombstone!" Joyce cried, reaching his side. "My God, are you okay?"

"Fine, Tomboy," he said. "Fine." He wasn't sure he was ready to believe that yet. His knees now, as reaction began to settle in, felt terribly weak, and his breaths came in short, almost panting gasps. He looked at her. Her dress uniform was disheveled and she'd lost her hat. His eyes widened as he saw a bright smear of blood on her jacket.

"It's not me," she said, reading his expression.

"You're okay?"

"Yeah. What about the admiral?"

"Damn. I don't know. I don't *know*!" They needed a doctor. No . . . they needed a *Navy* doctor, someone off the *Jeff.*

Nearby, Boychenko was standing again, staring around at the carnage with an expression as dazed as Pamela's. Several soldiers, eyes nervously on the building and the milling, panicky crowd, started to urge him away to safety, but he shrugged free and walked over to Tombstone.

"Captain Magruder," he said, the words heavily accented. He took Tombstone's hand in both of his, shook it, then pulled the American close and hugged him. "*Spasebaw.* Thank you, for my life. That was very brave deed."

"It was nothing," Tombstone said. "I was running for cover and tripped."

Bochenko blinked, looking puzzled. He probably didn't speak enough English to be able to understand more than a word or two of what Tombstone was saying.

"Is Admiral Tarrant? . . ."

"He needs medical help. A hospital."

"We do what we can."

One of his security men tugged at the general's elbow, imploring him with his expression to hurry. Tombstone could understand their worry. There might well have been more than three assassins, *should* have been, in fact, given the number of Boychenko's guards.

As they hurried him away, Tombstone moved to the far side of the stage and found Abdulhalik sitting up, one hand clutching a shoulder soggy with blood. "Lie down," Tombstone told him. "Damn it, get down!"

"Yes, sir."

Sandoval was lying nearby, his eyes wide open in death. Whitehead was dead as well. Damn . . . *damn!*

The security man complied and Tombstone used a length of cloth torn from the man's sleeve as a pressure bandage on Abdulhalik's wound. It looked as though the bullet had smashed through his chest, high up near his shoulder, shattering his scapula but, so far as Tombstone could tell, missing his lung. At least there was no blood in his nose or mouth, and he seemed to be breathing okay.

"Tatars," Abdulhalik said, his voice weak.

"Sorry?"

"Damned . . . Tatars. Descendants of the Mongols. You know Genghis Khan?"

Tombstone kept working, tying the packing in place with more strips of cloth. "Not personally. I never met the man."

"Think . . . Crimea is their . . . homeland."

"It is, from what I've heard." He'd read the history in a guidebook several days ago. Before the Russian Revolution, the *first* revolution in 1917, the Crimean Peninsula had been settled largely by Tatars—as Abdulhalik had said, descendants of the Mongol hordes that had swept across southern Russia in the thirteenth century. Crimea had been their final stronghold in Russia until the time of Catherine the Great, and they'd still been a significant part of the population well into the twentieth century. After the Communists had taken over, Crimea was redesignated as a Tatar Autonomous District.

Then had come the Second World War, and the invasion by Hitler's legions. Crimea had been occupied, then liberated, but with liberation came persecution. Stalin accused the Tatars of collaborating with the Nazis and used that excuse to exile all of them to central Asia. The ban against their return to Crimea had been lifted in the 1980s, and they'd been returning ever since, in larger and larger numbers. Many were now demanding that the Crimea be returned to them, as an autonomous district or as a free homeland.

Those demands, Tombstone reflected, would muddy the waters a bit but had no chance at all of being realized. Neither the Russians nor the Ukrainians were willing to relinquish the embattled little triangle of land, and for damned sure they weren't going to turn it over to the Tatars.

Looking up, Tombstone watched as soldiers picked up one of the bodies of the would-be assassins. "You think they tried to kill the general to get their homeland back?"

Abdulhalik tried to shrug and winced with the pain. "Ah! Well, it makes sense, yes? There are several radical Tatar independence groups. Any could have done this to further their cause."

"Maybe, but that doesn't mean they did it." He shook his head. "What would they achieve by killing Boychenko? Besides getting themselves stepped on, I mean?"

Abdulhalik didn't answer. He was unconscious. Tombstone finished his bandaging job and signaled for a stretcher team as they approached the stage. Joyce joined him a moment later.

"You look thoughtful," she said.

"Hmm. Abdulhalik thinks this was the work of a Tatar nationalist movement."

"Terrorists?"

"Yeah. But it just doesn't make sense."

"Terrorism doesn't make much sense."

"No, I mean, this is really far-fetched. What could they hope to achieve with this? If I were a terrorist group who wanted the Crimea back, but with no chance in hell of seeing my aims realized . . ."

His voice trailed off as he followed the chain of logic.

"Come on," he said.

"Where are we going?"

"The helicopter. That's probably where they're taking Boychenko, and I want to get there before they take off."

"Why? Are you hitching a ride back to the *Jeff*?"

It was a tempting thought, though Tombstone and the other Navy personnel ashore, except for Tarrant's staff, of course, were all supposed to remain in Yalta while the UN people took charge. But Tombstone had other ideas.

"No. I want to get on the radio. I think we may have problems."

She had to hurry to keep up with his long pace as he strode toward the east side of the palace. "What kind of problems?"

"I think Boychenko was only one of several targets," he told her. "And I'm afraid the *Jeff* might be next on their list!"

CHAPTER 17
Thursday, 5 November

Major Yevgenni Sergeivich Ivanov divided his attention between the radar display and the view out the cockpit. Flying a high-performance attack aircraft at extreme low altitude was always a challenge; he was skimming the waves of the Black Sea at an altitude of less than fifty meters, where the slightest hesitation, the least miscalculation would slam him and his aircraft into the sea at Mach 1.1.

He was flying a MiG-27M attack aircraft, hurtling along at just above the speed of sound, the variable-geometry wings swept back along the aircraft's fuselage like the folded wings of a stooping hawk.

Ivanov was an experienced pilot, as experienced as any in Soviet Frontal Aviation. At thirty-eight, he was old for a combat aviator, but he'd been flying aircraft of one type or another for over fifteen years. His first combat missions had been over Afghanistan. Later, he'd volunteered for a special Frontal Aviation program that transferred him temporarily to navy command, and he'd spent five years learning how to land on the deck of the new Soviet nuclear aircraft carrier *Kreml*, then teaching other, younger aviators how to do the same.

With that experience, he was part of a very special

fraternity, one of the smallest and most demanding in the world, the brotherhood of pilots trained to operate off the deck of an aircraft carrier. He'd flown off the *Kreml* in the Indian Ocean, during the India-Pakistan crisis, and again in the great naval battle off the Norwegian coast, the engagement during which the carriers *Kreml* and *Soyuz* had both gone to the bottom. With his ship shot out from beneath him while he was in the air, Ivanov almost hadn't made it home. Short on fuel, he'd nursed his damaged aircraft back across Norwegian and Finnish territory to land at a small airstrip outside of Nikel.

For a time after that, he'd been back in FA—Frontal Aviation—on more traditional assignments, flying ground-attack missions for Krasilnikov against the Leonovist rebels. With two of the former Soviet Union's three aircraft carriers destroyed, and the third kept in careful seclusion in its port facilities at Sevastopol, everyone in FA assumed that the Russian aircraft carrier experiment was dead. If nothing else, Russia was no longer a world power, neither able nor willing to project military force to some far-off corner of a hostile globe. Something as large, as expensive, and as complex as a nuclear-powered aircraft carrier was a serious drain on the military's fast-vanishing resources, and with no strategic purpose to its existence, it would soon be consigned to the wrecker's yard.

And that, Ivanov reflected as he glanced briefly left and right, checking the positions of the other MiG-27s in his attack formation, would have been a tragedy. *Pobedonosnyy Rodina* was a proud, noble vessel, for all that he'd never yet left port for more than a brief Black Sea shakedown. Operation *Miaky* had given him the chance to live again.

Ivanov had developed a feel for carriers during the years he'd served aboard them in the naval aviation program. Despite the long-standing rivalry between the Fleet and Frontal Aviation, he liked carrier service. *Rodina* deserved better than rusting away at his moorings or being broken into scrap to feed the starving, inefficient civilian industries ashore. His affection for carriers and his love of naval flying were shaped, as much as anything else, by the knowledge that he was part of that elite fraternity shared by only a tiny handful of aviators from Russia, Great Britain, France, the United States, and the very few other countries whose navies operated aircraft carriers.

Fraternity. The word he used was *bratstvo*, "brotherhood." He'd heard, though, that the Americans had begun allowing women to fly carrier aircraft. He snorted behind his oxygen mask. Women? The very idea was preposterous. During the long Soviet reign, women had been promised full equality with men, but that was an idea that had never really been reflected by the real world, one composed more of words than of substance. In the years since the collapse of the Soviet government, there'd been an ultraconservative backlash against the whole concept of women's rights; female equality with men was an idea linked inextricably in the public mind with the Communists, and there was a tendency now to relegate women to the kitchen and a select few professions outside the home—actresses and street sweepers and doctors and the like.

Ivanov grinned. Like most fighter pilots of his acquaintance, he thought of women as simple and delightful perquisites of his profession, the faster and hotter the better. As far as he was concerned, women belonged in bed, naked and with legs welcomingly spread, not in the cockpit of a jet aircraft.

He thought he would like to meet some of the American women aboard the *Thomas Jefferson*, however. If even half of the scandalous stories he'd heard were true . . .

Such a meeting seemed unlikely at best, just now. Once again, politics and the relentless tides of history were about to bring the American and Russian navies into conflict, and if he met an American fighter pilot at any time in the near future, it would be as an opponent, a minute, wildly twisting speck trapped in the targeting reticle of his MiG's HUD.

Pathetic . . . the thought of women attempting to meet men on equal terms in combat. The idea was ludicrous in ground combat, since women were so much weaker than men; it was even more ludicrous in air combat, for the demonstrable fact that women simply didn't have the brains for the highly technical aspects and details of flying high-performance jet aircraft. He'd heard that several American women had been shot down over the Kola; if Black Flight encountered any today, it would be an even more complete slaughter. In the Kola, the Americans had been flying against second-rate units and rear-echelon squadrons, the leftovers after the debacle in and around Norway. Black Flight, and the attendant formations code-named Bastion and Flashlight, were made up of combat aviators scoured from Loyalist units all over Russia and were comprised of the very best of the best.

"Black Leader, this is Bastion One-one-seven" sounded in his headset. "Do you read me? Over."

"Bastion One-one-seven, Black Leader reads. Go ahead."

"We are being painted by American radar, almost certainly from their naval AWACS."

"What about ECM?"

"We have been jamming steadily for fifteen minutes, sir. The Americans have been increasing the power of their scans and at this point are probably burning through our interference. They will not be able to judge our numbers, but they know we are here, and probably where we are going."

"That does not matter. They will not be concerned with us unless they believe us to be threatening their battle group."

"Just keep your ears sharp, Yevgenni," the voice of Captain Oleg Nikiforov added over the tactical channel. "Once they figure out what we're up to, they will be after us like a cat pouncing on mice."

"The cats will find they've cornered a pack of wolves, Captain," Ivanov replied, and he heard the others chuckle in response.

As a military pilot, he had a healthy respect for American naval aviators—the men, anyway; he'd flown with them in the Indian Ocean and against them off Norway and could accept, with some few unspoken reservations, the fact that they were the best in the world. This time around, however, it was going to be different.

There would be no massed attacks against layered American carrier battle group defenses, for one thing. That type of antiquated strategy had been dictated by the old Soviet military command, back when they'd been faced with the problem of how to wage war in the air, on the land, and both on and under the sea against a technologically superior enemy, overcoming them with forces whose *only* advantage lay in their numbers. No, the first direct attack against the Americans would come only after their battle group had been seriously weakened.

And weakening their forces was precisely the objective of today's low-level raid.

Ivanov thrilled to the sheer, joyous power of his machine. He was never more alive than when he was in the cockpit of the sleek attack aircraft, peering ahead across the broad, wedge-shaped nose known affectionately to the aircraft's pilots as *utkanos*, the duck nose. The MiG-27, known as "Flogger-D" in NATO's code, was a venerable aircraft by now; it had entered service with Frontal Aviation in 1974, and for most of that time had been the mainstay of Soviet air-to-ground attack. Most pilots held a genuine affection for the machine; up until its appearance, odd MiG designation numbers had been reserved for fighters, while even numbers identified attack planes. Like the American F-111, however, an attack plane with the completely inappropriate F-for-fighter designation, the MiG-27 carried a somewhat confusing identifier. Pilots who liked the way the plane handled, however, insisted that it was as fast and nimble as most fighters and therefore carried exactly the right ID. Indeed, besides his main armament of air-to-surface missiles, the MiG carried both two AA-8 infrared-homing missiles for air-to-air dogfighting, as well as a powerful six-barrel rotary cannon for close-in work. At need, the MiG could play the fighter's role, though Ivanov knew he would be at a disadvantage if he found himself tangling with American Tomcats or Hornets.

That was what the MiG-29s in Bastion were for.

He checked the flight's position on his terrain-mapping radar. Less than ninety kilometers to go. It was too late for the Americans to stop them now, even if they guessed what their true objective was.

There was still one remaining chance that the attack would be aborted, and it was time now to find out, one way or the other. Reaching down, he dialed his radio frequency selector to the channel assigned for Operations.

"Tower, Tower, this is Black One. How do you read me? Over."

"Black One, Tower. We read you."

"Dostoyevsky," he said, the writer's name serving as a code informing Operations that the attack group was on course, on time, and ready to proceed with the mission. The reply would be either "Tolstoy," which would mean abort and return to base, or . . .

"Chekhov," the voice said. "I say again, Chekhov."

"Confirm Chekhov," he replied. The mission was on! "Proceeding as ordered."

Switching back to his tactical channel, he contacted the other five aircraft of Black Flight. "The word is Chekhov, men," he said, and the relief he felt as he said it was almost palpable.

"Excellent!" Piotr called. "I've been wanting to do this for a long time!"

"Radio silence from now on," he warned. *"Vsevaw harashiva y pabeda!"*

Good luck, and victory.

The flight of deadly MiG-27s arrowed toward the still-invisible coast of Turkey.

0957 hours (Zulu +3)
E-2C Hawkeye Tango 61
Over the Black Sea

"Dog House, Dog House, this is Watch Dog Six-one. Do you copy, over?"

Lieutenant Arnold Brown checked again the sweep of green-white fuzz and blips on his main display screen. There was no doubt about it. Something big—several somethings, in fact—were moving out there, over one hundred miles to the southwest.

"Watch Dog, this is Dog House," the voice of the Operations watch officer replied. "Go ahead."

"I have a contact, designated Mike One-five, bearing two-zero-five, range one-zero-eight. There is heavy, repeat, heavy ECM, but I believe the contact to be multiple air targets down on the deck."

"Copy that, Watch Dog. We've got your screen up here in front of us now. How long you been tracking them?"

"Five, maybe six minutes, Dog House. I wanted to make sure I wasn't picking up waves."

"Met says the sea's flat and calm today, Watch Dog, so whatever you have, it's a hard target. Besides, I doubt that the Ukes are jamming to keep us from seeing waves off the Turkish coast."

"Ah, roger that."

Brown puzzled a moment at Ops' assumption that the targets were Ukrainian. On their current heading, they could have come from either Odessa or Sevastopol; the reciprocal of their course drew a line lying almost directly between those two cities on the map. They could as easily be Russian aircraft as Ukrainian.

The real question, though, was what were they up to? With all of that jamming, it was clear they didn't want the Americans—or anybody else, for that matter—to see what they were up to. They weren't threatening the CBG. They weren't anywhere *near* the battle group. If Brown had been ordered to take a guess, he'd have sworn they were lining up for an attack on the Bosporus.

"Watch Dog, Watch Dog, this is Dog House."

"Dog House, Watch Dog. Go ahead."

"Hey, Twenty XO is down here, and he wants to know if you think those bogeys are setting up for an attack on Istanbul."

Brown grinned. Twenty XO meant Commander Grant, the executive officer of CVW-20.

"Tell the Coyote that that's a big-time roger," he said. "Either Istanbul or the straits themselves would be my guess."

"Could it be a practice run, Watch Dog?"

"Dog House, there's no way to tell that until they goddamn launch!"

"Ah, copy that. Wait one, Watch Dog."

"Whatcha got, Lieutenant?" Lieutenant Commander Jake Garner, Watch Dog Six-one's commander, asked over the ICS.

"Bogeys on the road to Istanbul, Commander," he replied. "I'm on the horn to *Jeff* and they have me on hold."

"What, the Russkis are attacking Turkey?" Garner asked. "That doesn't make much sense."

"Could be a training exercise," the enlisted radarman at Brown's side put in. "You know, our subs are always practicing attack runs on friendly ships, just for practice, like."

"Yeah, but then the target doesn't *know* he's the target," Brown said thoughtfully. "If I were the Turkish air defense command, I'd be freaking right about now, but good."

"Suppose it's not for practice?" Garner asked. "What could they be after down there?"

"We have some UNREP ships coming through the straits about now," Brown said. He punched several keys, changing the scale of the radar map display until the Turkish coast in the vicinity of the northern mouth of the Bosporus was just visible. Though the storm of radar interference extended all the way to the mainland, it was thin enough in the south for him to see strong returns from several ships emerging from the straits. Most of those would be Turkish vessels, but one bore the ID tag of an American UNREP fuel tanker, the *Falcon Patriot*. "I suppose if they were mad at us for some reason, they might be after our UNREP."

"That doesn't make sense," Garner said.

"I know. What the hell are they after down there, anyway?"

"What the hell are they after down there, anyway?" Lieutenant Brian Crosby asked aloud, and Coyote was forced to
agree. As nearly as they could tell through all of the snow
and clutter, a number—possibly a large number—of unknown aircraft were bearing down on the entrance to the
Bosporus Strait. The CBG was already beginning to pick up
the frantic and uncoded radio cries of Turkish air control
officers and pilots, who believed themselves to be under
attack. No one had yet ventured a guess, however, as to what
actually might be going on.

Coyote watched the confused tangle of blips on the main
display in Ops and swore softly. What, he wondered, would
Tombstone have done in this situation?

But Tombstone was ashore, with the transfer ceremony
well under way, and Coyote as Deputy CAG bore the
responsibility for deploying *Jefferson*'s air assets.

Lieutenant Brain Crosby was the Ops duty officer at the
moment, and he was watching Coyote now, obviously more
than happy to allow the acting CAG to make the tough calls.

"Okay," he told Crosby. "Who's in place who could go
take a look?"

"Well, we've got BARCAP One here," Crosby said,
indicating an oval "racetrack" path marked on the screen
south of Yalta. "That's Two-oh-one and Two-oh-five, Batman and Libbie."

"But they're covering the ceremony and are in place to
escort the helo back here."

"Yes, sir. Then there's BARCAP Three, over here to the
east. They're out of the running. It'd take half an hour for
them to get down to where the action is. BARCAP Two is
up here, to the west. They're in a pretty decent position for
an intercept, actually. Ten, maybe twelve minutes."

"Who is it?"

He checked the duty board. "Two-one-eight and Two-one-oh. Dixie and Badger."

Dixie! Shit. Tombstone had recommended that Dixie be kept clear of anything but strictly routine patrolling for a few days, at least until he'd had time to settle down after the helicopter shoot-down incident. But sending him to get a positive ID . . .

On the other hand, it would take Batman longer to reach the bogeys and there was still the need to cover that helo flight.

No. It would have to be Dixie.

And maybe, just for a backup, he could redeploy Batman and Libbie to cover Dixie and Badger. BARCAP Three could be routed north to take BARCAP Two's place off Yalta. He glanced at the Air Ops clock on the bulkhead. Yeah, that would work. The ceremony wasn't due to end for another half hour or so. The Yalta party could stand to be uncovered for a few minutes, anyway, especially since all of the activity seemed to be way the hell and gone off to the southwest, near the mouth of the Bosporus.

Of course, the jamming and unknowns down there could be some sort of diversion, designed to get him to leave the Yalta ceremony unguarded, but he didn't think that was the case. It didn't feel like a diversion—a judgment based on a number of years of combat experience—and, even if he was wrong, even if Yalta was the real target, BARCAP Three would be close enough to station to employ their AIM-54s in . . . what? Make it ten minutes.

"Okay," Coyote said, deciding. "Here's what we do. Tell BARCAP Two to hot tail it down there and give us a fly-by ID, pronto. Nothing fancy, just a probe, shake 'em and see what rattles. If he can get close enough to eyeball 'em, we'll have some answers."

"We'll have some answers if they take a shot at him, too."

"There is that. Tell Batman and Libbie to leave station and fly overwatch for Two. And have Three leave station and take over for One. Got it?"

"Got it, sir." He shook his head. "Damn, it's getting busy this morning."

Coyote snorted. "What I'm worried about is how much busier it's going to get. I want to know what those—"

He broke off in midsentence, eyes widening. "What is it, sir?" Crosby asked, looking at him.

"I just had," Coyote said slowly, hoping desperately that he was wrong, "a horrible thought about what those bastards might be after! . . ."

0959 hours (Zulu +3)
Tomcat 218
On CAP

"BARCAP Two, BARCAP Two, this is Dog House," the voice of *Jefferson*'s Air Ops watch officer said over Dixie Mason's headset. "Come left to two-two-zero and punch it."

"Two-one copies," Dixie replied. He brought his stick over, watching the heading numbers on his HUD flicker to the right as he swung the Tomcat into a southwesterly heading. "Coming to two-two-zero and going to Zone Five."

"Two-two copies" sounded over the Ops channel. Tomcat 210 was flying Dixie's wing, with Lieutenants Cunningham and Burns in the cockpit. He shoved the throttle forward through the last of the detents, reveling in the familiar surge of power as the aircraft's afterburners kicked in, rocketing him past the speed of sound in seconds.

"What do you think the hurry is, Dixie?" his RIO called over the ICS from the backseat.

"I expect they'll tell us when they get around to it, Mick," Dixie said. "Anything on your scope?"

"Someone's still jamming the hell out of it, off to the west, somewhere. Maybe a Hawkeye could see through this shit, but I can't."

Dixie's RIO for this flight was Lieutenant Commander Kevin Moss, handle "Mickey," a young, sandy-haired guy who nevertheless passed for what the squadron thought of as "an old hand," since he'd been flying with the Vipers for almost a year now. For the past several days, ever since the helicopter incident when Cat had told him flatly that she wouldn't fly with him again, Dixie had been paired off with a succession of RIOs from the duty pool. He was beginning to suspect that they drew lots every day, with the loser assigned to backseating with him. The only qualification seemed to be that the man assigned as his RIO had to be more experienced than he was. It was humiliating . . . and unfair, and Dixie had had just about enough.

At least CAG had allowed him to keep flying. If he'd been ordered to stay on the deck, he'd be approaching critical mass just about now.

"BARCAP Two, this is Dog House" sounded over his headset. "We've got bogeys about two hundred fifty miles southwest of your position, and we need a positive ID. Deputy CAG wants you to go check them out."

"Roger, Dog House," Mickey replied. "We're on the way."

Dixie felt the tiniest bite of worry. A positive ID?

With the Tomcat cruising comfortably at Mach 1.5, they would be close enough to the intruders to get a visual in about twelve minutes, and this time Dixie was going to make damned sure of his target recognition.

At least this time the target wasn't likely to be U.S. Army helicopters.

1004 hours (Zulu +3)
Black Leader
North of the Bosporus Strait

Ivanov pulled back slightly on the stick, bringing his MiG's altitude up to just under two hundred meters. He could see the Turkish coast ahead; they were well into Turkish airspace now, and he could imagine the faces of the Turk air force officers turning purple as they screamed for identification. Casually, he glanced left, then right, searching the skies. He could see vapor trails on both sides, but those were almost certainly other aircraft of the attack group. They'd be scrambling interceptors by now at half a dozen nearby air bases, but it was already too late.

"Black Leader, this is Flashlight." Radio silence had been broken now. If the Turks didn't know they were here before, they certainly did now. "The target is illuminated."

Ivanov flipped a line of switches, checking his laser targeting pickup. A light winked on and a tone sounded in his helmet; his number-one AS-14 missile had registered the hot, optically invisible pinpoint of laser light gleaming on the target, now less than thirty kilometers ahead, and was tracking it.

Not much longer . . .

His MiG-27 was carrying a warload of two AS-14 air-to-surface missiles, the laser-guided monsters known in the NATO lexicon as "Kedge." His port-side missile had a solid lock on the target now, though it was still just beyond the weapon's twenty-kilometer range. Somewhere further out and higher up, "Flashlight," another MiG-27 with a laser designator pod, was illuminating the target for the entire attack squadron.

The blurred impression of water flashing beneath Ivanov's keel flashed suddenly from blue to browns, grays, and greens. He was over the beach now, thundering above peasants' stone huts and tangled complexes of larger-scale architecture. Black Flight's sonic booms must be rattling windows in their wake. For several seconds, he hurtled above the brown-streaked earth, and then he was over water once more, this time flashing low above the dark waters of the northern mouth of the Bosporus Straits. A pair of ships appeared ahead, a long, gray, knife-prowed destroyer and a far larger and clumsier-looking tanker, painted black with a white superstructure. Ivanov glimpsed the American flag fluttering from its truck.

Then he was past both vessels. He glanced down at both his radar display and his threat warning indicators, half expecting the Turkish destroyer to pop a SAM up his tailpipe, but there was no reaction from the surface.

Perhaps they'd managed to catch Turks and Americans alike by surprise.

A warning light winked on. He was within range now of

the primary target. Since Turkish interceptors would be in the area at any moment, the mission parameters called for launch at maximum range. He double-checked his target lock, then brought his thumb down on the firing button. "Black One, missile away!" he called.

His MiG lurched skyward as the Kedge missile, weighing some six hundred kilograms, dropped from his left-side inlet duct pylons. Its solid-fuel motor ignited with a yellow-white flash, and though the engine was supposed to be smokeless, condensation in the air boiled into a sharp, white contrail arrowing out ahead of the hurtling MiG.

"Black Three," Mikhail Mizin, his wingman, called. "Missile away!" A second contrail chased the first, swooping low toward the surface of the strait before leveling off just a handful of meters above the water.

"Black Two! Missile launch."

"Black Four. Aborting run. I have malfunction. . . ."

Damn . . . that was bad luck, but not unforeseen. Russian military technology tended to be blunt, tough, and simple; when it had to be complex, as in the case of MiGs or AS-14 missiles, there was always a stubbornly unpredictable but high chance of equipment failure of some sort. That was why attacks like this one were planned with multiple redundancy in mind. Each aircraft in Black Flight would loose one of its two missiles, then loiter until the damage could be assessed. If necessary, the second missile would be used on the primary target; if the initial attack proved successful, they would be free to seek targets of opportunity for their second shots, before turning back for the north and home.

He checked his indicators, noting that the missile was running hot and smooth. Flight time to the target would be just over one minute. . . .

CHAPTER 18
Thursday, 5 November

The newest and northernmost of the three bridges spanning the Bosporus was crowded this morning, with cars, trucks, bicycles and scooters, oxcarts, and even people on foot. The big show—the passage of the American aircraft carrier the week before—had drawn a much larger mob, but there was always heavy traffic both ways over the span, crossing in a few moments from one continent to another.

The bridge was of the same general design as others among the world's largest spans—the Golden Gate, the Verrazano Narrows, and, longest of all, the Humber Bridge in northern England. It consisted of a gently arcing deck suspended from two massive cables. Each of those main cables was just less than a meter thick and composed of hundreds of tightly woven wire ropes; the cables, in turn, were draped from two towers rising from either side of the strait's main shipping channel. The towers were paired, hollow-core, reinforced concrete pillars straddling the suspended deck; the span between the two towers across the channel was just over a thousand meters.

The first Kedge missile arrowed south across the waters of the Bosporus, scant feet above the dark and oily waters. Striking the base of the westernmost of the two huge concrete towers, the warhead triggered, one hundred kilograms of high explosives detonating in a savage blast, raising a vast cascade of white spray and hurling chunks of concrete far out into the water.

Three seconds later, a second missile struck the eastern tower. Those towers, designed to exacting engineering specifications to support tremendous weight or withstand hurricane-force winds, were simply not designed to absorb that brutal and sudden a punishment. With both northern legs of the suspension system damaged, the span between them sagged. The hangers, the vertical wire ropes support-ing the deck, began snapping, first one by one, then in rippling, crashing volleys. The deck itself was composed of many individual sections like shallow boxes and paved over with a one-and-a-half-inch layer of mastic asphalt; the design provided flexibility, as it had to on an engineering project of such scope, but it also allowed the two explosions to generate shock waves that rippled out from the towers, with the deck itself convulsing in a titanic game of crack-the-whip.

Vehicles and people alike were scattered like toys as the asphalt flexed, tossing them into the air and smashing them down again. A third missile detonated against the eastern tower, somewhat higher up the leg than the first blast, gouging through to the pillar's hollow core. With a vast and thunderous shudder, the northern leg of the tower shattered, cross struts crumbling, suspension cables writhing, hangers snapping apart like rapid-fire gunshots. Three more missiles arrowed in out of the north in rapid succession, two striking the span near the eastern side, the third hitting the western pylon once again. The deck tilted even more precipitously to the north, spilling vehicles and people into the yawning gulf below.

With the failure of the northern half of the suspension rig accelerating, the southern half began to go, too. The eastern tower sagged heavily toward the north, an avalanche of splintering concrete cascading into the water. The entire thousand-meter-plus center span of the northernmost of the Bosporus bridges whipsawed back and forth, the oscilla-tions building until the main cables snapped, spilling the box sections of the deck into the strait far below.

The navigable channel up the center of the Bosporus was not wide, a few hundred yards across at most, and as the smoke and spray cleared, observers aboard nearby vessels could see that it was almost completely blocked by fallen deck boxes and a vast and incoherent tangle of wire rope. Miraculously, there *were* survivors, struggling in the wreckage as small craft moved in to begin rescue efforts; the screams of the injured mingled with the continuing splash and crack of falling concrete, and the mournful hootings of ship horns.

Almost immediately, a Turkish naval vessel, the guided-missile patrol boat *Gurbet*, moving toward the center of the channel at high speed, shuddered, then slewed to a dead stop, two of her four propeller shafts fouled by the unraveling strands of wire rope that stretched above and below the surface of the water like a deadly trap designed expressly for ships.

Clearing out that tangle of debris would require a major engineering effort . . . and weeks, possibly months of time.

And until the wreckage of the fallen bridge could be cleared, no vessels would be passing between the Black Sea and the Sea of Marmara . . . or to the Aegean Sea beyond.

1006 hours (Zulu +3)
Tomcat 218

At eight thousand feet, Dixie and Mickey flashed southwest between the impossibly blue sky above and the deep, ultramarine sea below. Glancing right, he could see "Badger" Cunningham and "Red" Burns off his starboard wing in Tomcat 210.

"I'm making multiple bogeys ahead," Mickey said. "At least ten . . . ah, make that twelve contacts in three groups."

"Roger that, BARCAP Two," Watch Dog replied. "We've got them."

The radar picture ahead was clearing slightly as the

Tomcats drew closer to their contacts, until the F-14s'
AWG-9 radars gave a better picture than the more powerful
but far more distant electronics of the orbiting Hawkeye.
With the onboard data link, Tomcats and Hawkeye could
share an incredible volume of two-way data, all of which the
Hawkeye was relaying immediately to the Combat Information Centers aboard both the *Shiloh* and the *Jefferson*.

"Shit," Mickey said. "I wish I could see! It looks like the
bogeys are inside Turkish airspace. Tango Six-one! Do you
make some of those bogeys going feet dry over the coast?"

"Ah, roger that, Two. We're having a little trouble sorting
it out. Some of those contacts might be Turkish air force."

"Oh, yeah. Hell, I don't know what it is I'm seeing up
here. It looks to me like an attack run, though."

"Roger that."

What was happening? Dixie wondered. The nearest
contact was just one hundred miles ahead now, invisible to
the naked eye but clear enough on Mickey's display, despite
the jamming interference. Moments before, *Jefferson* had
alerted the BARCAP flight that a pair of EA-6B Prowlers
were on the way as well. The ECM gear on those babies
would be enough to burn through any jamming, as well as
provide electronic cover for the Tomcats. Four more Tomcats, BARCAP One, and the two aircraft covering the
Prowlers were on the way as well, but BARCAP Two would
be in position to get an ID on the unknowns long before
anybody else could reach the area.

Dixie's Tomcat was carrying a standard Barrier CAP
interception warload—four AIM-54C Phoenix missiles,
two AIM-9M Sidewinders, and a pair of AIM-120A AM-
RAAMs. The Sidewinders were strictly for close-in work,
of course, and the radar-guided AMRAAMs had a killing
range of about thirty miles. At one hundred miles, however,
the bogeys were comfortably within kill range of the
AIM-54s, which had the astonishing ability to reach out and
touch someone 120 nautical miles away.

But the Americans hadn't been attacked, yet—were not
even being threatened—and so no "weapons free" had been

granted by Ops. They would need a visual identification first.

Still, Dixie thought, something must have really stirred them up back at the bird farm, using aviator's slang for the carrier. BARCAP Two's patrol area had been seventy miles southwest of Sevastopol, and about fifty miles west of the *Jefferson*, positioned to spot and block any hostile aircraft approaching from the general direction of Ukraine and the northwest. BARCAP One, however, Batman and Libbie Bell, had been patrolling north of the *Jeff*'s position, just off the Crimean coast. Their primary mission of Barrier Combat Air Patrol included the secondary mission of covering Boychenko's helicopter when he flew from Yalta to the carrier. If Ops was pulling them out of position, something *really* hot must be on.

Something that was a direct threat to the *Jefferson*, her battle group, and her mission.

They would know in a few more minutes.

1006 hours (Zulu +3)
Black Leader
North of the Bosporus Strait

Ivanov brought his MiG higher and dropped his left wing, staring down at the destruction wrought by Black Flight's salvo of missiles. Perfect . . . perfect! Three-quarters of the center span was gone; he could see pieces of the deck strewn across the shipping channel like tumbled-down dominoes, and the northern main suspension cable had parted like a thread, spilling a forest of hanger cables and unraveling wire rope into the water. The southern halves of the two towers were still standing, and the suspension cable between them was still above water, but the northern halves were shattered, one fallen completely, the other half gone, like a jagged, broken tooth. The water between the towers was a seething cauldron of dirty foam, struggling antlike forms, ragged chunks of steel deck segments, and floating debris.

Smaller craft would continue navigating up and down the Bosporus no doubt, simply by avoiding the center channel, but larger, deeper-draft vessels—such as the monstrous three-hundred-meter-plus bulk of an American nuclear aircraft carrier—would be unable to pass without risking serious damage to screws, shafts, and keel.

"Tower, Tower, this is Black One," he called over the radio. "Come in!"

"Black One, Tower. Go ahead."

"*Seagull!* I say again, *Seagull!*"

The word was the title of one of Chekhov's more successful plays and was the code for the mission's success.

"We read you," Tower replied. "Proceed to *Uncle Vanya*."

And that code phrase, the title of another well-known Chekhov play, gave Black Flight and Flashlight permission to engage targets of opportunity.

"Affirmative, *Uncle Vanya*," he replied. He nudged the rudder pedals and felt the sudden pile-on of positive Gs as the MiG-27's nose swung toward the west. Pulling back on the stick, he sharpened the turn as he passed over land once more, bleeding off both velocity and altitude as he brought the aircraft around 180 degrees. He was traveling north once more, flying less than a hundred meters now above the gray-brown, building-dotted terrain.

"Black Leader, Bastion," a voice called. "We have red intercepts incoming, bearing zero-nine-five, range three-zero kilometers. Blue intercepts incoming, bearing zero-one-eight at one-five-zero kilometers."

"Black Flight reads you, Bastion. Take out red intercepts first. The blues can wait." The color codes referred to nationalities—the red of the Turkish flag, the blue of the American Navy.

"Black Leader, this is Flashlight. Secondary target is illuminated."

He checked his readouts, confirming target acquisition and lock on his second AS-14. Range ten kilometers . . .

"Firing missile!"

Again, the MiG-27 bucked skyward as though kicked from below and behind as the three-hundred-kilogram missile dropped from its launch rack. The engine ignited, sending the deadly package streaking toward the north.

"Target lock!" Piotr added. "Firing missile!"

1007 hours (Zulu +3)
U.S.S. *Falcon Patriot*
The Bosporus Strait

Captain Richard Calvin walked out onto the port-side flying bridge and leaned over the railing, craning his head for a long, searching look aft. He wasn't sure what those flyboy idiots were playing at, but someone had just flown a pair of high-performance jets over his command so fast and so low that his bridge windscreens had rattled, and he didn't care for *that* one bit.

Falcon Patriot was a brand-new member of the old Falcon Leader class, a tanker of 42,369 tons, with a length overall of 630 feet and a transport capacity of 225,100 barrels—very nearly ten million gallons. Despite her long-term charter through the Maritime Administration, she was a civilian vessel, owned by Falcon Sea and operated by Seahawk Management.

Normally, smaller oilers were used for Underway Replenishment of naval vessels at sea, but the unusual isolation of the *Jefferson* battle group inside the Black Sea had called for special measures, and the *Patriot* had been taken off her normal duties as a prepositioning shuttle tanker in the Med and assigned UNREP duties. She mounted two fueling stations abeam, one port, one starboard, allowing her to pass fuel to two ships at once.

Calvin didn't like jet jockeys. More than once, while the *Falcon Patriot* was attached to the Sixth Fleet in the Med, frisky Tomcat pilots had made low passes over his command, rattling windows and upsetting crockery in the galley. He had a reputation, he knew, among the various commanding officers and high-ranking brass clear up the ladder to Sixth Fleet HQ at Gaeta, Italy, for his loud and pointed complaints after each such incident.

Damn it, you *didn't* play games with ten million gallons of highly flammable petroleum products. If the pilot of one of those sea-skimming aircraft had been just a hair off, his plane and the *Falcon Patriot* would have gone up in a fireball that would be seen and heard clear back to Istanbul, and the burning oil might block the straits for days.

Brady, the ship's second mate, was already on the wing, looking aft through a pair of watchstander's binoculars.

"What the hell were those two playing at?" Calvin demanded.

"Damfino, Skipper," Brady replied without lowering the binoculars. "But if I didn't know any better, I'd say someone just stole themselves a bridge."

"Huh? What's that supposed to mean?"

"We heard that thunder aft a moment ago, right?"

"Yeah, just after those jets went over. Sounded like a sonic boom."

"Maybe." He sounded doubtful. "I been taking a look-see through these. I can't see the bridge back there."

Calvin could still hear thunder tolling in the distance, a kind of faint *thump-thump* that hung above the still waters of the Bosporus. Or was that the continuing roar of the jets in the distance? He glanced up. An unusual number of white contrails were scrawled across the blue sky this morning, aircraft at high altitude. Exercises of some sort, most likely.

He held out his hand for the binoculars. "Lemme see a minute."

This far north of the third Bosporus bridge there was little to see of the structure—a long, gray, spidery shadow on the horizon. Focusing the binoculars, he thought he could see one of the towers . . . but he couldn't be sure. There was a fog or ground haze moving in, and the area close to the water was obscured. It almost looked like smoke. . . .

He couldn't hear the thunder any longer.

"Did you get a look at those planes, Captain?" Brady asked. "They weren't ours."

"What do you mean, not ours?" Calvin had been buzzed by U.S. Navy jets often enough during fleet operations with them that he'd simply assumed that this was more of the same. He'd never paid much attention to the different classes of aircraft, though.

"They weren't ours," Brady insisted. "I used t'be in the Navy, remember. Navy planes are painted gray, dark on top, light underneath. These were kind of brownish. Couldn't see any Navy insignia, either. . . ."

"Maybe they were Turks," Calvin suggested. He lowered the binoculars, thoughtful.

"What the hell is that?"

Brady said the words in such a curious, unexcited manner that Calvin simply glanced toward where he was pointing. He could see something moving across the water, something small and dark and very, very fast—

He realized what it was just as it flashed past the port side of the *Falcon Patriot*'s bridge and slammed into the hull amidships. The explosion followed instantly, the detonation sending a rippling shudder through the tanker's deck. A ball of black and orange erupted from forward as Calvin and Brady both were pitched to the deck.

"*What the bloody hell*—" But Calvin's words were lost in the thunder of the blast, followed in an instant by a hurricane roar of furiously burning aviation gasoline. The missile had ruptured Three-port, loosing a torrent of JP-5 and igniting it.

A second missile—he *thought* it was a second missile, though in the thunder and boiling smoke he couldn't be sure of anything—struck forward. He could feel the ship lurch to starboard with the impact, could feel her bows drifting. . . .

Smoke was pouring aft across the bridge wing, so thick now he could scarcely see more than five feet. On hands and knees to avoid being pitched over the safety railing by further explosions, he crawled toward the bridge door, tumbling inside as Brady staggered in close behind him. The bridge watch, most of them, were on the deck; the helmsman was still at the wheel, clinging to it as if to life itself. The broad, slanted windscreen had shattered, the safety glass spilling across the bridge deck like millions of tiny glass spheres. Smoke made visibility worse, if anything, inside than out.

"Johnson!" he yelled at the helmsman. "Bring her to port! Full speed!"

The helmsman gaped at him, unseeing, uncomprehending. Heaving himself up off the deck, Calvin staggered to the wheel, shoved Johnson aside, and shoved the throttles forward. He could still feel the bite of the rudder as he spun the wheel left; tankers were ponderous beasts and slow to respond to the helm, but the *Falcon Patriot* had enough way on that she ought to be able to get clear of the shipping channel.

Calvin had several goals in mind, all urgent. The missile or missiles had struck the *Patriot*'s port side; by bringing the bow to port, he could slow the flooding somewhat and possibly keep the damaged hull sections from tearing themselves apart as they plowed ahead through the water. Too, the vessel was currently in the deepest part of the navigable channel; if she sank here, salvage would be difficult at best, and her hulk would block the channel for weeks, maybe months. If he could steer her to the shoal water to the west, however, he could ground her keel on hard bottom, keeping the channel clear and also making salvage and on-site repair efforts easier.

"Mr. Brady!"

"Yes, Captain!"

"Pass the word for all hands to abandon ship."

He could *feel* the pain in his ship, feel her wounds in the way she was shuddering and grinding with the turn to port. The *Falcon Patriot* was finished; she would break apart soon if she didn't burn to a cinder first. His instrumentation showed that automated fire control systems were engaged, but the flames from amidships were so hot, so violent, he knew that any firefighting efforts mounted by the automatic systems or by his twenty-man crew were doomed to failure. Better to get his people off now, while they could.

"Aye, aye, sir," Brady replied. He reached for the intercom mike.

"And Brady . . ."

"Sir?"

"Make sure you have a head count before you go over the side. I don't want anybody left behind to fry!"

"Yes, *sir!*"

Another missile struck, the impact smashing at the bottoms of his feet through the steel deck. Damn, what *was* this? Someone was deliberately slamming missile after missile into his vessel! All he could imagine was that a full-fledged war had just broken out, and the *Falcon Patriot* was squarely in its eye.

The fire forward was so thick he could not see where they were going. Heat was blasting back at the face of the bridge, turning the compartment into a furnace. He kept his eyes on the compass, however, bringing the ship around into a more and more westerly heading, praying that she stay afloat and responsive to the helm for just a few more precious moments. . . .

1008 hours (Zulu +3)
Air Ops
U.S.S. *Thomas Jefferson*

"It's confirmed, Commander," Lieutenant Crosby said as he hung up the telephone handset. "At least a dozen Russian aircraft just hit the northern Bosporus bridge and dumped it in the water. The *Falcon Patriot* was hit and is afire. Her skipper appears to be trying to put her aground near Sariyer, but her cargo is going up in flames."

Coyote felt a dawning horror . . . not just at the lost of the UNREP ship—though that was certainly a factor—but at what the attack meant. The *Falcon Patriot* had been carrying almost ten million gallons of fuel—three million gallons of aviation gasoline, and the rest diesel fuel for the nonnuclear elements of the carrier battle group.

Without avgas, *Jefferson*'s aircraft would not fly. Worse, while the *Jefferson*, the *Shiloh*, and the attack subs were all nuclear powered, the battle group's guided-missile destroyers and frigates were powered by gas turbines fired by diesel fuel. With their current stores, they could operate under normal routine for perhaps another ten days . . . but then the entire carrier battle group would virtually have to shut down completely. And if they found themselves in combat, making rapid surface maneuvers and flying aircraft off the roof round the clock, that ten-day leeway would be cut back to two to four days at the most.

And after that time, *Jefferson* and her escorts would be little more than large, expensive, and utterly useless toys, locked into the Black Sea by the closing of the Borporus Strait.

It was impossible to escape the obvious conclusion—that someone, Russians or Ukrainians, had just found an indirect but deadly means of rendering the CBG impotent.

"Deputy CAG?"

He turned. "What is it?"

Crosby was holding out a headset. "Sir, CAG's on the line. Something's going on ashore."

Coyote felt cold. Had the attack on the Bosporus bridge been timed to coincide with an attack against the UN party ashore?

He took the headset and slipped it down over his ears. "CAG? This is Coyote! What's happening?"

"Coyote!" Tombstone's voice sounded distant and static rough. "There's just been an attempt on Boychenko's life! The Ops duty officer just told me you pulled our air cover out! What the hell's going on?"

Oh, God, no. . . .

"Tombstone, we've got trouble, big-time. We picked up a flock of bogeys heading toward the Bosporus." Quickly, he told Tombstone about the reshuffling of the three CAP groups, explaining that BARCAP Three would be on station south of Yalta in another few minutes. "But things have already started going down," he concluded. "We've just had a report that unidentified aircraft dropped the northern Bosporus bridge across the channel, and fired on one of our UNREP ships."

"Sounds like someone doesn't want us leaving," Tombstone said. He sounded grim.

"That's the way it looks. We have BARCAP One and Two investigating, but it's going to be another few—"

"Coyote!" Crosby said. "BARCAP Two's engaging!"

He gestured toward a speaker mounted on the bulkhead, and Coyote became aware of the crackle of voices emerging from it. "*I'm closing, I'm closing with bandit India-three,*" Dixie's voice was calling. "*Range seven miles!*"

"Watch yourself," another voice, the voice of the air control officer aboard the Hawkeye, warned. "You have multiple bogeys swinging in on your six."

"*Okay! Okay, I see him!*" Dixie replied.

Damn. *Who* did he see, Coyote wondered? The guy he was chasing, or the "multiple bogeys" closing on his tail?

"*Badger!*" Dixie's voice called, suddenly anxious. "*Badger! Where are you?*"

"*Missile! Missile! Bandits have launched!*"

"We confirm bandit launch at one-zero-zero-niner and thirty seconds," one of Crosby's officers said. "Weapons free!"

"Gotta go, Tombstone," Coyote said into the headset's mike. "Looks like we have a situation developing here."

"Go take care of it. We won't be moving until we know we have air cover."

"We'll keep you posted. You keep your head down, Stoney, you hear me? The natives aren't as friendly as we thought."

"Roger that." He could hear Tombstone's grin on the other end of the radio link. "And you take care of my boys and girls! You've got the wing, Coyote."

"I copy. Dog House out."

"*I've got one on my tail!*" Dixie was calling from the bulkhead speaker.

"*Break left, Dixie!*" Badger replied. "*Break left! Fox two!*"

It sounded like Dixie and Badger had just flown smack into a full-fledged dogfight.

CHAPTER 19
Thursday, 5 November

The bandits had dropped out of nowhere, it seemed, coming in between Dixie and the now-distant *Jefferson*, their approach masked by jamming and the confusion of the moment.

"Break left, Dixie!" Badger yelled in his earphones. *"Break left!! Fox two!"*

The cry Fox two warned that Badger had just released a heat-seeking Sidewinder missile; his order to break left meant either that he was trying to set up a shot, with Dixie pulling the bad guy into position when he swung left, or that any other maneuver might expose Dixie's hot exhaust to the Sidewinder . . . and break its lock on the bandit with some rather serious consequences for Dixie.

Hauling back and to the left on his stick, he pushed the rudder over and dragged the Tomcat around in a hard turn to port. Sea and sky tilted on end, and both he and Mickey began grunting heavily, fighting against the rapid buildup of G-forces in their lower bodies. As his F-14 came around through nearly 180 degrees, he caught a glimpse of his pursuer, a black, winged speck a mile and a half behind him, reaching hard to match his turn.

"I see the missile!" Mickey yelled. "I see it! Coming in at seven o'clock! Pop flares!"

"I'm on it." Dixie hit the flare release, spilling a line of white-hot flares to confuse the incoming heat-seeker. A moment later, the missile streaked past, flashing beneath the Tomcat's belly and off to the right.

"Suckered him!" Dixie yelled.

"Who *are* these guys?" Mickey wondered, twisting in his seat to get a better look at the other aircraft.

"Don't know," Dixie said. He kept the stick hard over, maintaining a steady eight Gs of acceleration in the turn. "Where the hell is Badger?"

"There. Nine o'clock, coming in on the bandit's six."

"Thank God. . . ."

"Badger missed. That bandit's popping flares, too."

"Let's see if we can help." Leveling off at ten thousand feet, Dixie sent the Tomcat arrowing back toward the other aircraft.

The bandit was coming toward them, nose on. They only had a second in which to register each detail as it flashed past, but Dixie recognized the bandit as soon as he could make out its twin stabilizer configuration and the widely separated engine nacelles. Back in fighter school, he'd studied silhouettes, films, and photos of all possible aggressor aircraft, and he knew that one well.

MiG-29, "Fulcrum" in the NATO code list of hostile aircraft. A deadly aircraft, capable of Mach 2.23 at high altitude, of climbing fifty thousand feet in one minute, of outturning, outclimbing, and outmaneuvering nearly every combat aircraft in the Western arsenal.

Moments later, Badger's gray Tomcat approached, still trailing the bandit, wings folded back like those of a stooping eagle. Mickey had five more bandits on radar within twelve miles, closing fast, and plenty more within a thirty-mile radius. "Hey, Dixie!" he said. "We've got bandits all over the sky! I'm not sure I like these odds!"

"You wanna go to Phoenix, man?"

"Damn, I don't know." They had weapons free, but the big Phoenix missiles were long-range, stand-off weapons, designed to knock down attackers threatening the battle group. The strategic situation was still murky; just who was attacking whom here?

"Hey, Mickey! You get a good look at that red bird we passed?"

"Sure did, Dixie. MiG two-seven, no bout a-doubt it."

"Pass the word to 'em back at the farm, will you? I don't think they'll believe me."

"I think they'll believe this one, Dixie. Only question is, was it a Russki or a Uke?"

"I couldn't see a roundel or a star, could you?"

"Negative. He was going too fast."

Damn. It was frustrating to be in combat with someone . . . and to not even know who it was you were fighting! The assumption back aboard *Jefferson*—both in the briefings and in the bull sessions in the squadron ready room—had been that the likely aggressors today, if indeed anybody came out to play, would be Ukrainians bent on jumping the gun on the Russians before Boychenko turned the Crimea over to the UN.

The aggressor aircraft appeared to be forming up in a loose-knit cloud to the west now, moving in a more or less northerly direction. As Dixie studied the pattern on his Vertical Display Indicator, he had the impression that he was looking at essentially a *defensive* formation, that the attacks he and Badger had endured had been launched by hostile barrier forces to keep them from breaking through to the main body.

"BARCAP Two! BARCAP Two! This is Dog House!"

"Yeah! Go ahead, Dog House!"

"We're reading at least ten bogeys in your vicinity! Break off! Break off and RTB. Repeat, break off and RTB!"

"First sensible advice I've heard all day," Dixie said over the tactical channel. "It's gettin' too damned crowded out here!"

"Roger that!" Badger's voice came back.

A warbling tone sounded in his headset. Threat warning!

"Hey, Dixie!" Mickey called from the backseat. "They've got us painted!"

"I hear it." That particular warning chirp—and a red light winking on the threat display on his instrument panel—

indicated that a hostile aircraft had just established a radar lock on their Tomcat.

"Okay, Dixie," Badger called. "The bandits've got missiles inbound at three-zero-two . . . looks like AA-9s. You got 'em on your scope?"

"We have them," Mickey replied. "Range . . . two-five miles."

"Yeah, I think they just popped those things to scare us," Red Burns said from Badger's backseat.

"They're doing a hell of a job," Mickey said. "Let's didi out of here, man!"

"I'm with you, brother." Dixie brought the stick over again, swinging the Tomcat into a northeasterly course . . . back toward the *Jefferson*.

AA-9 Amos was the NATO designation for the Russian equivalent to the Navy's AIM-54 Phoenix, a large missile with a range of at least eighty miles and active radar homing.

"What's the range on the missiles, Mickey?"

"Nine miles." The RIO sounded tight, and totally focused on his rear-seat console display. "Let's go to burner."

"Zone five, now!"

The Tomcat's twin afterburners kicked Dixie hard in the back. The aircraft's computer swung the wings all the way back as they passed Mach 1.5. Moments later they slipped past Mach 2; the Tomcat's maximum speed at high altitude—say, at forty thousand feet—was Mach 2.34. At their current altitude of twelve thousand feet, the air was denser and sound traveled faster; Mach 2 was about the best that they could manage.

The AA-9 had a speed of about Mach 3.5, so there was no outrunning the thing in the short run. The long run was something else again, however. At Mach 3.5, the missile would cover nine miles in something like twelve seconds, but its speed relative to the Tomcat was only Mach 1.5—eleven hundred miles per hour, give or take a bit, at this altitude.

An old, old Navy saying from the days of sail held that a stern chase was a long chase. At a closing speed of eleven hundred miles per hour, the missile would eat up that nine miles in about thirty seconds . . . a small eternity when it came to combat in the air.

"You got an idea about who they're hunting?" Dixie asked. Likeliest, of course, was that one missile had been tossed at Tomcat 218, and another at 210.

"One's definitely got our name on it," Mickey said. "I think the other one's tracking Badger."

"Fun for everyone," Badger said. "Fun the whole family can enjoy!"

"Yeah, well, it's time to start partying," Mickey said. "Dixie! On my call, break right hard! I'll release the chaff!"

"Roger that." He tightened his grip on the stick, trying to ignore the unsettling prickling sensation at the back of his neck. There was a terrible temptation to turn in his seat and try to *see* the incoming missile, but Mickey had a much clearer and surer picture of what was going on showing on his rear-seat display.

Range was down to one mile. Three seconds . . .

"Popping chaff!" Mickey yelled. "Break right."

Chaff could be released both from the front seat and the back. Mickey was dumping clouds of aluminized mylar slivers to leave Dixie free to concentrate on the turn. Reacting at an almost instinctive level to Mickey's call, Dixie hauled the stick right and kicked in the rudder, diving with the turn in order to pick up a critical bit of extra speed.

The G-forces piled on, crushing Dixie down against the hard back and bottom of his seat. For just a moment, his vision narrowed slightly, the only warning he was likely to get of the blackout he would suffer if he didn't ease up a little. He held the turn as long as he could, willing the missile to miss them. By turning into the missile, he was using its greater speed to defeat it, since it could not turn at Mach 3.5 as sharply as he could turn at Mach 2. The chaff gave it a choice of radar-bright targets, enough to confuse its microchip brain and maybe give Dixie and Mickey an extra second or so to break out of the cone of its radar vision.

The explosion jolted Dixie as hard as kicking in the afterburners had, a solid thump from aft and left, accompa-

nied by a piercing note, like the ricochet on a TV Western.
For a moment, the controls went soft and he was afraid that
they'd gone dead . . . but then he felt them biting the air
again. He scanned his threat warning panel. No fires . . .
no flameouts . . . no electrical failures. Christ, what had
just happened?

"Mickey! You got any damage readouts?"

There was no answer from the backseat.

"Mickey! Yo! What's happening back there?"

He checked the small rearview mirror, then twisted in his
seat, trying to see aft, but the layout of the F-14 cockpit was
such that it was almost impossible for the front-seat man to see
his RIO, with his own ejection seat back and the RIO's
instrument panel between them. If Mickey was slumped down
or forward . . .

"Mickey!"

Still no answer. He turned again in his seat, this time
trying to check both wings and his stabilizers. Yeah . . .
they'd taken some shrapnel, all right. The trailing edge of
his left wing was showing some pretty bad damage; the
inboard high lift flap was shredded, and there was damage
both to the spoilers and the maneuver flaps as well. Three
thin, smoky white streams from beneath the center of his
wing were almost certainly avgas leaking from his port-
wing tank. He was conscious now of a shrill whistle, the
sound that all combat aviators recognize at once as air
escaping from their pressurized cockpit.

"Dixie, this is Badger! Do you copy?"

"Yeah." He blinked behind his helmet visor. Things had
happened so quickly that he was a little surprised to find that
statement true. "Yeah, Badger, I'm here. I think we got a
little shot up. And Mickey's not answering."

"Hang on. We'll be there in a sec."

"What about the other missile?"

"It's gone." Dixie could hear the relief in Badger's voice.
"We outran the sucker."

AA-9s packed enough solid fuel to give them a flight
time of about two minutes. If the target aircraft could stay

ahead of it until its fuel was exhausted, the missile would fall into the sea.

"What's the gouge? Where're the bad guys?"

"I think we're clear. Batman and Libbie'll be here in a few minutes. I've got you in sight now. Coming up on your five."

"The damage is on my port side," Dixie told him. "I think I'm losing fuel from the left wing."

"On your six and low. Coming around to port. Yeah, buddy. Looks like you took a near one. No blast damage, but your belly and left wing got peppered by shrapnel. So did your left stabilizer. Looks to me like it missed you, but the proximity fuse triggered the thing right under your wing."

Looking left, he could see Tomcat 210 coming up from behind, just off his wingtip.

"Can you see Mickey?"

"We see him," Red replied. "Head's slumped forward a bit. Can't tell from here how bad he's hit."

"Is his oxygen mask on?" Dixie was worried about the pressure loss in the cockpit.

"It's on." Red told him.

"How's she handling, Dix?" Badger added.

"Okay, I think." Cautiously, he played with his stick, testing the feedback. "I get a bit of flutter when I try giving it some left maneuver flap."

"Okay," Badger said. "Let's not try anything fancy. We'll escort you back, nice and easy. You can punch out when you're close to the *Jeff*."

"Not if Mickey's still out of it," Dixie said, determination giving his voice a hard edge.

"Right. Shit, I wasn't thinking. Okay, Dix. Let's come to zero-five-five, and maintain four hundred knots."

"Copy, Badge. Zero-five-five at four-zero-zero."

"Let's take 'er home."

1014 hours (Zulu +3)
The White Palace
Yalta

Tombstone was alighting from the CH-53 helicopter when he heard the thunder of approaching aircraft. At first, he thought it might be BARCAP Three, which Coyote had told him was coming, but then he realized that the sound seemed to be coming from the Crimean Mountains . . . from *north* of Yalta.

The sound might be an echo. Sound did strange things between sea and mountainside. But too many strange things were happening this afternoon for him to be willing to take chances. He waved at the helicopter's crew, gesturing for them to get out of their aircraft and take cover. After a moment's hesitation, they scrambled out, and together the men started running toward the White Palace.

The jets appeared with almost magical abruptness, howling in from the mountains, passing above the White Palace complex at an altitude of less than two hundred feet. The planes were so low that Tombstone could look up and see individual pilots, could see the sun-glint of canopies and dark visors, could see the numerals painted on their noses and the prominent red stars on stabilizers and wings.

MiG-29 Fulcrums. Some of the best fighter planes in Russia's inventory.

Dropping down a shallow embankment that might offer some cover if the MiGs started dropping nasty stuff, Tombstone stared after the jets. They were breaking formation now, far out over the sea. He glanced at his watch. BARCAP Three wouldn't be in their patrol position yet. He didn't think the MiGs were headed for the carrier. Where . . .

Yes. Two of them were swinging around in a full one-eighty, streaking back toward the White Palace. They came in low, wingtips almost touching; he saw the flicker of their rotary cannon, tucked away at the root of their port-side wings, before he heard the shrill whine of high-speed gunfire above the thunder of their strafing run.

An explosion sounded an instant later, a dull boom echoing from the improvised landing pad on the east side of the palace. The incoming jets lifted slightly, white vapor blossoming off their wings in the moist air as they increased their angles of attack . . . and then they were howling overhead, rising swiftly as they climbed the face of the mountains inland. A missile streaked into the sky after them, trailing smoke—a Grail or other shoulder-launched anti-air missile released by one of the soldiers on the ground—but it had been fired too late . . . or possibly without a firm heat source lock, and it twisted away after a few seconds of flight.

Rising from his hiding place, Tombstone jogged back toward the helicopter. As he'd feared, the Sea Stallion had been the target of that strafing run. It rested at a sharp angle now, with flames and black smoke licking from its port-side fuel tank sponson. If there'd been any doubt at all that those MiGs were hostiles, it was gone now.

There was still a lot of confusion on the palace grounds, with civilians and reporters milling about with aimless and seemingly random blunderings, and Russian soldiers standing in almost comic attitudes of readiness, obviously with no idea what was happening or what they were supposed to do. First the attack on Boychenko, and now this. The entire area was a scene of utter confusion.

Pushing through the crowds, Tombstone made his way toward the back of the White Palace. He could see Boychenko standing there at the top of the broad stone steps, surrounded by aides and guards, hands at his sides, looking up with an almost boyish expression of slack-jawed wonder as six MiGs roared overhead. Tombstone walked closer and several of the guards swung their weapons to aim at him.

Boychenko gestured sharply and snapped something in Russian. The guns were lowered.

"General!" Tombstone called. "Were those planes yours?"

The general looked at him and blinked. "*Nyet* . . . no," he said. "Not mine. Is navy."

"You didn't order that overflight by those MiGs?"

"No. Did not . . . order." His face creased with puzzlement. "They *attack*!"

"General, hostile aircraft have just attacked one of the bridges over the Bosporus and blown it up. Did you order that attack?"

Boychenko blinked helplessly at him a moment, and Tombstone wondered how much English the man could really understand. Then the general shook his head, a jerky side-to-side motion. Probably, Tombstone thought, he understood English better than he could speak it. "Did not order that! No!"

Boychenko gestured swiftly to Natalie Kardesh and spoke rapidly to her in Russian. She turned to Tombstone. "The general wants me to ask you . . . did you just say that his aircraft attacked the bridges over the Bosporus?"

"Tell him yes. We don't know yet if the aircraft were Russian or Ukrainian." He jerked a thumb skyward. "That overflight, though, was by aircraft with red stars. Russians. The general says they were navy?"

"MiG-29s with fleet," Boychenko said, nodding. He didn't look happy. "Admiral Dmitriev's command."

"Ask him," he told Natalie, "if it's possible that the Russian navy could have been behind that attempt on his life? Or Dmitriev?"

"Is possible," Boychenko said slowly, following the conversation.

One of Boychenko's aides, a major named Fedorev, nodded agreement. "I'm afraid that with Admiral Dmitriev, almost anything is possible. He is . . . ambitious."

Tombstone was beginning to fit the larger parts of the puzzle together, but he was still missing a lot of the pieces. This had the earmarks of an attempted coup. If this Admiral Dmitriev was trying to take over the Crimean Military District, it might make sense to combine an assassination attempt with an attack.

But why the Bosporus bridge? That made no sense at

all . . . unless they wanted the *Jefferson* and her consorts trapped in the Black Sea, and somehow that made even less sense than the attack itself.

He cocked his head. "Tell me. Is this Admiral Dmitriev . . . is his full name Nikolai Sergeivich?"

Fedorev nodded. "Yes, Captain. How did you know?"

"I flew with a Nikolai Sergeivich once. In joint operations in the Indian Ocean. I was wondering if it was the same man." The Nikolai Dmitriev he'd known had been a hard, resourceful, and skillful tactician. If he were now the enemy . . .

Tombstone didn't like that thought at all.

"The helicopter's totaled," Tombstone said. "We're not getting back to the carrier that way."

Fedorev wrinkled his brow. " 'Totaled?' "

"Wrecked. Finished. We have several hundred UN and American military personnel here, plus a bunch of civilian reporters from several countries. What are we going to do about them?"

Natalie consulted briefly with Boychenko, then nodded at Tombstone.

"The general says that when they know just what Dmitriev is up to, we will be informed. Until then, at least, and obviously, we are all the general's guests. We can stay here at the palace, or return to Yalta."

"Somehow," he said, "I don't think that's going to be good enough. If it was Dmitriev who tried to knock the general off here, he must know by now that he didn't succeed."

That, in fact, was the best explanation Tombstone could think of for the attack on the helicopter. Abdulhalik had said the would-be assassins were Tatars; had they killed Boychenko, the murder could have been blamed on Tatar nationalists. There would have been watchers, however, who would have reported by now that Boychenko was still alive. The air strike had probably been set as a backup plan, a way of keeping the general from escaping Yalta for the relative security of the *Thomas Jefferson*.

But that meant that hostiles were probably already on their way to finish the job the Tatars had botched.

"Tell the general," Tombstone said, "that we don't have much time. I'm going to round up the Americans and UN people. Tell him to get his army personnel assembled. I figure we have an hour, maybe less, before all hell breaks loose."

"Yes, sir."

"Sir," the aide, Fedorev, said, as Natalie spoke to the general. His use of the honorific was immediate and natural, unthinking. "Is there anything special you need?"

"Access to a radio," Tombstone replied. "I'd better talk this over with the *Jefferson*."

He was beginning to formulate an idea, but he couldn't develop it further until he knew what was happening at sea.

One thing he did know: The *Jefferson* battle group and the men and women aboard were in a war zone once again, and God help anyone who tried to get in their way!

CHAPTER 20
Thursday, 5 November

Dixie frowned. "Hey, Badge? I got another problem here."

"What is it, man?"

"My wings won't swing forward. Can't tell whether it's the computer or the wing hardware, but they won't budge."

The F-14 Tomcat's variable geometry wings were designed to fold back at higher speeds to increase maneuverability and decrease drag, and swing forward at low speeds to provide additional lift for takeoffs and landings. Normally, the aircraft's central air data computer, or CADC, began swinging the wings forward when the plane's speed dropped below three hundred knots. They were at 275 knots now as they circled in the Marshall stack, but Dixie's wings stubbornly remained folded in the full-back position.

"Try the override."

"I did. No go."

"Shit. How do you feel about a negative-turkey landing?"

Dixie chuckled nervously. "I think I can handle that."

Some Tomcat pilots overrode their computers during the final approach to the carrier, subscribing to the popular and loudly voiced belief that a Tomcat with its wings extended forward looked like a big, ugly, long-necked bird—"turkey mode," as they called it. A Tomcat could land with its wings folded back but had to maintain a landing speed of 145

242

knots on the approach and touchdown instead of the 115 knots of a wings-out landing.

"Two-one-eight" called over his headset. "Deck clear. Charlie now."

That was the signal for him to break from the Marshall stack formation and start his approach for the trap. They'd kept him in the racetrack-shaped loiter course for nearly twenty minutes while they brought other aircraft down; now it was just him, Badger, and Batman still up, with the other two Tomcats staying aloft both to provide security for the ship and to help talk him down if necessary.

God, he wanted to be down. His Tomcat had begun shuddering ominously during the long flight back, the vibration growing worse and worse as he descended to five thousand feet and becoming especially pronounced when he worked the flight controls, opening the flaps or spoilers. Normally, his CADC handled all such minor flight adjustments from moment to moment, as well as controlling his wing geometry, but he was having to make all corrections by hand now. According to his instrument readouts, his CADC was still operational, but its commands weren't reaching his wings . . . and each manual input seemed to increase the vibration from his left control surfaces. Sweat was pooling inside his oxygen mask now; he could taste it, feel its slickness between skin and rubber. His hands were sweating, too, inside his gloves, and he resisted the temptation to pull them off and wipe his palms on his flight suit.

His entire career in the Navy, it seemed, had focused his life to this moment when everything was riding on his skill and training. He'd always told himself that because he was black he had to be better than anyone else he was flying with, sharper, more skillful, more aggressive. The problem was that a lot of his bravado had been empty. Oh, sure, he'd known he was good, but in a superficial way that had been challenged, and seriously shaken, by the helicopter incident.

This was where everything he'd learned was laid out for all to see—bringing a crippled aircraft down onto a carrier deck at sea.

Turning to port, he came in astern of the carrier, following her wake, cutting his speed further now to 230 knots. "Two-one-eight, call the ball," he heard over the radio. That was the voice of the Landing Signals Officer, the LSO, standing on his platform on the carrier's port side aft, just left of the spot where Dixie wanted to set his damaged bird down. He could see the "meatball" now, the green bull's-eye of the Fresnell landing system tower that revealed, by appearing to move above or below a pair of horizontal dashes, whether he was staying in the correct glide path or not. To the right, aft of the carrier's island, the laser landing system beacon showed a dazzling green, giving him his choice of input. So far he was right on the money.

"Tomcat two-one-eight, ball," he called back, identifying his aircraft and alerting the LSO that he did have the ball in sight. "Point five." That last told them he had only five hundred pounds of fuel aboard. Prior to leaving the Marshall stack, he'd jettisoned much of his remaining fuel, as well as the missiles slung from his belly and wings. A lighter aircraft was easier to wrestle down, and if he did slam into the deck too hard, it would be easier on the *Jefferson*'s flight deck if he wasn't packing almost a full warload and tanks filled with JP-5.

The carrier was riding calm seas half a mile ahead, looking terribly tiny and isolated now against a very great deal of blue.

"Roger ball," the LSO replied. "Just bring it in nice and easy, Dixie. Everybody's turned out for the show down here, so let's show them what a real hotshot aviator can do, huh?"

LSOs, Dixie had learned soon after becoming an aviator, possessed an uncanny knack for instant psychoanalysis and treatment. The best ones didn't say very much at all, but what they did say was exactly right to correct a problem, or calm shattered nerves, or snap a pilot's mind back instantly to where it belonged. The duty LSO had just reminded Dixie that he had a bunch of people down there pulling for him . . . something he'd lost touch with over the past few days.

It was a good feeling. A *warm* feeling.

"What's the met rep?" he asked.

"Sea state calm, wind easterly at five knots," the LSO replied. "Carrier's at fifteen knots. Easy trap."

"Right. Keep your heads down, everybody."

"Deck going down. Power down . . . just a hair."

He eased back on the throttle and gave it a bit more flaps. Speed one-sixty . . . he was coming in too fast! He dropped the throttle another notch. . . .

"Don't overcorrect. Power steady."

The deck was rushing up at him now, much faster than he'd ever remembered in making an approach before. Then the carrier's roundoff vanished beneath the Tomcat's nose and he saw his own shadow flashing along the dark steel deck ahead of him.

His wheels struck the deck, a savage clang and jolt. His hand slammed the throttle full forward and his engines thundered with renewed life and power, ready to take him off the deck again in a touch-and-go bolter if his tail hook failed to connect.

But at the same moment as his engines howled to full power, he felt his tail hook snag one of the cables stretched taut across the deck, and his body surged forward hard against his harness. He cut his power back to a grumbling idle as a deck director and a gang of Green Shirts ran toward his aircraft. To the side, he saw other people running toward his aircraft, including the brightly clad fire detail and a number of rescue personnel and duty hospital corpsmen. The yellow-painted mobile crane stood ready close by, but there were so many people on the deck that it would have been difficult for it to get through. That sort of display was against regs, but nobody seemed to care this morning.

Easing back, he spit out the wire, then followed the deck director toward a waiting slot aft of the island. He cracked his canopy as a plane crew chief popped his access steps. He reached up, yanked off his mask and helmet, and gulped down cool, delicious air.

It had never tasted so good.

"Nicely done, sir," the plane chief said as he leaned in and safed the ejection seats. "Welcome home!"

"Give me a hand with Mickey," he said.

"That's okay, sir," a hospital corpsman said, scrambling up alongside the chief. "We've got him. You just take care of yourself. Are you all right?"

"Yeah. Yeah, I think so." His knees felt weak, his legs shaky. Helping hands unfastened his harness and helped him out of the cockpit.

"Well done," someone called as he set foot on the deck.

Someone else clapped him on the shoulder. "Good job, Dixie, bringing old Mickey Moss back!"

"How is he?"

"Can't tell yet, sir," a corpsman said. "He's alive. Can't find any bleeding. Side of his helmet's dinged. I think a piece of shrapnel must have whacked him." Several rescue people worked together to ease a board down behind Mickey's back and strap him to it. With his head and neck immobilized, they began lifting him out of the cockpit and into a Stokes stretcher.

"Dixie!"

He turned and found himself face to face with Cat Garrity. She threw her arms around his neck and kissed him, quick and hard. People standing nearby cheered or clapped or laughed.

"That was some damned good flying," she told him.

He grinned at her. "Does this mean I'm off the shit list?"

"Dixie, my man, I'll fly with you anytime, anywhere!"

He felt like he was *home*.

1235 hours (Zulu -5)
Yalta
Crimea Military District

Gunfire crackled in the distance—the expected attack by Dmitriev's naval forces. For Tombstone, it was a particularly helpless feeling, to be trapped at the palace with a group of nearly thirty American service personnel, with a pitched battle being fought nearby and nothing that he could *do* to help himself or the others.

His first consideration, certainly, was the treatment of the men wounded in the assassination attempt. There were four dead—Captain Whitehead, Special Envoy Sandoval, and two civilians. Wounded, besides Admiral Tarrant, were a Lieutenant Billingsly from OC, one Marine private named Garibaldi, five civilians, and Jorge Luis Vargas y Vargas, Sandoval's personal aide.

Ambulances had shown up within twenty minutes of the shootings, and doctors and medical assistants had provided first aid, but Tombstone had not authorized the release of any of the wounded Navy personnel to the local civilian medical authorities, and the senior UN people had requested that Vargas be taken to a Navy ship as well. The Russians had not been insulted; in fact, they'd been relieved, for facilities at the Yalta hospital, between casualties from the Russian Civil War and the ongoing critical shortage of medical supplies, were already strained to the limit.

The shortcomings in the Russian medical service were legendary, of course. Earlier, a Russian doctor, a woman named Vaselenova, had complained about it to Tombstone as she'd prepared an IV saline drip for the wounded Admiral Tarrant. He'd watched in horror as she'd stropped the tip of a disposable syringe needle on a whetstone, then dropped it into a pot of boiling water. *"Da, da,"* she'd said a few minutes later, using a spoon to fish the needle out of the water. "There is never enough of what we need. Plasma. Penicillin. Clean sheets at hospital. Beds. Scalpels. Needles. *Especially* needles. There are never enough."

So the medics had treated his wounded as well as they could, but left them in one of the sitting rooms in the palace, which had been transformed into a makeshift temporary hospital. If they could just establish communications again with the CBG . . . if they could arrange at least for helicopters to fly in and carry off the wounded, they could receive decent treatment aboard ship. The *Saipan*, especially, the MEU's Tarawa-class LHA, had a three-hundred-bed hospital aboard, with some of the finest military medical facilities afloat.

If they could just reach her . . .

That, he decided, was a large part of the feeling of helplessness he'd been enduring over the past several hours. It had him pacing restlessly back and forth at the top of the steps to the palace, with occasional stops to stare out across the blue of the sea at the southern horizon . . . and the battle group invisible beyond it.

Pamela had been able to read what he was feeling, even if he hadn't put those feelings into words. "You know," she told him, "that there are some things even the Navy can't fix."

He wished she would lay off the Navy. For some reason, the pride he felt for the Navy, *justifiable* pride, had always seemed to grate on her. He guessed that was one of the incompatibilities she'd talked about at the restaurant. He'd known they had differences, but he was willing to try to work them out.

It still galled him that Pamela didn't exhibit the same willingness.

There'd been little enough time to worry about that since the attack, however. In the two and a half hours since the assassination attempt, Tombstone had managed to round up all of the Americans in the party and get them into one place—a difficult operation in itself, given the confusion that seemed to be gripping everyone in the White Palace complex. He'd put Chief Geiger in charge of all personnel, including the officers, by declaring him to be "chief of the boat" and delegating to him the responsibility of keeping everyone together and out of the Russians' way.

Chiefs did not outrank officers in the command hierarchy, but Tombstone had found long ago that they often outranked them in sense. Almost immediately after making the assignment, he'd overheard a brief exchange between Geiger and Commander Sedgwick, who wanted to go up the beach with a party of Marines to find a place where Navy boats could come ashore and take them all off. Geiger had said, simply, "The captain wouldn't *like* that, sir," in his characteristic deep-throated rumble, and that had been the end of it.

Kardesh he kept with him as his personal translator, while Tomboy Flynn became his aide. Tomboy made herself invaluable by taking on the duties to which he had originally been assigned—serving as his liaison with the nearly one hundred press and TV news representatives who had become his personal responsibility.

Both women carried out their assigned tasks with quiet efficiency. Kardesh spoke excellent Russian—her mother, she told him, was Russian—while Joyce proved to be a born public relations expert, fielding questions and handling complaints with a light, personal touch that Tombstone knew he never could have managed . . . even if he'd had the time.

And he'd been working with Pamela a lot during the past few hours, too, trying to set up a radio connection with the battle group. The available Russian equipment, it turned out, didn't have the range to reach American aircraft which were, in any case, below the horizon, and they didn't have the codes—for reasons that were fairly obvious—that would allow them to tap into U.S. military communications satellites.

American Cable News, however, had equipment that was better in some respects than that of the American military. They'd originally flown into Simferopol Airport with a vanload of sophisticated electronics, including a satellite uplink that gave immediate and secure communications with ACN headquarters in Washington, D.C. It had been a fairly simple task, then, to organize a patch to HQ-NAVTEL, the Naval Telecommunications Command headquarters in Washington, which in turn routed the communications channel through a MILSTAR communications satellite relay to the U.S.S. *Thomas Jefferson*.

It was a roundabout method of talking to the CBG's bosses Stateside. Tombstone was reminded of the story of Marines during the invasion of Grenada in 1983 who'd lost radio communications with the rest of their unit a few miles away and had used a credit card to place a telephone call to Camp Lejeune, South Carolina, which in turn relayed their fire-support request to the appropriate units in the field. The tale was possibly apocryphal but had enough of the ring of truth about it to make him suspect that it was at least based on a true story.

The faster they could get Tarrant and the others mede-vacked back to the *Saipan*, the better. They'd been able to stop the bleeding and to give him saline—what medical personnel would refer to as a BVE, or blood-volume expander—to help make up for the lost blood, but he needed more blood, and even if they'd had access to Russian blood supplies, Tombstone knew he'd be happier trusting Tarrant's life, through cross-matches and donor blood, to Navy doctors and corpsmen who weren't forced by necessity to recycle their disposable equipment.

"How is your admiral?" Pamela asked him, as they waited for the communications patch to go through.

"Stable. We need to get him to some decent medical facilities, though."

"There's a pretty good hospital here in Yalta, I hear."

Tombstone made a face. "If we have to. But they're crowded. Besides, 'pretty good' in Russia, with all of the shortages and problems they have here, isn't even in the same league with Navy medicine."

She sighed. "Matt, you have such complete and un-bounded confidence in the Navy."

He shrugged. "I suppose I do. It's a confidence based on . . . what? fifteen, eighteen years of experience?" He nodded toward a small group of naval personnel, including Joyce and Natalie Kardesh. Sykes was there, and Lieutenant j.g. Vanyek, looking vulnerable and scared. They were sitting on the grass talking together. "They're good people," he said. "Whatever you think of the organization as a whole, it's composed of good people who know their jobs and do them."

"Why?"

"What do you mean, 'why'?"

It was her turn to shrug. "Matt, you must know they're abandoning you here."

"I don't know any such thing."

"Come on. Step out from behind the uniform and take a whiff of the real world. Do you seriously think they're going to risk a three-and-some-odd-billion-dollar nuclear aircraft carrier to rescue thirty-some men and women? At a risk of a hundred million per sailor? I don't think so. You and I both know how Washington works. They're not going to lift a finger to get you out unless they can make political capital on it, and I can tell you from personal observation that the tone back in the States right now is for us to stay the hell out of the Russian war."

"The public usually supports military personnel in the field," Tombstone said stubbornly. "They wouldn't like it if Washington left us stuck out here."

"Really?" She cocked her head. "Remember a little picnic in a place called Vietnam? They—the people who put you here, I mean—they don't care. And as for John Q. Public, well, I think Norway and that battle up in northern Russia frightened a lot of people, let them see how terrible, how destructive and deadly modern warfare really is."

"Mr. Magruder?"

Tombstone turned to face one of Pamela's ACN technicians. "Yeah, Ted?"

"We have your line. A guy named, uh, Coyote is waiting to talk to you."

"All right! Thanks!"

He nearly sprinted to the mobile communications van, which was now ringed by determined-looking U.S. Marines. When he took a headset from another ACN tech and held it to his ear, he could hear a faint hiss of static, but the line was unusually clear. "It's encrypted, sir," a Navy radioman sitting at the console said. "You can talk in the clear."

"Thanks." He pressed the transmit key on his mike. "Coyote, Coyote, this is Tombstone. Do you copy?"

"Loud and clear, Stoney," Coyote's voice came back. "I gather you guys had to go around Robin Hood's barn to get this comm hook up."

"That's affirmative, and I don't know how often we'll be able to do it, or for how long. Direct, tight-beam satellite feeds are hard to trace or jam, but there are some ugly customers hereabouts who might like to try."

"Roger that."

"Any ideas about getting us out of here?"

"We're working on it, Stoney. Air superiority is a problem right now."

"Understood."

"So is Washington. We've not had any clear direction as to what we're supposed to do. I can tell you right now that if it was up to the people here on the *Jeff*, they'd declare war on Russia right this minute, for knocking out the bridge, stranding you guys, taking a shot at one of our planes, wounding the admiral . . . and probably for conduct unbecoming, as well. But the five-sided squirrel cage is being slow just now."

"What's happening with the chain of command?"

"Okay. Captain Brandt, as Tarrant's flag captain, just got a brevet promotion to admiral. Confirmed through Naples about fifteen minutes ago. He's taking over the entire battle group, but he'll be under the command of Admiral Collins, who's senior."

"Right." Rear Admiral Frederick Collins was the commanding officer of MEU-25, together with Marine Colonel Winston Howell, who commanded the MEU's ground troops. From what he'd heard, Howell was a firebrand who'd won the Congressional Medal of Honor in Vietnam, while Collins was a more cautious, conservative type.

"Commander Hadley's got the ship, though he's pretty junior, too. I've been confirmed as CAG. Sorry, Stoney, but you're out of a job. At least until we work out a way to get you guys out of there."

"No problem, Coyote. I think I'll have my hands full here."

"Right. We're on full alert, of course, and flying full coverage patrols. Lots of intercepts, too. The Russkis are testing us . . . or maybe trying to use up our JP-5. We'll keep flying as long as we can, though."

"We're going to need to work on getting the shore party back to the ship," Tombstone told him. "The admiral needs medical help, better medical help than they can give him here, and we have some other wounded as well. We also have a large number of civilians. They might be allowed to leave from the Simferopol Airport, but I'm not holding my breath."

"I wouldn't, Stoney. Last we heard here, monitoring Russian radio, the military was shutting down all commercial flights, 'for the duration of the present emergency.'"

"Did they say what the emergency was?"

"No. They're managing to say it's Ukrainians and foreign mercenaries both, without releasing anything definite. Oh, and Boychenko has been branded a traitor. Our old friend Dmitriev is in charge of the Black Sea Fleet, and he's declared himself the legitimate military governor. No response yet from Krasilnikov's people. At least, none we've heard."

"Okay. I think we're going to have to assume that we're stuck here for a while, though I want you to keep working on a way of getting the wounded off. Maybe at night, by submarine."

"We'll look into it."

The crump and rumble of heavy gunfire—field artillery, possibly—sounded closer and louder, lending a new sense of urgency to the conversation.

"Okay, Coyote. I don't have much time. The way I see it, either Washington comes to our rescue, or we're going to be left on our own out here while they argue about it."

"Is this a multiple-choice test? How many guesses do I get?"

"We have to start planning for what happens if they hang us out to dry."

"Agreed."

"Okay, here are some possibilities. . . ."

Together, they began discussing options.

1630 hours (Zulu –5)
Flag Plot
U.S.S. *Thomas Jefferson*

"Attention on deck!"

Coyote and the other staff officers standing around the large chart table snapped to attention at the call of the sailor standing guard outside the compartment door. Captain—no, Coyote reminded himself—*Admiral* Brandt walked in, followed by several of his staff aides, looking grim.

The assembly had been called earlier that afternoon and included not only *Jefferson*'s department heads, but the skippers and senior staff of several of the other ships in the squadron, including those of MEU-25. Steve Marusko was there, as skipper of the *Guadalcanal*, as was Colonel Winston Howell, the commanding officer of MEU-25's Marine detachment. Admiral Collins was conspicuous by his absence. He was still aboard his flag, the *Guadalcanal*, and had delegated his interest in the planning session to Howell. In a way, Coyote thought, that was good. They could brainstorm some rather wild possibilities here, without being immediately overruled by the conservative MEU commander.

"At ease, gentlemen," Brandt said. Walking to his accustomed place at one side of the chart table, instead of Admiral Tarrant's usual spot at the head, he nodded to the others in the room. "Okay, people. We've had to endure a lot of sudden changes, and chances are this is just the beginning. I'd like to tell all of you, before we set out, that I have no idea how I'm to fill Admiral Tarrant's shoes. I'm not half the man he was, not half the strategist, and I'm feeling a bit out of my depth. I'm counting on each and every one of you here to see me through this thing, to help keep me from making an ass of myself and putting this battle group in jeopardy."

He paused a moment, looking from face to face. "Okay. We're here, as you all know by now, to discuss our options.

I don't need to tell any of you, I'm sure, that our situation as of this morning is not very promising. Some of us have been working on the various alternatives that have presented themselves, however.

"Let's hear from you first, CAG."

Coyote hesitated. It was the first time anyone had referred to him officially by that unfamiliar title, and he still wasn't very comfortable with it.

Of course, he thought, Jeremy Brandt must be having the same problem with his new role as admiral and CO of the whole battle group.

"Our major problem," he told the others, "isn't tactical. We're more or less hamstrung until we get definitive orders from Washington, and it could be a day or so before that happens. In the meantime, all we can really do is button up and maintain our own operational security.

"We are, however, maintaining full CAP coverage, and we're continuing to fly ASW patrols. We are also beginning to make plans for some sort of operation aimed at getting CAG—Captain Magruder, I mean—and the rest of the Americans ashore out of hostile territory." He smiled. "We've code-named it Operation Ranger, after John Paul Jones's ship."

"I thought that was the *Bonhomme Richard*," Commander Barnes, the Air Boss, said.

"Just for his big I've-not-yet-begun-to-fight engagement," Coyote said. "Before that, his ship was the *Ranger*."

He pointed to the large chart, which showed the Crimean coastline. *Jefferson* and the other ships of the CVBG, along with the vessels of MEU-25, were all plotted, along with the current CAP tracks and ASW patrols. A number of points had been marked in red, extending in a ragged arc along the battle group's perimeter.

"Our principal tactical problem is the Russian overflights, of course," Coyote continued. "Their attempted overflights. In the past five hours, our aviators have carried out seven interceptions of various Russian naval aircraft, ranging from MiG-29s to a Badger-G attack plane."

During the bad old days of the Cold War, encounters between Russian reconnaissance aircraft probing both the material and psychological readiness of the American carrier defenses had been common. Most aviators had treated it as a kind of a game, a way to show off to the Russians and even pick up a souvenir or two. There'd been plenty of cases of trades arranged by sign language or radio between bomber and Tomcat crews—a Russian fur cap for a copy of *Playboy*, for instance. For the most part, though, the Russian bomber pilots had tested the American defenses, noting how soon they were intercepted by the Tomcats and how far they could press the Tomcats before being forced to change course. There'd been several accidents during the closest of those encounters, but no cases of missiles or gunfire exchanged.

The situation was far more uncertain here, with the Americans completely in the dark about Russian intentions. Any of those approaching aircraft could be loaded with ship-killers intended for an all-out assault on the *Jefferson*. Each had to be met and, if possible, turned aside.

"We've met each Russian approach and turned it aside without incident, but it's forcing us to use our aircraft fuel reserves at a rather alarming rate. We've been putting aircraft off our flight deck nonstop now for, let's see . . ." He checked his watch. "For two hours, now. It seems likely, to Ops, at least, that the Russians are deliberately forcing us to expend our fuel reserves. They blocked the straits in the first place. They know we're not getting any more fuel. Now they're trying to get us to expend what we have."

"Setting us up for an attack, CAG?" General Howe asked.

"Maybe. Or maybe just to leave us helpless. Without air, of course, we're just so much gray-painted metal."

"What about our UN assignment for keeping the peace?" Marusko wanted to know.

"That'll be up to Washington, Steve," Admiral Brandt replied. "The transfer of control to the UN didn't legally take place this morning. Washington might want to take that as an excuse to back out now. On the other hand, we could get a directive anytime telling us to start bombing Sevastopol until the bastards yell uncle.

"In any case, our first priority, after the security of the battle group and MEU, of course, is to get our people off the beach." Brandt looked at Coyote. "You said you've been discussing this with CA—with Tombstone."

"Yes, sir. We've discussed several possibilities. One urgent note. We need to get the wounded out, including Admiral Tarrant. Stoney was wondering about subs, or a quick helicopter in-and-out."

"I don't want to send our subs that close inshore. Not in Ivan's backyard." Brandt looked at Marusko. "How about it, Captain? Can you get them off with your helos?"

"If Coyote's people could give us air superiority, both over the beach at Yalta and in a secure corridor all the way back to the battle group, certainly. A piece of cake. If not, well . . ." He shrugged. "We all know what happens when helicopters tangle with interceptors."

The attempted joke fell flat in the room, eliciting no more than a forced chuckle or two.

Brandt looked at Coyote. "How about it, CAG? Can you deliver on that air superiority?"

"Well, sir, we're not going to manage it without a fight. While they've been probing our defenses, we've been probing theirs, seeing how close we could get to the beach. Every time we get within, oh, forty, fifty miles of the coast, though, we find ourselves facing MiGs. Lots of them. It's kind of a standoff right now, you see. If they try to force our defenses, we open fire and we're in a shooting war. Same for us, if we try to force our way through to the beach. And until we get clear orders from Washington . . ."

Brandt nodded. "I think we're all aware of that particular handicap. I had quite a long session with Admiral Scott this afternoon. He tells me there's a special briefing of the President's advisory staff scheduled for this morning, Washington time, and they'll be going over their alternatives. But he also told me that the atmosphere back there is a bit panicky. No one in the administration wants to get into a

fight with the Russians. At least, no one wants the responsibility of being the one who gives the order. We may be on
our own out here for quite a while."

Brandt paused for a moment, as though gauging the
feelings and attitudes of each of the men standing around
the Flag Plot table.

"I do not happen to believe, however, that we should be
sitting around on our hands just because Washington is. I
want each department represented here to begin working up
a list of working options, based on the possibility—no,
belay that, the *probability*—that we're going to have to
fight to get ourselves out of this damned mess . . . and to
evacuate our people ashore."

"Getting out of this," Commander Jeffries, the senior Air
Ops officer, said thoughtfully, "could require something
other than fighting Russians."

"Who'd you have in mind, Bill?" someone asked, and the
others laughed nervously.

"The Turks, actually, since they're the ones who aren't
letting us into their waters or airspace. Has anybody
considered the possibility of putting the MEU-25 Marines
ashore at the mouth of the Bosporus?"

"Write it up," Brandt told him. "All of you, I want a major
brainstorming session out of each man here. Let's see
exactly what our options are."

"I vote we dig a canal through Turkey," Lieutenant
Commander Arthur Lee, the head of the CAG Department
intelligence team, said.

"Nah," Barnes said, arms folded, shaking his head. He
nodded toward the chart. "Dig it through the southeast
corner of Bulgaria and that little bit of northeastern Greece.
Shorter distance. We're out sooner."

The others laughed, and some contributed their own
outrageous suggestions, including sinking the entire Crimea
to remove that peninsula as a source of conflict. *They're not
licked yet*, Coyote thought with a flash of pride. *Not if they
can still joke about it.*

They were going to need a sense of humor to sustain them
for these next few days. Nothing, not defeat, not fear, not the

threat of an enemy attack, sapped a unit's morale like being left hanging in the breeze by one's own superiors in the chain of command.

What the hell are they thinking about in Washington? he wondered.

CHAPTER 21
Friday, 6 November

In silence, the men and women at the table watched the screen, where the hard, drawn-looking face of Vice-Admiral Dmitriev was looking back. He was sitting in a somewhat shabby-looking office, his hands carefully folded on the desk in front of him. He was speaking English—very good English, with only a trace of an accent—and he was speaking deliberately and with evident precision.

"Accordingly," he was saying, "I am assuming command of the Crimean Military District. General Boychenko has been declared an enemy of the state and will be arrested as a traitor as soon as he can be found.

"American forces in the Black Sea area of operations, specifically the aircraft carrier *Thomas Jefferson* and the battle group with it, have been neutralized. This was necessary because they had already established contact with the traitor Boychenko and were intervening in Russian internal and security affairs."

Admiral Thomas Magruder listened to the tape, like the others, with no outward show of emotions, but he felt a sharp pang of worry. His nephew, the last he'd heard, had gone ashore with a party of Navy and UN personnel to prepare the way for Admiral Tarrant to receive the surrender of the Crimea and, as far as he knew, they were still ashore, trapped by Dmitriev's coup.

Within twenty-four hours of the attack on the Bosporus bridge, this tape had been delivered to the White House by the Russian embassy in Washington. The President had seen it. His advisory group was reviewing it, looking for answers to seemingly unanswerable questions.

"We wish to stress that we have not intentionally fired upon American ships," Dmitriev's image continued. "The tanker sunk during the attack on the Bosporus bridge was attacked by accident . . . much as happened to the American helicopter in Georgia a few days ago. We apologize for that incident. We have also just recently learned that one of your helicopters was destroyed on the ground near Yalta. Again, that was a case of mistaken identity. We regret these attacks and stress that they were accidents, the products of the well-known fog of water.

"At the same time, however, we must stress our resolve. These are dangerous times for our government, for the safety of our people, our land. We cannot allow foreign powers to hinder our great purpose or to intervene in our internal affairs."

"Watch it," Herb Waring said, speaking quickly as the figure on the screen paused to draw breath. "Here it comes."

"But we do . . . have a proposition for you," Dmitriev continued. "One that we hope you will be inclined to accept, Mr. President, as a means for both of us to resolve this unfortunate and unnecessary confrontation in which we find ourselves. Boychenko's mistake, his *treason*, was in handing over sovereign Russian territory to foreigners, hoping that they would guarantee the Crimea's security. This, you must understand, is no different a situation than if one of your generals turned, say, Florida over to Russian forces for safekeeping.

"But we can work together. We *should* work together, in the interests of world peace. In fact, we would welcome your help fighting against the Ukrainian invasion when it comes. There is an excellent possibility, Mr. President, that simply the presence of your carrier battle group in our waters, coupled with your declaration to stand by the rightful, popularly elected government of the Crimea, will be enough to discourage Ukrainian aggression.

"I would also remind you of the Ukrainian genocide already committed against Russian citizens in eastern Ukraine. If they are allowed to invade the Crimea, I can only expect that—"

"Shut that thing off," Samantha Reed said. This was the third time they'd played the tape through, and by now they were beginning to know large parts of it by heart.

"The rest of it's flag-waving and grandstanding," Secretary of State Heideman said. "With a fair amount of heart-thumping thrown in gratis."

"The guy's insane," Waring said, shaking his head. "The President would never go for something like this."

"I don't know," Reed said thoughtfully. "We should at least consider the offer. Discuss it. It may be the only viable option we have."

"*Excuse* me," Admiral Scott said sharply, "but did I just hear that tin-plated neo-Communist dictator try to extort American military help? Those bastards just hijacked an entire carrier battle group *and* a Marine Expeditionary Unit and are holding them and something like thirty thousand of our men and women hostage! We do not make deals with terrorists!"

"Of course we do, Admiral," Reed said testily. "We do it all the time. We just cloak the reality behind negotiations and settlements and new breakthroughs in the peace process."

"Good God, Madam Secretary—"

"Now hear me out!" Reed insisted. "This may not be the disaster the rest of you are making it out to be."

"What?" Scott said. "Is this a new way you have of cutting back the Defense Department? Give our carriers to the Russians?"

"Admiral, I will remind you that you work for me! If you can't accept that, if you can't live with my standards, then you are welcome to tender your resignation."

"No, ma'am," Scott replied, his jaw stubbornly set. "You're going to have to fire me, because right now it looks to me like I'm the only one looking out for the interests of our people over there."

"Our people should be safe enough, Admiral," Waring said. "Dmitriev's not crazy enough to launch an attack on a carrier group, not as weak as his forces are right now. All our boys need to do is sit tight . . . maybe withdraw to a Turkish Black Sea port, and they'll be fine."

"Has anyone bothered to ask the Turks what they think of that?" Lloyd said quietly.

"They still refuse to admit our ships into their waters," Heideman said glumly. "We have people talking to them. They'll see reason, we think, but it might take time."

"That's not likely," Scott said. "Damn it, they have a war on their hands now. Don't you see? Russia just attacked Turkish territory. What . . . Roger? How many civilians died in that attack?"

"Last number I saw was eight hundred," Lloyd replied. "That'll go up, though. They're still fishing bodies out of the Bosporus."

"Well, why are the Turks mad at us?" Reed wanted to know. She spread her hands. "This puts us and the Turks in the same boat. Russia attacked both of us!"

"They, ah, may think that we provoked that attack, Madam Secretary," Heideman said carefully. "They may be trying to distance themselves for that reason."

Scott snorted rudely. "Ankara may also still want to salvage their relationship with the Russians."

Lloyd nodded. "The admiral's right. Remember, the Turks need the Russians to help control the Kurd arms-smuggling on their border. There are factions in the Turkish government that would accept a Russian apology for the 'accident' on the Bosporus in exchange for an air strike or two against Kurdish camps in Armenia."

"So where do we stand, then?" Reed wanted to know. "You're telling me there's no way we can get through and resupply them?"

Scott looked at Magruder and nodded. Magruder pulled a sheaf of plastic binders from his briefcase and passed them out to the others at the table. "These, Madam Secretary," he said, "are our estimates of the CBG's capabilities. In short, we estimate that they can continue normal flight and patrol operations for ten days. If, however, they are forced to fight a major battle—if Dmitriev launches an air strike against the *Jefferson*, for instance, and they have to beat it off—that operational window drops to three days. Less if they use mass attacks continued over a period of time, which is traditional Russian strategy."

"What if operations are rationed?" Waring asked. "You know, not flying any missions at all unless they're absolutely necessary?"

"Mr. Waring, that ten-day estimate takes into account only 'necessary operations.' Minimal CAP—that's Combat Air Patrol—with enough aircraft up at any given time both to give warning of an approaching hostile force and to be able to meet it in the air. Hawkeye and Prowler electronic surveillance flights. We *have* to have the E-2Cs up round the clock, or we're sailing blind. Viking and helo ASW flights go off round the clock, too, covering the entire battle group from hostile subs. Anything less . . ." He stopped and shrugged. "We might as well hang out a sign. 'For sale. Used aircraft carrier. You haul it away.'"

"What about hardware?" Waring asked. "Missiles, stuff like that?"

"One major engagement could expend nearly everything they have aboard, sir. But aviation fuel will be their major worry. Even at best, in peacetime with a slow ops schedule, a carrier's JP-5 stores are only good for a couple of weeks."

"And Dmitriev knows that," Scott added, "I don't believe for one second his claim that the attack on our UNREP tanker was an accident. The bastard was trying to sink her, partly to help block the channel, partly because he knew she represented an additional two weeks of flying time for our carrier planes."

"How about food and water?" Heideman asked.

"That won't be a major consideration, at least not for a while," Magruder told him. "They make their own fresh water. They may run out of fresh fruit and stuff like that, but they can go for a good many months with onboard stores."

"Look, the fact of the matter is we can't give in to Dmitriev's demands," Scott said. "That's extortion, pure and simple."

"Well, what would you have us do?" Reed demanded. "We can't go in and get them out. You say they can't last for long without fuel and supplies. The Turks won't let them into their ports. I see no alternative but to recommend that they cooperate with the Russians!"

"Madam Secretary," Scott said. "Do I need to remind you that these people have *attacked* us? Sunk a civilian ship working under charter with our fleet? Blockaded that fleet? Strafed one of our helicopters assigned to UN duty? Fired on our aircraft? Threatened us with an attack against that fleet?"

"Then give me an alternative that I can present to the President!"

"Simple," Scott said, folding his arms across his chest. "We send in the Marines. Secure the whole of the Dardanelles Straits, from the Aegean to the Black Sea. Send in Seabee units and SEALs to blast the wreckage out of the channel. We move another carrier—the *Eisenhower* is already in the Med—into the Aegean and fly support missions across Turkish territory, and to hell with what Ankara says. We can also fly aerial refueling missions off the *Ike* and extend the *Jefferson*'s onboard stores.

"Meanwhile, the Marines hold the channel open against possible repeat Russian attacks until the wreckage is removed and our ships and people are out of that death trap!"

"The Turkish government may take a dim view of our invading their territory," Heideman said.

"Then they can provide access to our ships," Scott said. "Also, we have MEU-25 already in the Black Sea, with the *Guadalcanal* and her escorts. They would be in an excellent position to grab the Black Sea end of the Bosporus and begin clearing operations. I would suggest bringing in MEU-21 for operations on the Aegean coast."

"The Army should have a piece of this," General Kirkpatrick, the Army Chief of Staff, said. "Ranger units to seize key airfields. The 101st to grab Istanbul and its approaches. This thing is *do*able."

Reed looked at the general with distaste, then turned to Admiral Scott. "Surely you gentlemen aren't seriously suggesting we declare war on Turkey? The last I heard, they were on *our* side."

"That seems to be debatable, Madam Secretary," Scott told her, "at least in view of their refusal so far to allow us overflight privileges or access to our battle group. I believe an amphibious operation may be the only way to secure the safe extraction of our people."

"The worst aspect," Admiral Magruder pointed out, "is the length of the entire Dardanelles-Bosporus channel. It's three hundred kilometers—make that a hundred eighty miles—from the Aegean end of the Hellespont to the Black Sea end of the Bosporus. Most of that is the Sea of Marmara, in between the two, but we'd still have several hundred miles of coastline to secure, a mammoth operation. And it's not like we'd be facing some third-rate, minor country, either. We've counted on Turkey as NATO's right flank for so long that we've equipped them pretty well. Worse, we've trained their people pretty well. An op of this scope would be no walkover."

"You're not suggesting that we give up, are you, Admiral?" Scott asked sharply. Magruder heard in that tone a bit of desperation; Scott needed support here and was afraid that Magruder was backing off.

"Certainly not. But there are other governments in the area that we could approach. If we could convince Greece and Bulgaria to go along with us on this, we might manage an air-mobile op against just the Black Sea end of the Bosporus. We could land north of Istanbul just long enough to clear the shipping channel."

"We'd still have the problem of extracting our ships," Scott said.

"But it would buy us time and open some new possibilities, I think."

"There's also," Kirkpatrick said, "the option of striking directly at the problem. Hit the Russians, threaten them with an expanded war against a real enemy, not just Ukrainians or other Russians. Hit 'em and hurt 'em until they yell uncle and let our people go."

"Difficult, General," Scott said, "without a nearby base of operations. Or are you suggesting we invade Russia from eastern Europe or the Baltic?"

"Unacceptable!" Reed said sharply. "Remember, the whole point of this exercise is to avoid becoming involved in a war over there. It would be easier and cheaper to go ahead and let the Russians have our damned ships!"

"Gentlemen," Waring said, shaking his head. "I have to weigh in and say that I'm completely opposed to any operations against Turkey anywhere along those straits. There's historical precedent not to try something like that, you know. Anybody here remember Gallipoli?"

"What's that?" Reed asked him. "A city?"

"A battle, Madam Secretary," Magruder said. "In World War I."

"That," Reed said with a lift of her chin, "was a bit before my time."

Gallipoli had been one of the bloodier failures of the First World War, an attack by Great Britain against Germany's Ottoman Turk allies in 1915. Brainchild of the British First Lord of the Admiralty, one Winston Churchill, the idea had been to land on the Gallipoli Peninsula at the Aegean mouth of the Hellespont and seize the straits, isolating Istanbul from the Asian portion of the Turkish-Ottoman Empire, knocking the Turks out of the war, and opening a new line of supplies to the embattled Russians. Simple in concept, the plan had been wrecked by hesitation and slow-moving commanders. After seizing a beachhead with few casualties against light opposition, the invasion force had failed to move inland off the narrow thrust of the peninsula; the Turks had closed them off, and there'd followed an extended battle by attrition.

Some 252,000 men had become casualties on the Allied side alone. Nearly as many Turks had been killed or wounded as well, and the entire operation had accomplished exactly nothing. The most skillfully handled part of the

entire campaign had been the British evacuation of the
beachhead at the end, early in 1916.

"Gallipoli failed," Magruder said carefully, "because of a
failure of nerve and of vision on the part of the people
running it. It was a fine strategic concept, with a major
screwup in the execution."

"If you ask me," Gordon West, the White House Chief of
Staff, said, "this whole thing has been one colossal screwup.
I know the President isn't going to want to get into any
major military operation until we know just what went
wrong in there. This, this could have an incalculable impact
on his image."

Scott snorted loudly. "We're not talking about public
opinion polls here, Mr. West."

"We are talking," West said with a quiet, deadly earnest-
ness, "about the President of the United States, and his
perceived effectiveness as a world leader. I'd say that is at
least as important as the safety of your precious aircraft
carrier."

"Perhaps, gentlemen," Waring said, glancing back and
forth nervously between the two men as though he feared
they were about to come to blows, "and Madam Secretary,
ah, perhaps it's too soon yet to make any decision at all. I
mean, a rash decision now could have unfortunate effects on
all concerned, on the President, and on the *Jefferson* and her
escorts. If we wait, the situation may resolve itself."

"I might remind you all," Admiral Scott added, "of the
service motto of the British Special Air Service, the SAS.
'Who dares, wins.' This isn't a time for halfhearted measures, fixing the blame, or mealymouthed political shenani-
gans."

Reed shook her head. "Mr. Waring, I cannot in good
conscience recommend any act that will deepen our military
involvement in that region." She looked pointedly at Scott.
"We will *not* send in the Marines and risk this, this *incident*
escalating into a major war."

Admiral Magruder looked up. "Madam Secretary, excuse
me, but you're suggesting we do nothing? What about our
people?"

"There are times, Admiral, when political expediency must take precedence. For the good of the country."

"You're suggesting that we abandon them? Let them just, just hang out to dry?"

"There are wounded personnel ashore," Admiral Scott added, his voice growing harder, angrier. "Including the commanding officer of that battle group. So far, the Russians have not even been willing to discuss allowing us to extract them. That's a problem quite separate from the larger one of our battle group being trapped inside the Black Sea. Madam, we can't simply turn our backs on them!"

She drummed her fingers briefly on the tabletop. "I will remind you, *both* of you, once again, Admiral Magruder, Admiral Scott, that I will happily accept your resignations if either or both of you cannot see things my way. I need team players here, not dissent. Not squabbling. My recommendation will be that we engage the Russians in a meaningful dialogue. Perhaps something can be negotiated. We should tell Dmitriev no right up front, but keep the door open for further bargaining. I think we can work something out, given time.

"We should also, Mr. Heideman, continue our talks with Ankara. If we can secure rights to berth our ships in one of their Black Sea ports, in Sinop, possibly, the entire problem goes away. Don't you agree?"

"Oh, absolutely, Madam Secretary."

"In any case," Waring added, "we can extend those negotiations as long as is necessary. Long enough to see what the Russians do. Long enough for the President to garner support for military intervention, if necessary."

"That raises an interesting possibility—" Gordon West said.

But Magruder leaned back in his chair and closed eyes and ears alike. He recognized the signs. This discussion was going to continue throughout the rest of the morning, possibly into the afternoon as well, but nothing would be decided, nothing accomplished. A wholehearted advocate of the necessity of separating military from government and keeping them separate, he nonetheless resented it, resented

it deeply, when the civilian bureaucrats in charge regarded
military men and women as expendable pawns. The same
sort of thing had happened time after time in the past. The
U.S. government had known there were still POWs in
captivity in North Vietnam and Laos when the Paris peace
accords had been signed, but in the name of political
expediency and a crumbling presidency . . .

Sometimes Magruder, patriot that he was, felt deeply
ashamed for his country.

CHAPTER 22
Friday, 6 November

Medium shot of a large, imposing, white building sur-
rounded by trees. UN troops, wearing bulky flak jackets and
blue helmets, are everywhere in evidence. Cut to medium
close-up of Boychenko, speaking earnestly with a U.S. Navy
captain and an enlisted woman.

"In the historic city of Yalta today, the chaotic disinte-
gration of the Russian Federation took yet another step into
anarchy, as Russian naval forces in the Crimea refused to go
along with General Sergei Boychenko's plan to turn the
region over to UN forces."

Cut to long shot of Russian soldiers moving cautiously
along a street, using abandoned vehicles or fallen rubble for
cover. Cut to blurry view of a jet aircraft streaking
overhead, then back to another long shot of soldiers in the
street. Two men drag a wounded comrade to shelter.

"The mutiny has precipitated sharp fighting between
army units loyal to Boychenko, and naval infantry and air
force units under the command of Vice-Admiral Nikolai
Dmitriev. Casualties are reported to be heavy.

"Dmitriev has declared Boychenko to be a rebel in the
employ of antigovernment forces and has assumed full
command of all military units in the Crimea, this in the
wake of the attempted assassination of Boychenko during
UN ceremonies here yesterday morning. Authorities believe

that attempt was probably instigated by Dmitriev, though spokesmen for the Black Sea Fleet's commander deny it."

Medium shot of UN soldiers near the White Palace. Cut to a view of the wreckage of a large helicopter on the palace grounds.

"In the meantime, some one hundred UN personnel, including a contingent from the U.S. Navy's *Jefferson* battle group, now steaming offshore, have been trapped in Yalta by the rapidly escalating hostilities. All flights out of the area have been canceled, and military helicopters have been grounded. Dmitriev has threatened to shoot down any foreign aircraft in the region, fearing, perhaps, Boychenko's escape."

Cut to long shot of an older Russian woman with a small child, huddled against the side of a building. Zoom in on her age-wrinkled face as she stares apprehensively up at the sky. Cut to medium shot of a wood-frame house burning, then to several long shots of civilians in small, desolate groups. Some look fearful, some angry. Most look bewildered or simply numb. Cut to tight closeup of the first woman's face. She is crying.

"For the people of Yalta, and the entire Crimea, the war goes on . . . and the killing . . . and it doesn't really seem to matter who is fighting whom.

"For ACN, this is Pamela Drake, reporting live from Yalta."

2135 hours (Zulu +3)
Tomcat 216
The Black Sea

Dixie held his Tomcat, his new Tomcat, steady at five hundred feet, a sea-skimming altitude that would put him in a vulnerable spot if the Russians jumped him but that might give him and the seven other Tomcats flying in an extended formation with him a critical few more minutes of evasion from Russian radar.

It was fully dark, with sunset having taken place four hours earlier, the sky partly cloudy, and the new moon just two days away. He couldn't see the water flashing beneath his F-14's belly, couldn't see anything, really, except the mingled cool green-yellow glows of his cockpit instrumentation lights, his vertical and horizontal display indicator screens, and his HUD.

His pulse was pounding; he could feel it in his throat, against the collar of his flight suit. It felt good being on a full op again, instead of flying racecourse ovals over featureless spots of ocean on CAP.

Cat Garrity was riding backseat with him again, and that felt good as well.

"Coming up on the way point, Dix," Cat told him over the ICS. "We have unknown aircraft in the vicinity, at two-seven-oh to three-three-five. No sign that they've noticed us yet."

"Rog. Maybe they can't see in the dark, huh?"

"Don't count on it. Our Prowler friends can only jam them so much. When they get close enough, they'll see us."

Two separate flights of EA-6 Prowler ECM aircraft had departed from the *Jefferson* an hour earlier. One had cut inland, flying straight north and crossing the coast near Gurzuf. The other had paralleled the coast, jamming hard and recording any radar sites careless enough to paint them and give away their own positions. The first group was code-named Spoiler, and their job was to literally stir up an enemy response, attracting missile fire and interceptor squadrons, if possible, in order to clear the path to Yalta from the sea. The second group, Pouncer, would provide selective ECM jamming coverage for the rest of the aircraft, as well as loosing deadly AGM-136A anti-radiation cruise missiles. These weapons, called Tacit Rainbow, actually patrolled large sections of sky, detecting and storing the locations of all radar and radio emitters in the area, until, on command, they were directed against a selected target— even some minutes after that target had stopped transmitting. They'd proved themselves superbly effective in the

Gulf War and elsewhere at knocking out hostile radar arrays and weapons-targeting systems.

"I've got two more unknowns at two-zero-eight," Cat told him. "They're up high. Looks like a search sweep."

"Rog."

He was absolutely dependent on his RIO in a night operation, as dependent on her for radar information—both that picked up by the F-14's AWG-9 radar and that relayed to the squadrons from the E2-C Hawkeyes orbiting far to the south—as he was dependent on his instruments now to tell him how high above the water he was flying and in what direction.

"Way point one," she announced. "Come right to zero-zero-four."

"Zero-zero-four," he echoed as the F-14 tilted sharply to the right. "Coming around to new heading . . . now."

"We should have the coast in sight."

He glanced up, peering past the reflections on his canopy and out into the darkness. "Got it. Funny. The place is still lit up like Christmas."

"The Crimean Riviera, remember? They probably don't shut down for anything short of a power failure."

He could see the lights of Yalta ahead, smeared into a gradually thinning glitter of light inland and cut off sharp and hard by the curve of the coastline. Triple A—antiaircraft fire—was already floating into the sky from several points inland, along the mountain chain that pinned Yalta to the shore.

"Okay," Cat told him. "We're going feet dry. Swing us into the racetrack now."

"Rog." Lights swept beneath his aircraft. He looked behind and to either side, trying to spot Badger and Red, flying his wing, but he couldn't see their aircraft. They were flying loose wing, perhaps a mile to his right and slightly behind.

He'd studied maps of the Yalta coastal area thoroughly and knew that the White Palace where Captain Magruder and a number of other Americans and UN personnel were trapped was just up the coast to the east . . . just about *there*, in fact. The light show was dazzlingly beautiful . . . and deadly. Some of those slowly drifting globes of light— they looked like softly glowing tennis balls—seemed to be chasing one another in gently arcing lines across the sky only a few feet away, close enough for Dixie to reach out and catch one.

Their distance and their slowness were illusory. They were close, within a mile or so, but traveling fast enough to punch clean through his wing if they struck it. Proximity fuses could trigger them to explode within a set range of several meters, peppering his relatively fragile and vulnerable aircraft with white-hot shrapnel.

An explosion rocked his Tomcat . . . and another. Once he heard a sharp *ping* of metal on metal, but after a heart-stopping moment of scanning his damage indicators, he decided that it had missed anything vital. The Tomcat was rocking now with the gentle throb of aerial explosions. Streams of tracer rounds, green and yellow, floated and arced across the sky.

"So what do you think, Cat?" he asked his RIO. "Are we at war yet?"

She laughed. "I don't know what Washington has to say about it," she said, "but *I* was at war with those bastards the moment they shot our people."

"You don't think it was a terrorist attack, like they're saying?" Everybody in the battle group, it seemed, had been watching the ACN broadcasts, live, since the ships were all set up to receive satellite news feeds. It was a little eerie, Dixie thought, that he'd been seeing news programs broadcast from this spot on the Crimean coast just a few hours ago. He'd been watching the TV monitor set up in the Vipers' ready room, and the explosion of cheers and applause when Tombstone appeared briefly in one of the shots had been thunderous.

Washington might be undecided as to how to handle the Crimean mess, but every man and woman aboard the ships of CVBG-14 and MEU-25 was ready to go in now and kick ass until their people were returned safe.

The flak was growing thicker toward the mountains . . .

but had vanished along the coast west of Yalta. That in itself was a warning.

"Yeah, that's where they're coming from, Dix," Cat told him. "I've got four, no . . . make that five bogeys coming in at two-eight-five, range fifty-two miles. I'm getting radar tone." There was a pause. Then, "Missiles! We have missiles incoming!"

"Tell me when!"

Seconds dragged past. "Hold it . . . hold it . . . okay! Zone five and break left!"

Dixie threw the F-14 into a hard turn to port, slamming the throttle forward to the final detent. As acceleration crammed him down against his seat, he looked up . . . and saw two bright stars curving through the night sky, coming straight at his head.

"Dropping chaff!" Cat said . . . and the missiles streaked past, passing beneath the aircraft and out over the sea.

Dixie kept the afterburner on as he straightened out on a new heading, flying directly toward the oncoming wave of hostiles.

"Poor Man, Poor Man," Dixie called over the radio, using *Jefferson*'s code name for this op. "This is Air Hammer One-three! We are taking fire!"

"Poor Man" had been adopted from the name of John Paul Jones's most famous command, the *Bonhomme Richard*. "Air Hammer, this is Poor Man," replied the voice of *Jefferson*'s Ops watch officer. "We copy Hammer One-three taking fire. Can you confirm? Over."

"Poor Man, Hammer One-four," Badger's voice said. "We confirm."

"Poor Man, Hammer One-one," Batman added. "Missile launch confirmed. The bastards are shooting at us, too!"

"Air Hammer, this is Top Hat," a new voice said . . . Admiral Brandt, speaking from *Jefferson*'s CIC. "We confirm hostile action at twenty-one-forty hours. Weapons free. I say again, weapons free!"

"Music to my ears," Dixie said. "I'm tired of being shot at."

"Radar lock," Cat said. He heard it, the shrill, chirping

warble in his ear. "Let's see if we can discourage them, Dix."

"I'm with you."

"Shall I do the honors?"

"By all means."

"Okay. Bring us left a bit. There. That's it. Hold it steady." He could hear the flick-flick-flick of console switches as she armed the Tomcat's AIM-54C missiles. "I have target lock, smack on the leader. I have tone . . . Fox three!"

The Tomcat bucked skyward for a moment, even though Dixie had been ready for it, as the 447-kilogram missile dropped clear. Its exhaust flared a dazzling, blinding white as the missile slid off the F-14's wing and Dixie found himself staring briefly right up its tailpipe.

"Shit," he said, blinking. His night sight was gone, shattered by that flare of light.

Cat guessed what had happened. "Next time—" she said.

"Don't look," the two of them chorused together, completing her statement. He blinked hard several times. He could still read his instruments well enough, and that was all that mattered.

"Target two . . . lock," Cat said. "Fox three!"

This time, Dixie closed his eyes as the Phoenix missile blasted away from the F-14 and streaked into darkness.

They were carrying a total of six Phoenix air-to-air missiles, a full load; their AWG-9 radar was capable of tracking six targets and the missiles assigned to them simultaneously.

It was, Dixie thought, a strange kind of warfare. He couldn't see the targets, wouldn't have been able to see them even in broad daylight at a range of over fifty miles. Cat chose the first two targets; the aircraft's fire control computer chose the next four, in decreasing order of threat to the aircraft. The elapsed time between her first Fox three and her last was just thirty-eight seconds.

Her first missile, flying at better than Mach 5, covered the forty-eight miles to the first target in a little over forty seconds. He saw the detonation when it went off, a tiny flash in the night far to the west. Her second missile hit, the third missed—evaded by some spectacular aerial maneuvers by the target—and then in rapid-fire succession, the fourth, fifth, and sixth AIM-54s all struck home.

Within the space of a minute and a half, Dixie and Cat had just launched six million dollars' worth of technology, destroying five aircraft worth some twenty-five times the total cost of the AIM-54Cs.

There was no way of knowing at this range whether or not those aircraft's pilots had managed to eject or not.

"Poor Man, this is Air Hammer One-three," Dixie called. It was strange, but he didn't feel the elation he'd expected. The engagement had been so distant, so . . . clinical. "We're five for six and dry."

"One-three, hold one."

"Copy."

It wasn't until sometime later that something else occurred to him: They'd just scored five kills, technically qualifying him as an ace. He didn't feel like an ace; Cat had fired two of the missiles, and four had been launched by the aircraft's computer. Over the tactical channel, he could hear bursts of radio chatter from other aviators as they launched on the unseen enemy.

"Fox three! Fox three!"

"That's one! I saw it hit!"

"God, look at those flames. I've got a MiG here, going down in flames!"

"That's Fox three for Hammer Two-two."

They sounded so distant, so isolated. It seemed a cold and lonely way to fight a war, and he was glad Cat was with him.

"One-three, this is Poor Man. We copy you dry. Hold your position. The helos are going in."

"Roger that. Hammer One-three, maintaining position."

This was the part of Operation Ranger that he'd not been sure he could handle. With no missiles remaining, his only weapons were the F-14's guns, weapons useful only for extremely close-ranged combat—at "knife-fighting distance," as aviators liked to say—and then only when you could actually see the other guy. But the operational plan had called for two flights of Tomcats, Air Hammer One and Air Hammer Two, to move in over the Crimean coast and, once the weapons-free command had been given, to down enough enemy aircraft to keep the rest cautious. If they turned tail and fled for the *Jefferson* now, the enemy would follow . . . and blunder into the flight of helicopters off the U.S.S. *Guadalcanal* that even now ought to be streaking through the darkness toward Yalta at wave-clipping height.

By maintaining position, the two Tomcat squadrons presented a formidable wall of radar targets that *ought* to keep the enemy guessing . . . and at a distance. Not all of the F-14s had launched; half were holding their warloads in reserve. Dixie and Cat were relying now on Badger and Red to cover them with their load-out of Phoenix missiles.

Nonetheless, Dixie felt naked, orbiting through the night without a missile left to his name.

2144 hours (Zulu +3)
Yalta
Crimean Military District

"Are you sure you want to go through with this, General? There's still time to get out."

Tombstone watched Boychenko's mouth quirk upward at the corner as PO/2 Kardesh translated for him. Her Russian was precise, fluid, and glib.

"I . . . am sure," Boychenko said, his accent thick. "Is my gift to you, for save my life." He hesitated, frowned, then said something quickly in Russian to Kardesh.

The woman nodded, then looked at Tombstone. "He wants to know if our battle group will have fuel enough to carry out this operation, with all of the flying that's going on now."

Tombstone glanced up at the dark sky, laced with the colorful streams of antiaircraft tracers. It was strange to think that his people were up there, Batman and Brewer and Nightmare and Dixie and all the rest.

"Tell him we'll have enough to take the facility," Tombstone said after a moment. "But it's essential that we secure the Arsincevo complex, or this whole exercise is going to do nothing but leave our planes grounded and our ships helpless. Make sure he understands that. I also want him to understand that we'll be attacking a pretty fair-sized Russian force. Russians against Russians. I want to know if he can trust his people."

"Aye, aye, sir."

After Boychenko replied at length, she delivered the translation. "He says he understands the risks and thinks that Arsincevo can be taken. He also says that his troops, specifically, the 4th *Spetsnaz* Fleet Brigade and some attached support units, are loyal to him, personally."

"A *Spetsnaz* brigade? That's what . . . a thousand men?"

"Twelve hundred, in this case, sir, plus a piece of a transport company and some other odds and ends he's scraped up in the last couple of days."

"He understands that we won't be able to evacuate them as well."

Another brief exchange in Russian.

"The general says, sir, that they are loyal to him specifically because he promised to find a way for them to go home. They don't want to stay here in the Crimea. After Arsincevo, they will cross the Kerch Strait and hook up with Krasilnikov forces there. He . . . he does say they don't know he will be leaving them."

"Yeah." Tombstone took a hard look at Boychenko, wondering what kind of man would simply abandon his men in the field. Granted, his own death sentence had already been signed, most likely, and his execution at the hands of Krasilnikov's agents would not serve any real purpose beyond the traditional honor of the captain going down with his ship.

Still, what kind of cold-blooded bastard did it take, Tombstone wondered, to use troops as fanatically loyal as his were supposed to be and then calmly walk away from them while they were carrying out his last set of orders?

The thunder started far out over the sea as a faint, distant

rumble, then swelled rapidly to a shrill, booming crescendo
that rattled the windows of the White Palace. Tombstone
looked up but saw only afterburners, brilliant, paired eyes of
white-orange light gleaming in the night as they streaked
low overhead.

Hornets. With *Jefferson*'s two Tomcat squadrons serving
as FORCECAP to keep the enemy from striking either
the American ships or the rescue helicopters, it fell to the
F/A-18 Hornets of VFA-161 and VFA-173, along with the
A-6 Intruders of VA-84 and VA-89, to deliver the massive
air-to-ground strike necessary to let Boychenko's troops
break free of their death grip with Dmitriev's naval infantry.
The Hornets howled, two by two, above Yalta and the White
Palace, vanishing into the darkness above the mountains to
the north. Seconds later, he could hear the thunder of their
bombs and air-to-surface missiles.

It was almost time.

Pamela and Joyce both were standing on the palace's
south patio, a few yards away, apparently deep in conversation. Tombstone wasn't exactly looking forward to what
he had to do now, but there would be no better time.
Excusing himself from Boychenko, he walked toward them.

"Well, ladies," he said. "Are you ready to say farewell to
the sunny Russian Riviera?"

Both women turned to him, and both looked angry. "I *beg*
your pardon, Matt?" Pamela said. "We're going with you."

As he'd expected, they were going to give him an
argument.

"Negative," Tombstone said. He nodded toward the sea.
"We'll have helos touching down in just a few moments,
and I want all unnecessary personnel on board."

"Is that what I am, CAG?" Tomboy demanded. "'Unnecessary personnel'?"

"Tomboy—"

"Damn it, sir, my assignment was here, with you."

"Your assignment as press liaison can continue as you
escort Ms. Drake here to the *Jefferson*. Take good care of
her."

"Now just one goddamn minute, Matt," Pamela said.

"You've been talking about your career. Now we're talking about *mine*. There's a story to be covered here. I'm a reporter. And you have no right to stop me from doing my job."

He looked at Pamela. "This is an evacuation, damn it. The Arsincevo is a military operation and there will be no—"

"If you will check your orders, Captain," Pamela said, ice and steel in her voice, "you will see that ACN personnel are not under your military command, or even the UN's. We're free agents, and we can come and go as we please."

"And if I'm still press liaison," Tomboy added, "my place is here. Keeping an eye on *her*."

The two women exchanged glances . . . and a "I-guess-that-told-him" nod. Tombstone sighed. There was no time for argument, and he had no patience at all with political correctness games.

He pointed at Pamela. "You. You're quite right. I can't give you orders, but you will stay the hell out of the military's way. Got me?"

"Certainly, *Captain*." She gave him her sweetest smile. "Oh, and will you still be requiring assistance from the civilian sector for your communications?"

He grinned. "That's a negative. They're flying in everything we need. *You* I don't need, and if you give me half an excuse, I'll fly you out of here, orders or no."

She started to open her mouth and he held up his hand. *"And*, Ms. Drake, if you insist on staying ashore, you will follow my orders regarding where you can and cannot go, what you may and may not film. I'm not going to telegraph my plans to Dmitriev on the ACN nightly news."

Pamela started to respond, then nodded. "Okay, Matt. You're the boss."

Tombstone shifted his finger to Tomboy. "*You*, at least, are an officer in the United States Navy and subject to my orders. You will return to the carrier immediately and report for duty with your squadron."

Her eyes widened. "Tombstone—"

"That's an *order*, Flynn. They're going to need every

aviator they can get up there. I want you flying an F-14, not wading around in the mud with the grunts."

He was remembering that cold tundra in the Kola, and Tomboy on the ground with a broken leg.

"What about you, CAG?" Tomboy demanded. "*You're* an aviator."

He jerked a thumb over his shoulder, taking in Boychenko and the Marines and a number of Russian soldiers standing on the patio nearby. "I'm also the architect of all of this. I've got to see it through . . . and someone ought to stay with it on this end to make sure the Russians carry out their part of the bargain." Even yet, he didn't entirely trust them.

"This is not fair. If you're trying to send me someplace *safe*—"

"There is no *fair* here, Commander. And the front seat of an F-14 isn't exactly what I would call safe. This has nothing to do with PC or me trying to protect you. It's what's best for all of us. Our ship. Our *shipmates*." The fewer people he had to worry about . . .

Besides, he *was* concerned about her safety. Charging around in the dark behind enemy lines with a bunch of Russian special forces and U.S. Marines wasn't the sort of thing she'd been trained to do.

He was carefully ignoring the fact that that sort of activity wasn't listed on his job description either.

Tombstone thought she was going to keep fighting him, but then she took a deep breath and let it out in a sigh. "Aye, aye, sir." She sounded resigned.

"As for you," Tombstone told Pamela, "if I thought I'd get away with it, I'd have you hog-tied and dragged on board the first helicopter to hit the LZ."

"I'm glad to see you know your own limits, Matt."

He was about to give her a sharp reply when he heard the distant flutter of rotors. He turned, staring out to sea. Moments later, the helicopters materialized out of the night in a throbbing of turning rotors, the far-off *whup-whup-whup* cascading swiftly to a droning thunder. There were five of them, big, gray CH-53 Sea Stallions off the *Guadal-*

canal, and they came in hot and hard, flaring out one after another as Marines and sailors directed them in with flashlights used as landing signal wands. They settled onto the beach, their rotor washes setting up great, wet swirls of sea spray and blown sand. As soon as the first helo touched down, its rear ramp dropped open and a dozen U.S. Marines spilled out, taking up defensive positions around the aircraft. Waiting men, crouched nearly double to avoid the descending tips of the slowing rotor blades, hurried down the beach, carrying the wounded men on stretchers. Hospital corpsmen dashed out to meet them, beginning to check each man as the stretcher-bearers continued carrying them up the ramp and into the aircraft's cargo compartment.

Admiral Tarrant, still unconscious, was first up the ramp.

Tomboy was gone. Pamela still stood at his side. "Seriously, Pamela. This could be your last chance to get out of this hellhole."

"I told you, Matt. You have your career. I have mine."

He gave a short, hard nod, then left her, trotting down the beach toward one of the helos.

"Captain Magruder?"

A hard-looking man in camouflage fatigues and a floppy, broad-brimmed booney hat, with an H&K MP5 submachine gun slung over his shoulder and his face blackened with paint, approached him. He was carrying two heavy-looking canvas satchels.

"I'm Magruder."

"Ellsworth," the man said. "Got your satcom shit here."

"Great." Magruder's eyes narrowed. The man wore no insignia at all but was carrying enough grenades and other gear in his combat load-bearing vest to equip a small army. "Ellsworth. You're a Marine?"

Ellsworth grinned, his teeth startlingly white in his paint-blackened face. "That's a negative, sir. I just work with 'em now and again. And . . . you can just call me Doc. Everybody else does."

A SEAL. He had to be, with that outfit and that cocksure attitude. Tombstone pointed back up the beach. "We're getting ready to move out, Ellsworth. Get the satcom up to that BMP."

"Right, Captain."

Nearby, Joyce Flynn stopped at the ramp long enough to give Tombstone a long, indecipherable look. He waved, and she tossed her head, obviously still angry, and strode up the ramp.

Moments later, the last of the civilians and evacuating UN personnel were on board. The Marines on LZ perimeter defense, who were joining the shore party, leaped to their feet and scrambled up the beach as the helo pilots set their rotors spinning faster once more. Sailors on the beach waved all-clears with their flashlights, and one by one the CH-53s rose off the sand, hovered momentarily, then swung their bows toward the night and the sea and vanished, swallowed by the darkness.

Tombstone watched with a terrible, icy apprehension. It was impossible to see those big CH-53s lifting off from their makeshift LZ without remembering that Operation Eagle's Claw, the failed Delta Force op to free the American hostages in Iran in 1980, had used Sea Stallions as well. Military operations *never* went entirely as planned, and mechanical or human failures were constants in any endeavor as big and as complex as Operation Ranger. The entire operation could fail right here, right now, if one of those big aircraft crashed, if two collided in midair, if the enemy attacked . . .

"I like her," Pamela said.

He turned. He'd not noticed her approach. "She's a good person."

"I wish you hadn't split us up. I was just getting to know her."

"You could have gone with her, you know." She gave him a warning look, and he held up his hands. "Okay! Okay! But, anyway, I *had* to split you two up. I had the distinct impression you were joining forces against me."

More aircraft thundered overhead . . . A-6 Intruders, this time, on their way to hit Dmitriev's positions north of Yalta. It was time to move out, before the attacks ran out of steam, before Dmitriev's fighters broke through the American air perimeter, before Boychenko's people just plain ran out of time.

Boychenko had rounded up a fair-sized transport convoy—Zil trucks, mostly, but an odd collection of other mismatched vehicles as well, including ZSU-34-4s, BMP personnel carriers, and even a T-80 tank. They were parked along the highway on the north side of the palace complex, engines idling, ready to go. It would be a long and dangerous passage, especially if Dmitriev's people figured out what Boychenko was up to. The coast highway followed the Crimea's southeastern coast for nearly 120 kilometers to the point where it joined highway M25 east of Feodosija, then turned east for another hundred kilometers the rest of the way to their final destination.

Two hundred twenty kilometers—over 130 miles. A four-to five-hour trip, calculated by the best highway speed of the slowest vehicles in Boychenko's convoy.

If nothing went wrong. If they were able to break away from Dmitriev's troops and searching aircraft.

If . . . if . . . *if* . . .

CHAPTER 23
Saturday, 7 November

Starshiy-Leytenant Anton Ivanovich Kulagin stood to attention and saluted his superior. "We cannot confirm the reports, Comrade Admiral," he said. His uniform, usually spotlessly immaculate, was mussed, and there was a smudge of something, smoke or grease, on his face. "But it appears that Boychenko has escaped."

Dmitriev swiveled in his chair to face the young officer. "How?" The word was flat and emotionless.

"Sir, the Americans launched a heavy air strike against our positions in the mountains above Yalta. Under cover of that strike, they landed a number of helicopters at the White Palace and evacuated a large number of people. Their wounded, the UN people, their naval UN attachés. We cannot confirm that Boychenko was among them, but—"

"But we must assume that he is." Dmitriev closed his eyes, suddenly very tired. Boychenko would not have missed his opportunity to flee to asylum with the American battle group.

"Yes, sir. Casualties were light among our ground forces, moderate to heavy in the air. We lost twenty-five aircraft of various types, mostly interceptors."

He looked up. "Twenty-five? So many?" That was nearly twenty percent of all of the combat aircraft they possessed, gone in a single engagement!

"Yes, sir. And several more damaged. Colonel Vorodin reports twelve American aircraft shot down, but we have no confirmation on that as yet. Fifteen of our pilots are dead or still missing." Kulagin paused. "The Americans, it seems, possess a considerable advantage in their Phoenix missiles."

"*Da.* Those monsters." Once again, the Americans had shown the value of their undeniable technological lead in weapons systems. An air-to-air missile that could guide itself across nearly two hundred kilometers at five times the speed of sound . . .

He shook his head. The best in the Russian arsenal still could not match the AIM-54C.

"And the rebel forces?" he asked. "Surely they did not evacuate all of them by helicopter?"

"No, sir. In fact, our observers reported that a number of Americans remained behind when the helicopters left."

"Indeed!"

"Yes, sir. American Marines. Our scouts were not able to get close enough to formulate a detailed report, of course. We don't know how many remained ashore."

"American military forces are helping the rebels." Dmitriev's fingers drummed rapidly on his desktop. "What do they hope to achieve? They will be trapped in Yalta—"

"Sir . . ." Kulagin stopped, obviously afraid.

"Go on, go on. Nothing you say can be worse than the news that we've lost so many aircraft."

"Sir, shortly after the helicopters left, the rebel forces evacuated the palace as well. They appear to be retreating up the coast road."

The news struck Dmitriev like a physical blow. "*What?*"

"Yes, sir. We estimate fifteen hundred rebels, mostly from the 4th Fleet *Spetsnaz,* are now on the road."

Dmitriev got up and walked around his desk. A map on the wall next to his office door showed the entire Crimean Peninsula and the northern third of the Black Sea in considerable detail. Pins with colored tags had been stuck into the map at various points, marking ground forces, while the American fleet's movements had been drawn in with broad strokes of a blue felt-tip pen.

"That is an interesting detail, Anton Ivanovich," he said. "You are sure of this?"

"Yes, Comrade Admiral. At last report . . ." He leaned forward, his forefinger brushing the town of Alusta, twenty-five kilometers up the coast from Yalta. "They were here. That was perhaps an hour ago. Vorodin reports attempting to launch an air strike on the convoy, but American carrier aircraft continue to provide cover for them. His aircraft have not been able to get close enough to attack."

"The coast road." Dmitriev's thoughts were spinning. "The coast road." *Where are fifteen hundred rebel soldiers going?* His eyes followed the coast road to the northeast, to Feodosiya, where it swung gradually eastward across the Kerch Peninsula.

"Kerch," he said abruptly. His finger came down hard on the seaport city at the easternmost tip of the peninsula, overlooking the narrow Kerch Strait that connected the Black Sea with the Sea of Azov to the north. The strait was only five kilometers wide at that point, separating the Crimea from the Taman Peninsula . . . and Russia proper. "Kerch," he said again, turning to Kulagin. "They are going home, as Boychenko promised them."

"Then we have won, Comrade Admiral!"

"Hardly!" Turning from the map, he hurried back to his desk. There was much to be done.

"But if the rebels are fleeing—"

"An hour ago I had a report from our aerial reconnaissance unit," Dmitriev said. "The American battle group is now moving northeast at full speed."

Kulagin remained in front of the map, studying it carefully. After a few moments he said, "The Americans are going to Kerch as well?"

"Yes. It is obvious, no? They intend to provide naval transport for Boychenko's troops across the strait. It could be that Boychenko plans to cut a deal with Krasilnikov." *Probably by painting me as a bungler*, he told himself, but he was unwilling to voice the thought to his subordinate.

"But we have naval facilities at Kerch. And a battalion of naval infantry."

"Exactly," Dmitriev said as he picked up the telephone on his desk. He punched a button. "Vasily! Get me Yevtushenko at Kerch! I don't *care* what time it is! Get him!" As he waited for the connection to be made, he looked at Kulagin. "And Anton! While I discuss this with Yevtushenko, call an assembly of all ship captains. In the main briefing room down the hall, three hundred hours."

Kulagin's eyebrows crept up his forehead. "All captains? A sortie, Comrade Admiral?"

"A sortie. With speed, we can catch the American battle group against the Taman Peninsula, while Yevtushenko deals with Boychenko's soldiers ashore. If we cannot use the American carrier group, we can destroy it . . . a demonstration that should impress our Ukrainian friends. More likely, we will actually be able to force their surrender, and *that* would be a prize indeed to present to Krasilnikov!"

"But, sir! An American battle group!"

"Don't you see, Anton? They have been flying air operations steadily since Thursday morning. Since before that, even, if you count their ASW and fighter patrols. They were in combat Thursday against our Bosporus strike force. And this evening they mounted a major operation that must have involved *all* of their air assets. And with their lines of supply cut, they simply do not have the reserves of aviation fuel necessary to continue operations much longer. Even an American aircraft carrier battle group cannot fight for long without fuel for its aircraft!"

"We don't know how much they still have, though—"

Dmitriev laughed. "They do not have enough, and that is all we need to know! That, and the fact that we know where their carrier force is going . . . straight into the pocket south of Kerch and the Taman Peninsula! We will trap them, force them to use the last of their aviation gasoline . . . and then we will have them! Go now! Quickly!"

"*Da,* Comrade Admiral!"

It was, as the Americans might say, a long shot, but they might just be able to pull this off. . . .

Tomboy guided her F-14, nose number 207, into position astride the slot for catapult two, following the arm and hand motions of a Green Shirt on the deck in front of her. The cat shuttle was run back, and she heard the thumps and clanks as the deck crew attached it to her nosewheel. It was still dark, with sunrise another ten minutes away, but the entire sky was alight with a deep blue radiance that clearly illuminated the activities on the deck.

She felt again the familiar thrill of anticipatory excitement, waiting for the cat shot.

"Ready to roll back here, Tomboy," her RIO, Lieutenant Bruce "Hacker" Kosinski said from the backseat.

"Okay, Hack. You keep your eyes peeled back there. We're going to be knee-deep in Russian interceptors as soon as we hit the coast."

"Roger that."

She thought again of Tombstone ashore. His order still rankled, and since returning aboard late last night, she'd had to watch herself to keep from sounding short or sharp with Hacker or her other fellow NFOs. She glanced down at the map clipped to a board attached to the right thigh of her flight suit. A carrier's chief strength, outside of the obvious punch and counterpunch represented by her aircraft, was her speed. *Jefferson* had covered 150 miles during the night and was now less than forty miles south of Kerch, well into the broad, open bite that stretched along the southeastern coast of the Crimea and down the western coast of Caucasian Russia.

"Hey, Tomboy."

"Yeah?"

"You think this thing's gonna work?"

"Of course it will," she replied. Her earlier bad humor, she realized, was rapidly dissipating. She couldn't help grinning behind her face mask as she added, "We're about to go take a bite out of Crimea."

Hacker groaned appreciatively. Thunder boomed from the right as Tomcat 201—Batman and Malibu—roared off Cat One and into the early morning sky. White-shirted checkers paused, crouched low, as Batman's F-14 howled off the bow, then continued their inspection of Tomboy's aircraft. A Green Shirt standing to starboard of her cockpit held up a board reading 65000. She nodded and signaled OK, the tally matching her figure for the Tomcat's full-loaded weight. An ordie held up a bundle of red-tagged arming wires and she counted them off. A standard intercept warload: four Phoenix, two AMRAAM, and two Sidewinder missiles, correct. She gave the Red Shirt a thumbs-up and he dashed away, getting clear.

The deck officer signaled for her to wipe her controls and she did so—flaps, ailerons, spoilers, rudder—as White Shirts checked each movement, then signaled OK. Another signal, and she eased the throttle forward, feeling the raw thunder of the F110-GE 400 engines building as she took them all the way up to full military power. The checkers watched carefully, then signaled thumbs-up.

All clear, ready for launch.

Another Tomcat was being rolled onto Cat One and hooked up as steam swirled off the slot from Batman's launch. The nose number was 216—Dixie and Cat. Tomboy caught Cat's eye in the other aircraft's backseat and waved; Cat tossed back a jaunty salute.

The pace of launches was rapid this morning—one every forty-five seconds to a minute. The deck crew scurried about, sometimes appearing to be some sort of huge, brightly colored colonial or amebic creature moving with urgent purpose rather than a scattered group of tired, hardworked men and women.

"Green light," Hacker called.

"Good. Let's grab us some sky!"

"Fine. But no more Crimea puns. Please!"

"Deal."

The launch officer took a last look up and down the deck

and around the Tomcat. He looked up at Tomboy and saluted.

She returned the salute. The launch officer dropped to his knee, pointing down the deck as the Green and Yellow Shirts nearby crouched low. He touched his thumb to the deck. . . .

Acceleration—a momentary surge of pressure and noise as she sank back hard against her ejection seat—and then the dark gray of the carrier's deck was gone and she was soaring out over the open sea. She pulled back on the stick, climbing, climbing. Glancing back over her shoulder, she saw the *Jefferson*'s bow dwindling with distance. The rescue station helicopter was a tiny toy well off the carrier's port side, its rotors sparkling in the sun. To the north, *Shiloh* and *Decatur* held station. Beyond that was the forbidding-looking coast of the eastern Crimea.

Tomboy held her climb, taking the aircraft past eight thousand feet in seconds, rising swift and clean out of the Earth's shadow. Sunlight exploded around her, warm, golden, and glorious.

She hated like hell to admit it, but Tombstone was right. *This* was where she belonged.

0744 hours (Zulu +3)
Near Arsincevo
Koroh Peninsula, the Crimea

Tombstone stood on the low hill, peering through binoculars at the tank farm below. It was typical of such facilities the world over, endless rows of squat, cylindrical tanks painted a drab olive color, together with the tangle of piping, fractionating towers, compressor buildings, flare towers, and furnaces that marked a petroleum refinery.

Arsincevo was a small town, a village, really, on the southern outskirts of the sprawl of Kerch. The naval port was directly on the north, almost adjacent to the tank farm, while a major airfield was visible to the northwest. By the dazzling light of the new-risen sun, Tombstone could see

Kerch itself to the northeast, a drab-looking city separated by the sparkling blue waters of the Kerch Strait from the gray strip of land marking the western tip of the Taman Peninsula. Where much of the southeastern coastline of the Crimea had been devoted to resorts, health spas, and recreational beaches, the eastern end of Crimea, the Kerch Peninsula, was nearly entirely given over to the Russian military.

In particular, there was a Black Sea Fleet port at Kerch itself, together with a major refinery and military petroleum storage facility at Arsincevo. A major pipeline from the rich oil fields of the Caucasus came through the town of Chuska on the Taman Peninsula, then crossed the strait underwater, emerging south of the Kerch naval base and running through the Arsincevo refinery complex. The storage facilities here held millions of gallons of diesel fuel for the Black Sea Fleet ships deployed at the base.

And some of those tanks, according to General Boychenko, held several million gallons of aviation fuel, a formulation identical to the JP-5 used by U.S. Navy aircraft.

CBG-14 might have been left to its own devices by Washington, but they were about to demonstrate that those devices could still be very effective indeed.

"Hey, Captain Magruder?"

It was Doc Ellsworth. During the drive up the coast from Yalta, Tombstone had been able to draw the young man out a bit more. He'd been right in his guess that Doc was a SEAL, a member of the elite Navy commando unit descended from the famous UDT frogmen of World War II. He was serving now as part of a Marine Force Recon unit; SEALs and Marine Recon often teamed up in four-man units for special ops.

"Whatcha got, Doc?"

"Trouble. Coming out of the Kerch naval base and headed this way."

Tombstone nodded. "Okay. On my way."

He was tired, though the pump of adrenaline had been keeping him going since yesterday. It had been a long, long night.

The coming day promised to be longer still.

Polkovnik Yuri Nikolaivich Yevtushenko was riding with
his head and shoulders above the circular commander's
hatch in the turret of his BTR-60 as the armored personnel
carrier crested the ridge north of Arsincevo. It was a
glorious morning, the sun sparkling off the sea, though a
low line of dark clouds to the north held the promise of rain
later.

On the highway ahead, the BTRs of the reconnaissance
platoon were stirring up a cloud of dust. Turning in his
steel-ringed perch and looking back past the heads of the
naval infantry commandos riding on his command vehicle,
he could see the rest of the column strung out on the road
behind him, six amphibious PT-76 tanks and a long line of
personnel carriers.

"We're all here, Comrade Colonel," one of the soldiers
said, shouting to make himself heard above the roar of the
armored car's engine. The others laughed. "None of us has
left yet!"

"Well, then," Yevtushenko said, grinning, "perhaps I'd
better get into uniform!" Ducking back below the hatch, he
removed his regulation steel helmet and pulled out his beret,
the famous black beret of the Russian naval infantry, and
donned it at a jaunty angle. Rising again in the hatch, he
grinned at the soldiers and tossed them a strictly nonregu-
lation one-fingered salute.

"Ah!" one shouted. "Now I *know* we are going into
combat!" He removed his own helmet and pulled his beret
out from inside his one-piece, light-camouflage uniform. In
seconds, the others had done the same. Russian military
uniform doctrine specified steel helmets for naval infantry
troops, but the black beret was such a beloved and distinc-
tive part of their uniform by now that most commanders had
long since given up trying to enforce that regulation. In fact,

the *Morskaya Pekhota*, the naval infantry, was an elite combat unit, classified as a "Guards" unit, in fact. As such, they were permitted to wear their berets, with the red triangular patches peculiar to the Russian marines, and at any desired angle, shape, or position on the head, a bit of unit nonconformity surprising for an otherwise superbly disciplined force.

The morale of the men was good, and Yevtushenko was pleased at that. In a civil war—or a mutiny—it was never possible to know ahead of time exactly how the troops would react. Often they had friends, even family, among the troops on the other side.

Fortunately, in this case, at least, the enemy forces were composed mostly of *Spetsnaz*, and there was little love lost between the Russian special forces and the marines. *Spetsnaz*—the name was a contraction of the Russian *Spetsialnoye Nazranie*, "Special Designation Forces," and they technically belonged to military intelligence, the infamous GRU. Naval *Spetsnaz* units worked closely with the naval infantry, providing frogman and reconnaissance forces, but Boychenko's Bodyguard, as some of the men jokingly called the 4th Black Sea Fleet *Spetsnaz* Brigade, were army, participants in the sharp rivalry between naval and army units throughout the Russian military. Yevtushenko had explained the situation carefully to his men—itself something rare among Russian military commanders in any service—telling them that Boychenko's people wanted to abandon the Crimea to the Ukrainians.

Perhaps a quarter of Yevtushenko's men were native to the Crimea, and many others had wives or sweethearts here. His own wife and twelve-year-old son lived in base housing at Glazivska, just a few kilometers north of Kerch. He and his people were *not* simply going to abandon their homes and loved ones to the Ukrainian genocides.

And if protecting those homes required in some left-handed fashion that they fight fellow Russians, so be it. He'd explained that by stopping—or at least punishing—the mass defection of Boychenko's men, Krasilnikov would be made to understand the larger issues at stake here, perhaps even be induced to send more men to the Crimea's defense.

And as for the rumors that U.S. Marines were helping Boychenko's troops, so much the better. The *Morskaya Pekhota* would have them for breakfast . . . then turn and crush the Ukrainians if and when they dared set foot on Crimean soil. It was unfortunate only that Boychenko himself, at last report, had escaped to refuge with the American fleet, coward and deserter that he was.

Scouts had already reported on the rebel position, occupying a low ridge not far from the Arsincevo refinery and storage facility south of Kerch. American fleet units were reported approaching from the south. Yevtushenko's unit—a reinforced battalion—was not enough to block a major amphibious assault, but they could certainly spoil the enemy's plans to cross the straits at that point.

Thunder boomed overhead, and he looked up. MiG-29s, a flight of six of them, howled overhead, their bellies bristling with missiles.

He was eager for this coming clash. Boychenko's force did not stand a chance.

CHAPTER 24
Saturday, 7 November

By 0830 hours, the U.S. Marines were firmly ashore, moving onto and across the beach by a variety of means. Dozens of LVTP-7 amtracks, each carrying twenty men, churned through light surf at nine knots toward the beach. As their tracks hit sand, they lurched up out of the water like prehistoric beasts rising from the sea, grinding inland in a meticulously planned double envelopment that secured both the undefended beachhead and the refinery complex at Arsincevo. A public beach south of Kerch was designated Red Beach. Moments after dawn, LCACs—Landing Craft Air Cushion—howled across the surf in billowing curtains of spray, then drifted across the beach shelf over self-generated hurricanes of windblown sand. As each hovercraft settled down onto collapsing rubber skirts, bow and stern ramps dropped to disgorge twenty-four troops or as many as four vehicles. The first amtracks growled ashore at 0750 hours, just twenty minutes after sunrise.

Overhead, Marine helos clattered through the air, racing inland to touch down and disgorge Marine strike teams at key points around the tank farm and the naval base. Marine Harrier jets and Cobra gunships joined with the F/A-18 Hornets off the *Jefferson* to hit the Kerch airfield and various military facilities all over the eastern end of the peninsula. Others were precision-blasted by cruise missiles launched from the carrier group's attack subs, a storm of robotic killers droning in on stub wings to seek out SAM sites, radar complexes, command posts, communications centers, and even individual vehicles with deadly precision-ist accuracy. Larger or more dispersed targets were hit repeatedly by A-6 Intruders of VA-84 and VA-89, flying mission after low-level mission off the *Jefferson*.

These attacks, particularly the air attacks, were not intended to destroy all opposition. Indeed, the strike planners had recognized early on that there were simply too many targets to hope for a clean sweep. Rather, they had been designed to throw the defenders into disorganized confusion for a critical several hours, isolating them from outside communications, and misleading them as to the exact scope and target of the Marine incursion.

Since the 1970s, U.S. Marine doctrine had stressed the MAGTF concept, or Marine Air-Ground Task Force, as a means of providing combined arms—sea, air, and land—at all levels of Marine unit deployment. The largest MAGTF unit was the Marine Expeditionary Force, or MEF, which consisted of an entire Marine division, an aircraft wing, and ancillary support units, with a total of over fifty thousand Navy and Marine Corps personnel deployed from a task force consisting of about fifty amphibious ships. The recent operation in the Kola Peninsula had been carried out by II MEF.

Next in size and complexity was the Marine Expedition-ary Brigade, which deployed fifteen thousand Marines and six hundred seventy naval personnel—not counting the ship's crews—from twenty-one to twenty-six amphibious ships. It consisted of a Regimental Landing Team, a reinforced aircraft group, and support units.

Smallest of the deployable MAGTF units in the Marine Corps was the MEU, the Marine Expeditionary Unit, composed of a Battalion Landing Team, a reinforced heli-copter squadron, and an MEU Service Support Group. Total strength, not counting the Navy crews of its four to six amphibious operations ships, totaled 2,350 Marines and 156

Navy personnel. Colonel Winston Howell commanded
MEU-25's ground forces.

Twenty-five-hundred–odd men was not much of an
invasion force, but they had the advantages of speed and
surprise, backed by the tremendous sheer firepower of
CVBG-14. MEU-25 had shifted position during the night,
keeping pace with the fast-moving carrier group. The LPH
Guadalcanal, the LHA *Saipan*—only recently detached
from service with II MEF—and the LPD *Shreveport* made
up the core of the naval half of the MEU, together with
several other amphibious vessels, a scattering of supply
ships, two Perry-class frigates, and the guided-missile
destroyer *Isaiah Robinson*. Another advantage was the wing
of twenty CH-53A Super Stallions. Normally, an MEU
included only four of the smaller CH-53E Sea Stallions,
relying for most of their air-mobile needs on twelve of the
older CH-46 Sea Knights. The helicopter carrier *Guadalcanal* had been recently attached to MEU-25, however,
specifically to carry out the Marines' mission in Georgia,
and the Super Stallions aboard were a welcome addition to
an operation that in most other areas was already feeling the
pinch of limited supplies and assets.

The air attacks on various Russian installations had been
continuing since well before 0500 hours. The first helo-
borne troops were disembarking at a dozen different locations half an hour before sunrise. By the time the amtracks
were coming ashore, the most stubborn defenses had
already been overrun or neutralized. Resistance was fierce
in spots, but only briefly. When a pillbox or heavy weapons
site pinned down an advancing Marine party, Cobra gunships or Harrier jump jets would appear within minutes,
blasting the site with Hellfire missiles, Zuni rockets, and
high-speed 30mm rotary cannon fire.

In most areas, the Russian defenders had fled the fire and
death raining from the predawn skies. Marines entered the
outskirts of the Kerch naval base on foot at just past 0830
hours to find it deserted, with half a dozen guided-missile
corvettes and patrol boats, a couple of armed tugs, and a
Riga-class frigate, all of them aflame or already settled into

the dark, shallow waters of the port, as oil-black smoke stained the blue morning sky.

Throughout the landing area, prisoners were rounded up and interrogated. Morale among the defenders, it turned out, was low, though a few elite naval infantry troops were defiant and possessed undeniably high spirits.

Navy and Marine Corps public affairs officers had already characterized the landings, however, as "meeting little opposition" and "suffering only very minor casualties," all in all a "remarkably clean and uncomplicated, surgically precise strike."

0835 hours (Zulu +3)
Above Arsincevo

Tombstone lay flattened in a pool of near-liquid mud, facedown, hands clasped over his head, as the ground beneath him bucked and rocked. Thunder passed, caressing him; he looked up and saw smoke boiling into the sky.

"God*damn* it, Matt!" Pamela screamed from her patch of mud a few feet away. "Tell them we're on *their* side!"

"Rule number one of combat, miss," Chief Geiger growled from close by. "Friendly fire *isn't*."

Slowly, Tombstone rose to his knees, staring after the departing aircraft in time to see sunlight flash from the wings of the two A-6 Intruders that had just spilled an avalanche of high explosives—a "force package" in the sterile lexicon of official DOD reports—across the top of the ridge.

There was nothing, *nothing* more demoralizing in warfare than being attacked by your own side.

Rising unsteadily from the mud, he jogged toward the smoke. Boychenko was there, pointing and giving orders as Russian soldiers trotted toward the crest of the ridge. Several vehicles had been hit on the road and were burning furiously, including, he noticed, the ACN van. *Oh, God, no. . . .*

But there were no bodies, no screaming wounded. He

spotted PO/2 Kardesh standing near the general. "Natalie!" he called. "Anybody hit in that attack?"

She shook her head. "I don't think so, sir! But the general asked me whose side those Intruders were on. He says some of the men are a little shaken by that attack!"

"I can believe that." Fortunately for the rebel column and its American auxiliaries, the Intruders had dumped their load on the vehicles, which had been standing empty along the Kerch Road, on the west side of the ridge.

"Tell him he's *got* to get the panels out!" Tombstone told her.

"I did! He said this ridge is too exposed, that we have to try moving closer to the refinery. Otherwise, we're going to get flanked up here."

God save us from military geniuses. . . .

Natalie blinked at him. "Pardon, sir?"

He hadn't realized he'd muttered the thought aloud. "Never mind. Come on. Translate for me."

Tombstone could hear the sound of the ground battle developing up ahead, on the east side of the ridge, a sharp rattling and cracking of automatic weapons. As they reached General Boychenko, he was conferring with several of his officers. He looked up from a map as Tombstone and Natalie approached. "Ah, Captain Magruder," he said, raking Tombstone with his eyes. "You . . . are one of us now, *da*?" He added something in Russian, and his officers chuckled.

Tombstone looked down at his full dress uniform ruefully, now so coated with mud that he was very nearly as well camouflaged as the *Spetsnaz* troops in their camo fatigues. Both of his shoulder boards with their four broad gold stripes were gone, and he'd pocketed his medals during the drive from Yalta. His uniform was no longer blue, but a smeared mix of black and clay-brown. It felt as though his face were probably colored the same way.

"General," Tombstone said. "If you don't get those marker panels out, we're going to be one big, happy bull's-eye on top of this hill." During his planning session with Coyote, they'd agreed that cloth ground panels—

parachute material or canvas or whatever else could be scavenged for the purpose—would be laid out in the shape of large Vs, visible from the air, identifying Boychenko's column. If there'd been time, he would have insisted that Vs be painted on the vehicles as well, but they'd been on the move, on the run, really, all night.

And now it was too late. He was just glad no ACN people had been in that van when the Intruders had struck.

Natalie translated, then gave Tombstone Boychenko's reply. "He wants to know if we aren't in communication with our ships."

"Tell him yes, we are, but things are pretty confused out there right now. With so many planes in the sky, it's hard to coordinate. All of these ridges up here look pretty much the same from the air."

Boychenko nodded. "We are . . . how you say? Stuck." He pointed to the map, then told Natalie something in Russian.

"He says that an armored force coming out of Kerch has spread out along the east side of this ridge." She pointed to the map. "Here . . . and here. *Between* us and the port. He says they're naval infantry."

"*Morskaya Pekhota,*" Boychenko added for emphasis, making a face. "Like American Marines. Good soldiers."

"He says the lead elements of his column have been skirmishing with them for several minutes now. That's what the gunfire is, over the top of the ridge. He says there's no way to go through, and he doesn't think we can go around. He wants to know if helicopters can come here to pick us up."

Tombstone looked up. Contrails were twisting wildly through the sky high overhead. One contrail ended in a fleecy white puff, from which a black streak emerged, arrowing downward toward the sea.

"Not until we have air superiority," he replied. "And probably not until we do something about that naval infantry. The helos can't touch down if they're under heavy fire from the ground."

Boychenko looked grim as Natalie passed on Tombstone's assessment. A moment later, she told him the general's reply. "He says . . . he says he hopes we can use rifles as well as aircraft, because we're in the infantry now. He cannot promise us a way through to the beach."

On the other side of the ridge, to the east, the crackle of small arms fire was increasing.

0840 hours (Zulu +3)
Over Arsincevo
Crimea Military District

In the skies over Kerch and Arsincevo, the real battle was beginning to take shape. As Tomcats and Hornets flew constant patrols, shielding the Marine landings, the ships offshore, and the attack and support aircraft that were backing up the landings, two major groups of Russian aircraft approached, one from the north, coming in low across the Sea of Azov, the other from the west, bursting across the Crimean Mountains and streaking straight for the fleet gathered in the shallow gulf between the Crimea and the Caucasus.

The Americans struck the first blow in the aerial engagement, loosing their AIM-54C Phoenix missiles while the enemy was still eighty miles away. The survivors pressed on, however, their numbers only somewhat thinned.

At 0840 hours, the Russian aircraft, now numbering about forty, mostly MiG-27 Floggers and MiG-29 Fulcrums, hit the wall of American fighters—a total of sixteen Tomcats and fourteen Hornets flying in four squadrons. Marines on the ground looked up in something like awe as white contrails crawled and scratched across the sky, etching out twists and turns and occasional deadly plunges toward the earth on smoke trails turned black.

The twisted mass of contrails thickened, swiftly tangling into what aviators referred to as a furball.

In the skies above the Kerch Peninsula, aircraft and men were dying.

So far, the information supplied by the Russians through
Captain Magruder had proven accurate. South of the naval
base facilities at Kerch, and just offshore from the tank farm
and refinery complex at Arsincevo, an enormous offshore
fueling dock was connected to the shore by a bridge and a
massive bundle of petroleum loading lines. The dock
approaches had been carefully checked by the frigate *Leslie*,
making certain that the shipping channels were clear and
deep enough for the supercarrier's ponderous draft. Two
hours earlier, a shore party of fuel handlers from the Air
Wing's V-4 Division—"grapes" in Navy parlance, because
they wore purple jerseys during flight deck operations—
together with a security detail of Marines off the *Jefferson*,
had boarded the offshore dock and begun readying it for
fueling operations.

Commander Tom Hadley stood on the starboard side of the
Jefferson's bridge, looking down at the fueling dock . . .
and out across the water beyond to the shoreline a mile
away. *This* was the key moment in Operation Ranger, the
whole point of the raid, and the time when the huge carrier
was at her most vulnerable. He'd brought her into the
narrow waters between the Taman and Kerch Peninsulas,
facing south with her starboard side toward the landing
beaches to the west. The shore party was hooking up the
fueling lines now, swaying the ends up to *Jefferson*'s
starboard fuel ports and locking them home. A Seabee crew
ashore had already identified the storage tanks containing
high-octane aviation gasoline, while Lieutenant Commander Volkwein, senior officer of V-4, had pronounced the
avgas "sweet" and up to *Jefferson*'s demanding standards.

Now all they had to do was pump nearly three million
gallons—about nine thousand tons—of the highly flammable stuff on board.

All flight deck operations had been suspended, of course, and the smoking lamp was out throughout the ship. More worrisome, Hadley had ordered the automatic fire control computers for *Jefferson*'s three CIWS defense systems switched to standby mode. If something triggered the Close-in Weapons System's radar-linked computer while it was on active, it would acquire the target and open fire by itself within two seconds, loosing a stream of depleted uranium shells at a buzz-sawing fifty rounds per second . . . and possibly ignite the gasoline fumes spilling from the carrier's starboard side.

That meant, however, that for the critical thirty minutes or so necessary for the transfer of fuel from shore to carrier, the *Jefferson* would be relying solely on its fighter cover for defense from enemy aircraft.

Of course, the carrier always relied on her aircraft as her first and primary line of defense; CIWS, pronounced "sea-whiz" in Navy-speak, was strictly a last-ditch defense against missiles or aircraft that had "leaked" through the outer defensive perimeters and approached to within fifteen hundred yards of the carrier. But this close inshore, this close to the battle, with a defensive perimeter as tight and as restricted as this one, they were taking a terrible chance.

Hadley paced the bridge, anxiously watching the sky.

0904 hours (Zulu +3)
Tomcat 216
Over Arsincevo

Dixie couldn't see the enemy plane yet, but he could follow the symbol marking it on his HUD, shifting from left to right as the other pilot tried to position himself for a launch.

Tomcat 216 was momentarily alone; Tomboy and Hacker in 207 had dropped back a few miles, deploying in a "loose goose" formation that gave the defense maximum flexibility. The attackers, as nearly as Dixie could tell, weren't even employing wingman tactics. Possibly, the volley of Phoenix missiles had so broken up the approaching formations that only scattered, individual aircraft were left.

"Damn!" Cat said from the backseat. "This bastard's taking us head-to-head! Range five miles!"

"Going for Sidewinder," Dixie said, flipping a selector switch. He still had two Phoenix missiles left from his original four, but he wanted to save those for a difficult shot or longer-ranged targets. The AIM-9L was an all-aspect heat-seeker, meaning he didn't have to be looking up the target's tailpipes in order to get a solid lock. Still, head shots were risky, and in more ways than one. Since the target gave off far less heat from its forward aspects than from its tail, it was always easier to elude an incoming heat-seeker by dropping flares.

"Range three miles!" Cat warned. They were closing rapidly.

He heard the warble in his headset, indicating a heat-seeker lock. "I've got him!" Dixie yelled. "Fox two!"

0904 hours (Zulu +3)
Flogger 550
Over Arsincevo

Major Yevgenni Sergeivich Ivanov had been holding his MiG-27M steady, angling toward the oncoming American aircraft until he saw the flash of its launch, just three miles ahead. There was no buzzing tone warning of a radar lock, so the incoming missile had to be a heat-seeker. He held steady for another three beats, then pulled back sharply on the stick, going into a steep, twisting climb as he triggered a string of flares. At twelve thousand feet, he flipped the MiG over onto its back, dropping out of a perfect Immelmann that put him well above the American, and slightly to the right. From here, looking down on the enemy, he let his port-side AA-8 Aphid missile "see" the F-14's heat plume and triggered the launch.

As soon as the Aphid slid off the launch rail, Ivanov

rolled hard to the left, trading altitude for speed as he plummeted toward the sea far below.

While the American was dealing with the heat-seeker, perhaps he could slip through down on the deck.

0905 hours (Zulu +3)
Tomcat 216
Over Arsincevo

"We missed," Cat said. "He suckered us with a flare."

"I'm going after him," Dixie said. His heart was pounding, his breath coming in short, hard gasps behind his oxygen mask.

"Watch it, Dix!" Cat warned. "He's launched!"

"I see it!" Dixie adjusted his course slightly, angling straight toward the oncoming missile, holding steady for an agonizing three seconds . . . then cutting back on his throttle while simultaneously popping flares.

Another few seconds passed, and then the missile streaked past, a hundred feet off; there was a loud thump from astern as the AA-8's proximity fuse detonated the warhead, but no indication of damage. Dixie rolled hard to port, pulling the F-14's nose around, centrifugal force mashing him down into his seat as he whipped around through sixty degrees of the compass. He'd lost sight of the other plane.

Now where the hell? . . .

"Tomboy, this is Dixie! Where are you?"

"About five miles behind you, at base plus five." That put her at eight thousand feet, slightly above 216.

"We just missed a Flogger coming through the line! Did you see him?"

"Negative on that, but we'll keep an eye out."

"Rog." He thought the Flogger must have dived; that's what he would have done in that situation—give the opposition something to think about, then head for the deck, where the ground clutter might hide him from enemy search radar. "I think he's on the deck. What's your warload, now?"

"We're down to one AIM-9," Tomboy replied. "We're empty on the 54s."

"Shit. Okay. If you spot him, coordinate with Cat. We have two Phoenixes left, and maybe we can take him if you can spot him."

"I copy."

Dixie pulled into a turn, giving Cat a chance to probe the entire area with the F-14's AWG-9, as well as to query the Hawkeyes that were orbiting further south, outside of the main battle area. The AWG-9 had the impressive capability known as "look down-shoot down," meaning it could pick a target out from the background clutter even when it was mingled with returns from the sea or ground. But Cat would need time to narrow her beam and carry out a search.

The problem, he reflected, in fighting a major engagement in such a tightly confined area was that you didn't have much of a second chance against leakers. Once they slipped past you, they were into your inner defensive zone in minutes or seconds, and then it could well be too late.

They *had* to find that Flogger, and fast!

0906 hours (Zulu +3)
Flogger 550
Over Arsincevo

Major Ivanov had pulled out of his dive a scant five hundred feet above the sea, then dropped even lower, skimming above the fuel tank farm of Arsincevo at an altitude of less than fifty meters. He swung left, avoiding the fractionating towers of the refinery. Directly ahead, the sea was crawling with ships, boats, and the odd-looking tracked vehicles the American Marines used as landing craft.

There were targets there . . . tempting targets, but Ivanov was after bigger game. He'd already noted the position of the biggest game of all, a big, fat aircraft carrier slipping in close to the fueling dock off Kerch.

He was carrying two AS-7 air-to-surface missiles under

his MiG's wings, the kind of big, ugly ship-killers that NATO called "Kerry." If he could slip *that* pair of ship-killing one-hundred-kilogram warheads into a carrier while it was taking on fuel . . .

And he was now well inside the Americans' fighter envelope. It was certainly worth a try.

0906 hours (Zulu +3)
Tomcat 216
Over Arsincevo

"Got him!" Cat called. "He slipped past us after he popped that Aphid."

"Where is he?"

"Down on the deck, like you said. Bearing zero-five-five. *Shit!*"

"What?"

"He's locking onto the *Jeff*!"

"Guide me onto him, Cat. We've got to take him down!"

"Right. Tomboy, this is Cat. You copy?"

"Cat, Tomboy." Her voice sounded strained, as though she were enduring a high-G turn. "Copy."

"Tomboy, we've spotted our leaker." Cat gave her the coordinates of the Flogger that had broken past. "It looks like he's trying for a radar lock on the *Jefferson*!"

"Okay, Hacker and I've got him. You're a little closer, though, and I need a minute to lock him with my Sidewinder."

"Just cover us, Tomboy," Dixie said, "in case we miss this one. We're not getting another chance!"

0907 hours (Zulu +3)
Flogger 550
Over Arsincevo

Range three miles—practically point-blank—and if that
carrier was taking on fuel, as Ivanov thought it must be, the
detonation of two antiship warheads ought to send up a
fireball powerful enough to shake the *dachas* at Yalta.

He heard the tone of radar lock, and his thumb came
down on the firing switch. There was a hard bump as the
first four-hundred-kilogram Kerry dropped free, its solid
fuel motor igniting. Instantly, Ivanov locked with the second
missile. Fire!

Two ship-killers accelerated to Mach 1 in seconds,
streaking across the sea toward the helpless supercarrier. . . .

CHAPTER 25
Saturday, 7 November

"He's launched!" Cat yelled. "One . . . no, two cruise missiles, in the air!"

"He's fired on the *Jefferson*," Tomboy echoed over the tactical channel. "Cat! Take them!"

Dixie yanked his thumb off the firing button that would have released one of his two remaining Phoenix missiles. In the backseat, Cat wiped the lock they'd just achieved on the Russian Flogger and was shifting instead to the two tiny, fast-moving blips streaking out in front of the MiG.

The AIM-54C—together with the Tomcat's AWG-9 radar-fire control system—had been designed with two specific missions in mind. One was the standoff intercept, allowing the Tomcat to target and kill enemy aircraft approaching from a range of 120 nautical miles. The other, however, was dictated by the ever-changing requirements of modern naval warfare. Cruise missiles—large, relatively slow, but extremely deadly ship-killers like the AS-7 Kerry—had emerged during the past three decades as the single deadliest threat to surface ships. The Phoenix and the look down–shoot down AWG-9 had been designed with the express capability of tracking and destroying large missiles in flight.

But with the high speeds and short response times that characterized modern warfare, success or failure often hinged on one man's reactions, on his experience, on his training, and on his ability to separate a great deal of confusing, even conflicting information, analyze it, and do the right thing instantly.

Dixie didn't have to think it through; he *couldn't*. Traveling at the speed of sound, the AS-7s would travel the three miles to the *Jefferson* in just over thirteen seconds. He was five miles from the Flogger—a flight time of a hair under five seconds for a Phoenix—but in five seconds, the Kerrys would have traveled almost half the distance to the carrier. Dixie had less time than that to decide that the Kerry missiles had to be his target and not the Flogger, to abort his launch on the MiG, and to let Cat lock onto the missiles and fire both AIM-54s.

"Take the missiles!" he yelled at Cat, an instant after Tomboy's order.

But she was ahead of him, already punching the new target into the computer. "Fox three!" she yelled, and a Phoenix shrilled off the Tomcat's launch rail. "Fox three!" she yelled again, and their last missile streaked after its companion.

Dixie found he was holding his breath. He could see neither the Kerry missiles nor the MiG that had launched them, but he could see the *Jefferson* less than ten miles ahead, huge and gray and vulnerable.

And somewhere between him and the carrier, four missiles were flying a deadly, high-speed race.

0907 hours (Zulu +3)
U.S.S. *Thomas Jefferson*
Arsincevo fueling dock

"Missiles incoming!" the voice of someone in CIC yelled over the intercom. "From the southwest!"

Hadley spun just in time to see a white flash above the water halfway between the beach and the fueling dock; he heard the crash of the explosion a moment later. A second missile, dragging a vapor trail through the air, arrowed across the water toward *Jefferson*'s exposed starboard side. At the last instant, the missile seemed to skip, rising high; the maneuver, often programmed into antiship missiles, was designed to bring it down on the relatively unarmored topside of the target, rather than into steel-plated sides.

The maneuver took the Kerry out of a direct flight path into the carrier's fueling port, where grapes were still frantically pumping avgas aboard, but would bring it down squarely in the center of *Jefferson*'s four-acre flight deck, where one Hawkeye, three Hornets, and four A-6s were being refueled and rearmed after the day's early morning operations. A detonation among those aircraft would cause a major fire on the flight deck, a fire that would spread instantly to the avgas fumes to starboard. . . .

The Kerry had just reached the apex of its climb, coast, and dive when the second Phoenix missile streaked in from behind. The explosion felt as though it had struck the bridge, a savage *bang* that shattered windows and knocked several of the bridge watch-standers to their knees.

Hadley stood there for a long, desperate second or two, waiting for the far larger roar of exploding aviation fuel to follow. The roar did not come, and after a moment he allowed himself to breathe again.

God in heaven, but that, that had been *close*. . . .

0908 hours (Zulu +3)
Tomcat 207
Over Arsincevo

Tomboy hauled her F-14 into another hard turn, trying to follow the fleeing MiG as it twisted hard toward the north. She was three miles behind it now, and it was little more than a speck . . . though Hacker had a solid lock on the aircraft with their AWG-9.

Unfortunately, she had only the one Sidewinder left, and the target was jinking so sharply across the folded landscape that she was having trouble getting a lock.

Tone! "Fox two!"
Her last missile streaked toward the target.

0908 hours (Zulu +3)
Flogger 550
Over Arsincevo

Turning in his seat, Ivanov saw the missile arrowing toward him. Cursing, he dragged his aircraft hard to the left and punched in the afterburners—normally not a good idea when being pursued by a heat-seeker, but he needed altitude, fast, and the only way to get it was—as the Americans said—to "go ballistic."

As he climbed almost vertically, he cut his burners and released a string of flares, letting his MiG fall over onto its back with the nose pointed almost directly at the approaching Tomcat. The Sidewinder, deprived of its easy, hot targets, nosed over as it simple-mindedly pursued a flare, missing Ivanov's aircraft by a generous margin.

He grinned into his mask. This American, whoever he was, was good. Schooled in the warrior's mentality, Ivanov welcomed this head-to-head exchange, the chance to test himself against another expert aviator. He was glad he wasn't facing one of the rumored female pilots employed by the American battle group.

That would have been too easy, no challenge at all. . . .

0909 hours (Zulu +3)
Tomcat 207
Over Arsincevo

"He's coming at us, head-to-head!" Hacker warned.

"I think he wants to play chicken," Tomboy replied. "Hold on!"

She pulled the stick back, climbing fast; the enemy plane went into a climb at almost the same moment, and the two hurtled skyward, twisting as they passed, rolling into the deadly aerial maneuver known as a rolling vertical scissors. For an agonizing second, MiG and Tomcat flew back-to-back, practically canopy-to-canopy, and Tomboy could pull her head back and look "up" into the Russian's cockpit, only a few deadly yards away. . . .

0909 hours (Zulu +3)
Flogger 550
Over Arsincevo

Ivanov looked "up" and found himself scant yards from the American Tomcat; he could see the pilot and his radar intercept officer, their helmeted, visored heads tipped back to return his stare. He was so close he could actually read the lettering picked out on the F-14's fuselage, just beneath the canopy: CDR JOYCE FLYNN "TOMBOY." Behind was LT BRUCE KOSINSKI "HACKER."

He frowned, puzzled. He could read English lettering fairly well. He knew the name "Bruce," but "Joyce"? What kind of a man's name was "Joyce"?

It sounded almost like a *woman's* name. . . .

0909 hours (Zulu +3)
Tomcat 207
Over Arsincevo

For several deadly seconds, MiG and Tomcat rolled around one another as they continued their climb, still canopy-to-canopy. Tomboy cut her power and let her aircraft slew sideways, coming within a hair of stalling and going into a pancake dive.

That second or two was all she needed, though, as the MiG continued its climb, rolling onto its back and twisting clear of its aerial embrace with the Tomcat.

She'd anticipated his break; ninety percent of being a good tactical combat flayer was being able to guess what the other guy was going to do and matching or countering the move almost before he made it. Her port engine stuttered, dangerously close to a stall, but she nursed the throttle, felt the engine resume its accustomed thunder, and watched the Flogger drop across her gun sight.

Tomboy had already shifted to guns, since her M61A1 was the only weapon she had left. Reacting instantly, and at a range of less than fifty yards, she squeezed the firing button on her control stick; the six-barreled cannon howled, sending a tight-spaced volley of 20mm rounds into the Flogger's left wing, sawing through from front to back in a splintering, slashing burst. The skin of the wing pocked, then shredded; fuel from the wing tank gushed into the air, then ignited in the hail of white-hot shells. A fireball erupted scant yards from the nose of Tomboy's F-14 as the Flogger disintegrated. Jagged fragments hurtled past her head; shrapnel pinged and rattled from her aircraft's skin—and then she was hurtling through the fireball with a hard jolt and smashing through into open sky.

"Whee-ooh!" Tomboy exulted, her voice shrill. "Got him!" Then, sobering as she eased into a gentle turn, she said, "Did you see a chute?"

"Negative," Hacker told her. "I didn't see anything but fire."

"Too bad," Tomboy replied. "He was *good*."

0910 hours (Zulu +3)
Near Arsincevo

By now, Tombstone knew that he simply was not cut out for life as an infantryman. In the sky, strapped into the cockpit of an F-14, he had an impressive array of sophisticated electronics and high-powered weaponry at his command, available literally at the touch of a button. His machine *spoke* to him, in the warble of warning tones and flashing threat indicators, in the yellow-green glow of radar blips scattered across his VDI, in the feel of the aircraft as he pulled it into a turn or nursed it out of a plunging, hell-bent-for-leather dive through thirty thousand feet.

Here, in the mud and cold and blood of man-to-man combat, there was nothing to speak to him but his own pounding heart and his own ragged fear. Combat, for the aviator, still possessed something of the romantic, medieval flavor of single combat between knights. Here, though, there was no glory, no romance of single combat. There was only stink, pain, fear, and death.

Tombstone and several other naval personnel were huddled inside the partly wrecked stone building just below the crest of the ridge overlooking Arsincevo, not far from the spot where Tombstone had first seen the storage facility. A dead Russian lay faceup in the mud a few feet away. He was naval infantry, wearing a one-piece light-camo jumpsuit, his black beret lying by his side. His eyes, wide open and very, very blue, stared sightlessly at the sky.

Stoney had appropriated the man's AKM assault rifle and a canvas pouch with five spare magazines, fully loaded, but his mind was full of images of the Russian he and Tomboy had killed in Kola. There'd been nothing romantic about that encounter, either, and he was not eager to get into a firefight.

Pamela and several members of her ACN crew were sitting on the ground nearby. No one had been hurt, and all were accounted for, but they seemed a bit lost now that they didn't have their van of high-tech electronics.

He walked over and slumped down at Pamela's side. "Sorry you came?"

"Are you looking for some kind of victory?" she asked him. "All right. I'm sorry I came. I'm sorry I ever heard of this godforsaken place. Satisfied?"

"I wasn't looking for satisfaction," he told her.

"What are you looking for?"

"I don't know. I know I wish you'd flown out on that helo." He hesitated, wondering if he should say it. "I still love you, you know."

She didn't answer, and Tombstone knew that their relationship was truly over.

Gunfire continued to bark and crackle from the east side of the ridge, Boychenko's *Spetsnaz* holding off yet another charge by the naval infantry. One charge, a few minutes ago, had come close to sweeping over the defenders' position; that one Russian marine had actually made it all the way to the American position, shouting the naval infantry's battle cry *"polundra"* — very roughly translated as "Look out below!" — before a U.S. Marine had shot him.

It was the only time all morning that any of the Americans had actually gotten into the battle. Tombstone had ordered everyone in the group, including the Marines and the SEALs, to stay out of the fighting if they possibly could. Their small numbers could add nothing to the larger battle raging up and down the ridge around them; their participation would only guarantee that some of them would be killed.

And at the moment, Tombstone could see nothing in this desolate and war-torn country worth dying for.

He was giving a lot of thought to alternatives, just now. The SEAL, Doc, was in a corner on the other side of the wrecked house, still trying to raise someone on the satellite communications gear, but so far he'd only been able to pick up coded transmissions. He'd hoped to reach *Jefferson* directly, but either the signal was being jammed, or human error had put the carrier on a different channel from the one he was trying to reach. Those channels that they were able to listen in on either weren't picking up their transmissions, or else those transmissions were being ignored in the general confusion of the moment.

Nothing, he reminded himself, *goes as planned in war.*

The problem was, there were several tanks coming up the east side of the ridge, four of the odd-looking PT-76 amphibious tanks designed to swim rivers. Those tanks, along with a number of armored personnel carriers, were still positioned squarely between Boychenko's *Spetsnaz* and the American beachhead. The *Spets* forces had not expected heavy fighting; the idea had been for them to serve as a blocking force on that ridgeline and to provide perimeter defense as the Americans pulled out, not fight a major ground action with elite forces. Boychenko seemed less than eager to press the attack.

But if he didn't, Tombstone and Pamela and Natalie and the rest were likely to be guests in this country for quite a long time to come.

"Hey, Captain!" Doc called suddenly.

"You get 'em?"

"Still can't raise Ops, but I think we're tapped into the aircraft tactical channel. I can hear the pilots talking to one another."

"You can!" Tombstone sprang to his feet. "That's great. Let's hear!"

Doc led him to the wall where the satcom device had been set up, its small antenna pointed carefully at a particular patch of sky in the south. He took the headset Doc handed to him and pressed it against his ear.

"Tomboy! Tomboy!" was the first thing he heard. "You okay?"

"I'm okay, Dix," was her reply. "Just a little singed on the outside!"

Quickly he pressed the transmit key. "Tomboy! Tomboy! This is Tombstone! Do you copy?"

There was a moment's pause. Then, *"Tombstone?"* He could hear the surprise in her voice. "Is that you?"

"I see you strapped on your Tomcat, like I told you to," he said, using the incident at the palace to positively identify himself.

"Damn it, Tombstone! Where are you? What are you doing on this channel?"

"I'm on the back side of a ridge west of Arsincevo. We're having a little trouble getting through to the beach. Think you can help us?"

"I'll see what I can do. Give me your tacsit."

He began describing their situation.

Tomboy was out of missiles, but she still had the Tomcat's left-mounted M61A1 20mm rapid-fire gun, and almost five hundred rounds remaining of her original 657. She dropped through the sky, leaving the furball of the mass aerial battle above and behind, flashing in an instant low above the row upon row of fuel tanks, and the twisted, black columns of smoke marking dozens of raging fires.

That ridge . . . that would be where the Boychenko Russians—and Tombstone—were holding off the approaching naval infantry detachment.

"Okay, Tombstone," she said. "I see the ridge. Talk to me."

"We've got three, maybe four PT-76 tanks," he told her. "They're on the east side of the ridge, moving toward the top in a line-abreast formation, about two hundred meters from the crest. I can see them pretty well from here. Doesn't look like there's too much ground cover, so you ought to have a clear shot."

"I think . . ." She stared ahead through her HUD, straining to see.

"Watch it, Tomboy," Hacker called from the rear seat. "I've got a Gun Dish paint!"

"Ah, Tombstone, this is Tomboy," she called. "Your band of gypsies happen to have a Zoo in the parade?"

"That's a negative, Tomboy. No Zoos."

"Okay. We've got one in the area. If you see it, give me a yell, will you?"

"Will do."

There they were. She could see the tanks now, four of them stretched out in a line almost directly ahead. She only had an instant to react, and she had to aim and fire by instinct. Her thumb closed on the trigger, and she felt the vibration as her six-barreled Gatling gun screamed white death at four thousand rounds per minute.

A white cloud appeared on the naked slope of the ridge just short of the first amphibious tank. Holding the aircraft steady, she walked that cloud along the slope, sending it smashing into the first tank, then adjusting slightly to the left to hit the second.

At better than four hundred miles per hour, she roared overhead so fast that the terrain was a gray-brown blur, though she had a brief instant's impression of men in camouflage uniforms on the ground, some running, some falling, some simply standing and staring up at her with mouths agape. One tank, at least, was burning, and she thought she'd hit another one, but now she was out of sky and out of time. She pulled back on the stick, climbing hard.

0913 hours (Zulu +3)
Near Arsincevo

Tombstone and Pamela were peering over the shattered wall of the building when the Tomcat rose from behind the crest of the ridge, a huge, gray bird riding fire and thunder. An explosion fireballed on the ground beyond the crest.

"You know, Matt," Pamela said as the F-14 clawed for sky, turning back over the Arsincevo Valley with sun flashing from its wings, "I'm beginning to think *she's* more your type. I think you must have a lot in common with her."

Tombstone looked at Pamela, defensive . . . and then he saw her tired smile. He grinned, a bit ruefully. "Maybe you're right. I *do* like her style!" He still couldn't deny the feelings he had for Pamela, but he was able to accept the simple, cold fact that their relationship really did have no future. He understood, he thought, what Pamela must have been going through and why she wanted to end their relationship.

And maybe, after all, that would be best.

Tomboy was bringing her F-14 in for another strafing run. He stood up behind the wall, exposing himself to fire from below so that he could see. Dust and smoke erupted from a third PT-76; from further down the valley, a squat, ugly-looking tracked vehicle with a low, open turret slewed quad-mounted 23mm cannons and opened fire.

"Tomboy!" he yelled. "ZSU on the road—"

"I'm hit! I'm hit!" he heard her calling. White smoke was streaming aft from her Tomcat as she hurtled past the east face of the ridge, angling toward the sea eight miles away.

"Tomboy!"

"I'm . . . okay," he heard her say. "We're okay, but I don't think we're going to make it back to the *Jeff.*"

"Get some altitude!"

"Already on it."

He could see the F-14 coming up now. It was hard to see, but he thought one of the engines was out. The smoke streaming off the aircraft's tail was thicker now.

"Okay," Tomboy said. "We've got an engine fire. We're definitely not going to make it to the *Jefferson.* She's still taking on fuel, and they're not going to let us come anywhere near her with a dinged Tomcat. I think we can make it out over the sea, though, and eject."

"Good luck, Tomboy," he said. "Hey . . . this time try not to break your leg when you punch out, okay?"

He heard her laugh . . . but he also heard the worry behind it. "Don't worry, Stoney. You take care of yourself. See you back aboard the carrier!"

"See you aboard. . . ."

He watched her Tomcat, dwindling to a speck in the distance, still climbing, still burning. . . .

0945 hours
U.S.S. *Thomas Jefferson*
Northern approaches to the Bosporus Strait

The broad, calm waters of the Bosporus spread out ahead of the *Jefferson* as the great carrier slowly cruised southwest into the straits. The same pilot who had guided them through weeks before, Ismet Ecevit, was again on the bridge, stoically at his place alongside *Jefferson*'s helm. If he felt any distress, any injury to his national pride after the events of the past weeks, he gave no sign at all.

Tombstone leaned forward in the chair, the raised, leather-backed chair that had the word CAPTAIN stenciled in bold letters across the back, and grinned.

They were leaving the Black Sea at last.

"Glad to get out of this pocket?" Admiral Brandt, standing at his side, said with a smile. "I seem to remember you weren't too thrilled with coming in here, a couple of weeks ago."

"Yes, *sir*," Tombstone said. "It's going to be real good to get home."

They were going home. It still seemed hard to believe, but the orders had come through from Washington only a few hours after U.S. Army engineers and Navy Seabees had reported the Bosporus Strait clear to navigate.

The Battle of Kerch, as it was being called now, had ended in a clear victory for the American battle group and MEU-25.

Tomboy had taken a lot of good-natured ribbing once she and Hacker were back aboard the carrier. The F-14 Tomcat had been designed strictly as an air superiority fighter— "not one pound for air-to-ground," as the slogan had insisted during the aircraft's design and testing. Still, she'd handled the big machine as an appallingly effective ground-attack aircraft, something quite outside its normal purview . . . and hers. Her impromptu strafing run was credited with breaking up the naval infantry attack on Boychenko's position; the Krasilnikov forces had fled moments later, opening up the way for the evacuation helicopters off the *Guadalcanal* to move in. They'd touched down on the ridge above Arsincevo minutes after Tomboy's strafing run; Tombstone had made it back to the *Jefferson* only ten minutes ahead of Tomboy and Hacker, who were plucked from the sea south of Kerch by one of the carrier's SH-53 rescue choppers.

By then, the U.S.S. *Thomas Jefferson* was underway again, cruising south at a brisk clip with her aviation gasoline tanks full once more. With another sixteen days' worth of fuel for her aircraft, clearly any attempt to stop her would be foolhardy. Tombstone, pausing only to take a quick shower and put on a clean uniform to look the part, had assumed command from the ship's Exec; Admiral Brandt had transferred his flag to the *Shiloh*, and so Tombstone had been left in command of the carrier, a command confirmed—at least temporarily—by Washington a few hours later.

The sea battle that had followed had been almost total anticlimax. Dmitriev's small and ill-prepared carrier force had been steaming around the southwestern tip of the Crimea, obviously hoping to trap the battle group at Kerch, but by the time the two squadrons came within range of one another, Dmitriev had only a handful of aircraft left, and his huge *Pobedonosnyy Rodina* was literally a sitting duck.

The battle was over in minutes and was resolved even before Coyote could order an air strike by A-7s and Hornets. The Los Angeles–class attack sub *Orlando* had been lurking unseen and unheard in the deep, dark waters south of Sevastopol and had picked up the approaching rumble of the *Rodina*'s screws almost as soon as she'd left port. Over one hundred miles away, four sub-launched TLAMs— Tomahawk Land Attack Missiles—had burst one after the other from *Orlando*'s vertical launch tubes, driving up through the water on rocket motors that hurled each twenty-foot-long cruise missile into the air at a fifty-degree angle. The solid motors burned out and fell away; the cruise missiles, gulping air now, steadied on course at altitudes of only a few feet, arrowing toward the distant Russian carrier at Mach 7.

The *Pobedonosnyy Rodina* never had a chance. Her escorts turned back even before the huge vessel capsized beneath a funeral pall of roiling black smoke.

One of the oil-covered survivors pulled from the Black Sea by one of *Jefferson*'s helicopters hours later had been one *Vitse-Admiral* Nikolai Sergeivich Dmitriev, encountering the *Jefferson* for the second time in his career. He'd requested asylum as soon as he was aboard.

Tombstone wondered what he and Boychenko had been talking about in the week since.

Turning in his seat, he could see a great crowd of *Jefferson*'s enlisted men and women stretched across her deck in a shoulder-to-shoulder line, walking slowly down the deck, their eyes on the Kevlar-coated steel at their feet. Occasionally, someone in the line would stoop, picking something up off the deck. The exercise was called a Foreign Object Damage walkdown, an FOD for short, and it was the most efficient way the Navy had come up with yet to clear the flight deck of every single dropped nut, lost tool, or anonymous chunk of metal that might be sucked into an aircraft's jet intakes during flight ops.

Small things could do tremendous damage, all out of proportion to their size. It was literally true that a thirty-five-cent bolt sucked into the air intake of a Tomcat on the deck could ruin a thirty-five-million-dollar aircraft—at least to the point where a set of turbine blades had to be pulled and replaced and the compressors checked for damage. A single million-dollar Phoenix could take down a thirty-million-dollar jet a hundred miles away.

A single carrier battle group could change the politics of a nation.

Strategically, the raid on Kerch had been a pinprick, inconsequential in any larger scheme of things, but it had demonstrated the resourcefulness and will that were by now defining characteristics of the United States Navy. It had also broken the air power of the Black Sea Fleet; at last report, Ukrainian landing craft had been coming ashore at Mikolaivka and Kacha, just north of Sevastopol, and were on their way to overrunning the entire peninsula. The UN had protested, insisting that the Crimea was under UN protection, but no one seemed to be paying any heed.

The loss of the Crimea might well be the final blow to Marshal Krasilnikov's hard-line rule of what was left of Russia. No one could know with any certainty, however, what the future held for that unhappy country.

Tombstone, however, knew *exactly* what was in store for him. It was the end of the twentieth century, the beginning of a new era . . . a new world. For a long time, he'd wondered whether technology and events had already passed him by, whether or not it would be better if he accepted that he'd gone as far in his naval career as he could. Civilian life, sometimes, looked pretty good.

But he knew now that that was not for him. The special fraternity with the men—and women—who sailed and flew with him was something he would not easily be able to lay aside.

He looked around the bridge of the *Thomas Jefferson*, caught Brandt's eye, and winked.

The *Jefferson* might still have three thousand miles of open ocean between her and her home port, but Tombstone Magruder knew that he was already home.

NOW AVAILABLE IN HARDCOVER

STATE OF

EMERGENCY

A NOVEL BY

STEVE PIECZENIK

PUTNAM